E.T. GUNNARSSON

Forgive Us

A BOOK BY BRAGI PRESS

Second edition

ISBN: 978-1-7363773-4-5

Editing by Alison Rolf, Alison Rachel Editing
Proofreading by Alison Rolf, Alison Rachel Editing
Cover art by Zealous"

This book was professionally typeset on Reedsy.
Find out more at reedsy.com

1054709

For my mother and father

Acknowledgement

Firstly, I have to give thanks to my mother and father. Without their love and support, *Forgive Us* wouldn't exist. From reading the first drafts of the early chapters to putting "the end" after the final page, they were the most crucial drive in creating my first book. Love you guys.

Of course, I have to give thanks to my long-time friend Logeenth Rao. Without many years of practice writing with him, I wouldn't have had the skills or courage to start typing the first words in this book. Thanks, bro, and good luck in your writing adventures.

My sincere thanks to my friends Caleb Tackett and Chris Cardella, who spent many conversations with me discussing and brainstorming ideas for *Forgive Us*. Their contribution to the design of the book's story gave me a conceptual foundation to build on.

I am grateful to Adrienne Pohrte, who spent many hours editing and criticizing an early version of *Forgive Us* before it even got to an editor's desk. Thank you.

Joe Vazquez at Joe Vazquez Photography took my profile picture. Thanks Joe! You can find more of Joe's awesome pictures at silverbackclicks. smugmug.com.

Robert Williams created the awesome original cover art, which gives a fantastic representation of Rose. You can find more of Robert's artwork and contact information at rdwstudio.artstation.com.

Zealous" created the current cover art after winning a cover competition at https://99designs.com/.

Finally, I am super grateful to my editor, Alison Rolf at Alison Rachel Editing. Thank you for all your work to perfect my book. And, of course, thank you for my newfound hatred of passive voice. You can connect with

Alison at reedsy.com/#/freelancers/alis-c.

Memory

Silent, empty, and cruel. This was the nature of the wasteland.

The wasteland was a vast expanse of ruins, sand, and dying life beneath a polluted sky. This was the new world. It was created by humanity in 2079, and it was the world that they now had to brave to survive.

The downfall of the old world happened slowly. Humanity did not know it, but their cunning and technology became their undoing. In the great battle between Mother Nature and humanity's dominion, there was no winner.

The sound of a thunderous engine erupted throughout the eerie wasteland as a motorcycle sped along the ancient roads. Upon it was a survivor, alone and braving all odds. His name was Oliver, a thirty-six-year-old man who had grown up in the old world.

Oliver was a refugee from the wild and untamed lands near the Rocky Mountains. He fled East, guided by the hope that the East would be better, though he could feel in his gut that it wouldn't be. The only solace he had were stories from traveling caravans and survivors who spoke of growing settlements in the East.

Oliver was pursued. Not by man, not by beast, but by time. Starvation, dehydration, exposure, all of these were barely kept at bay by luck and experience. His current and most dangerous pursuer was the weather.

The pollution haze above blocked out the sun. As night approached, the world slowly became pitch black and freezing cold. The darkness parted before the headlights of his motorcycle, yet Oliver felt vulnerable.

Parallel to the road were telephone poles, some of which had tilted or completely fallen to the ground. The surrounding wasteland was desolate and empty, occupied by rocks and sand dunes.

Oliver wore an old-world smart suit that was on its warmest setting. He also wore a coat made out of animal hide over his smart suit. He had traded for it a while ago, and it had saved him from freezing to death many times already. Still, he shivered.

A gas mask covered his face. It was vital for survival in the wasteland; without it, the toxic air would corrode Oliver's lungs. It was old and worn, created in a factory in the old world. Still, it worked much better than the makeshift masks that most people wore. Finding filters for the gas mask was easy; they were everywhere.

There was a grim face beneath the intimidating gas mask. Oliver's brown eyes reflected a man whose past was full of pain and hardship. Through the visor, they seemed tired. The light that most people have in their eyes was dim in Oliver's. He also had deep curves between his brows and fatigued laugh lines. His skin was dark and covered in colored blotches, irritated and damaged from the wasteland air.

Oliver focused on his current task: finding shelter for the night. Such searches were often painful since he had to be picky about the buildings he used. Some were too unstable to hold up against the wasteland's extreme weather; some were too hard to get into, others occupied.

He paused at a fork in the road, gazing down each path. After a few seconds, Oliver turned the motorcycle right and sped off. The sand-covered asphalt in front of him rose into a hill. Oliver followed the road and arrived at a parking lot. In front of him was an old, wooden church that was leaning to one side. A few cars sat parked in the parking lot, their paint stripped by sandy winds and their frames rusted out by time. The church itself had shattered windows and holes in every wall. Oliver had to make do. It was too dangerous to search for better shelter with night fast approaching.

The thunderous engine cut out as Oliver parked and turned off his motorcycle. The world became silent again. Only faint wind could be heard in the absence of the engine's power. Oliver turned on a flashlight that was attached to the side of the gas mask. Next, he grabbed his gun off the back of his motorcycle. Holding it with two hands, he turned toward the church. Oliver's boots met the ground with quiet clicks. These were combat boots, tough and made for smashing jaws.

He swallowed nervously. Though anxious, Oliver felt safe with his Railshot Rifle in hand. It was beautiful, a flawless combination of a railgun and a shotgun. He checked the top port of the gun before entering the church. The gun had plenty of scrap metal in it, ready to shred flesh and bone instantly. Next, he checked the round blue energy meter above the trigger. Oliver felt sure there was enough charge to keep him safe.

He moved toward the entrance. The flashlight pierced the darkness, allowing him to see the gnarled and twisted vines covering the church. They looked so dry that it seemed like they would crumble to dust if Oliver touched them. The twin doors that blocked off the entrance to the building posed no challenge. One was hanging weakly from its hinges, while the other had broken off and now laid on the floor.

Step by step, he entered the church, walking over a fallen door and looking up into the steeple. The lonely church bell still hung far up there. It was rusty, kept in place by a few frayed ropes, gently moving back and forth. Each time the wind gently moved it, Oliver heard a distant "ding" from the steeple.

The bell seemed so lonely. It was a reminder that this place was once the center of a community. Where were they? He assumed that they were all long gone, lost to the last twenty years.

The interior of the church was desolate and destroyed. The hard, wooden floor inside had a layer of sand and pebbles. Each time Oliver took a step, a quiet crunch followed.

There were broken benches and piles of rubble everywhere. Oliver wondered if any ghosts still sat on those benches. Were they at peace, or were they suffering? Many parts of the walls and roof had collapsed upon the altar and benches lining the church. Oliver looked around cautiously, taking in the looming structure.

Here was once a holy site that held peace, now defiled by the wasteland. To Oliver, all of it was just firewood.

The place was empty of any living presence. The only recent trace of human activity was a single piece of graffiti over the altar. Oliver examined the graffiti, stepping upon the altar to wipe some dust off of it.

"GOD HAS ABANDONED US!"

Oliver frowned and stepped down from the altar, turned around, and started to gather pieces of wood. The graffiti was unsettling. Oliver breathed uneasily as he moved around. Once he grabbed enough pieces, he formed them into a campfire at the center of the building. Oliver took off his backpack and laid it beside him. It was an old, rugged backpack that held most of his belongings. There were some holes in it, and its fabric was so worn down that the once blueish fibers were black and dirty. The backpack held a bedroll, food, gas mask filters, incredibly precious bottles of water, and bags of scrap metal.

He dug inside the backpack and pulled out a tesla lighter. It was old, given to him when he was younger. On one side was a company logo that was almost invisible from wear. He flipped the cap open and turned it on. Arcs of energy formed between two metal rods, the arcs humming and dancing.

Oliver lowered the lighter down to the campfire. First, there was smoke, then after a few moments, a small flame appeared. Oliver nurtured the flame until it engulfed the small campfire. Once it was going, he unstrapped the bedroll from the backpack and laid it out beneath a bench near the fire. Oliver felt happy as he basked in the warmth of the fire; his shivering slowly stopped as he turned off his flashlight and sat down.

The church creaked and moaned from the rough winds outside. The sounds made Oliver uneasy. He stared at the fire, his face wrinkling in thought as he contemplated the church. People still clung to Christianity in the new world, though their beliefs had changed over the past two decades.

Many were afraid of old churches. Some said that God had punished humanity for their sins. Sin was thought to be the reason why the world was like this now. Many believed that the Devil lived in old holy places like this church. Oliver didn't believe in all those stories, but the idea still creeped him out. He imagined the evil, horned demon dancing in the shadows with the flickering flame, laughing at his ignorance and plotting to steal his soul.

While warming up from the heat of the campfire, Oliver gazed at the device on his forearm. It was a Smartwrist, similar to a smartwatch from the early 21st century. He turned it on and checked the time. It was nine o'clock, three hours until midnight. New year, new century, same problems. People used to celebrate the new year, drink, and make merry. Not anymore.

With nothing else to do, Oliver decided to eat dinner. He grabbed the backpack and dug through it, procuring a vial with a full meal inside of it. Processed cubes of synthesized meat and vegetables composed the meal, food from the old world. He frowned bitterly under his mask as he looked at the vial. Oliver unscrewed the lid, quickly lifted his gas mask, emptied the vial, and put his mask back on in one swift movement. Instead of throwing away the vial, he put it back in his backpack for later use.

Oliver looked like a chipmunk with so much food in his mouth. Stuffing too much food into his mouth was a bad habit Oliver had; as a matter of fact, he used to be called "Chipmunk" by his family. The artificial food tasted like stale popcorn. Oliver's metal teeth chewed through the stuff easily. While he was eating, Oliver thought about his last visit to a dentist in the old world.

He remembered having his teeth pulled out to be replaced by 3D-printed metal teeth that wouldn't break or decay. The pain from the procedure was brutal and lasted a few days after the surgery. For many, it was once a rite of passage, marking the transition from teenager to adulthood. Everyone went through it, and, in Oliver's opinion, he was happy to have metal teeth. Suffering tooth decay from the inability to deal with his hygiene was the last thing Oliver wanted. They looked like real teeth anyway and didn't turn yellow.

Oliver's gaze shifted to the doorway of the church. Outside, there was the darkness of a polluted world. There was no grass, but there was still some life, mostly brown, dry, and barely alive. The winds were blowing fiercely as always. A blackish color tainted the air, and waves of dust sailed over the ground with the tremendous force of the wind.

A discontented exhale left his lips as he closed his eyes. Oliver tried to remember a time when the sky didn't constantly have a dark haze over it. Growing up in a cramped apartment, Oliver heard stories of when there were still green fields and blue skies. He believed the stories only because he had seen pictures that captured those forgotten times, though some doubts lingered in his mind. No matter how hard he tried, he could never recall a bright, sunny day. All that came to mind was the sky darkening as time passed.

He struggled to remember a day when he didn't have to wear a gas mask to go outside. Oliver recalled that every indoor space had a sort of airlock before anyone could enter. He would walk in, have doors closed behind him, then have the room completely emptied of air and refilled with filtered, clean oxygen in a few seconds.

Oliver checked the time again. Two hours until the new year. He put more wood on the fire to push the biting cold away.

A pained moaning interrupted the peace as the sparks and flames engulfed the new fuel. Oliver let out a startled gasp, holding his breath and looking toward the sound. Far away outside the church, Oliver could hear footsteps approaching. Oliver barely made out the shapes of figures in the darkness outside, human shapes with extra arms, faces, and body parts fused into them. They were human mutants, the fiendish nightmares of the wasteland.

Oliver hastily stood up and snuffed out the fire in front of him with a boot before laying down flat. He reached out for his weapon and held it, his heart throbbing with dread. The noise and the moans were the worst part. The faint silhouette of their horrid, mutant forms was all Oliver could see in the darkness as memories of being chased, attacked, and more slowly crawled back and made his skin feel cold. They came close to the church, horribly close. Their footsteps and hoarse breathing filled the air.

Oliver heard bodies brush against the sides of the church as they walked past, their footsteps passing slowly and beginning to fade. Oliver carefully stood, proceeding to investigate the church. Had he been seen? Did they know he was here? Nothing. Nothing seemed to be hiding among the ruins, and he heard no more sounds outside. A relieved exhale left his lips as he returned to the fire and knelt beside it, trying to start it again.

Abruptly, footsteps quickly approached from behind. Oliver swung around with his gun ready as he heard them. At the same time, something his size crashed into him, causing him to see stars.

It knocked the gun out of his hands and sent Oliver to the ground. He landed with a pained grunt. In an instant, his knife was in his hands. Despite his surprise, Oliver immediately retaliated against the figure he could barely make out.

The beast shrieked as he plunged the blade blindly into its body. Its arms thrashed, mouth gnashing at Oliver. He stabbed again, then again, the thing falling on top of him. Its shrieking grew higher in pitch, a rough hand striking Oliver in the head. The strike made him blink, stunning him but not stopping him from stabbing.

With a tremendous kick, Oliver threw the creature off and began stomping the monster into the floor. Every smack made it squirm less, its whole body growing still after a while. As he stopped, Oliver heard a rasping breath from it. He stomped again out of spite. Oliver wasn't going to give it mercy. He lifted his mask and spat on the dying creature. As he did, he caught a whiff of its rancid, sweaty smell.

Oliver listened to the creature as it occasionally let out pained squeals. He started the campfire again, the flame slowly growing from the church's dried, ancient planks. In the light, Oliver could make out the creature dying before him. It was a mutant, shaped like a human with a face fused partly into its shoulder. A useless limb extended from its belly, while a stunted leg dangled from the calf of its right leg. Stab wounds covered its body, blood seeping from each.

Oliver relished its suffering. He watched it trying to fight again, weakly twisting and squirming. It growled and gurgled, painfully bleeding out. After five minutes, it gave in and collapsed completely. Once the mutant was dead, Oliver remained wary of any more creatures. Fortunately, none came to avenge the mutant that he had just killed.

Oliver felt a stinging sensation on the side of the head where the mutant hit him. He rubbed it, causing his face to scrunch as he winced. It must've been another mark.

"That's going to bruise," he whispered to himself.

His skin was rough and covered in scars, damaged from the toxic air and the violent wasteland. Even if it did bruise, it wouldn't stand out.

He checked the time again — only forty minutes to midnight. The wind outside began to batter the creaking church. The structure's stability was questionable, but there was no option to find shelter in another building. Oliver moved his bedroll under a bench and got inside of it, keeping his gun close at hand.

He played games on his Smartwrist to pass the time. Oliver felt a sinking sensation of emptiness when his thoughts dwelled on these games. In his youth, games and social media were a major part of his life. Oliver had followers, friends, and people that he still kept in touch with years after losing face-to-face communication. Sometimes, Oliver had met his old friends in virtual worlds. The thought caused his fingers to meet the port where the VR chip went, the object that connected the Smartwrist to the VR equipment he once had.

The world felt more desolate than it already was when these thoughts of loneliness came to him. He remembered virtual games too and how many hours of his life he lost to them. Gaming was a happy memory that made him smile when thinking about all the friends he had made, especially those from strange places. Now, survival was lonely and harsh. Whenever humans met one another, it was either shoot or run.

The last thirty-five minutes passed in the blink of an eye, and before Oliver knew it, the last minute before New Year arrived.

As the last minute dwindled, Oliver released a relaxed, drawn-out exhale. He counted it in his head, one Mississippi, two Mississippi. Oliver mumbled it under his breath until the last ten seconds. He turned off the Smartwrist and lifted both arms in the air with spread fingers.

"Ten, nine, eight, seven, six, five, four, three, two, one... HAPPY NEW YEAR!" he whispered as loudly as he dared.

The year was 2100, and Oliver was still alive.

Guardian

7:32 AM, May 13, 2154

Rose sat with her toy rabbit in her arms, watching London from her seat on a decaying, rusty car frame. The rabbit was an old, worn, hole-filled toy with stuffing leaking out of it. Rose didn't mind its age, hugging the old toy and taking comfort in it. The rabbit once had a baby blue color but had since been worn down to a gray color. There were stitches in it, keeping its one remaining ear together.

In front of her was London, tending to a campfire and cooking breakfast. He was a rugged forty-five-year-old man with aching joints and tired eyes. Their breakfast was impaled above the fire on a makeshift spit, a skinned and gutted mutant animal. It resembled a squirrel, except it had rough skin with patchy fur. It was missing a tail, had a second deformed face on the right side of its head, and had a stub for a right hind leg. It wasn't a pretty animal, but it was protein once the fire purged the diseases it carried and seared its flesh to perfection.

"London, what is that?" she asked curiously, tilting her head.

London turned his gaze to her, pausing to think while letting out a "hmm" sound. Rose was around the age of nine and was curious about the world around her. She was especially interested in the old world. London always gave her books on the topic. He was also fond of stories describing what life was like seventy-five years ago, in a different age.

"Well, the books I've shown you might say that it's... a squirrel? Or a rabbit? Maybe a groundhog. I don't know, old-world books only talk about old-world animals, Rosey," he told her.

"It has to have a name!" she responded and crossed her arms.

"What would you call it?" London asked, raising a brow.

"Uh.... How about a Sqabbit?"

"Eh, I don't like that name. I found it near the hole where it lived."

"Oh! I know! Ground chiprabbit!"

London let out an amused chuckle and shook his head. He lifted the spit and examined the cooked rodent, its flesh slightly burnt and rendered completely safe by the fire. Casually he procured a knife and began slicing it, separating meat from the bone.

"I like Sqabbit better," he said.

"Hey! You don't like my names," Rose pouted.

"I do! Better than what I can come up with. I just call it breakfast."

London gave Rose a handful of sliced-up meat. She took off her gas mask and pulled down her patchy hoodie; her short, strawberry-blonde hair flowed freely as she ate. London taught Rose to eat quickly, to put the gas mask on when she needed to breathe, and then eat again. It was the only safe way to eat, and London did the same. His hair was barely visible since it was so closely shaven, though there were some apparent gray hairs. He made sure that they always had short hair, keeping Rose's hair at her neck and typically tying it up.

Their meal was satisfying, though there wasn't enough to fill them up. Hunger was a prominent, horrible feeling in the wasteland; a catch like this was a lucky and rare one. Rose despised synthesized food, so she was grateful for real food. Their bodies reflected the wasteland's harsh conditions; both were a bit bony from years of going consistently without a full meal. Even though food was always a challenge, London did his best to make sure Rose ate more than he did to grow unhindered. Keeping her fed was one of his greatest worries.

Once finished, they secured their gas masks tightly and saved the leftovers, no matter what they were. London walked over to her and began to tie up her hair, making two small buns of hair that were hard to grab.

"What do we say, Rose?" London asked after the meal was over.

"Thank you," she said a bit reluctantly.

London finished tying up her hair.

"I know, manners are hard," he remarked.

"Why do we have manners?" she asked in a fussy voice.

"Well, Rose.... Manners are from the old world. It made you a better person to have manners, and people liked you more when you had them. People didn't like it when you chewed with your mouth open or weren't respectful when asking for things. It doesn't change now, Rose. Always be respectful." he explained.

"I think they're stupid."

"I don't care," London said, laughing at the reaction he saw under her mask.

Rose's lips tightened in annoyance as she tried to come up with a response. London watched as her face turned a faint red color through her visor; her expression was the funniest part for him. She finally came up with a response and attempted to use it. Before she could, London cut her off.

"Come on, get your stuff. We should get moving," he said, gesturing to her little backpack.

Rose grumbled and did as London ordered.

Between both of them, there were very few items to be found.

London wore clothing that covered him from head to toe, made from the hides of wasteland animals. Across it was scrap armor, created with the rusted metal of old-world items such as shopping carts. He also had a worn, old-world gas mask with a slightly cracked visor. On London's back was a patchy backpack. It was full of food, water, general supplies, and had a bedroll on top. Some other things also hung off the backpack, like the frying pan he had just used. The most important things London had in the backpack were books.

He also had a pistol built from wood, metal, and old plasma pistol parts. It was sturdy for being made of so many different parts but still inferior to factory-made pistols. His main weapon was a bat, with a taped-up handle and plenty of mean bits on the shaft. There were screws, nails, and a metal chain wrapping its length in pure, punishing pain.

London put his backpack on and helped Rose gather her stuff before he snuffed out the campfire.

Rose wore clothing similar to London's but tailored for a little girl like her, such as an old-world hoodie and a gas mask. Finding gas masks for her size was hard, so she had a makeshift one, which was arguably in better shape than London's. Rose's little backpack carried fewer things than London's and also had some books.

Her weapon was an incredibly sharp knife made from some wood, tape, glue, and a piece of metal crafted into a blade. He had been trying to get her a gun, but it was difficult to find something in working condition.

"Hey, Rose, when we get somewhere safe, do you want to practice shooting again?" he asked.

"Yeah! Guns are a little scary, but they're fun!" she replied enthusiastically.

London cracked a smile.

"What are the rules, though?" he asked.

"Oh... uh... it's not a toy!' she began to list, "Use it for defense and hunting. Don't waste ammo. Know where your finger and the trigger is. Keep it loaded, and keep it clean."

London nodded his approval and began to walk down the road with Rose at his side. She held the bunny in her hands and skipped beside him. Today, the wasteland winds blew softly with a delicate touch, the pollution haze giving way to some sunshine. Due to the haze, the world was always a sickly gray or brownish color; London hated it. He knew it wasn't always like that.

He didn't like how dreary and barren it was, how still and unmoving the world's decaying ruins were. London hated it because Rose had to grow up in this world. There were other survivors out in the wasteland, but many didn't accept people into their groups or were distrustful.

The asphalt road beneath their feet was cracked and sinking into the embrace of the earth. Occasionally, there was a weed that feebly clung to life through the cracks, small things that were frail. They also passed the ruins of collapsed buildings and occasional billboards too. As the pair followed the road, they passed the rusty shells of cars that used to run by themselves.

Their engines were run by the thing that brought so much pollution and destruction to the planet.

"London?"

"Yes, Rosey?"

"You told me about cars, how they used to take people around. How did they move?" she asked, looking up at him.

The answer was simple, Ignium. London thought about all the books and experiences he'd had throughout his life with Ignium. He read that it was invented around the late forties and widely implemented around the early fifties. It was energy cheap as dirt, easy to make, more efficient than other energies, and easier to manipulate.

Ignium became widely used and replaced electricity, even opening up a whole new field of science focused on Ignium and its strange physics. Gradually, Ignium replaced everything in terms of power and energy and was used in everything and anything. Ignium soon appeared in cars, devices, weapons, houses, everywhere.

"Well, in the old world, there used to be this kind of energy called Ignium. Remember when I told you about electricity?" he began.

"Yeah, I do. It goes zap!" She said with a giggle.

"Well, Ignium was the 'new' electricity back around 2050, a hundred years ago." he explained, "It was easy to make and easy to use! They used it in everything, like in cars. I use Ignium to power some of our things, like my pistol," he told her.

"Cool!"

London frowned as he remembered its downside. It was toxic, a heavy pollutant much worse than most pollutants. Scientists discovered that in the early sixties, but massive corporations, governments, and more depended on Ignium. They covered up any research that painted Ignium in an evil light. By the time the results became clear of what Ignium could do to the planet, it was too late to stop using it.

"Don't be too excited. Ignium is also toxic. But, with our gas masks, we'll be okay."

"Are you sure?" Rose asked.

"Yes."

As London walked, he touched his gas mask lightly in contemplation. People had to wear gas masks in the late sixties, and they became a fashion. Research put into gas masks around this time made them exponentially better. It was the reason he only had to replace his filters every week instead of every few hours. London recalled reading that the mid-seventies was when many buildings had air filtration units installed inside of them.

"I'll teach you all about Ignium some time, Rose," London said.

"Really?" she asked with an excited bounce.

"Yes, if we find someplace safe. Hopefully, an old-world bunker," he said.

London didn't tell her Ignium's entire history yet, though he was nearly an expert with how much he knew. London recalled that from the forties to the seventies, civilization aimed its focus on innovation. With Ignium leading the way, technological progress exploded, causing the world to change quickly.

Tremendous progress in agricultural and medical technology made the population skyrocket. As the population grew, so did the consumption of resources and the usage of Ignium. Around the late sixties, resources began to run dry, and with it the stability of world peace. Meanwhile, throughout the sixties to the seventies, heavy pollution darkened the world, making it colder, and destroying it all at once. This destruction created the world that London and Rose now lived in.

With such massive populations and over-consumption, nations went to war for resources. These wars were bigger than any war that had ever been waged in history, a war that ended with the downfall of man. After all the nuclear, bio, genetic, and chemical warfare, most world governments fell apart. Law and society followed, leaving the remainder of the population to collapse beneath hunger, sickness, and anarchy. In the end, the remains of man and a toxic world were all that was left. This was the world London grew up in, and this was the world Rose was growing up in.

London readjusted his backpack as they passed the ancient remains of an automobile power station. Rose looked over at it, taking it all in for a moment. The main building resembled an ancient gas station, though it was collapsed and covered in sand. The pumps were outside, but instead of gasoline or electricity, they pumped out Ignium.

"What do you think a bunker would be like, London?" Rose asked.

"Well, maybe there's a bunker deep underground in the East. People went to bunkers in the old world to survive. There's probably food, water, clean air, hot showers, everything. Maybe there would be books, too?" he explained.

"I'd like that; what do you think a shower is like?" Rose asked with a thin smile under her mask.

"I don't know... I know it'd be warm. Maybe it's relaxing. Wet too."

Rose giggled at his response.

The most London ever had regarding a warm, relaxing bath was a tub of cold water a long time ago, and he could scarcely grasp it in his mind. People in the old world always had hot water, and London was envious.

The pair continued wandering along the road. London knew his way around the world, using methods like determining the sun's position to know which direction he was going. They always headed to the East. Long ago, he read about old-world bunkers and was told of their wonders by someone, and it became his life's goal to go to one. When Rose came into his life, that goal intensified with the intent of protecting her.

London contemplated the fact that Rose had never had a place to stay and call home. His expression turned to a frown, and his doubt blossomed. Could he find an old-world bunker? Could he protect Rose? Could London teach her to survive? Could he even get them to an old-world bunker? These thoughts turned London sour when they came. He shook his head as if he could shake them from his mind.

The further they walked, the more buildings there were. London didn't like the ruins of ancient man. Dark memories were all that he had of them, and the further they ambled, the more cautious he grew.

"Look! Do you think that place has things we can take?" Rose remarked, pointing at a building.

London looked over to the building Rose pointed over to, another automobile power station. This one still stood, though heavily worn down. Graffiti covered it wall to wall. Surrounding it was a heavy chain link fence with barb wire running the whole perimeter. London saw that the Ignium chargers were gone. Wooden planks covered each door and window, though some ropes led to the roof and the chance of an easy entrance.

"Maybe, do you want to check it out?"

"Yeah!" Rose said, jumping a bit.

"All right. Let's be careful; remember the rules of a new place." London said.

Bread

11:32 AM, April 13, 2185

Thirty-one years later, Simon ran his fingers through the hydroponically grown potato plant's green leaves, admiring it before moving on. His face was expressionless. There was a focused air about him as he walked down the greenhouse of the Agricultural Sector.

As he did, he looked up through the glass of the greenhouse's roof, gazing past the UV lights lining the framing. He had a touch of a smile, a nostalgic feeling holding him as he looked up. There was the universe and the stars. They were beautiful, all that could be seen through the glass as the greenhouse rotated. He adored all of it, even though he had come here to fix the lights.

He was born and raised on a great space station called the Arcadis Station, which currently was the home of around two thousand people. The space station itself was a gigantic construction by the United States government back in 2077, launched in 2078 into space, bringing hundreds of people on board. These people were called the Raptured, the few saved from a dying earth. The space station used what many other Raptured stations used: centrifugal force to produce artificial gravity. The Agricultural Sector used this gravity to its advantage, specifically built where the gravity was the most effective.

Sometimes, Simon stopped to fix or replace a UV bulb. Strolling to the end of the last row, he turned around with a satisfied smile. Simon hated his position on the space station; most of the Workers did. It didn't matter

17

though, a fine job was a fine job, and that was his solace. Simon breathed in the filtered, recycled air with a relaxed expression.

Having finished his tasks early before the 1200 hours lunch call, Simon walked to the middle of the greenhouse and gazed out into space. With the constant rotation of the Arcadis, one never ran out of views. He stood there and contemplated freedom, admiring the stars as the station rotated.

After a few minutes of thought, Simon's expression soured, his nose wrinkling and smile fading as he caught a glimpse of an obscene sight. Earth, the damned home planet. He remembered when he was younger and still had to attend the Education Sector. Like every generation passing through the Education Sector, Simon and his classmates were taught of a time when Earth was green and blue. They had proof through pictures; his friends had doubts that they were even real.

Seeing Earth now filled him with bitter hatred for the ancestors who destroyed Earth. He looked across what used to be blue seas, green landscapes, and a sky full of clouds. Instead, what he saw was the eternal haze of pollution. It loomed over the planet, dark and sinister. Occasionally, his eyes saw strangled seas and barren landscapes through the haze. That was enough stargazing for now.

Simon walked to the door and opened it. Once outside, he proceeded throughout the complex hallways of the Agricultural System. It was a maze of many halls. On either side, there were greenhouses, each blocked with ID access doors. While he waited for the lunch call, Simon greeted his fellow workers as they passed by him.

It wasn't too long until an automated message rang out across speakers all around the space station. They were controlled by the station's AI named "Genetrix." The Workers somewhat relied on her for scheduling but did come up with mocking nicknames for her like "Naggy" based on her repetitive commands.

"All Workers report to the Nutritional Sector for lunch." the feminine robotic voice said.

In response, a wave of the entire Worker population began traveling to the Nutritional Sector. Simon joined the masses, falling in with the flock.

Everyone knew most of the space station like the back of their hand and navigated the complex maze work with ease. They formed lines as they surged to lunch, behaving almost like ants in the way they efficiently moved.

The Nutritional Sector was a massive place that expanded over the many years the station had spent in space. There were dozens of mess halls split between the populace. The Workers had the most mess halls since they were most of the population.

Simon followed the rest as he entered mess hall four and shuffled down the line toward the food stations. At each station, people scanned their Individual Chips. Once registered, they received a plate, food, and water, and were sent along to a table.

Everyone had an Individual Chip. It was a small chip that acted as a sort of registration for the population of the Arcadis. It was placed in the right forearm and used for many purposes on the ship. Everyone had a number, and it was almost amazing that the Workers didn't address each other by assigned numbers instead of their real names.

The food stations were placed along one wall of each mess hall and provided all the nutrition that the population required. After waiting in line, Simon needed only a moment to receive his portion. A plate dropped down a chute and softly landed in his hands; a machine immediately gave him food and water following the biological statistics provided by his Individual Chip.

It was all boring, artificial food portioned to a precise amount; the water was purified water, recycled from everywhere in the station.

Overseeing all the lines were Peacekeepers. They wore gray, smooth armor along their entire bodies and had full visor helmets. In their hands were tesla batons. Simon had never been in trouble enough to be hit by one, but he certainly feared them. Most Peacekeepers were bored and paid little mind to people like Simon as they watched for troublemakers to beat bloody.

After leaving the line, Simon took a moment to examine all the seats open for selection. A table near one of the gigantic windows looking out to the stars was his usual table. The table was empty, so he was alone as he approached it and sat down.

Once he sat, his gaze became filled with a full view of space. With a content exhale, Simon began to pick at his food. All the food on the station was much like Earth food before the Raptured left.

On Earth, plants were grown in incredibly efficient greenhouse skyscrapers, while the meat was grown in meat farms. All the foods were then taken to factories to be broken down and synthesized into artificial food. Artificial food was healthy. With every aspect of it subject to control, each bite became a mouthful of nutrition and vitamins. The only unhealthy part was the preservatives used to make food last forever, but that wasn't something the people on the space station had to worry about.

The proper amount of food was always created to sustain the population. There was, of course, an extra supply of emergency food. The downside of artificial food for Simon was that it was dull and lacked any natural feeling. He mechanically chewed as he ate. With no smell and barely any taste, his food was just cubes of "meat" and "vegetables." If he was lucky, he might've found some "fruit."

Since the food was so boring, Simon's mind turned to his thoughts. Thoughts gave way to imagination. Simon ogled the view with an entranced stare. Space was his greatest fascination, and he always wished that he was on a colonist ship going out into the galaxy to find new homes for humanity instead of here.

The Arcadis Station itself was one of many vessels tasked with waiting for a time when they could clean Earth and make it habitable again. At twenty-four, Simon was part of the fourth generation born on the Arcadis. To him, returning to Earth seemed like wishful thinking. The Developers, the station's brains, still said that the pollution was the same as it was a hundred years ago when the station took off. This knowledge turned any idea of return into hopeless dreams.

"Hey, Simon!"

The words startled Simon as his friend, Albert, threw himself onto the bench beside Simon. Albert grew up with Simon and was his lifelong friend, even attending the same classes and often the same jobs. Albert looked at Simon with a smile, the kind Simon could only attribute to being his.

"Hey, Albert," Simon said after swallowing his food.

"Are you going to the Thrash Games tonight?" Albert asked, happily digging into his food.

"I was thinking about it. I'm on the fence, might just go to my quarters instead," Simon replied.

"Don't be like that, man!" Albert said and tapped his friend's shoulder with a fist, "It'll be fun. I heard they might serve alcohol."

"Alcohol is crap here, Albert." Simon groaned and rolled his eyes.

Simon was right; alcohol was terrible on the station. So rarely was alcohol served that Simon doubted that they would serve it at the Thrash Games tonight. He never drank it anyway. It was a waste of time in his eyes, and most of the alcohol came from the station's black market. No one could really trust that market.

"Bah, you're no fun," Albert said, dismissively waving his hand.

"I know," Simon replied with an amused smile.

They paused for a moment to eat.

"You ever gonna sign yourself up for the Population Maintenance Program?" Albert asked with a smug half-smile.

"No, why?" Simon replied.

"Aw, c'mon. The Developers would love you. You're the perfect example of a Worker," Albert told him.

"We're all genetically modified, Albert. All of us are 'perfect' examples," Simon said, rolling his eyes.

Everyone on the ship, including the trio, was genetically modified from gestation. Every person was grown in a lab through in vitro fertilization. Because of this, none of them had genetic diseases or very few genetic-related issues. They were also modified to function better, though there was a regulation for the Developers to keep true to the human form.

"It would be fun. I hear all sorts of rumors about it," Albert said.

"Rumors are not facts," Simon replied, slapping the table with his palm.

Before they could carry on, another person joined them at the table. It was Thaddeus. He was massive compared to most people, a muscular powerhouse often tasked with heavy labor. He was a friendly man, and as soon as Simon met him, they connected.

"Hello, guys!" Thaddeus said, his voice powerful and deep.

"Hey, Thaddeus, anything new?" Simon asked.

"No, just the normal heavy work," he replied.

"Are you gonna watch the Thrash Game tonight?" Albert asked.

"Yeah, are you guys?" Thaddeus said.

"I am. Simon's still on the fence."

"You should go, Simon. It'll be fun," Thaddeus stated.

"Well, sure. If you're going, I'm in." Simon told them.

They began eating together, Simon daydreaming while Thaddeus and Albert indulged in rumors. Rumors were a part of the Worker class's culture; it was often that you could find a quiet conversation regarding rumors between two Workers during their off times. Simon didn't care for rumors. Most were untrue or too risky to talk about.

The conversation became hushed as Albert lowered his head and spoke.

"Did you hear that the Leaders eat real food?" Albert told Thaddeus.

"Really? Not like this synthesized shit? Like real food?" Thaddeus asked with slight amazement.

"Yeah, the three Workers that spoke about it got sent to the 'Deck.'" Albert whispered.

The Deck. The harsh prison of the Arcadis. It was formally called the Behavioral Mending Sector, which was a fancy name for it given to it by the Leaders. It was a prison area attached to the ship where the artificial gravity didn't work. There, no gravity was torture. Each cell was similar to solitary confinement. Prisoners seldom were given food and water, and there were also no toilets or showers.

Being sent to the Deck was equivalent to a death sentence. Being sent there the first time came with the removal of identity and proof of existence. The second time meant getting shot out into space. Law was strict in a place like this, and for good reason. Even so, most of the Workers still thought the punishments were too harsh.

"Bullshit! The Leaders eat what we eat, and you know it." Simon asserted.

"Keep your voice down!" Albert hissed.

"Want to get us sent to the Deck?" Thaddeus asked.

"Bah, bullshit. Almost as dumb as last week's rumor about Earth being habitable again. You can see the whole thing outside the window for crying out loud." Simon said with a reluctantly low voice.

"You like to eat what they tell you," Albert stated.

"I don't eat nonsense." Simon retorted.

"Who knows, Simon, lies are easy to swallow," Thaddeus told him.

Simon snorted.

"Yeah, that's why we talk about rumors day and night," he said.

They paused for a moment, then Simon continued.

"Why can't we talk about anything interesting? Like the universe, Earth's history, the colony ships going out and exploring?" he asked both of them.

"He's right. Why don't we?" Thaddeus followed.

"Never really put thought into it," Albert said with a shrug.

Before they could carry on, the commanding, robotic voice of Genetrix echoed throughout the station.

"All Workers report to the appropriate Tasking Stations for their assignments," she said.

"Well, that was lunch. See you guys at the game tonight." Thaddeus said, standing up and walking away.

"See ya. Simon! Ay, Thaddeus, wait up!"

Simon waved to them before he stood up. He had eaten his fill of food, a perfect portion as usual. He put his dishes away in a machine that zipped them away for cleaning and reuse, afterward going to a Tasking Station. The Tasking Stations were little consoles specifically located where the Workers resided, automatic machines that would scan the Individual Chip and assign a task for that person.

He joined the lines flocking to the Tasking Stations, waiting patiently. As soon as Simon got to one, he scanned his forearm and waited for a moment. The machine lit up and assigned a task.

"Worker 4221, Oxygen Maintenance Sector, filter cleaning," it told him.

Dawn

Eighty-five years earlier, the morning sun rose over the Eastern horizon. Rays of sunlight barely pierced the pollution haze. The winds had calmed down since the day before, leaving the wasteland still, silent, and undisturbed. Oliver woke up slowly, unwilling to open his eyes. A beam of sunlight shone through a hole in the wall, hitting his visor. Oliver groaned grumpily and sat up, immediately bumping his head on the bottom of the bench he slept beneath.

With a loud thud, he jolted awake.

"Fuck! Ow!" he cursed, rubbing his head.

Oliver shuffled out from beneath the bench. He felt stiff and slow. He stretched and yawned, his joints clicking and popping. Even with the smart suit on its max heat setting, it was still cold.

He checked the Smartwrist, finding that it was seven in the morning. Oliver lowered it and looked around. The mutant's corpse was still there, its battered body now sitting in a small pool of blood. It smelled disgusting. It was somehow overpowering enough to get through his gas mask. He did his best to ignore it as he ate breakfast and planned his day.

The normal agenda was all that he could conjure to mind. Travel further East, find water, food, supplies, and try not to die. Oliver smirked over the last step. A dose of humor that got him going in the morning.

Next, Oliver checked that he had all his belongings with him. He rolled the bedroll up and attached it to his backpack; after, Oliver rummaged through the backpack and made a mental note of its contents. Finally, he checked the filters of his gas mask and the condition of his gun.

Once he finished breakfast, he put on the backpack and immediately departed. His motorcycle awaited for him like a faithful companion. Oliver walked over to it, brushing off some sand before sitting down and starting the motorcycle. The Ignium engine came to life with a roar.

So much power in his bare hands felt good. It made him grin. He revved it a bit before turning and driving down the hill. Ten miles an hour, twenty, forty, sixty, all the way up to ninety. Oliver sped along the old-world roads, flying through the other fork in the road and continuing East.

The sunrise made the pollution haze ahead light up in bright colors of orange and red. It was stunning. It felt exhilarating to drive so fast, to feel the wind of such speeds, and to see ruins zip by and disappear. Oliver passed digital billboards that no longer worked, rusty and empty cars, and utility poles.

The thrill of the ride made the empty feeling of venturing into the wasteland fade. He didn't think of the dead trees that he passed, all of which lived and died in a polluted world. Moments like these made it, so it didn't feel like driving on a corpse that succumbed to the virus of humanity.

Occasionally, Oliver would have to go off the road to avoid fallen trees, potholes, and rocks. The earth he drove onto was hard and crunchy; a cloud of sand kicked up whenever he went off-road. Oliver couldn't help himself as the dirt ahead rose into a bump. He drove full speed despite the risk, flying over it and getting some air.

"Fuck yeah!" Oliver shouted mid-air.

The thrill passed as Oliver went back onto the road.

Oliver zipped past cars, trucks, and more poles. Sometimes there would be a skeleton on the side of the road, its bones bleached and half-buried by time. Oliver chose to ignore them. The bleak landscape began to feel endless as he sped along.

A shimmer in the distance broke up the mundane wasteland. Oliver slowed down and squinted to see what it was. He could make out two figures beside the remains of a tipped-over truck. He slowed down even more before finding a spot to park the motorcycle, shutting off the roaring engine, and hopping off.

He grabbed his gun and checked it again — plenty of ammo, plenty of energy. Oliver began to walk forward, sneaking toward the two figures. He saw that they were men, standing at the end of the truck's trailer. One man had his hands up in the air as the other man pointed a gun at him. Oliver broke into a jog, then a sprint as he ran towards the man with the pistol. He caught the tail-end of the dispute as he drew near.

"No more funny business! Give me your shit, or I'll melt your ass!" the man with the pistol demanded.

Oliver's heart was pounding with excitement and fear, his breath quickening. He had no idea what was going to happen. Would the man drop his weapon as soon as he saw Oliver? Would he shoot on sight? Oliver's thoughts rushed.

Oliver's boots crunched as they hit the ground, clicking as he went onto the asphalt part of the road. He went behind a car that was half-sunken into the side of the road, pointing his gun at the pair.

"Put the weapon down!" he ordered.

The man with the gun turned and looked at him, the two men staring at him in complete surprise. Oliver kept his gun on the man with the pistol, aim at the ready. He didn't even have a second to think as the man shot at him. The pistol, powered by Ignium, heated its shot in the blink of an eye and sent a molten mass of goo at Oliver.

Oliver ducked and dove behind the car. The other man ran inside the trailer of the truck as the battle broke out. Oliver stayed behind his cover as more molten goo flew toward his cover. It sizzled and burned, melting through the frame of the car and burning holes into the dirt beside him. Oliver was patient, waiting for a pause in the shooting.

Abruptly, as soon as the bursts stopped, Oliver popped up. He pulled the trigger, immediately aiming for where the man was taking cover. A massive surge of Ignium energy surged through the gun, sparks lighting the barrel up. Metal scrap left the gun, shredding everything in front of Oliver in an instant.

The truck's side became filled with holes, some of which went straight through and out the other side. At the same moment, the man let out a painful scream. In retaliation, more molten masses of goo sent Oliver back down for cover.

Oliver peeked for a moment, spotting the man turning tail. He bolted into the wasteland, shooting a couple of shots back to cover his retreat. The ragged clothing the man wore became stained with blood. A piece of shrapnel had pierced his side. Oliver was unsure if it was lethal but didn't bother to pursue him.

Oliver jumped over the car, avoiding the scorching puddles of goo. His gun was up and ready as he approached the trailer. The second man came out with his hands raised.

"Holy shit, you save–Woah! Wait! Wait! Don't shoot!" he said.

"Weapons! Drop them!" Oliver barked.

The man was wearing a makeshift mask, something more common in the wasteland. Oliver thought it looked peculiar. It had attachments, much like the flashlight on the side of his own. His clothes were ragged like the first man's clothes, made out of the hide of wasteland animals. Around his waist was a tool belt that had a few tools on it.

He watched the man pull out a knife and drop it on the ground. The tools in the tool belt followed.

"Do you have a gun?" Oliver asked.

"Yes, the other guy made me drop it already," he said, pointing to a simple pipe rifle lying on the ground.

Oliver carefully walked over and took it, hanging it off the side of his backpack while keeping his gun pointed at the man.

"Why shouldn't I shoot you? Why was that guy pointing his gun at you?" Oliver asked, his finger hovering over the trigger.

"Woah, Woah! Calm down! I got plenty of reasons for you to keep me alive!"

"Tell me now!"

"All right! All right! He wanted my stuff. Said he was hungry and thirsty and threatened to shoot me if I didn't give him something."

"Why shouldn't I do the same?" Oliver asked.

"Don't! Don't! I can help you. I got shelter, a place to hide out from Doomstorms and shit!"

"Doomstorms?"

"Yeah!"

Oliver narrowed his eyes in confusion. It took him a moment to recognize the name. It was the name used often by other wasteland dwellers. Doomstorm was the name used for the most extreme weather the wasteland had, sandstorms that reached into the sky, and shredded paint. Doomstorms could rip weak buildings apart and even pick up cars. They were unpredictable and fast, often killing wastelanders caught in the wrong place at the wrong time.

"I can find my own damn places to hide," Oliver said, moving forward with the gun.

"Wait! Wait! Hold on! I have water, fresh and enough for both of us!"

Oliver paused.

"What?"

"Yeah, yeah! I have a windmill not far from here, along with that house. It pumps water daily, fresh, and clean. It'll probably last for decades, maybe a century."

"Bullshit!"

"It's true! I'll take you to it right now."

Oliver considered for a moment.

"Stay right here," Oliver ordered him.

He nodded before Oliver left him standing there. Oliver ran off and retrieved his motorcycle, mounting it and starting the thundering engine. A few moments after, he drove back to where the man stood, his gun rested on part of the bike, and ready to fire. Oliver half-expected the man to run before he arrived and was surprised by his cooperation.

"Take me to it."

The man began to walk. Oliver drove slowly behind him. They moved down the road at first, then turned right into the wasteland and over the sandy dunes. The trip lasted for at least an hour. It consisted of the man walking and Oliver following on his motorcycle with a vigilant stare. The sun was halfway across the sky when the top of a strange pillar-shaped object over a dune caught his eye.

"Is that it?" Oliver asked.

"Yes," the man replied.

The pair moved forward and up a hill, a strange sight awaiting Oliver at the top. Below him, in a basin of earth, was a windmill. It was the kind of windmill built on stilts, the kind you'd find in the wild west. It tilted slightly. Rusty metal sheets its frame, all securely nailed into the legs of the structure. The blades of the windmill spun slowly, moving with the wind.

The pair moved down the hill, allowing Oliver to take a closer look. The entire thing was hand-made and built on top of an old-fashioned water pump dug out of the ground. Plastic jugs were strewn about, knocked about by the wind. Oliver looked up at the tall mass, mouth agape.

"I'll be damned," Oliver said, "This is yours? And the water's clean?"

The man nodded.

"You built this?"

"Yes, I built it up from a water pump. I think it was one of those pumps used for cattle in the old world. I came here a long time ago and found it half-buried in the ground. When I dug it up, I found out that it was hand-powered; but now the windmill does all the hard work," he told Oliver.

Oliver could hear it squeak as it spun. His eyes trailed across it all, following the pipes and mechanisms inside the protective metal sheets encasing the whole thing. It seemed sturdy and built to withstand Doomstorms. Oliver noticed a shovel propped up inside it, likely used to keep sand from burying the structure.

"What's your name?" Oliver asked.

"Sam. Yours?"

"Oliver. Sorry for almost shooting you back there."

Oliver didn't mean the apology and was still considering shooting the man. The only reason he didn't was that he needed the water and the shelter. It was best to get on Sam's good side, which was especially easy since Oliver just saved him from being melted. Regardless, he kept his gun ready.

"Ah, don't worry about it. I understand." Sam told him.

"Where's that shelter you told me about?" Oliver asked.

"North of here. It's really a shack.. or a cabin. Whatever you want to call it. It has a storm cellar, too; I hide down there when the weather gets bad."

Oliver smiled broadly beneath his gas mask, cheering inside his mind.

"Well, if you will, then lead the way," Oliver said, gesturing Northwards with his gun.

"All right. Promise not to steal my things?" Sam asked with a thin smile.

"If I wanted to steal anything, we wouldn't be talking," Oliver sternly said.

Oliver warily followed Sam with the bike as they left the basin and moved into the wasteland. As they moved, Oliver took notes of different landmarks to help find his way around. He noted cars, houses, odd-looking rocks, anything to prevent himself from getting lost.

It turned out that the windmill was somewhat out of the way from civilization, hidden from the rest of the world. Eventually, they found a road and began to follow it. After passing the shell of a car, Oliver could make out a structure in the distance.

It was a small wooden shack, sticking out like a sore thumb in the empty expanse. Around the property was a half-buried fence. Most of it had fallen, though there were still some patches of barbed wire. Behind the shack was a small entrance. Oliver assumed it was the storm cellar with an Ignium generator beside it. On the side of the shack, there was a hard clay chimney sticking out of the side.

They continued on the road until they went up to the front of the shack. Oliver parked his bike underneath the canopy above the door, shutting it down and getting off.

"Welcome to my humble abode," Sam said, opening the door and walking inside.

Oliver followed him inside and took the whole place in. It was an utter mess, cluttered to the brim. There was garbage, furniture, tools, everything of every kind laid in every corner and space. Oliver could trace out the paths made by Sam over time to navigate the small structure.

"Take a seat anywhere you'd like," Sam told Oliver, wading over to a sort of kitchen area.

The kitchen was the only "'empty'" space in the whole building. It had an old metal stove attached to the chimney going outside, one of the old kinds found in cottages. Oliver had only seen such stoves in pictures and barely recognized what it was.

It appeared that's where Sam would cook and heat the structure. Beside it, there were cabinets with rubbish piled inside and outside of them. Scattered throughout the whole area were cooking items like pots, pans, knives–all old and worn.

After a nod of understanding, Oliver tried to find a spot to sit. To him, it felt that there was so much stuff that it gave him a headache. He settled on a small, dispirited stool against the wall. He put his backpack beside it and sat down, looking around.

Under his breath, without Sam hearing it, he mumbled, "For fuck's sake, Sam."

"How long have you lived here?" Oliver asked.

"Uh... Couple of years. Don't remember, actually. Maybe ten years or so? It's hard to track time these days, you know?"

"I get you. It's 2100 if you wanted to know. New Year's was yesterday."

"Wow, it's been that long?"

"Yeah. Did you grow up in the old world?"

"I was born 2072. I was young when it all fell apart."

"Where did you live before?" Oliver asked.

"Denver, near the mountains." Sam replied, "Yourself?"

"Austin, down in Texas," Oliver told him, shifting on his stool.

A thud echoed from the other side of the kitchen wall. Sam went over to the window and looked through the curtains, gazing through the cracks of the planks covering the glass. He could see only sand and could hear howling wind from the other side.

"Storm's coming," Sam stated.

Ruin

Fifty-four years later, London was tugging at a hatch atop the building. He heaved his full weight on it as the metal groaned. It didn't budge.

"Damn it..." he whispered as he took a breather.

He gazed at Rose for a moment as she curiously examined the remains of an Air Filtration Unit. She was all over it. Like a bloodhound, she was examining every angle of it, from top to bottom. He smiled and then proceeded to work on the hatch again.

London tugged against it, letting out a loud grunt as he put more effort into it. Abruptly, the hatch opened with a deep metallic pop, with London falling onto his behind as immense effort led to clumsy success. He sat there for a moment with an astonished look beneath his mask.

"You got it open!" Rose said, skipping over to peer down the hole.

"Careful, don't fall down. I've no idea what's down there," London told her, holding out his hand in front of her.

"Do you think there are magazines down there?" she asked, gazing at him with a joyful gleam in her eye.

"Who knows? Maybe there's a delicious one-hundred-year-old bag of snacks too?" London said.

"Ewy! I hope there's something better."

"Food is food. We can only find out. I'll go down first."

Atop the roof were a tent's remains, made with four metal posts held down by heavy concrete blocks and a blue, ripped tarp attached to the top. Rose watched as London stood up, grabbed some ropes made out of old clothes, and placed them beside the tent.

London tied the rope around a post and had Rose stabilize it, even though her tiny mass would barely hold it if anything happened. He took the risk, though he was worried. London took comfort in recalling that getting on the roof wasn't too much of a hassle, even with sheet ropes leading up to it.

He tossed the rest of the rope down the hole and sighed sharply, mentally preparing himself. Before descending into the depths of darkness below, London paused to grab his flashlight. It was an old cracked flashlight, one of the small ones made in the previous century.

Through growing up in the wasteland, London had developed claustrophobia. It was always scary to go into a new place, especially using this method. There was no telling what range of monsters, traps, and other deadly things hid in the shadows. Despite his best efforts and experience, he breathed sharply as intense anxiety gripped him.

The building was similar in design to an ancient gas station from the early 21st century. It had shelves lined with dust, a collapsing ceiling, and a counter with a shelf canopy for holding cigarettes. London fought the darkness with the flashlight; his eyes took a moment to adjust to the gloom.

London was taken aback by what he saw. There were the remains of residence everywhere, the leftovers of the people that once lived here. There was garbage from corner to corner, scrap as far as the floor went, and rubbish stacked in piles.

He gazed at unpowered freezers along one side of the charger station, filled with piles and piles of empty cans and food containers. There were the remains of automobile parts on one side. TVs, computers, and other electronics piled up against the walls. Mattresses lined another area while garbage bags and boxes were strewn across the floor, each full of junk.

"Hello?!" London called out.

No such luck. It seemed empty to him. London was simply amazed by all the miscellaneous items his eyes could catch. He slowly panned the flashlight around and found more things such as office furniture, entertainment items like darts and board games, and tons of other objects. Regardless of all the items inside the structure, it was vacant as far as he could tell.

"Rose, come down! It's safe." London said, looking up the hatch.

Rose strolled over to the hole and peered down before climbing down beside London.

"Woah!" she blurted out, her young eyes trying to take it all in.

"Stay close to me. We don't know who was here before."

Rose nodded and kept very close to London, so close that she almost touched him. London began to take cautious steps forward into the embrace of the dusty darkness, guided by the illumination of his flashlight. They began to sweep the main lobby of the charging station. As they did, they found nothing particularly dangerous. After a while, Rose was allowed to explore the many piles of garbage, curiously grasping and examining everything she could lift.

London allowed her curiosity to bloom. To London, knowledge was one of the greatest powers in the wasteland. It was true in the old world, and it was true now. His attention was focused elsewhere, especially on the search for valuable items. London grabbed anything that could be deemed useful, such as a few books, magazines, and Ignium batteries.

"What is this, London?" Rose asked.

London looked over.

"An old smartphone, Rosey. Nothing useful to us,"

She gazed at it, proceeding to take it apart to see what the inside looked like.

Meanwhile, the light led London forward until something caught his eye, causing him to pause to see what it was. London grimly stared, eyebrows creased in observation. All over the dusty and rotting walls were words. They were scribbled, spray painted, drawn, and carved everywhere.

London gazed at it all, murmuring the words under his breath.

"See you soon..." said one wall.

"Love you!" there was in red.

"Where are you?" in faded blue.

"Please come home." another in worn pink.

"They're outside."

"Hello, world!"

"They keep me awake."

This building gave London the creeps, giving him a spine-tingle, unlike most buildings.

"There are eyes outside."

"Come home, please!"

"We won't last long."

London walked over to one of the freezers, spotting some ancient fridge magnets spelling out 'hungry' with the R on the ground.

"Love didn't conquer them."

Multiple scribblings of "bad" littered the wall.

"They're at the door. They'll be in here soon. Love you, xoxo." was the last thing London found.

London quivered slightly as a chill shot through him. He ambled over to Rose and scavenged with her, keeping close, making sure she was safe.

"Do you hear anything, Rose?" London asked.

"No, why?"

"This place is odd."

"It's creepy! But I found books!"

"Oh? Let me see." London said, Rose pointing him over to a pile of books she had been creating.

He walked over to the pile and began to sift through them. London found magazines, entertainment books, workout books, and coloring books. He decided to keep some and even toyed with the idea of staying in this place for a while. London sifted through the pile, turning it upside down.

"What's this?" Rose asked aloud as she picked up another magazine.

"What is it?" London responded, looking over.

"Hunks and twi-" she began, gazing over the cover which showed a muscular, half-naked man.

"Oh no, that's not for you!" London said, snatching the magazine from her hands.

"Wait! What is it?!" Rose asked in complete confusion.

"Something that's not for little hands like yours," London said, disposing of it while trying to keep himself from laughing.

"Why?"

"I'll tell you when you get older." London said, "C'mon, let's keep scavenging."

They continued scavenging, finding more books, food, and some hidden water bottles. London ventured into the charging station's back areas, finding himself grateful for his gas mask after visiting the remains of the bathrooms.

With every step, London could not get rid of shivers down his spine. Unease stayed with him in every inch of the building, and there was a sense of building dread in his stomach. He did not allow Rose to stray too far.

The words on the walls occasionally appeared in different areas, speaking of nonsense or warning. London could only infer that whoever lived here spent their last days waiting to be found by a greater evil, all the while losing themselves to madness. Rose could sense London's unease and hung on to the safety of his presence. They moved forward step by step, clearing the place out and viewing all remnants of the past.

To London, there was something slightly beautiful about the remains they found. Though they were creepy, it caused a state of remembrance of the past. In a way, London revered the past ancestors; their pain reminded him that they were human too; everyone was and is. Each piece of junk, scribbling here and there— it all spoke and told London of their humanity.

Rose did not imagine it as London. The only thing she saw was the curiosities of a bygone age, something amazing to be found in everything. Any piece of junk that told London of humanity told her a story. To the people of the past, the things they interacted with weren't so special and never given too much thought. Rose, on the other hand, could only dream of seeing how things were made, used, and discarded.

Another step forward met the pair with surprise as they entered the last room. London opened the door to the storage room, only for a pure shock to slap him in the face as a body fell out from the door. It hit the ground with a thud.

Rose squealed and stumbled back, London immediately swinging his baseball bat down upon it. Each inch of it landed perfectly, producing a squelching sound.

The body was still, but the sight of it was ghastly. London could barely make out anything human about it. It was a monster, with three arms and a face fused into one shoulder. It had lumps and tumors everywhere and decay spanning parts of its flesh. There was a blade sticking out the top of its head, seemingly from a trap.

"What is that?!" Rose exclaimed, eyes wide.

"Calm down, Rosey, calm down," London said, putting a reassuring hand on her shoulder after checking that the abomination was dead.

"What is that thing? It's scary."

"It's something from another time, Rose. A monster. Don't worry; it's dead."

"Are you sure?"

"Yes."

He dragged the body aside and slumped it in a corner. After it was out of the way, London peered into the storage room alongside Rose.

"Do you see what I see?"

"Food! And water!" Rose declared, going in immediately.

"Woah, woah!" he stumbled after.

"What?"

London pointed to a long chain with a broken end hanging from the ceiling. The light allowed them to make out what killed the mutant from before. It was a bladed trap, meant to swing down and potentially behead anything that triggered it.

"Remember, don't rush into a place without caution. It's okay, at least it was triggered before."

"Sorry, London," she said, looking down.

"Live and learn, Rosey."

London began to examine the storage room. It wasn't too large. It was a room the width of a human arm span and the depth of a small car. It had shelves on either side full of items, London checking every inch. There were food and water containers, all of them empty. The only good thing they found was Ignium batteries, placed on the top shelf.

They took the Ignium batteries, somewhat disappointed with the haul. Hanging on the wall opposite from the door was a clipboard detailing rationing and what supplies were here according to the last audit. He looked it over and found almost everything on the list missing, especially weaponry. It was rotten luck.

"That was a bad haul," London whispered. "But, you did well, Rosey," he said in praise.

"Thanks, London. Do you think we can stay here?"

"I don't know. I think we should move on. I don't like the look of this place."

"Yeah... Okay." Rose said, frowning.

"I'm sorry, Rosey, we'll find a place to call home one day," London said.

"I know... I just want it to come sooner."

"Me too. C'mon, up the rope."

Rose quickly climbed up the rope and onto the roof, London following after and taking a moment longer due to the weight he had to carry. He turned off his flashlight and adjusted to the brightness of the outside world. It was then that London's eyes met a gun.

"Drop your weapon and raise your hands," a woman said, pointing the gun straight at his head.

Circus

The metal crash echoed throughout the stadium.

The crowd erupted with cheers and jeers as the two combatants met each other. Simon sat and watched as the two began to battle it out. The Thrash Games wasn't his favorite form of entertainment, but it was a ship-wide holiday for most of the Workers.

Initially, the stadium and arena didn't exist. Its creation was a response by the Leaders to the population's desire to relive old-world sports and was only forty-three years old. The arena itself was a massive sphere. Centered in the middle of the Arcadis, it lacked the artificial gravity the rest of the station generated. Each Thrash Game hosted a new look for the arena, this time inspired by the meteor shower over Earth the previous month.

Rocks and obstacles floated around the arena— places to stand and bounce off of, allowing for all sorts of crazy maneuvers. The Thrash Games also had game modes such as Capture the Flag, Team Deathmatch, and more to entertain its fan base. This time it was Deathmatch, a gladiator game mode where two players fight until one loses.

Simon's eyes followed the combatants excitedly. Each had a full suit of armor styled like a spacesuit, both wielding melee weapons. Thrash Games players had sensors placed in their suits that detected stat changes. The inside of their visors displayed their stats, such as a health bar. In essence, the Thrash Games were an innovative combination of physical sports and game sports from Earth.

Albert had made sure Simon knew who was fighting. The Blue player was Catos Charnel, who wielded a twin-point spear. The Red player was Adonis Streets, who wielded twin swords.

Another crash led to another eruption from the crowd. The two players were constantly floating, using their suits to help them maneuver in zero gravity. Each was specific in the strategies they employed, the methods of movement they used, and how they used the environment. Simon always wondered how hard it was to think and fight in space where one could move in any direction.

"Go, Catos!" Thaddeus boomed.

"Kick his ass!!" Albert screamed, the most excited of the three.

"Hit him from above!" Simon shouted.

They sat in seats arranged all around the arena, attached to them by seat belts so they wouldn't float around. Vendors floated among the rows, giving out containers of sweets, mostly candies similar to bland sugar cubes or awful-tasting red licorice. All three of them had taken some containers, Simon occasionally eating a cube from his container.

"How low is Adonis?" Simon asked Albert.

"Uh... Hold on," Albert responded.

He quickly tapped the console on his armrest, a cheap device that buzzed to life upon touch. Albert put in a code and checked the statistics on a small screen.

"About 62%, Catos is down 54%, though he's making up for that fast," Albert said.

"He won the last tournament. He's winning this one. Get 'em, Catos!" Simon shouted.

There were a few teams that competed at every Thrash Games, each supported by different fractions of the Worker population. The naming of the teams was subject to those that formed them. The team favorite that Simon and his friends supported were called the Cargo Bears after the jobs the team members typically worked.

"Wait! Wait! Check this out. I think he's setting up his favorite move," Albert said, tapping Simon's shoulder to make sure he paid attention.

Simon watched as the two met at the center of the ring with clashing blades. Catos spun and blocked every strike by Adonis, equally dishing out his strikes. What Simon didn't notice were the intricate attempts that each employed to deceive one another. Adonis didn't notice either that for each strike he made, Catos was already four steps ahead.

Abruptly, Catos swung cross shoulder where Adonis blocked with his sword. At the same moment, Catos kicked out his right knee. As he kicked, Catos spun around and whacked Adonis across the helm with a fist before leaping off of him, bouncing off of a rock above and bringing down the spear straight into Adonis's back.

Albert watched as the 62% meter of Adonis shot down with each brutal strike until the final blow led it to 0%. The crowd exploded once more as Catos won the match, raising his arms in victory. A large hologram beamed into the center of the arena, spinning around. Upon it read 'VICTORY' in all capital letters.

"Hell yeah!" Thaddeus exploded, his voice thundering over Simon and Albert.

It took time for the crowd to calm. Meanwhile, the contestants left the arena through two different entrances. Before they left, Catos helped Adonis to his feet, the two shaking hands before floating in opposite directions.

"I'm going to go to my quarters Albert, swing by later if you want," Simon said once the two players parted.

"Aw man, you said you were going to watch."

"I said I would come. At least I'm here," Simon said.

"All right, night, man. I'll come over if I can," Albert told him.

Simon exchanged high fives with Albert and Thaddeus before he released his seat belt and floated away. The spectator areas had bars everywhere, allowing one to maneuver easily out to where there was gravity. The worst part about returning to normal gravity for Simon was just how weird it felt. He felt light as a feather and could not shake the feeling of being in zero gravity.

He left the arena. The cries and cheers of the crowd soon faded away as Simon clung to a railing. Soon enough, he regained his balance. His new task was to guide himself to the Residential Sector. The Residential Sector was one of the biggest sections of the Arcadis Station, divided into multiple parts. The Workers occupied the most space in the Sector.

The Peacekeepers, the station's security, were located in a different wing of the Residential Sector that only authorized people could enter. The most luxurious wing of the Residential Sector belonged to the Leaders who led the Arcadis. The Developers, the brains of the Arcadis who advanced technology, resided in the Development Sector.

He walked throughout the maze of halls, rooms, and glass tunnels that made up the Arcadis. Simon often paused to admire something interesting or simply to gaze out at space. Sometimes he wished he saw mountains, forests, and lakes instead of the great abyss of space. It was not that Simon disliked space, not in the slightest; it was boredom and envy. He had always seen space from windows and had a creeping feeling of being trapped in a cage for the last few months.

What Simon noticed that others did not was the increasing grip of the Leaders upon the governing of the station. More and more people disappeared, either shot out into space or sent to the Deck. Simon thought about it and recalled that he had not seen his usual co-worker, Jeff. Last he recalled, Jeff had told him some rumor about the Leaders having a change in leadership and that things were going to change. Things always changed is what Simon told him. Now Simon was slightly worried.

Another turn brought Simon down into the halls of the Residential Sector. He began to walk between the doors leading to cramped living spaces. Simon maintained a steady stroll down the hall until a loud ruckus in the distance caught his attention.

Curiosity got the better of Simon, and he slowly drew himself closer to the source. It took only a moment before he glanced down a wall with an open door. A messy pile of clothes lay in front of the entrance and Simon could hear screaming. A pair of Peacekeepers were raiding the room clean, one exiting with a woman in handcuffs in front of him. She struggled but was struck by a tesla baton each time she did. Simon hid before being caught peeking.

Such arrests had become more common since Jeff told him of the rumor. He listened down the hall for footsteps, prepared to look as if he had just unknowingly crossed the scene. Two more Peacekeepers came to the scene, and Simon could hear pieces of conversation.

"Any contraband?" the first one asked.

"Nothing much. Unauthorized digital book, some stolen tools, some plant, I don't know what it is. Probably something from the Agricultural Sector that she wanted for her room." the second one responded.

"What's the book?" the third one inquired.

"Something on history, let me check the title," the first one told the third, pausing to check before repeating the title, "*History Of Civilization Prior and During the Early 21st Century.*"

"Downloaded it without permission? Oh well, just helps us figure out holes in our digital security. Why would you even risk getting this book?" The second one said.

"Who knows, the Workers never make too much sense. That's why they do all the work," the first said and shrugged.

"Hah! Yeah, at least they're occupied. Nothing more boring than sitting on your ass all day hoping for someone to get caught doing something illegal." the third stated.

"Hey, you guys wanna watch the recording of the Thrash Games when we get off shift?"

Simon had heard enough. He slid away as sly as a fox, his footsteps silent as a ghost. Simon hurried back to his quarters, cautious of everything while trying not to look suspicious.

It didn't take long before he got to his door. Simon quickly slid his forearm into the Individual Chip scanner and walked into his room. A shuddering breath came from Simon as he closed the door behind him with relief.

In front of him was the entirety of what he owned. Living like every other Worker, Simon had a square, apartment-like room that was very simple and uncluttered. Built into the walls were a bed, shelf, cabinet, and desk to make the space smaller and more useful.

Just ahead of Simon was the reason this room was his favorite. Sprawling almost the entirety of the wall was a window that always had a magnificent view, especially from his bed.

To many, this room was like any other in the space station. For Simon, it was his home. After spending many years doing technical jobs, he knew how to make his small space larger.

After pacing around the room for a moment, Simon slowly went over to the air vent and unscrewed it. He snuck his hand in and reached, fingers slowly feeling out a square object. What Simon felt was the cover of a book, his fingers caressing the sides and the pages for a moment. On the Arcadis, there were only so many material books. Most belonged to the Leaders in a secret area of the Education Sector. The rest had been shot out into space.

When Simon was young, he became friends with the history teacher, who gave him this book before graduating from the Education Sector. At a time when shooting books out into space was common, Simon received this one. He had kept it safe ever since, and it was his most important secret.

He grasped the book and pulled it out, gazing at the title. It had golden letters and spelled out *"The Omnipotent Eye and Individuality by Carl Kavanaugh"* on the black cover.

It was a very old book from the early twenty-first century, discussing the Internet's inclusion in modern life. Specifically, it discussed government surveillance by devices and Internet monitoring, especially to curtail individual rights.

After a while, he sat beside the vent and began to read. Simon flipped through the pages as he had done many, many times before. It was his favorite book, mainly because it was the only one that wasn't controlled by the Leaders. Therefore, he knew it was real. He read it with the same enthusiasm as he did the first time he ever opened it.

Simon read for a while, soon being interrupted by a knock at the door.

Shopping

"Where are we going?" Oliver asked.

"To a town north of here," Sam replied.

Oliver stretched as they walked, feeling his joints crack and pop. He warily looked around the wasteland surrounding them, searching for any threat that might appear.

"Why?" Oliver asked, raising a brow.

"Uh, well... I've been looting there. I've been there a few times already, but it's a long task."

"So, this is just a looting run?"

"Sort of. I'm trying to find some stuff for a special project," Sam told him.

"A special project?"

"Have you ever heard of electricity?" Sam asked.

Oliver paused for a moment, looking blankly ahead as he thought about the word.

"You mean that stuff they used way back when before Ignium?" Oliver said.

"Correct."

"What about it?"

"Well, as you're well aware," Sam said, gesturing to the polluted sky, "Ignium is toxic in large amounts, like how it was used back then."

"Yeah," Oliver nodded.

"I was thinking humans are bound to rebuild civilization. I'm sure you've seen the tribes and caravans popping up here and there. Why should we use Ignium again after all the destruction it caused?" Sam explained.

"That... makes sense. What does electricity have to do with this, Sam?" Oliver asked.

"Well, I found some old information about electricity. I think that it could replace Ignium if we use it correctly. It's not as easy to make or use, but it's not toxic at all. I haven't shown you yet, but I've actually made some electricity. I was thinking if I could learn more about electricity, I could give humanity some hope, you know? I've been searching for the right material for a long time."

"You think this town has the right stuff?"

"Probably, but a bunch of buildings are half-buried. I've been digging out the hardware store for weeks. I just got to the door before I met you, but I need to blast the airlock before I can get in. So, I brought some of these," Sam said.

Oliver watched as Sam took off his backpack and opened it. He pulled out two round objects the size of tennis balls. They were little bombs, handmade with small smiley faces on them.

"Oh, fuck," Oliver said, blinking in surprise, "Nice touch with the smiley faces."

"Thanks," Sam replied, putting them back.

They continued onward through the wasteland. The pair followed a road going north, passing old cars and trucks. Sometimes they'd find a skeleton or the ruins of a half-sunken or half-collapsed building. The wasteland was quiet. The only disturbances were their boots and the wind. As Oliver walked, he barely noticed sand bouncing off his visor.

Soon, Oliver could make out the faint outlines of buildings on the horizon. Ahead of them was a small town that appeared to consist of over twenty buildings. Many of the buildings had sand piling up against them, while a few had sunken into the ground.

Oliver surveyed the town as they entered it. He looked at each store entrance, looking into the sand-filled ruins.

"You never quite get used to them, do you?" Sam remarked, gesturing to the ruins.

"No, you don't. Where's the hardware store?" Oliver asked.

"Down the street. Careful, I have a couple of traps around here."

Oliver looked at him, moving his head forward and raising his brows.

"And you didn't think to tell me that before we came here?"

"I forgot to mention it," Sam said, chuckling.

Oliver shook his head. They approached an old brick hardware store that was half-buried in the sand. Oliver examined the exterior, walking side by side with Sam before looking at him.

"Where's the entra- Woah!"

Oliver fell down a hole in the front of the hardware store, landing with a thud in front of a door.

"Fuck! Oliver, are you okay?" Sam asked, sliding down into the hole beside him.

Oliver groaned and sat up.

"Fine, I'm fine. Just wasn't looking where I was going," he told Sam, looking up, "Fuck, this is deep."

"You can guess why it took so damn long to dig it," Sam said.

"No shit."

"Right, I'll get this airlock busted down. You might wanna stand back." Sam said, gesturing for him to move back.

Oliver climbed out of the hole and watched as Sam set down the backpack. He took out one of the smiley bombs and attached it to the door with something sticky. As Sam lit the fuse, he grabbed the backpack and ran out of the hole. The pair ran and dove for cover a few moments later.

A dozen seconds after they hit the ground, an explosive sound echoed loudly from the hole. Flying smoke and debris followed it. They stopped and looked at each other, both of them laughing as their faces lit up with excitement. They quickly hopped over their cover, running over to check out the results.

"Damn!" Oliver remarked.

The door had been completely blown inward, ripped from its hinges. The second door of the airlock remained, though clearly damaged. Sam repeated the same process as before, attaching the second smiley bomb to the door and running as soon as he lit the fuse.

More debris and smoke flew from the hole as the explosion demolished the second door. The pair returned to the hole, high fiving each other in giddy excitement. There was nothing like blowing things to smithereens. Oliver slid down the hole first, the pair holding their guns ready and turning on their flashlights.

The dust was still settling as they entered the structure. It was dark and cramped. At the front of the store was a cash register, half-covered in sand. Oliver looked over at the sand, following it to the store window. It appeared that the front window had broken some time ago, allowing sand to flood into the building.

Oliver moved his light to the rest of the store. The rest of the building consisted of shelves, many of which were empty as the light revealed them.

"What are we looking for?" Oliver whispered, glancing at Sam.

"Anything. Place seems empty, but keep a lookout. I've found two mutant nests in this town before," Sam replied.

Oliver nodded and moved further into the small expanse of the hardware store. Most of the shelves were lined with dust, vacant of the bounties of the old world. He walked along the rows of aisles, shining a light down each until he got to the other end of the building. Once Oliver searched the main building, he moved to the back portion of the store.

First, he opened the bathroom and searched it. Loud slams echoed through the structure as he kicked open each stall door, gun ready to fire as he checked each stall. Once the bathrooms were clear, he searched for a back room. After a minute, Oliver found a door near the right rear of the hardware store. It was locked.

He had no trouble at all kicking it down, the entire door bursting off the hinges and landing in a cloud of dust. Oliver walked forward, finding himself in a large room full of wood, metal, and other supplies. At the end of it was a garage door. He walked into the room, searching every crevice and corner.

As he searched, he found a skeleton in between two piles of wood. It caused him to jump a bit, a startled gasp escaping his lips.

"Sam! It's all clear!" Oliver shouted.

"All right! What's the backroom looking like?" Sam asked.

"Lots of good shit!" Oliver told him.

Oliver knelt and examined the body. Its bones still had decayed strips of flesh hanging off of them, covered by torn clothing. Oliver's eyes trailed down until it saw a couple of empty jars and then a large needle.

"Gah! Fuck!" Oliver hissed, stepping back at the sight of the needle.

At the same time, Sam entered.

"What? You good?" Sam asked.

"Just... I'm fine; it's just a needle," Oliver told him.

"Wait, you're afraid of needles?" Sam asked, trying to contain his laughter.

"Shut up," Oliver said.

"You are!" Sam said, bursting into laughter

Oliver sighed and shook his head, walking out of the room.

"Oh, come on! It's funny, Oliver!"

"Shove it, Sam!" Oliver said, throw a fist in the air.

Sam continued to laugh for a few minutes until he calmed down. After, he joined Oliver and gave him a duffel bag that was folded into his backpack.

"Here. Pack as much as you can into this." Sam stated.

Oliver nodded and began moving throughout the store. His hands were greedy, stuffing anything he saw into the bag. Ignium batteries, chains, wires, tools, everything he could grab was stuffed into the bag. After an hour, the bag was half-way filled.

Sam came back with his bag full of supplies, grabbing the one Oliver filled in the other hand.

"All right, this should be plenty. Can you grab one of the boards back there and bring it with us?" Sam asked.

"Sure," Oliver replied.

He walked into the back room, grabbing a large board and heaving it onto his shoulder. Slowly and steadily, he walked out of the hardware store, the door being the most difficult spot to traverse

Soon, the pair were leaving the town behind and moving back into the wasteland. They breathed heavily as they strained under the weight of their loot.

"It's a bit less than I expected, but this is a damn good haul," Sam remarked.

"It's fucking heavy," Oliver groaned.

"Preaching to the choir," Sam replied.

Refugee

10:32 AM, May 13, 2154

London dropped his baseball bat on the ground and raised his hands in the air slowly. In front of him stood four people, each armed with a different weapon. Rose was grabbed and put aside. They took her knife and rabbit, keeping a gun on her. Under her mask, her eyes were wide with fear.

"Turn around and put your hands on your head, slowly," the woman in front of him ordered.

He did as told. They took his baseball bat, plasma pistol, knife, and backpack before placing him beside Rose. She gazed at him with terror in her eyes, close to tears.

"What should we do with them?" asked the woman.

"I don't know. Maybe shoot 'em? They could be spies for Patria," a man responded, shrugging.

"They're not," said a man with an elderly voice.

"How do you know?" asked the woman.

"Her," he replied, pointing at Rose.

The group all looked among each other. London had no clue what they meant by spies or Patria. He planned for the worse; to tell Rose to run while stepping in front of a hail of bullets. London watched as the woman walked up to him, placing her makeshift pipe pistol against his chin.

"Who the hell are you people?" she asked in an aggressive tone.

London stared directly back at the woman. She was shorter than him with a mask as shoddy as her weapon.

"I'm London. This is Rose," he answered calmly.

"Where do you come from?" she asked.

"The West, we are nomads," London replied, keeping things simple.

"They're not Patrians," the elderly man stated.

"How can you be sure? They could be trying to fool us with her!" she said, gesturing at Rose.

"I just know. We'll keep an eye on them," he replied.

The woman stepped back and lowered her gun, looking London over with suspicion. By now, the tenseness of the group had faded a bit, only lingering like a bad smell. The old man approached, eyeing London through a military gas mask with a friendlier expression.

"Your name is London, eh?" asked the old man.

"It is."

"And you, my dear, are Rose?"

"Y-Yes, sir." Rose stuttered.

"Well, I am Reginald. I somewhat lead this wonderful group," he told them in a friendly voice.

"A pleasure," London replied distrustfully.

"This is Alisa. Forgive her for being a bit tense with y'all. She's our guardian. Best gun skills I've seen out of any woman," the man said, Alisa and London exchanging nods.

Alisa was a short and sturdily built woman, with a gas mask with a full-face visor with a large crack going across it. In terms of quality, it seemed like it barely worked. London could see that she was ill-tempered, with a seemingly permanent scowl on her face.

"Archie is our best scavenger," Reginald said as he gestured to Archie.

"Ay! Nice to meet you!" Archie told London with an enthusiastic voice.

Archie seemed very thin and scrawny, even for a wasteland survivor. Though scrawny, he was light and spry as if he could climb anything. His gas mask was similar to Alisa's, though it seemed to be in better condition.

"You, too," London said plainly.

"Tommy, well, we don't know much about him, but he's proven to be an asset to the group."

Tommy idly waved at London, standing near the ropes which led to the roof. He had goggle visors and carried the biggest pack out of everyone. Tommy also had the biggest build of them all and was likely able to crush skulls with his bare hands.

"We have two more down below. I assume y'all cleaned out this here building?" Reginald asked.

"Yep, nothing much down there except trash," London told him.

"Where are y'all heading? West seems a bit far off from here."

"We're going to the East. I'm trying to find a better place for her," London said, gesturing to Rose.

"Well, as luck would have it, we're heading East too. Y'all are welcome to join us. The territory ahead is pretty dangerous."

London looked at Rose, his eyes asking her for an answer. She nodded a plain 'yes.' It would be nice to have a group to protect them, and they seemed to know the area ahead. It didn't take him more than a few seconds to come to an answer.

"Sure, we'll come with you."

"Wait, what? They're coming with us now? Come on, Reginald, we don't know who they are," Alisa protested.

"They're unarmed, Alisa, and one's a child. I'm sure we can handle them. Should we leave them to the Patrians instead? Y'all know what they'll do to them, especially her. Have mercy for Pete's sake," Reginald told her.

Alisa scoffed and accepted the old man's words with a shake of her head. She and Archie began to walk behind London and Rose, Reginald leading them down from the roof. It took a minute before they all got to the ground. As they did, London met a surprising sight as soon as his feet touched the ground.

In front of him was an elderly woman in the strangest form of wheelchair he had ever seen. Holding the entire thing up were spider-like legs made from various parts and powered by a small Ignium engine. It had a seat made out of the old parts of a lawn chair. The machine also had a little table extension attached to the left armrest, an ashtray, and a cigarette box resting on it. In the back, on the other side, was an umbrella with a bug light.

The woman sitting on it was very old and frail, with an oxygen mask on her face instead of a gas mask. It was one of the old world ones found in hospitals, attached to an oxygen tank in the back that pulled in air, filtered it, concentrated it, and kept her alive. London had no idea what to call the wheelchair other than "spider chair."

Standing beside her was a man similar to London in build but a bit shorter than him. London took note of the supplies he had, mainly medical.

"London, Rose, meet my beloved wife, Margaret, and our medic, Finlay," Reginald said.

"Reginald, are these more folks escaping the Patrians?" the old woman asked, her voice sounding electronic.

"No, my dear. Nomads, but surely in danger from the Patrians."

"Well then, I'm glad to see some new faces in our little group."

"A pleasure to meet you, madam." London said, "Rose, what do we say?"

"Nice to meet you!" Rose squeaked.

"Hey, I'm Finlay, as you know. If you guys need any medical assistance, I'll give it. You guys aren't Patrians, and you don't seem to be tribals either, so that's enough for me."

"Thank you," London said.

"All right, people, we need to get moving if we're going to cross the city today. I want us to stick together; we'll be moving pretty slowly. Finlay, Archie, you guys in the back. New people in front of them, then Reginald and Margaret. Tommy, you're with me in the front, " Alisa told everyone.

The group left together just as quickly as they met. London was surprised that they didn't shoot them on sight. He was wary without his weapons, feeling naked without any protection. Rose held London's hand as they walked, gazing around in distress. Some of the group occasionally gave the pair suspicious looks, projected mainly at London.

They moved into the city ahead. Ruins enveloped them as they marched. Office buildings sat crumbled, fast food joints slumped along the road, and empty, dreary shopping centers surrounded them as they pushed on. The street harbored cars from decades before.

The cars were rusty, picked over for parts, left to be hollow husks.

Meanwhile, the ancient buildings surrounding had their paint stripped off long ago by extreme weather, left empty and dull. London had hoped at the beginning of the day to avoid a place like this.

For hours they trekked through vacant streets and collapsing ruins. London's anxiety grew more intense. As they moved, he noticed small things like the mechanical clicking of the old woman's arachnid wheelchair. Every dark corner among the buildings felt as if they had monstrosities lurking within, even though London counted on it being his imagination. Still, anxiety asked him, "how do you know?"

The rising sun began to loom overhead, each ray it produced trying to pierce through the haze in the sky. Yet, the bleak streets felt no safer. Eventually, the over-looming sun began to set, and the group's objective shifted to finding shelter. London shuddered and placed a protective hand around Rose as mutant birds cawed overhead. He couldn't shake the feeling of stalking eyes deciding over which parts of their bodies were the juiciest.

"Reginald, where are we stopping today?" Alisa asked.

"Office or apartments, somewhere high off the ground," Reginald said, eyeing the surrounding structures.

"There! That could work!" Archie said, pointing at a building.

It was one of those forgotten office buildings, likely housing an extension to some giant company. The structure was barren, worn by at least a century of hazardous weather. Countless Doomstorms had destroyed most of its windows, and it looked like it was tilting slightly. It seemed safe enough for the group.

"Good pick, Archie. Let's go, everyone! Archie, go find a way upstairs," Alisa said.

Archie took off into the building, swift upon his feet and disappearing inside. London was surprised by his speed. The entire group slowly followed, having no trouble gaining access inside. Archie didn't take long to come back, leading them to a set of stairs. London expected to have to help them bring the old woman up each level. Instead, when the arachnid wheelchair got to the foot of the stairwell, it simply crawled its way up with complete stability.

They gathered on the fifth floor, Archie searching the building and finding it empty. Once settled, they made a campfire. The group gathered around the fire, London and Rose sitting in a corner with the others surrounding them. One of the group members always stood watch. The task mainly was staring down at the darkening streets or listening. Alisa seemed to be the most stubborn out of all of them, volunteering for most of the night.

As the night rolled in on the forlorn ruins of the city, the monsters of the night began to awaken. Shrill screams and horrid shrieks filled the air, packs of beasts marauding the city. The group set up a tent over the fire, shielding its glimmer from the rest of the world. Once settled, they began to eat and talk among themselves, sharing stories and igniting memories of their old ventures.

London took note of what they spoke of and who spoke to who. Reginald leaned on the wheelchair and whispered to Margaret, who sat with a smile, sometimes responding or sometimes looking at the group.

They both seemed very old and might've been alive in the old world. Margaret was the thinnest and frailest, with a boney frame. Reginald was nearly the same but still had muscle on him.

Alisa was on watch. London looked out to her, spotting her unchanging expression of attitude under her visor. She might've been shorter than London, but she was much wider and muscular, likely stronger than most of the group. She also wore a police vest, with scrap metal or tough material covering everything else.

Meanwhile, Archie and Finlay spoke, laughing like the best of friends. Finlay was like London and wore cloth clothing covered in packs and bags. Archie was taller than both of them but very thin. He also wore clothing similar to Finlay's, though without all the bags and equipment.

The one who didn't speak but instead stared directly into the fire with an empty gaze was Tommy. He wore thick swat armor mixed with scrap metal from head to toe. He was also taller and wider than the whole group and exuded an aura of dormant lethality that could awaken at any moment. London couldn't tell if Tommy could be trusted, struggling between discomfort and disregard.

Soon, the conversation hushed between Archie and Finlay after some joke. For a while now, Margaret had been staring at Rose with a kind look. She leaned forward in her chair and gazed at London, her sight fading with age.

"Forgive me, my memory is terrible. Your name was London, dear?" she asked.

"It is."

"Where do you come from, all alone with this child?"

"The West," London answered simply.

"The West? Any tribes, cities?" she asked, thinly smiling at his blunt answers.

"I come from the West, ma'am. I ain't got much to tell, sorry."

"We all have a story, dear. What is hers?" Margaret pointed to Rose.

"A long one," London said before Rose could speak.

"I understand. You may ask us any questions, dear. We will give you time to answer ours."

London paused and stared at the fire, dwelling on the question for a few moments. He then looked up at Margaret.

"Who are the Patrians?"

Spark

7:33 PM, April 13, 2185

Simon clapped the book closed. He scrambled to throw it back into the vent as he heard the knock, proceeding to hastily screw the vent shutter back on. The knock came again, this time more firmly. Simon walked up to the door and opened it with a button, relief striking him immediately.

"Hey, Thaddeus. Why aren't you at the Thrash Games?" he asked with a confused tone.

"Can I come in?" Thaddeus asked with soft urgency.

"Y-Yeah, sure," Simon replied.

He stepped back and let Thaddeus into his room. There was a moment of silence as Thaddeus looked over Simon. His eyes were wide, and his brow raised in concern, worrying Simon.

"Why are you here? Where's Albert? And why aren't you at the Thrash Games?" Simon asked impatiently.

"I don't know where he is. We were watching the fight after you left, halfway in. I don't know what happened, but the Peacekeepers came and took someone away. The people around them tried to fight back, and then there was a massive brawl. I left before I got caught up in the mess, but Simon, man, I don't know what's going to happen."

"W-Woah! What? Thaddeus, they're gonna arrest all those people!"

"There's nothing we can do about it. Albert disappeared before I even knew what was going on. They're probably gonna shut down the event," Thaddeus said.

"I saw a woman being arrested on the way to my room," Simon replied "Why?"

"I don't know, didn't stay long. Could've been a random raid, or someone could've spoken to the Peacekeepers. She had a digital book."

"Why did she have a digital book? And why would she be arrested for that?"

"Illegally downloaded, obviously. Why she had it is beyond me."

"How the fuck can something be illegally do-"

The robotic voice of Genetrix rang throughout the station. Her voice had the same robotic tone as every announcement. Even so, Simon couldn't help but hear the voice as piercing and cold. She was a cruel overlord.

"All Workers are to report to their designated quarters. Any Worker caught outside of their quarters will be detained," she commanded.

Thaddeus and Simon looked at each other. They were right; the Leaders shut down the Thrash Games. It would cause shock waves in the Worker community, and there would be rumors and arrests for weeks to come. The repercussions of the Thrash Games brawl would linger for months.

"Simon..." Thaddeus began.

"Thaddeus, get back to your room. It's no use finding Albert; if he's caught out, then he's caught," Simon said.

Simon led Thaddeus to the door, opening it and already finding people running past. Thaddeus shook his hand before leaving. Simon gazed outside at the chaos, watching as Thaddeus disappeared among the flooding crowd. Simon then closed the door and walked over to his bed.

Simon sat and stared at the door for a while, listening. Footsteps were constant as the crowd outside rushed, thinning out over five minutes. He awaited almost in anticipation for a different kind of sound. After a while, harsh footsteps from combat boots echoed as they ran through the halls. The Peacekeepers had arrived.

Now the long night began. In the far distance, the first crash rang. A door opened somewhere near his room, followed by a crash and a scream. Every crash made him tense up. Simon could only hope that they'd overlook him. He decided to lay down and cover himself with his thin blanket, trying his best to sleep.

Throughout the night, there were raids, which led to people randomly being arrested. The sporadic chaos kept Simon awake as he stared at the ceiling. He counted at least six arrests. He eventually fell asleep, awakened at random times at night by the chaos outside.

What was the meaning of this—Simon asked himself how many faces would be missing at the mess hall tomorrow? These questions lingered and pestered him in the restless hours of the night, growing worse each time a slam awakened him.

While he was awake, his gaze shifted between the ceiling to the room's window. The stars were kind and gentle in his eyes, unlike the Arcadis. To Simon, the stars were the food stores, and Simon was a rat in a cage. No matter, the stars lulled him back to sleep each time he woke up. Toward the end of the night, the chaos settled down, and there was silence.

"All Workers, good morning," the voice of Genetrix said, echoing throughout the Arcadis in the morning. "All Workers are to attend to hygiene before exercise."

Simon groaned and rolled out of bed, tired and angry. He almost cursed loudly at the voice. Lazily, he tended to the routines set up by the Leaders. Once twenty minutes passed, Genetrix rang out again and proceeded to give the population a morning exercise. Yoga and calisthenics, the usual.

"Exercises complete. All Workers are to report to the Nutritional Sector for breakfast."

Simon frowned in irritation. At least they could've made Genetrix talk normally. It sounded as if they tried to rub in the robot part. He went out through the door and joined the morning flood. As he followed the crowds, he looked at everyone. Each person seemed shaken from the night before, and Simon could already see that a few people were missing.

The ant lines formed again, and they shuffled out of the Residential Sector. They split up into different parts of the Nutritional Sector, Simon going to the normal branch he usually frequented. As he walked into the mess hall he usually went to, he noticed all the Peacekeepers.

There were normally a few per mess hall, watching over everyone. This time there were more than a dozen all around. The Workers were visually uncomfortable as they walked in, gazing at all the Peacekeepers.

The Peacekeepers had stern faces, and Simon felt as if they would beat any one of them for coughing in the wrong direction. Eventually, Simon got his food, walked to his usual table. Thaddeus was already there, and Albert was missing. Carefully, he sat down at the table, afraid to somehow offend a Peacekeeper.

"How did you make it through the night?" Simon whispered to Thaddeus, keeping his head low.

"Dude next door got detained. He went quietly, though. I hope they have mercy on him. After that, I didn't hear too much. It's better not to talk about him," Thaddeus replied.

It was considered bad luck among the Workers to talk about people sent to the Deck since they didn't exist anymore. Simon knew that those people would never register on a list as the same person again. Nobody was ever sent away just for talking about those people, but Simon faintly recalled it was a minor violation to do so.

"I heard a lot where I was. My night was crappy. Where do you think Albert is?" Simon asked him.

"I don't know. I hope he didn't go with the rest of them."

"Shit... Maybe."

Usually, they'd be discussing rumors and joking around, but instead, they ate in silence. Occasionally, Simon stared out the great windows and contemplated. He tried his best to avoid exchanging glances with a Peacekeeper. The lines were still going, everyone soon getting their meals. As he ate, Simon bent over his plate as if he could hide by doing so.

Typically loud chatter, laughter, and occasionally horseplay filled the mess hall. It was nothing like that today. Voices were hushed, some angry, some sad, some confused. Most people held their heads low, while the bravest of them all stared defiantly. Meanwhile, rumors bounced from table to table as the Workers whispered.

Simon was caught by total surprise as a plate landed beside his. He and Thaddeus both looked up, relief hitting them immediately. Albert made it through the night. Simon knew he had done nothing wrong; he would never.

"Albert! You made it through the night." Thaddeus stated with a smile.

"Are you okay, man?" Simon asked immediately.

"Yeah! Yeah, I made it." Albert responded with relief in his voice.

"Where were you?" Thaddeus asked, "I lost you when the brawl started."

"I was fucking getting myself out of there. I didn't want to get caught up with the rest. I didn't know what to do, so I ran to my quarters."

"You had us scared for a good minute!" Simon said, clearly glad.

"How many people got arrested last night?" Albert asked, "After the announcement, I heard all sorts of shit."

"No numbers yet. I'm sure someone will come up with something. The Leaders sure as hell won't tell us," Simon told him.

"Damn it all, why did they arrest so many? They need us, right?" Thaddeus wondered.

"There are a couple hundred of us. They don't need all of us. I'm sure we're just slaves to them, pieces of property," Simon said.

"They probably arrested forty people, I reckon!" Albert stated.

"Ten would have been enough to send all of us a message. I don't know if you guys can read it, but I think they just said we're fucked," Simon said.

"We'll make it through this. They can't send us all to the Deck, or shoot us all into space," Thaddeus reassured.

"No shit, brother," Albert said.

"I'd like to see them try," Simon followed.

They ate and murmured among themselves, as all the tables did. Thaddeus and Albert explained what happened from their perspectives, telling Simon how they thought the brawl broke out and what happened when the Peacekeepers stepped in.

Both Thaddeus and Albert were there when the brawl started. It began when a few Peacekeepers came to escort a Worker out of the arena. As they did, the other Workers tried to stop them, which led to the Peacekeepers beating a few people. Once the beatings started, chaos followed.

People were floating everywhere as the fight broke out. Workers and Peacekeepers floated through the air, exchanging blows back and forth. After a few minutes, a flood of Peacekeepers arrived into the arena and arrested everyone involved with the brawl. By then, both Thaddeus and Albert had left.

Thaddeus explained how he avoided the brawl, got to Simon, and survived the flood of people after the announcement. Albert told them how he escaped as soon as the brawl broke out and then described what it felt like running back to his quarters. Soon enough, their conversations came to an end.

"All Workers report to the appropriate Tasking Stations for their assign-ments, " Genetrix rang out.

Breakfast was over.

Storm

Sam looked out through the dirty window, peering between the wooden boards barricading it. The sun hardly illuminated the outside world, sunlight weakly beaming in through the window. Soft winds blew in the early morning, low currents of sand carried with them.

Oliver woke up on a pile of pillows and blankets. Slowly, he sat up and stretched. As he let out a muffled yawn, his fingers dug under his gas mask and rubbed his face. After enough time, he scooted over to the end of the pile and looked at Sam.

"What's the plan for today?" Oliver asked groggily.

"Well..." Sam responded, beginning to make breakfast, "We have breakfast to start with; then we should probably get some more water for the week; then check our supplies, and I might get some projects started."

"Are you really gonna try to plant those seeds you found?" Oliver asked, standing up and stretching again.

"No point in just letting them sit," Sam told him, "I was thinking of experimenting with some UV lights in the basement. It'll be impossible to grow them outside."

"Did you find out what they are?"

"Carrots, I think. Package is really worn, but if we're lucky, and if I remember how to grow them, we'll get carrots in no time."

"Hopefully,"

It didn't take long to prepare breakfast. As usual, it was tasteless, synthesized food warmed up on the stove and placed in whatever clean container Sam could find. He waded through the heaps of garbage to give Oliver his portion, both of them pausing to be grateful for food. They ate in silence. Afterward, Sam grabbed a few water bottles from their collection and gave one to Oliver.

"I want to get water fetching out of the way today before God decides to shit on our luck," Sam told Oliver.

"Doesn't He always?" Oliver replied, cracking a smile.

"Better not tempt Him," Sam said, chuckling.

Oliver grabbed his gear. First his backpack, then his Railshot Rifle, and lastly some minor things like ammo. He then went to the door, waiting for Sam as he checked the time on his Smartwrist.

Sam walked over a few moments after and gave Oliver two empty water jugs. He attached each to his backpack. Sam swung open the front door and led them outside. It was still somewhat dark. Oliver's motorcycle stood near the door, covered in a tarp to protect it from sand.

"You never really told me how you got so inventive, Sam?" Oliver asked as they began to walk.

"Inventive?" Sam repeated, narrowing his eyes at the strange question.

"You know, you create all these things and know so much about how old-world tech works," Oliver explained.

"Well, I used to be the 'engineer' of a group a long time ago. My father was an engineer in the old world. Taught me almost everything I knew," Sam responded as they left the property and began the journey to the water pump.

"Well, you must've been pretty popular," Oliver commented.

"I was. Fixed everyone's tools, weapons, made things. I think I was the most useful guy. I miss those days."

"It didn't last, did it?"

"No," Sam frowned.

"Yeah... I understand," Oliver responded.

They grew quiet as they followed the path to the windmill. This trip was done once a week and never got any easier. Fortunately, the two had never been attacked or disturbed while fetching water; regardless, Oliver always had his suspicions and rifle ready. His head was constantly on a pivot.

Oliver looked up at the hazy sky. The weather was calm, seemingly still. He hoped that it would stay that way.

Sam soon led them off the road and down toward some hills. The last time they were here, Sam had begun leaving small poles in the ground. The pair went from pole to pole, each having a different colored piece of clothing flapping in the wind.

It wasn't long until they arrived at the earthen basin that contained the windmill. It looked the same as usual, a towering structure of reinforced wooden struts leading up to windmill blades. Oliver walked up to it with Sam.

"Well, she's still standing. Let's get to work; I think the wind's kicking up," Sam said.

Oliver laid down the jugs beside Sam, who knelt in front of the spigot, beginning the slow process of filling all the containers. Oliver meanwhile stood watch, holding his Railshot rifle and looking all around. His eyes narrowed, and his lips pressed together with vigilant focus. He never liked how the landscape made a circular hill around the windmill, only dipping in the northern direction.

Gazing upwards, Oliver saw that clouds were gathering in the distance, and the winds were kicking up slowly. A frown appeared on his face at the sight.

The trickle of water echoed within the containers as they began to fill, Sam sighing patiently.

"Hey, Oliver, look, is that what I think it is?" Sam pointed out.

"What?" Oliver blurted out, turning around.

Sam pointed at where the water dripped onto the ground. An amazed expression formed on Oliver's face as he saw a small patch of grass. It was such a small and fragile patch, but to them, it was something grand.

"Grass?" Oliver said.

"Grass!" Sam repeated.

"It would be nice to see green like back in the day, you know?" Oliver said.

"It would," Sam replied.

"Maybe this is the beginning of that?"

"Maybe,"

Sam finished filling the first container and moved onto the second. Oliver watched as the water trickled into the container for a few seconds before turning. He had a stern expression, one that was focused and ready.

The winds continued to grow worse, and it looked as if the gathering clouds were coming closer. As Oliver gazed nervously at the weather, a shiny gleam caught his eye. It was on the top of the hill, like a piece of metal was reflecting the sun. It was hard to see, forcing Oliver to squint to see what it was.

A gunshot sung into Oliver's ears, causing his heart to skip a beat. A tight pressure was immediately felt on his right forearm, a tingling sensation spreading throughout the arm. Oliver fell backward a moment after losing his balance, eyes wide and mouth agape with complete shock and confusion.

Sam turned and dove over to Oliver, dragging him to the other side of the windmill while under gunfire. Bullets began to whizz toward the pair, hitting the windmill, the ground, and narrowly missing both of them.

"Oliver! Oliver, are you okay, Oliver?" Sam asked in a panic.

"Sam? What's happening?" Oliver asked, blood flowing from the gunshot wound.

"Stay with me, buddy! Can you still shoot?!" Sam said, tapping the side of his mask.

"Argh... I don't know; I can try." He groaned.

Oliver rolled over and crawled up against the windmill, laying on it and grasping his gun weakly. Sam pulled out his pipe rifle and began to check his side of the windmill, pulling back when bullets narrowly missed him. Oliver felt a burning sensation grow in his arm, making it so he could barely concentrate on the other side.

"How m-many are there?" Oliver asked.

"I see.... I see four, I think! One has me pinned down up on the hill; I think he shot you!" Sam replied, firing the pipe rifle.

"My gun is useless. They're too far away..." Oliver said, groaning as he began to feel throbbing pain, "How do we get them closer?"

"I don't know. There's no cover to run to."

"S-Sam?" Oliver called out.

"What?!" Sam responded, repeatedly firing and reloading.

Oliver could feel pain setting in, allowing a moment of comprehension. It was the worst pain in his life, beginning to sear like he'd relaxed an arm on a hot stove. Blood flowed freely and coated Oliver's arm, Oliver trying his best to stop the bleeding as bullets whizzed by. All while the chaos erupted, the wind grew worse as an approaching storm crawled nearer. Oliver's wound stung more as sand blew up and found its way into the wound.

"We need to run! I don't think I'll make it like this," Oliver told Sam.

"Grab the bandages in my bag! Apply them, and I'll see if we can get out of here," Sam said, turning so that Oliver had access to it.

With pained efforts and a dripping arm, Oliver shuffled over and opened the bag. For a few moments, he dug before clumsily pulling out alcohol and bandages.

Oliver poured on alcohol first, causing him to scream and thrash as pain erupted in the bleeding hole.

"Haargh!!!"

Oliver breathed heavily and gasped for air when the pain subsided, quickly grabbing the rags and hastily wrapping his arm to stop the bleeding. Each time the bandage wound across the injury, he hissed in pain. He tied the bandages off. Oliver paused for a moment, worried if the bullet was still in there.

"How's the wound, Oliver?!" Sam asked.

As he spoke, Sam kept their unknown enemies at bay with his weapon, occasionally switching sides of the windmill to fire at them. Sam hoped that they would run low on ammo, or at least try to flank them.

"Got it wrapped," Oliver replied.

Sam fired off a few more shots before turning to grab more ammo from his bag. As the shooting stopped, their enemies seized the moment, two people charging down the opposite hill.

One charged around the corner into Sam, readying to fire her weapon. Before she could shoot him, Sam tackled her. Both fell to the ground, struggling over life and death on the sandy ground.

Oliver, meanwhile, was caught off guard as the second person came around the windmill. As soon as the man ran at him, Oliver instinctively kicked at his weapon.

The boot crashed into the man's fingers and a popping was heard as bones broke.

"Fuck!" the man screamed in pain, holding his hand.

Oliver flopped himself forward and threw his whole body at the man in a sloppy take-down. Immediately the man fell, shocked by Oliver's attack. They grappled for a moment, then pushed each other off.

A brief moment passed before they scrambled for their guns. It was an intense race, the two crawling across the sand as fast as possible. They gripped the guns at the same time, turning and aiming. Luck was with Oliver as he pulled the trigger a second faster.

Power surged throughout the rifle, energy sparking from the wires in the barrel. The scrap metal contained inside slid forward into the magnetic embrace of the gun's mechanisms. In a blink of an eye, each shard shot out with incredible speed in a wide arc. They annihilated flesh and bone in a mere heartbeat; the man's chest, face, and arms became unrecognizable as his body fell limp.

Oliver's eyes widened in horror. His chest rose heavily and quickly. It was as if the whole world disappeared around Oliver, forcing him to face the terrible crime he had just committed.

"Oliver! Oliver, help!" Sam screamed, causing Oliver to snap back to reality.

"I-I'm coming!"

Oliver stood as quickly as possible, adrenaline and will pushing him forward. Sam was beneath the woman, holding her hands at bay and preventing a knife from being plunged into his chest. She was so focused that she did not see Oliver shuffle over and put the rifle to her head.

Before she could react, scrap metal snuffed out her life. The gun annihilated her head, her body falling to the ground with a pool of blood seeping forth from the gore.

"Come on, Sam! Let's go!" Oliver said, weakly pulling Sam to his feet.

They both took flight up the hill in the other direction, their enemies hot in pursuit. They reached the peak of the hill, both of them sliding down the sand on the other side and running into the wasteland. As they ran, Oliver hooked his gun onto his backpack.

After a minute, the other two people arrived on the other side of the hill and shot at them; they split for cover. Oliver felt the wound throbbing in agony as he ran, barely keeping himself together. He wobbled in each running step, dizziness claiming him. Oliver felt cold to his core but sweated profusely with a pale face.

Gunshots filled the air.

He heard his heart beating in a frenzy, the world beginning to disappear again. Oliver thought he could hear Sam calling, with gunshots ringing afterward. Sam's words became muffled as pure fear caused Oliver to flee as he had never fled before. He stumbled and fell as he ran for what seemed forever. Oliver didn't even look where his feet took him, the horror taking over as insanity.

Oliver's luck turned for the worst. He barely recognized it, but from the corner of his eye was a sight no man would wish upon his enemy. Reaching up into the clouds was a sandstorm, an impenetrable wall of wind and shredding sand. It was a Doomstorm. The worst of all storms was coming straight for Oliver. Panic again took Oliver as he took off in the other direction, stumbling and tripping forward as fast as possible.

The winds became violent and howled like a million wolves, sand hitting the visor of his gas mask. Oliver breathed heavily and let out a roar of effort as his will pushed him forward. All of a sudden, the sandstorm engulfed him, and the Doomstorm came thundering down upon him. The sand completely blinded Oliver. The wind knocked his body around. Raging gusts picked him up and flipped him repeatedly, rolling him across the sands.

Oliver cried out as doom enveloped him. He burst into a sprint and fell, stars lighting up in his field of vision. Oliver fell downward and began rolling, barely able to see what was going on. The last thing Oliver knew was the sensation of going down a hill, violently turning and tumbling until a thud made everything disappear.

March

The group became quiet. The question of "who are the Patrians" didn't seem to be a favorable one as they all exchanged glances. Some expressions were filled with contempt, while some were confused. Reginald and Margaret were the only ones to keep their cordial looks.

"Y'all really haven't been this far East before, have you?" Reginald remarked, raising an eyebrow.

London shook his head.

"Tell them, dear," Margaret said.

"Well, let me fill y'all in with the entire story. Y'all know we're heading to the East. Most of us come from different backgrounds, but we're all fleeing the same thing, which is Patria. The next best place to the other side of the world is New Uruk."

London nodded and listened, Rose sitting beside him and clinging on to him.

"New Uruk is the next city East of here. Alisa has been there, and Archie and Tommy are from there."

Tommy nodded in confirmation, still silent.

"Patria is the enemy of New Uruk. We've had a couple of run-ins with them individually and as a group, and they ain't the most hospitable if y'all know what I mean." Reginald continued.

"Why?" London interjected.

"They're a warrior society. Patrians trained new soldiers and maintained their territory through raiding parties, targeting anything that isn't Patrian. We're being chased by a group right now. We're just trying to beat them to New Uruk." Reginald told him.

"They're horrible people, too," Alisa added with a grim frown under her mask.

"They're well known for their violence and knack for enslavement. What most people talk about is their execution methods, but I don't want to scare your daughter." Reginald said.

London opened his mouth to correct him, paused, and then spoke.

"Oh, she's... Not my daughter. I'm just her guardian," London said quietly.

They all looked at each other in complete surprise. It seemed that none of the group had expected this.

"Well, we appreciate the honesty. How did y'all meet?" Reginald asked, leaning forward with his elbows on his knees.

"Uh..." London let out, reluctant to reply.

"You can tell them," Rose whispered to him.

"Well, Rose doesn't remember, but I met her at birth. I knew her mother well back home in the West when I was still part of my original home," London began, staring into the fire.

The entire group watched his expressions change as he related his past.

"Her mother and I grew up together in the same village. Of course, we married different people, but we were very close. She owned a food store, and I always helped her out when merchant caravans came through," London explained. "I remember when she found out she was pregnant. We weren't a very big settlement, so the news spread fast to everyone. The same night she found out our village had a party to celebrate."

He paused and readjusted himself on the hard cement. London smiled as he continued to speak.

"I remember the day I saw Rose for the first time. I watched her learn to walk, talk, and everything in between. I remember when I started teaching her to read." his grin becoming wider, "She was so happy."

Then a frown formed. It was clear that he recalled painful memories.

"I started protecting her since I left the village. I uh...." his voice quivered slightly, "It was probably the worst day of my life. This merchant caravan came in, the same as usual every month. Everyone in the village felt that there was something off, but, of course, we needed the trading to survive."

He paused again and tried his best to keep it together. As he spoke, mournfully gazed at the ground and fiddled with her fingers uneasily.

"I was carrying some supplies to the store when I watched the man her mother was trading with screaming at her over something. I think it was over some bad deal or something. He shot her, there and then. I couldn't do anything as they destroyed the store and then began to take the village down. Rose was with her father that day, doing some business on the other side of the village. His name was Craig. I ran and got to him pretty quickly."

"We three fought our way out of the village. I almost got shot a few times. He took a bullet to the shoulder. He succumbed to it a week later since we didn't have any medical supplies. He was a good guy. When he died, he made me promise to look after and protect Rose, and I have ever since." London became silent after.

"God damn..." Finlay said under his breath.

"That's..." Archie began, stopping himself immediately.

"... We're all lost for words, London. That's very noble," Reginald said after a while.

London nodded in acknowledgment.

After enough time passed, Alisa came in. She thought it was strange that everyone was so silent and somber.

"What's going on?" she asked.

Reginald shook his head. It was a subtle gesture that she would be told later, and now wasn't the time to repeat it.

"Right... It's time to hit the sack; Tommy, you're on watch," Alisa said, laying down on her bedroll and watching Tommy leave the fire tent.

"Y'all heard her. Don't let the bed bugs bite," Reginald said with a thin smile.

London got into his bedroll and laid down on his back, Rose doing the same behind him.

"London...?" she whispered.

"Yes, Rosey?" London replied.

"I don't like this place," she told him.

"Yeah, there could be bugs here."

"B-Bugs?!"

"Probably not. There might be some spiders around here. Maybe in our hair."

Rose gasped and looked up to her hair, bringing her hands to rub through it.

"Just kidding, I scared them all away," London whispered with a chuckle.

"Meanie!"

"Aw, c'mon. I thought it was funny."

Rose grumbled.

"Don't worry, Rosey, there's nothing that'll get you. Get some rest. We need it," he told her.

"Okay, good night."

"'Night, Rosey."

London closed his eyes and exhaled softly. As usual, the sounds of the night kept him up for a while. Remarkably, he drifted to sleep within an hour, unlike on other nights. It was nice until he fell into deep nightmares, eventually waking up from his first night terror and sighing lethargically.

Soon, the night passed, and the sun began to rise over the ruined city, barely piercing the pollution haze. London woke up, staring at the ceiling above him with an empty gaze. Everything from head to toe felt stiff as stone. With his sleeping bag well worn out, stiffness was the price for any amount of sleep.

Close beside him was Rose, still deeply asleep. London gently sat up, making sure not to wake her as he did. Every joint in his body protested against this, audible popping and clicking heard as he stretched. London looked around under the protection of the fire tent. He found that everyone else was still asleep in their tent rolls, including Alisa; Tommy was outside on watch in her stead.

With soft steps, London moved over to Rose in the corner. He sat down and moved the flap of the fire tent, gazing outside. Through the broken glass, he could see the dark streets below. A dark gloom enveloped everything. The entire city was like this as far as the eye could see, and even in the darkness, London could see all the ruin.

What caught his eye were the figures that darted back and forth among the buildings and streets. Beneath him, unknown to London, was a series of hunts and chases. Mutant animals ran after each other; some bolted for places to hide, while others idly patrolled between the cars, too large to be challenged.

There were screams and chaos in the distance, footsteps below them, and the occasional gleam of eyes toward London. He could even catch a rancid hint of mutant in the air through his mask. It was like sweat mixed with decay.

After enough eyes met his, London had enough of sightseeing and covered the crack with the fire-tent flap. He returned and held Rose until she awoke, whispering with her when she awoke as they waited for everyone else to rise.

"London?" she whispered when she woke up.

"Yes, Rosey?" he uttered.

"Are we safe?"

"We're still safe."

"Good. What's for breakfast?"

"I don't know. We'll see what our new friends want."

"Okay..." she mumbled, closing her eyes and cuddling against London.

It took some time for everyone else to wake up. There was a quiet hustle and bustle as each woke up one by one; whispers from all around the tent as idle conversations started. By then, Finlay had already started the campfire back up and was warming up some dried meat.

Alisa was the last person to wake up, a grumpy expression on her face from a night of standing watch. London felt a growing respect for her. He already felt forgiving for her tough attitude and rough exterior.

Tommy joined them as they gathered around the fire. They all held out their hands, warming themselves up and fighting the cold. It was usually cold due to the pollution haze, with mornings usually being the coldest part of the day. London shivered slightly even though he was dressed for the weather, rubbing his hands together. Eventually, Finlay served the food, everyone eating quickly and quietly.

Alisa wasted no time planning out the day ahead after eating, speaking with a grumpy and stern voice.

"All right, we need to get out of the city today," she said, "I've been through here before, and the quickest way out of here will be through toward the Northwest."

"Northwest? New Uruk is East, though?" Finlay questioned.

"Yes. I'm picking the quickest way out of the city. It'll only add a day to our journey." Alisa replied.

"It might throw the Patrians off our tails, too," Reginald added.

London sat silently and listened to their discussion.

"Yeah, plus we don't have to risk the damn mutants more than we have to. It's bad enough in the wasteland." Alisa said.

"We should get packing then!" Archie said with excitement.

"Right. Everyone pack your stuff; we're leaving." Alisa ordered.

London helped Rose gather her stuff. They only had their sleeping rolls out for the night, so it didn't take more than a minute. London helped the rest of the group take down the fire tent and bundle it up; its load divided among almost everyone. They all climbed down the same flights of stairs to the first floor, leaving the building and walking out into the street.

It was still a little dark even with the sun rising, though the very presence of sunlight was enough to scare off plenty of the mutants. Regardless, the group was a little tense and jumpy as they clustered together for safety in the middle of the street. They did not dare venture near buildings. They stayed clear of cars as well, checking under them as they passed.

As a group, the mutants avoided confrontation with them; instead, they hid in empty buildings and stalked them. From the corner of his eye, London could see shapes darting from shadow to shadow. It was unsettling. What made it worse was that they hadn't given his weapons back, leaving him with a naked feeling.

"Could I have my bat back at least?" London asked.

"Bit worried, eh?" Finlay said, smirking at him.

Alisa glanced back at London with a judging look.

"Let him have it, just not the gun," Reginald stated with a waving gesture.

Reluctantly, Alisa paused and gave him his bat.

"Nice weapon," she said with the smallest bit of friendliness she's shown him since they met.

London grasped it and spun it with a grin. It was firm and nice to handle. Some dried blood still stained parts of it from its last use. He let out a relieved sigh and continued walking.

They turned down another street. The city spread out before them, the edge of it hidden by tall buildings and the horizon. It would be a journey to just get out of the city itself, something London didn't look forward to. Their long march had begun.

Kindling

"Worker 4221, Waste Management Sector, robotic maintenance." the Tasking Station told Simon.

Simon looked around as the Tasking Station gave him his task. A Peacekeeper stood beside him, eyeing the line behind him with a menacing stare. Simon wasted no time getting away from him and out into the main hall connecting the individual mess halls.

"Stop!" a voice shouted at Simon.

He froze. Simon's heart plummeted to his stomach, pumping madly in fear. Did he do something wrong? What's going on? Should he fight? A Peacekeeper walked up behind him and circled around. He grabbed Simon's forearm and put his forearm against it. The Individual Chips registered each other and produced a "pling" sound.

"Worker 4221, that line," the Peacekeeper ordered, pointing to a line of other Workers.

Simon saw Thaddeus in that line, along with some other Workers. He joined the back of the line, Thaddeus glancing back at him with the same confusion. Lines assembled in front of every entrance, a Peacekeeper in front of each line. The Peacekeepers each shouted their destination and led their lines, firm in their commands.

"Waste Management Sector!" commanded the Peacekeeper for their line.

He pointed with his tesla baton, beginning to lead them away from the Nutritional Sector. They shuffled after one another, unsure of what was going on and questioning their safety. Simon leaned to the side and looked down the line.

"Psst, what's going on?" he asked the woman in front of him.

"I do-" she began.

"No talking!" the Peacekeeper ordered.

Simon became silent. They marched through the Arcadis, going to the opposite end of the station. This side of the station split into multiple levels. The top two layers were storage, while the Waste Management Sector was below them. The Waste Management Sector was also one of the few ways to access space, which led to rumors about the Leaders shooting people out to space in this sector.

The Peacekeeper led them into the Waste Management Sector, allowing them all to file in. They all knew their tasks. After the Peacekeeper barked an order and threateningly waved his tesla baton, they all set off to work.

The Waste Management Sector was quite large. It was a metallic, ugly room with three exits. Two were doors, and one was the large trash bay for launching trash into space. There were heaps of trash everywhere, dumped here by trash systems and robots.

It was where all the trash was sorted and recycled. Simon found it amazing how advanced the station's recycling was. Anything could be cleaned and reused or broken down and reforged. Simon knew the place inside out and what his job was here.

"Robotic maintenance," Simon told himself.

He walked to where the robots of the sector were housed and charged. There were ten robots in total that worked in the Waste Management Sector simultaneously. Each had a simple, fun name, which were acronyms for their tasks. Most of them were out working with the Workers already, sifting through the garbage and performing their tasks.

There was a massive robot sitting on its charging station, alone and dormant.

"Oh, big buddy. What's got you down, WRB-LT?" Simon asked.

Simon walked around it and examined it. Most of the robots had some kind of personality for more "human' interactions. The WRB-LTs, of which there were two, were shy and gentle, even though they were massive robots meant to recycle large heaps of trash. Simon reached out and opened the front of it, the robot humming to life and shyly beeping at him.

"Relax, relax, I'm just checking your body," Simon told it.

It shook slightly but allowed him in.

"Jeez, what have you done, buddy? Your trash filters and pickers are all busted up." Simon said, going out to look at it, "Did you try to take too much garbage again?"

It shrugged with massive mechanical arms, innocently lying to him. Simon chuckled and shook his head. He retrieved a toolbox nearby and walked to the bot. As he began to examine the robot, he heard a voice behind him.

"Ah, I see WRB-LT number two has another friend?"

"What?" Simon mumbled, turning around.

A man Simon didn't know approached. They had the same uniforms and haircuts. The man was roughly the same size as him, with green eyes different from Simon's brown. Both of them had brown hair.

"Oh, sorry, I didn't mean to surprise you. Robotic maintenance, too, I see?"

"Yeah."

"Well, I'm Thomas. Nice to meet you."

"Simon, nice to meet you."

The two looked at each other with confused expressions. They had never met and had never worked on the same robot with someone else before.

"Well, uh... I guess we should get working?" Simon suggested.

Thomas nodded in agreement. WRB-LT hummed excitedly at the two, knowing both as friends.

"You must've busted yourself up a lot to have both of us repairing you, WRB-LT," Thomas said.

"No shit, you fell apart recently," Simon added.

"I worked on him like..." Thomas paused, "Three months ago, I think."

"Damn, WRB-LT!"

The bot occasionally hummed in response, deeply thrumming with a shy tone. The two separated their workload. Simon worked on the interior, while

Thomas worked on sprucing up the exterior and a few circuits. All the while, the giant machine hummed happily. Occasionally, it would take a mechanical limb and mess with them, playfully poking them or misplacing tools.

"I have to say, holy shit. Did you see all the Peacekeepers this morning?" Thomas asked.

"Yeah. I assume you heard about the brawl?" Simon replied.

"All about it. I saw part of it myself. I was on the opposite side of the arena, though, and bolted out of there damn fast."

"The Leaders didn't like that."

"I can tell. I've never seen the Peacekeepers more entertained," Thomas said, both chuckling.

They continued working.

"I've never seen you on this job before," Simon remarked.

"I typically work in other sectors; I've been here like three times in my life," Thomas told him.

"Oh, well, nice to meet you."

"Nice to meet you too."

Simon glanced at Thomas once. There was a strange connection between them, something that they both noticed. Simon wondered if he felt the same about the Arcadis, especially the growing feeling of being trapped in a cage.

They quickly repaired the robot. The pair tested its replaced and mended systems, the robot humming with excitement. The two stepped away as it left its charging port and moved to a trash heap. It grabbed the heap and pulled it inside itself, sorting it all within thirty seconds and recycling it all.

"Hah! Nice," Simon said.

Thomas and Simon high-fived. After they repaired the WRB-LT, they moved on to some of the other bots, examining them and repairing minor issues.

"What do you think of the Leaders?" Simon whispered to Thomas.

Thomas looked around.

"Same as anyone. Powerful, scary, and I don't like them," Thomas whispered in return.

"I imagined..." Simon mumbled.

"You?"

"Tyrants."

"That's a better word."

They had entered dangerous territory. Though not stated as illegal, the very idea of this conversation could get either of them sent to the Deck. Regardless, there was a sense of trust between them. Simon thought it was strange. He couldn't talk to Albert like this at all, but this stranger was completely fine.

In some ways, Simon thought he was a rebel. Did this man share his opinions? Did he want freedom too? Did he want to explore the universe? These questions ran through Simon's mind as they finished their tasks. As soon as they finished, they went to a Tasking Station and got new assignments.

"Worker 4221, Agricultural Sector, hydroponic maintenance," the Tasking Station ordered Simon.

"Worker 4274, Nutritional Sector, system maintenance," the Tasking Station ordered Thomas.

"Well, at least I won't be far when lunch hits," Thomas said.

"Unfortunate that we have to split," Simon told him.

"What mess hall do you go to, Simon?" Thomas asked.

"Number four, where the Cargo Bears go."

"Oh? Cargo Bears? Personally, I'm with the Rocket Scorpions in number five," Thomas said.

"Guess you work with the station's controls a lot?" Simon pointed out.

"Yeah. Do you want to meet at lunch today?"

Simon paused before answering.

"Sure, my mess hall?" Simon asked him.

"Yes, if we're allowed to."

"All right, I'll meet you there. See ya, man."

"See you later."

They parted. Simon was fascinated by the stranger. Who was he? Why had he never seen him before? He was also a little paranoid. Was this a spy sent to watch him for the Leaders? Simon would keep that question in mind.

As boring as it was, Simon headed to the Agricultural Sector and did his work. Afterward, he was sent to the Storage Sector on the same end of the ship as before to repair another machine. He felt impatient. Simon was amazed to find himself expecting and hoping for the 1200 lunch call.

After successfully repairing the machine and checking up on some robots, he paced about until 1200. It took only five minutes before Genetrix's voice echoed through the Arcadis.

"All Workers report to the Nutritional Sector for lunch," she commanded.

Bunker

Oliver opened his eyes. At first, all he could see was blurry sand. His entire body ached. He noticed his gunshot wound; it burned like fire while also feeling wet to the touch. Oliver rolled over and looked around. He was surprised by the fact that it felt like recovering from a terrible nap.

There was a crack clean across his gas mask, though it didn't seem to let any air in. Oliver slowly tried to get on his feet, his balance failing and bringing him down. Instead, he crawled toward a wall. The Doomstorm still raged around him. Oliver's heart throbbed in fear, the howls of wind filling his ears and blinding sand hitting his gas mask.

Oliver made his way to the wall and leaned on the cement. He sat there for a moment, carefully grabbing the Railshot Rifle hanging from his backpack. After a few moments of gathering himself, Oliver took off the backpack, grabbed some scrap metal, and reloaded the gun. His hands were still weak, though it felt nice to hold the weapon. To be safe, Oliver replaced the gun's Ignium batteries. Oliver had just replaced the filters in his gas mask, so he didn't need to worry about them for about a week.

Minutes passed as Oliver sat and looked around in confusion. He couldn't recall a single memory of how he got there or one of where he was. All that came to mind was the attack and being shot.

Oliver paused and looked at the bandages around his forearm. They were red. Blood had drenched through them. He forced himself to stay calm, despite the alarming sight. On the other arm, his Smartwrist rested, half of its screen cracked.

"It ain't over yet," he whispered to reassure himself.

Oliver looked left and right. He was sitting on a road that went left into the wasteland and right into a tunnel. The wall he propped up against was just the entrance of the tunnel, ominous darkness meeting him further down. He had a choice between braving the wasteland or descending into possible death. Searching in the wasteland for something to keep him alive was pointless.

Instead, Oliver pushed himself up against the wall and stood uneasily. His legs were shaking, but he could still walk. Carefully, Oliver began to shuffle down the tunnel.

The foreboding darkness embraced him; Oliver glanced back as the light abandoned him. Quickly, he turned on his mask's flashlight. A cone of light appeared from it, illuminating the darkness of the tunnel. Uneasily, Oliver held his gun, looking back and forth. Slowly, step by step, he moved into the tunnel with a cautious stride.

The only sound in the gloom was Oliver's shaking breath. Dust particles slowly drifted past the beam of the flashlight, settling on the ground as he moved. Every step made an echoing click, every shuffle of gear horribly loud, and every scared breath was like a scream.

Eventually, his steps led him to a large ornate metal door. It was massive and could've at least fit a semi-truck if not larger. On either side of the door were two statues, men sculpted like Greek statues holding up the roof of the tunnel. At the peak of the door was a stone face, peering down upon the new guest.

With some further investigation and the flashlight, Oliver could see all the detail put into the door and the statues. The statues were naked and appeared as if they carried great strain on their shoulders. He didn't know how many years they had been holding up the tunnel, but it felt like they had been there forever. It was like the Greek gods themselves put these statues here for eternal punishment.

On the door, there were little carvings in the metal. Oliver didn't know what they were but could make out houses, people, dogs, and civilization. He followed the carvings up to the center of the door. There was a clear separation in the door, showing that it was a double door. Along the center was a massive mushroom cloud, what Oliver assumed to be an atomic bomb.

"What the...?" Oliver mumbled.

Were these carvings the story of the 21st century? He didn't know.

With the searing in his body growing worse, Oliver had no other choice but to try and get past the door. After a few cautious steps over to the door, Oliver noticed that it was already a little open. He took a moment to examine it before pushing it open, only making it budge an inch after using all of his weight.

An angry grumble came out of Oliver before moving forward. First, he had to squeeze his backpack through the crack, then himself. The gun fit, but Oliver's whole body was a different matter. The most difficult part was getting his head in, his gas mask getting caught against both sides of the door. With a loud "thunk" Oliver got through, popping out into the darkness and stumbling.

After brushing dust off of himself and putting his backpack back on, Oliver looked around. Amazement struck him immediately as his flashlight shone down a long hall. It was huge. Ornate pillars held up the tall ceiling in rows along either side, leading into more halls and making him wonder about the immensity of this place.

Oliver began to walk, looking around as he did. Occasionally, there would be statues and paintings between the pillars. The statues were unnerving. It was as if their eyes followed him.

Eventually, there came a crossroads in the halls. Oliver approached a brass sign nailed to one of the walls, blowing the dust off of it and trying to read. As soon as it was slightly disturbed, the rusty nails holding the sign gave way. The whole thing came crashing down. A large plume of dust rising up along with a crash that echoed down the halls.

Oliver leaped back as it hit the floor. He shone his flashlight around in fear, checking to see if anything heard him. There was not a single sound after the crash, just an eerie silence instead. Was this place empty?

There was no point in sticking around to find out if it was. Oliver checked the sign and tried to read it again, searching for something along medical lines. With some difficulty, he found directions to a medical area. Oliver looked up to his left, the sign directing him that way.

He took off down the wing, following the great columns that held up the strangely gigantic place. Oliver wasn't sure, but he assumed the place was built into the ground. Was this some bunker from the old world? Maybe, he thought, it was an ancient temple that nobody had ever seen before.

His arm dripped blood steadily on the floor, Oliver trying to move faster each time it did. He felt woozy, stumbling often. Sweat soaked his whole body; his heart throbbed faster as anxiety grew. He knew that if he didn't calm down, his heart would kill him faster. Oliver forcibly inhaled and exhaled, trying to control his breathing.

Signs led Oliver along. There were many wings, halls, and rooms that Oliver missed along the way. They all seemed amazing and interesting. What Oliver couldn't shake was the feeling of eyes following him.

There were no steps in the darkness, no figures, nothing to lead Oliver to think anything was here. No matter what, the belief that there was something remained unshaken.

Soon enough, Oliver found the final hallway that led to the medical wing. The entire place felt like a maze, and his blood was the rope back to the entrance.

Oliver had to follow the wall now. His body slid against it, all of his weight propped up along the cement. It was the only way to stay standing.

He entered the medical wing. A huge arch made up the doorway. The first room was a massive lobby, with chairs, couches, tables, and all sorts of objects inside of it.

Oliver shuffled across the room and down a much smaller hallway. He glanced into every room. Many of the doors remained, some with windows and some without. Inside the rooms Oliver could look into, he saw very little except for medical equipment.

He pushed forward, searching for a supply room, finding one at the end of the first hall. He opened the door and shone the flashlight into the darkness. A surprised gasp left his lips as the light met with a body sitting in a chair, staring at the door. It was only a skeleton.

"Holy shit... You scared me, buddy." Oliver muttered.

Oliver took two steps into the room and almost fell to his knees, mostly due to relief and blood loss. The storage room was untouched. He quickly took off the backpack, setting his gun aside and leaving the door open with a small crack. He then searched the room, grabbing anything he needed and slumping down on the floor.

With shaking hands, he began to peel away the soaked bandages, wincing in pain as he did. It went around and around until it was all gone and dropped on the floor. Oliver shone the flashlight on his wound, cringing as he did. The bullet hadn't gone through, lodged clearly in the flesh. He dreaded what would come next.

Carefully, Oliver grabbed a pair of tweezers and lifted his arm, letting out calming breaths. In, out, in, out. He shakily brought the tweezers toward the end of the bullet. Incredible pain shot through the arm as the tweezers disturbed the bullet. Oliver writhed as he tried not to scream, groaning quite loudly and kicking. His jaw clenched, and his eyes squeezed shut, gasping as he endured the pain. He stopped and grabbed a rag, stuffing it under his mask and biting it.

With difficulty, Oliver slowly wiggled the bullet out with the tweezers. Each left and right motion was agonizing. His flesh felt like it was searing, barely releasing the bullet.

Oliver threw the tweezers across the room in pain as the deformed bullet fell to the ground with a metallic "tink." It rolled away, going right under the door and out into the hall. With heavy breaths, Oliver calmed down and began to wrap the wound up again. He couldn't bear putting alcohol in the wound, so he just put it on the bandages.

It was just like before. Each time the bandage went around the wound, it stung. Oliver made sure it was tight. His entire body was shaking after, sweat still pouring from him. Regardless, Oliver was relieved.

For a while, he laid there and contemplated. The arm stung from the alcohol on the wraps, and his body was weak from blood loss.

After he took the rag out of his mouth, he shakily grabbed his backpack and opened it. His fingers searched around inside and pulled some food and water. The water was clear and refreshing as he drank it, and the food provided a sense of bliss. He was sure he hadn't eaten for a few hours. He tried to recall what had happened previously. Oliver remembered most of the day, from waking up, to going to the windmill, to the battle. His memory grew faint and was snuffed out somewhere after running over the hill and into the wasteland. A cold feeling grew in Oliver's stomach, fear being the only feeling he could remember after running into the wasteland. Out of many questions, one nagged intensely. Was Sam okay? Perhaps, he imagined, he could recover, find a way out of here, then find Sam. Logically thinking, Oliver believed that leaving here was impossible. Right now, his legs could barely hold him up.

An hour passed. Every minute that went by furthered Oliver's recovery. After thirty minutes, Oliver began to try his luck with standing. The first few attempts failed, though each one was better and better. Soon enough, with most of his weight on the wall, Oliver was on his feet. Slowly but surely, he began to walk around with a sluggish pace, exploring the room as he did.

There were a lot of shelves, containers, cabinets, and more. The room was large and full of supplies. Oliver wondered why there were so many supplies in a place that seemed empty. It appeared untouched, except by Oliver, who had gathered enough energy to start looting. His hands grabbed things greedily and stuffed them into his bag. After a while, his bag was full, and his legs couldn't take it, so he returned to sitting.

The wound still throbbed, though Oliver felt at peace. It was as if everything would work out fine. His hand came and touched the bandages. Oliver imagined the hole the bullet had made, wondering what it would look like if it had gone completely through. It was strange to think of a hole in one's limb, at least to Oliver.

Oliver's eyes followed the length of his arm, going to the blood trail from the bullet. It went from where he originally sat, trailing along the room and out the door. It was then that he heard it. The sound of bare feet softly slapping onto concrete, step by step, going straight for the door. Oliver's throat tightened as he struggled to his feet upon hearing the unexpected sound.

He looked around in alarm, grabbing his gun and aiming for the door. Quickly, he corrected himself and decided against the bad idea. Could he hide? Oliver examined the room, the footsteps stopping at the very front of the door. Before Oliver shut off his flashlight, he saw the faint shadow of a figure on the other side.

The figure emitted a rough breath as if its throat was full of gravel. It seemed to gurgle. Oliver fumbled around in the darkness, his breath quickening with panic. His hands met the cold touch of a cabinet door, Oliver leaving his backpack behind and quickly opening it. He stuffed himself inside of it with his gun, closing it shut and holding it.

Inside the cabinet, which felt incredibly small, there was only the sound of fearful breathing. The door to the room let out a chilling squeak as it opened, the same footsteps now entering the room. Oliver's breath cut out. Every closer step made him shrink in fear.

The footsteps and breathing stopped directly in front of the cabinet. The monster was just inches away from the cabinet, Oliver imagining monstrous hands reaching out for the handle. Only a moment away from being discovered, Oliver readied himself to jump out and start shooting.

Yet, the moment didn't seem to come. The thing outside simply stood there and terrorized Oliver with its gargling breath. His stomach twisted in dread, Oliver barely able to contain insane panic. Everything was quivering, from head to toe, and no matter what, his lungs did not dare take in air.

With no warning, there was a pause in the breathing, the footsteps beginning once more and departing. Soon, they faded away, and Oliver was left alone. Oliver sat for a while and quivered in the tight cabinet, reluctant to leave its safe embrace. He had to work up the courage to consider the thought.

Oliver's hands shook as he reached for the door and slowly swung it open, carefully scanning the dark room. His gun was in hand, ready for anything. The room was empty, leaving him alone in a maze. Oliver turned to his next task, escape.

Violence

2:43 PM, May 14, 2154

The sun bathed the ruins of the old world city in warm rays, warding off the night-time mutants. They hid in the shadows, waiting, planning, stalking. Some mutants were dumb and slow, wandering out into the streets during the day like zombies.

The group wasn't afraid of the slow ones. Ignoring the mutants, the humans pushed throughout the streets, sticking to the center of every road to be as far away as possible from the mutant packs hiding in the buildings on either side of them. Rose was close to London, looking around them in fear. London kept her close, assuring her that they'd make it out safely.

He firmly held the baseball bat in his hands. The group dealt with roaming mutants quickly and silently, bludgeoning and stabbing them before quickly moving on. They moved as quickly as Margaret's spider chair could move, all of them jogging past cars and corpses. If Rose became too tired or couldn't keep up, London picked her up and carried her.

Reginald's words repeated in London's mind. He had never seen Patrians or ever heard of them until now; regardless, he felt the same anxiety as everyone did. What they didn't tell him was how far away the pursuing raiding party of Patrians was. London was unsure if they even knew.

"Finlay," London began.

Finlay glanced back and slowed down slightly, allowing London to jog side by side with him.

"How many of these Patrians are chasing you guys?"

Finlay didn't respond for a moment, thinking about it.

"Usually, small raiding parties consist of fifteen men. We can expect around fifteen to twenty."

"Why are they chasing you?" London asked.

"This time?" Finlay responded.

"Uh... Yes, this time."

"We were out trading in an outpost in New Uruk a couple weeks ago. Of course, the people of New Uruk and Patria are at war with each other right now. We got caught up in a surprise attack there. Their little army split up to chase survivors, which led to this raiding party being on our trail for a long time now."

"How far away do you think they are?"

"Based on signs recently, a couple hours behind us. They've caught up with us once or twice, but that's where my job takes the spotlight. We've gotten out with only a few scrapes and bruises every time."

"All right, thanks."

"No problem."

Finlay went ahead again.

Hours had passed since they left the shelter of the ruined office building. They had stopped twice to ease their sore feet and have a snack break. When they stopped, London found that Archie and Finlay were the friendliest and most talkative. They were young and full of energy. London felt a little old, the thought of which caused him to chuckle a little.

They immediately took a liking to him. They were fascinated by his knowledge and tales of the old world and were even interested in his books. London learned that Archie had a hard time reading. He never learned how to read beyond small things like reading store signs or what kind of canned food he found. Finlay read almost as well as London did, something London expected from someone in the medical field.

"What is this book called?" Archie asked, holding a book from London's backpack during their second break of the day.

"Let me see," London said, leaning over.

"Oh, The History of Ignium."

Archie opened it and looked through it.

"Ay uh... London?"

"Yeah?"

"Can you teach me to read when we get to New Uruk?"

"Sure, no problem."

"Thanks, man."

They were soon ready to take off again. London put his books back in his bag, checked that Rose had gotten her snacks, and pulled everything together. He paused as he watched Alisa return from scouting.

"We need to go. Now," Alisa said with an urgent voice.

"What's going on?" Reginald asked.

"The fucking Patrians are behind us. Saw their banner in the streets behind us. Come on! Come on! Let's go!" she replied, gesturing urgently.

Everyone immediately rushed to gather their things. London put his backpack on and helped Rose put on hers before grabbing his baseball bat. After that, they were all moving, trying to put as much distance between them and the pursuing Patrians. London's thoughts rushed. The only thing that slowed them was the spider wheelchair.

"Come on, Rosey, come on," he told Rose as they moved.

The group had their weapons ready. They checked their guns, cocking them and turning off the safeties.

"This way!" Alisa ordered.

Tommy ran ahead of them as they turned into a building. They ran straight through it, going through the front door, through the first level, and out the back door. Then came an alley, which they followed to get to another street. Tommy crashed into one of the slow mutants as they went onto the street, London reaching it a moment later and swinging his bat at the downed creature.

It had tumors all over it and a misshapen leg that seemed to have a gnarled paw instead of a foot. Every screw and nail lining the shaft crashed into the head of the creature, the metal chain wrapping its length, adding to the strike. London blew straight through its jaw in one clean strike. He left it stunned by the brutal hit, continuing to run.

Howls and barking quickly closed in on the group as they went down another street.

"Go! Go!" Reginald shouted.

"Dogs!" Finlay cried out, pointing behind them.

From behind them came a pack of dogs. They were mangy animals, their hairless skin covered in tumors and scars. They also had scrap metal covering them, a makeshift armor that protected vital areas. Upon seeing the group, they howled and charged.

Finlay and Tommy stopped to turn around, firing their guns at the animals. The first one went down with a bullet through its head; the second one went down after four bullets. The third one caught up to them, throwing itself forward and clamping its jaws down upon London's leg.

"Aaarrgh!!" he screamed.

London fell forward as the animal squeezed its jaws shut and threw London around. Tommy got it off with a bullet and a punishing kick to its chest.

"Fuck! My leg!"

"London!" Rose screamed.

"Fuck! It's okay, Rosey, it's okay."

Finlay stopped and came to London's attention, kneeling by him and examining it.

"Hold still, hold still," he said and looked at the bleeding wound, "Can you walk on it?"

"It hurts like hell. I don't know if I can," London said, turning onto his boot and looking down at it.

The dog had bitten a massive, bleeding wound cleanly into his calf. They didn't have the time to patch it up as the Patrians weren't too far behind.

"Come on, come on, I'll help you up," Finlay said. "We have to move."

Finlay began lifting London, Archie coming to help as they both got him up. London placed pressure on his leg, immediately having pain shoot through him.

"Argh! I can't walk."

"We need to go!" Alisa said.

"Just leave me behind! Get Rose to safety," London said.

"No!" Rose said, "We're not leaving you!"

"Damn right. We're getting your ass out of here," Finlay said.

At that moment, Tommy went up to London and lifted him. The man easily hoisted him over his shoulder and began to run again.

"Let's move!" Tommy said sternly.

As they departed, spears and arrows hailed toward them. The Patrians had caught up with them. They shot at them with guns and makeshift weaponry. Some were pressure rifles, which used pressure to launch spears at the group. Others just had guns and bows.

"Go! Go!" Archie shouted, aiming and firing back from cover as the group moved.

"I'll cover you guys!"

All eight of them moved as fast as possible, bobbing and weaving out between ruins to avoid getting hit. All the while, they tried to protect Margaret, the spider chair going as fast as it could. Archie began running after them, an arrow whizzing through the air and hitting his shoulder. He paused in pain, crying out as it hit him before carrying on after the group.

"Archie! Are you good?" Finlay asked as he joined the group.

"I'm fine. It's just an arrow."

"Don't worry, buddy. I'll get it out."

Archie groaned in pain before responding.

"You better."

London glanced back at the Patrians as they chased after. They wore clothing that covered them from head to toe to protect them from the toxic air and weather. They had gas masks, with a few built into football and police helmets. Most of them had armor, some had padding, while others had metal to protect them. What they all shared was the same symbol painted on their chests and backs. It was a red, two-headed dog painted on a purple background with a gray border; the dog had pointed ears and seemed to be some kind of mastiff.

He assumed that was the symbol of Patria.

They were all caught in a cycle of taking cover and running, firing back at the Patrians. It was an uphill battle with eight of them and eighteen pursuers.

There were many close calls, arrows, and bullets barely missing their mark. The hardest part was protecting Margaret, who only went so fast.

It all seemed doomed. The group fired a few shots as they ran into the remains of a supermarket. Each of them bolted through the doors, Finlay and Archie stopping at the doors to delay the Patrians. As they got inside, Tommy put London on the floor and prepared his gun.

"Fat ass," he said with a half-smile, poorly trying to joke.

London looked up at him and couldn't help but chuckle.

"Sorry."

Rose came to London's side, hiding in fear against him.

A stalemate began between the two groups. The Patrians were stuck outside, and the refugees were stuck inside.

They started to run out of ammo, Archie's gun going first while a few Patrians ran out of spears and arrows. Meanwhile, Tommy was busy killing a small group of mutants who came out from the empty aisles.

Soon, the gunfire stopped as both sides ceased firing and came to a standoff. London had no idea what was happening. No one dared to make the next move.

While they stood and stared out, Finlay walked over to London and took off his bag. He examined the wound and took out one of the few bandages in his bag, moving London a bit before bandaging his leg. London hissed in pain each time the bandage touched his wound. Regardless, he was thankful. As Finlay bandaged London's leg, Rose hid her face in his chest while he hugged her.

"Thanks,"

"No problem," Finlay said, returning to the front doors of the supermarket.

Afterward, Finlay went over to Archie and pulled the arrow out of his back.

The standoff was slow as if time itself was moving slower in anticipation. The wind blew, kicking up sand at the anxious Patrians outside. Finlay, Archie, and Alisa occasionally peaked outside, also anxious in their hiding spots.

Twenty minutes droned on. No one moved.

Abruptly, gunfire erupted outside as smoke grenades landed and blocked out the entire parking lot. A loud truck was heard outside, along with a lot of screaming.

"Incoming!"

"Go! Go, go!"

Eventually, the gunfire stopped, and the chaos outside calmed. The group looked at each other, unsure of what just happened. They prepared to fire as they heard footsteps approaching.

"Anyone alive in there?"

At the same time, Archie, Finlay, and Alisa stepped out from cover with their weapons ready.

"Ain't you a sight for sore eyes," Finlay said, immediately lowering his gun.

"We heard the commotion and thought we'd lend a hand. Y'all ain't Patrians, are ya?"

"We're with New Uruk," Reginald said, "You came in the nick of time."

"What's going on?" London asked.

Rose peeked out.

"We've been saved!" Archie said, stretching his arms out in victory.

He hissed as he felt the arrow.

"Ow."

A man dressed in armor similar to the Patrians marched in. He had metal plates on him, a bullet vest, and a pipe rifle. On his chest and back was a different symbol. Instead of a dog, there was a red circle on his chest with four orange dots around it, the entire symbol having a blue background. It was the symbol of New Uruk.

Machination

Simon joined the lines shuffling to get food. He scanned his Individual Chip, got his food, and proceeded out of the line. Meanwhile, the Peacekeepers gathered around the mess hall, staring everyone down. As he left the line, Simon nervously glanced at some. As he sat at his usual seat, no one caught his eye or bothered him.

Eventually, Thaddeus and Albert joined him.

"How are you doing, friends?" Thaddeus asked in a low voice.

"Terrible," Albert whispered. "Almost got beaten by a Peacekeeper at my assignment today."

"I'm fine.... I may have gotten us a new friend." Simon said.

"Friend?" Thaddeus repeated with a squint.

"His name is Thomas. I met him at the Waste Management Sector."

"Who is this new friend?" Thaddeus asked.

"I just met the guy. I think he's trustworthy. Works similar technician jobs as I do. He expressed some interesting opinions on the Leaders," Simon detailed.

"Simon has good instinct, Thaddeus. Plus, we'll be careful," Albert said.

"All right," Thaddeus said reluctantly.

The group ate and watched the lines shuffling into the mess hall. Simon watched them intently. Each Worker was like a robot. Each one waited in line, flawlessly following the pattern of scanning their Individual Chip, getting a plate, and then getting food and a container of water before parting the line.

Simon was waiting for Thomas, trying to pick him out from the dwindling crowds. After a few minutes, he saw him. They exchanged eye contact, idly nodding to each other in recognition before lowering their gazes to avoid trouble.

Thomas followed the same pattern as everyone else. He immediately walked to the table where Simon was sitting, attempting to look casual as he did.

"Is that him?" Albert asked.

"That's him," Simon responded.

Thomas nodded to them as he sat down, slowly putting his plate on the table and looking at all of them.

"Wassup?" he said.

"Yo," Albert said.

"Hey," Thaddeus said.

"Hey, Thomas. Meet my friends. This is Thaddeus, and this is Albert. I've known Albert since we were kids, and Thaddeus I've known for a few years now," Simon explained.

"Hey, I'm Thomas. Nice to meet you two," Thomas said, nodding to both of them as they nodded back.

"You're not from this mess hall, never seen you before. Which one are you from, Thomas?" Thaddeus asked.

"Number five," Thomas responded.

"Rocket Scorpions!" Albert said a little too loudly, "Buncha suckers."

"Better than the Cargo Bears," Thomas replied with an amused smile.

"Boys, boys, we're not here to argue Thrash Game teams," Simon told them.

"Why is he here?" Thaddeus asked in a more serious tone.

"Simon invited me," Thomas replied.

"I wanted to talk about the Leaders," Simon said.

Albert's loud statement about the Rocket Scorpions had attracted the gaze of a Peacekeeper, though he was too far away to hear them. Thomas glanced in his direction and then lowered his head.

"I assume your friend here can be trusted then, Simon?" Thomas asked.

"Yes," Simon said.

Thaddeus didn't seem to trust Thomas, but he lowered his head to listen intently. Albert did so as well.

"All right, look..." Thomas said. "I'm sure you guys have heard a lot about the brawl at the Thrash Games."

The other three nodded.

"Yeah."

"I'll start simple. All these Peacekeepers and new rules aren't just a random, new punishment for that."

"What do you mean?" Thaddeus asked.

"I mean, things have been changing for months, even a few years. The brawl was just an excuse to change more things in a shorter period of time."

Thomas paused to eat.

"You may have heard the rumor about the change in leadership. It's true. Some new Leaders are controlling the station."

"We got some new ones, so what? What's with the Peacekeepers and the rules?" Simon asked.

"I'm not entirely sure. It's the rumors and civil unrest among us. There've been more events like the Thrash Games brawl, which were isolated. I'm sure you guys recall what it was like a few years ago? Only like four people got sent to the Deck a year. Now it's at least thirty a year. They're trying to keep us under control and failing."

"I'm sure they hid those other events. I haven't heard a lot about the civil unrest; what's that about?" Simon asked.

"As I said, rumors. For example, I've heard that the Developers are saying that Earth is habitable soon. It means we can get off this fucking station and do what we were intended to do. The Leaders don't want that. Why? I think it's because they're afraid to lose power once we get down to the surface, and they have everything neatly controlled up here."

Thomas paused to eat again.

"Every time a brawl or something happens, security will get worse and more people are gonna get in trouble. Simple facts." Thomas stated.

"Simple facts?" Simon repeated.

"Is there anything we can do? We can't just let them rule over us like this." Thaddeus insisted.

Thomas looked around again and then spoke even more quietly.

"We are doing something about it."

"What do you mean we? Who's doing anything about the Leaders? Who can?" Albert asked in a tone of disbelief.

"We. I know a lot of other Workers who don't like the Leaders. There's a secret group among us, doesn't have a name. I just call us the Defiants. Why make it complicated?"

"Creative name," Simon remarked with a snort.

"Thanks," Thomas said with a chuckle, "In front of the Peacekeepers, I call us the Electronic Repair Group. Makes us sound like we're just a group of technicians, isn't too suspicious."

"How does this work? You have secret meetings or something?" Thaddeus asked.

"Kind of. We use different methods to communicate. We get pretty creative to avoid detection."

"How do we get in?" Simon asked.

"Time," Thomas said, "I can put the good word in for you guys. Someone will give you instructions one day. You might meet in a hallway and walk past each other. That's what happened to me; walked past the guy I was supposed to meet, and he shoved a message in my hand as he walked past. It only had 'welcome' on it."

Thomas finished his food and downed all of his water.

"From there, I met people at mess halls, sometimes jobs if we're lucky, and pass secret messages around."

"Do you guys have a leader or something?" Albert asked.

"Nope. Just a group. We've been devising a way to overthrow the Leaders, but nothing so far. We're just trying to remain undiscovered."

"I might be able to help with that," Simon said.

"Maybe. Like I said, I'll put the good word in. Don't mention anything about this conversation to anyone outside this table. The Leaders do have spies."

Spies? Simon frowned. Anyone could be a spy: his friends, coworkers, anyone. Thomas was just about to continue as a Peacekeeper approached the table.

Tomb

Oliver crept out of the supply room, softly fumbling his way through the darkness. As he did, he heard the footsteps of the figure from where he came. There was no way back. Left with no other choice, Oliver had to follow the hall down to his left. He moved as quickly as he dared, soon turning on his flashlight and illuminating the darkness.

It didn't take long for the medical wing to be left behind. Oliver felt vulnerable. He jumped at every sound and imagined figures in the darkness. He listened, waiting for the horrible, gurgling breath of a mutant. It felt as if, at any moment, a claw would grab him from behind. Oliver continued moving, ignoring each room he passed.

He went right at another crossroad, then left at the one after. His breath quivered. Occasionally, he heard hoarse breathing and growls in the hall.

"Oh fuck... Oh fuck..." he whispered to himself in fear.

He stopped at a sign at another crossroad, brushing off the dust and reading the sign. To his right was a maintenance wing, ahead of him was a residential wing, and to his left was the atrium. Oliver looked up to his left. Perhaps he could navigate his way out through the atrium?

Oliver began to walk again, tiptoeing through the labyrinth. There were works of art everywhere. Statues lined the halls, paired with paintings and displays. The whole place was luxurious, with complex and intricate work put into everything, from the ceiling to the floor.

Soon, he approached a large arch. It was just as beautiful and detailed as everything else, with a large stone face watching from its apex. Oliver looked up at it and then continued. He stopped on a balcony, the flashlight on his gas mask shining ahead. The room he found himself in was massive. Two stories below him were giant bookshelves, a maze dotted with various sitting areas and little offices. Three stories above him was the ceiling, with a large chandelier hanging from it.

He could just make out a painting on the ceiling, something that appeared to be a copy of the Creation of Adam. Each deck of the layered room had archways, going to different parts of the bunker or to stairs leading up and down. Oliver shone the flashlight down into a maze of bookshelves. There were no figures down there, and there wasn't a single sound in the entire atrium.

Oliver decided to explore the library. He needed a break from moving anyway. Oliver walked around the balcony until he found some stairs, moving down each flight until he reached the bottom of the atrium. The bookshelves were even bigger than he thought, each one needing a ladder three times his height to reach the top.

It was dusty. A thick layer coated every book in the library. Oliver walked into the maze, pointing his gun down every path. After a while, he stopped and slumped into a chair inside a small, square sitting room built inside the maze. He needed rest. As Oliver sat there, he looked up at the bookshelves around him. There were all sorts of books. He saw books from almost any genre and date, ranging in size from little to big.

After a while, Oliver reached out and grabbed a book. He brushed the dust from the cover, all of it dropping to the floor in a pile. The entire thing was thick. It must've been at least seven hundred pages. He had no trouble reading, even with the crack across his gas mask visor.

Oliver flipped it around and read the title under his breath.

"*Electricity Before Ignium by Martin Lee.*"

Beneath the letters was a picture depicting an electrical motor from the 1800s, with an arrow pointing from it to a motor from the 21st century.

"Sam could use this," Oliver whispered, looking around before stuffing it into his bag.

Oliver stood and began to gather various books.

"*The History of the Engine.*" Oliver said, whispering each title, "*Nikolai Tesla's Stolen Ideas, The Lightbulb of the Modern Era...*"

Soon, his bag was overstuffed. It was heavy, filled with books and supplies. Oliver heaved it from the floor and swung it onto his back.

"Oh, hol-" he blurted out, stumbling slightly from its weight. "Fucking... You better appreciate these, Sam."

Break time was over. Oliver stood up with the new weight on his shoulders. He was tired, but he didn't care. He didn't want to sleep in this place. Oliver stumbled out of the maze, searching for a new sign to lead him out before walking down an archway, gun ready and flashlight on.

The breathing and growling in the hallways became audible again as he left the atrium. Each one chilled and terrified Oliver. He gasped each time he heard one, pointing his gun around in terror. Occasionally, he'd veer off course to avoid the various sources of raspy breaths.

"You're not dying today... No, not today. You are not dying today, Oliver." he whispered to himself, trying to stay brave.

Oliver continued down one hallway, finding another crossroad. He stopped and looked down each path. The left was clear. Ahead of him was clear. As he looked to the right, he jumped in surprise as his flashlight illuminated six idle figures. Oliver heard them react to the light. He turned off the flashlight as quickly as he could and slinked behind a pillar, hiding against it as the six fiends moved toward where he was.

They shuffled past him, growling, snarling, and gurgling. Oliver could make out their bodies as they went past. They were completely pale, their bodies covered in fused body parts and strange limbs. He swore he saw a hoof sticking out of one's back. The group went down one hall, allowing Oliver to carry on in another direction.

He wasted no time going down the hallway opposite from them. It caused him to get lost again, but it got him away from the beasts. Oliver came into a new wing of the bunker, being greeted by another archway and another stone face. Ahead of him were multiple doorways as the hallway split multiple times.

Oliver walked forward, shining his flashlight into the first room he passed. He saw a bed, clothing strewn about on the floor, a shower in the back, and some pieces of furniture. The next room was much the same, except a few pieces of furniture were turned over and broken. This must've been the residential wing.

It was creepy. Sometimes, there were skeletons in the rooms. Sometimes they were laid on beds, sometimes on the floor, and many showed signs of struggle before they died. People had lived and died in this place, trapped deep underground with a monstrous threat. Oliver also saw nests, collections of clothing, bones, mattresses, and more piled in various rooms.

Oliver continued as quickly as he could out of this wing, moving into another hall. It felt hopelessly futile, moving from hall to hall, wing to wing, completely lost and trapped.

He followed a hallway that opened up into a gigantic, cavernous area. Oliver shined his flashlight upward, the light barely able to reach the stone ceiling. He looked ahead of him, finding beach chairs and tables with umbrellas. The area was a massive expanse. A platform with little shops built into the walls was on one side, and a fence was on the other side.

Oliver walked to the shops first, looking into each. Most of them were closed with metal bars blocking entry, each of them made to resemble a shop in a mall. The ones Oliver could get into were empty, any pieces of food eaten and gone. He sighed and sat in a beach chair, taking another break.

Once he was able to stand again, Oliver walked over to the fence. Below him was a massive reservoir, with large water tanks built into the walls sucking in water over time. He knelt and looked at the water, only a few feet below him. It was brown and murky. On one side was a rusty staircase going into the water, disappearing into the abyss.

He stood and looked out into the water, unable to see where it ended. Even though it was murky, the sight of it was stunning. Oliver took it all in. As he did, he saw reflections in the water, pairs of dots shining back at his flashlight: one pair, two pairs, three pairs. Then there were twenty, thirty. Oliver stepped back. His eyes widened.

"Shit!" he cursed, immediately turning and running.

His boots echoed in the vast expanse, the only noise for a moment. Then there was splashing.

At first, he heard only the sounds of water dripping and wet footsteps chasing after him. Then came snarls and growls. His heart thundered in his chest, Oliver running so fast that it felt like he was flying.

It didn't feel like enough. He pushed himself hard, sprinting down the hallways he came from. It wasn't enough. He slid and turned, trying to throw off the growing horde behind him. It wasn't enough. The fiends from before came from the right, while the horde trailed him from behind, forcing him to take off down the hall to his left. It wasn't enough.

Another snarl, another growl, another hungry squeal. He didn't dare look back. Another left, another right! No, not that way! He turned to avoid more monsters. His arm burned, his entire body ached from the running. Oliver couldn't stop.

Oliver ran into the atrium, bolting through the maze of bookshelves. The creatures followed him. They flooded the maze, coming from the left, the right, and behind him. Oliver ran through it as fast as he could, getting grabbed a few times. He shook off each wet claw, screaming in terror.

He emerged from the shelves, continuing to run. The maze did little to stop the horde. He looked behind him, only to see a swarm. He turned a corner and ran up a flight of stairs, stopping at the top. The horde flooded in after him, crashing into the corner and flooding up the stairs. Oliver pointed his gun, pulling the trigger.

Once again, the barrel sparked to life, glowing in the darkness. The scrap metal inside fell into the magnetic embrace of the gun's mechanisms, flying into a hellish cone of doom. Oliver watched as the scrap metal shredded at least ten of the creatures, a few of them dying and falling down the stairs.

It was enough to scare the horde into a pause, Oliver taking off again with more distance between him and death. He did it again, shredding more monsters.

The numbers didn't seem to change. Another flight of stairs. He ran down a hallway and into another wing. He knew where he was, the medical wing.

Oliver ran past the rooms making up the wing, bolting straight into the lobby. He crashed into a fiend in front of him, using all of his weight to throw it aside. It gripped onto him, tripping him. Oliver turned and kicked it, blasting it immediately with scrap metal.

The gun came to life, shredding the fiend into mush. Oliver scrambled to his feet, the horde now just behind him.

He had to make it. He was so close. Oliver followed his blood on the floor, the trail he left when he came here. It was as if it was a guiding hand sent from heaven. Oliver turned into the crossroads with the broken sign. The sign was still there. Oliver tried to turn and fire again.

The gun was empty, no more scrap metal inside of it. Instead of letting out a cone of doom, it only sparked and fizzled out.

"Shit!" Oliver shouted.

He took off down the hallway to the door. He could see the metal doors ahead. As he ran, Oliver took off his backpack, carrying it and his empty gun. It was so close. Oliver felt his lungs burning, his heart throbbing in agony, and his body full of terror.

There it was. The door! Oliver threw the backpack through the crack, then his gun, then himself. The horde crashed into the door, the combined weight of the mutants closing it.

Oliver grabbed his stuff and stood, continuing to run. He saw the light ahead, the end of the tunnel. He ran and stumbled, blinded by the light as he ran into freedom. He made it.

"Oh, God! Oh, fuck! Thank you, thank you!" he cried out, panting and laughing.

He fell to his knees, resting his head on the ground and catching his breath. Oliver slowly rolled over and looked back at the tunnel, a broad smile on his face.

"Fuck all of you!" he growled, gesturing rudely to the tunnel.

Oliver laid there for a bit, panting and gaining his energy back.

The Doomstorm and the sandstorm brought with it was completely gone now. He looked around him. Where was home?

Trade

10:23 AM, August 12, 2154

"Excited for your first caravan ride, Rose?" London asked.

"Yes! I can't wait!" Rose said, excitement filling her voice.

London smiled as they walked out into the street. They were in the center of a bright, growing nation: New Uruk. It had been a few months since the patrol found and saved them, and a lot had changed since then. Both London and Rose had become citizens in New Uruk. Since their integration, London had joined the trading and water caravans that worked in New Uruk.

It was an okay job, in his opinion. It paid well too. He was paid in gas mask filters. They were common enough to replace money, and everyone needed them. Even if there were different types of filters and gas masks, they still held trade value. Regardless, caravan jobs were dangerous with attacks from Patria due to the war and wasteland scavengers trying to make a quick haul.

Grunting, London heaved a bag of supplies into the back of a wagon and moved to the front. He groaned slightly. His limp hadn't gone away. The wound dealt by the dog a few months prior had healed well, but he was sure he'd limp for the rest of his days.

Fifteen wagons lined the streets, surrounded by buildings on either side. There were merchant stalls, homes, workshops, and more lining the buildings. In between were citizens of New Uruk, walking around from place to place and doing their daily business.

Rose followed him as they went to a wagon second to the front. In front of each wagon were two large, boar-like beasts called Scab Boars. They were the size of cows and had tough leather-like skin covered in tumors and hard growths. They also had multiple tusks and the occasional fused body-part, such as additional, useless legs on their abdomens.

London helped Rose get up onto the wagon before going around to pet one. It looked at him with docile eyes, huffing heavily with a powerful breath. On the sides of its ribs and neck were holes, called "iron lungs" by the people of New Uruk. London looked over as it breathed. Every time it exhaled, the holes opened and let out toxic excess from the air, allowing it to breathe the polluted air.

He had read about iron-lung animals before. They were created in the old world by scientists trying to help animals survive in a toxic world. When humanity tipped over into chaos, these animals escaped labs and zoos and replaced old-world animals such as deer. They, alongside human mutants from mutation bombs, became the animal life in the new world.

"Pretty, isn't she?"

London looked up to see Alisa getting onto the wagon.

"Yes, indeed. Where did you get these two?" London asked.

"Bought them from a Scab Boar herder for a bunch of filters. We were gonna lose our jobs in the caravans if we didn't replace the two we lost in the last attack." Alisa said.

"How many filters?" London asked, raising a brow.

"Enough," she said.

"All right, it was needed," said London.

He stopped petting the Scab Boar and climbed into the back of the wagon. Rose, himself, and Alisa were the first to arrive at the cart. The group had split somewhat since they had arrived in New Uruk. Tommy and Finlay were sent to the war front to fight against Patria, Tommy as a soldier, and Finlay as a medic. Reginald, Archie, and Alisa had joined London in doing caravan work. Margaret usually stayed in New Uruk, dealing with trade coming into New Uruk.

Eventually, Reginald and Archie arrived. Archie hopped into the back with London, sitting on top of a large container.

"Ay, London, we're bringing Rose?" Archie asked.

"Yeah, she wanted to join us. We're going out to get water, so I assumed it was safe enough to bring her," London said.

"She's gotta learn the business." Reginald said, "She's a smart little girl. She can defend herself."

"Hey, I've taught her some stuff," Alisa said with a proud smile.

London grabbed some heavy gas canisters from Reginald and walked across the back of the wagon, attaching them to a mounted pressure spear-gun behind the driver's seat. There was a barrel of spears beside it, which were ammo for the gun. It was a device built to destroy enemy wheels or impale people, which worked well for the caravans.

Alisa and Reginald got into the driver's seat, with Reginald taking the reins. They patiently waited for the rest of the caravan to go. Meanwhile, each of them checked their weapons.

Alisa had an old, worn shotgun, a sort of bola for tripping people, and a wicked hatchet-bat. London still had his modified baseball bat but had traded his pistol for a more consistent crossbow with a bayonet. He added a quiver to the side of his backpack for its bolts. Archie had a single-shot pipe rifle and a knife. Reginald stuck with an old-world pistol, something he had a lot of practice and skill with. It didn't seem like it, but doing caravan jobs had made them somewhat wealthy.

Eventually, a man with a horn stood on the front caravan and looked down the line.

"Y'all got your backers tight?!" he shouted.

"Ay!" each driver, or Whip, replied.

It took a while for London to learn caravan slang, but he was almost as fluent in it as any other caravaner. A backer was the back of a wagon, generally for carrying goods or people, and tight meant full or ready. The drivers, like Reginald, were called Whips because of how they whipped the reins to make the Scab Boars move.

"Whips ready! Move out!" the man said, blowing a small horn.

After the horn blew, the caravan began to move. The wagons moved slowly as the massive Scab Boars heaved forward, grunting and letting out an "orf" sound from their iron lungs. Rose sat behind London against the front side of the wagon's back, looking up at him as he leaned on the spear-gun.

London gazed at the buildings they passed. The people on the street watched as the caravan departed, some waving as they watched their friends leave. There were merchants, workers, guards, and more scattered in the crowd. London could see people living in the old buildings as they passed, along with craftsmen doing their works and traders yelling out their prices. They turned left onto another street and continued out of New Uruk.

The nation centered itself in an industrial area inside of an old-world city. This area had large and strong buildings, both for enduring sieges and Doomstorms. Inside the old office buildings and factories were markets and entire neighborhoods. The largest building was a gigantic factory that had become the capitol building. Beneath New Uruk was an underground system where subway trains used to go, now occupied by the citizens. The underground was particularly useful for sieges and Doomstorms.

The caravan also passed buildings where they collected and cleaned soil used for indoor greenhouses. London had learned that New Uruk sustained its population through indoor farming. Since the pollution and Doomstorms were too harsh on agriculture, it was a perfect solution. Most of their supplies came from old-world greenhouse skyscrapers, such as UV lights and seeds; water came from the caravans.

"Hey, London, look," Reginald said, pointing to a building they were passing.

London looked inside. It was one of the newly made factories in New Uruk, producing weapons for the war. There was an entire workshop inside, full of Ignium powered machines with belt-drives to make everything move and work. Rose stood and stared at the factory with an amazed look in her eyes.

"Wow, that's amazing," London remarked.

"I thought you'd like it since you read them old-world books and all. People of New Uruk are learning from the past, and these factories are just how they were a long time ago in the old world." Reginald said.

"I can see. I've read some about factories. They kinda look like belt-driven machine shops, which are really old. I think before the twenty-first century."

"I didn't know that. Weird," Archie commented.

"Yeah, seems they're using Ignium for them?" London asked.

"Yep, good ol' Ignium. Heard they were trying to use electricity again," Reginald told London.

"That's hard to do, less information and less things to use," London stated.

"I think I've seen an electrical watch before; thing was broken," Archie remarked.

"Damn shame that electricity went out of fashion," London stated.

"Don't worry too much. We'll get it all sorted out and be using electricity in no time," Reginald stated.

The caravan carried on. Eventually, it came to the edge of New Uruk inside the city, stopping at a wall. It was a tall wall made out of concrete, scrap, tires, and junk with barb wire lining the top. The guards that met the caravan had a small discussion with the driver at the front wagon before moving the "gate." The gate itself was an old bus covered in metal with sandbags on top, a small Ignium-powered machine pulling it out of the way while several men pushed. Once it was out of the way, the caravan carried on.

They followed a specific route out of the city, passing patrols by guards and little outposts in buildings. It was relatively safe outside the walls except for the occasional mutant that wandered too close to human territory. There were traps everywhere, along with warnings made out of impaled mutant bodies and heads. The patrols out here knew the territory well and left a safe route for the caravans.

After an hour, the caravan made it outside of the city, leaving behind a very small outpost at the edge of it all. Now they were in the wasteland, heading south-west into the sandy openness. The wind was calm. Apart from the pollution haze, it seemed like a rather clear day. London had never been out with a caravan when a Doomstorm hit, and he hoped it would never happen.

London continued to rest on the spear-gun, eyeing the surrounding wasteland.

"London?" Rose whispered.

"Yes, Rosey?" he responded, looking down.

"Are there gonna be bandits out here?"

"Don't worry, Rosey. I told you, there hasn't been an attack on a caravan in a while, and there's plenty of protection where we're going."

She looked at him, London giving her a reassuring nod.

"Any news on the war?" Archie asked, laying down on a container on the back.

"Nothing much," Alisa said, "I haven't seen Finlay in a while, and Tommy I haven't seen since they sent him into the war."

"I heard that so far Patria and New Uruk were fighting over some expanses of land and small settlements out in the wasteland," Archie said.

"Poor folks. They're just trying to survive out there, and now they have to deal with the war," London said.

"That's the way it is. Best we can do is make sure the war ends quickly," Alisa said with an annoyed sigh, "I wish I was out there helping."

"I'm happy you're with us," Reginald said.

"Pisses me off that they won't let women join the war," Alisa said in an annoyed voice, "They need all everyone to beat Patria back."

"I don't blame you. The Patrians have a much bigger army than us, and they have lots of women fighting. I'm sure if we become desperate, then that rule will change," London said.

"Patria doesn't care about its people. People don't matter; their usefulness and ability to fight does. Not sending women to war is for their protection. Y'all haven't heard about the women they've captured from Patria? They ain't right," Reginald told them.

Alisa angrily furrowed her brow and looked at Reginald, barely holding her silence.

London looked up as they approached a wide, open plain. They were about an hour and a half out from New Uruk. In the middle of the plain was a building turned into an outpost, a huge field of water pumps behind it. He saw row upon row of water pumps, all of them pumping up water slowly from deep underground. Among the water pumps and the outpost were dozens of workers and guards, eyeing the caravan as it rolled in.

He watched as workers collected water from the pumps with machines, transporting them to large water silos at the outpost. London also saw a large, mobile drilling platform used to dig new wells for water pumps. It was currently dormant, parked on the other side of the outpost.

The caravan approached the water tanks.

"All stop! Whips ready to move, hands get your water!" said the front driver, blowing his horn.

The caravan came to a stop. One by one, each wagon moved forward beneath a water silo. The hands, or the workers of each wagon, hopped out immediately and began to work as a team to pump water into the containers that each wagon carried. It took around forty-five minutes to fill all the containers on each wagon. Afterward, the caravan had a fifteen-minute break before they carried on to deliver the water back to New Uruk. Once again, the front driver ordered them to leave.

"Y'all got your backers tight?!" he shouted, to which the Whips shouted, "Ay!"

"Whips ready! Move out!" he commanded, blowing a small horn.

Betrayer

3:34 AM, June 6, 2185

Albert was startled awake to the sound of his door opening. He sat up from his bed, looking as four Peacekeepers entered the room. They were armed with their tesla batons but didn't have them ready.

"Worker 4720, Albert, come with us," one said.

Albert didn't protest or say a word, simply nodding and standing up. The air felt tense, but none of the Peacekeepers seemed ready to beat him to a pulp. Instead, they escorted him out of the room and guided him through the Residential Sector. They walked through the maze-like hallways until they arrived in the Peacekeeper's part of the Residential Sector.

A heavy door marked the beginning of their area, heavier than those found in most areas of the Arcadis. It was closed as they got there. As they arrived, one of the Peacekeepers stuck her arm into a scanner in the door, the machine scanning her Individual Chip and opening the door.

The heavy door opened slowly, allowing the group in. Albert felt out of place and in danger. He swallowed nervously and held his breath. Peacekeepers slept in rooms similar to those of the Workers, Peacekeepers going out to patrol and returning from patrols, and Peacekeepers training. It seemed to Albert that they had nighttime and daytime squadrons.

Albert kept his head low. It took only a few minutes before they walked across the Peacekeeper Residential Area, stopping at another set of heavy doors. This time, they met other Peacekeepers who had orange bands around their wrists.

"Is that Worker 4270?" asked one.

"Yes, as the Leaders instructed," answered a Peacekeeper that was escorting Albert.

"You are all relieved then; enjoy your nights."

The four Peacekeepers that had escorted Albert nodded, turning him over into the hands of the special Peacekeepers before leaving. Albert assumed that these were some form of elite Peacekeepers, watching them open the door behind them. Once it was open, they led him inside.

Albert's jaw dropped as he saw what was ahead of him. Past the door was a hallway full of paintings with small, magnificent sofas beneath each one. The floor was white, clean, and shiny, unlike the worn, metal floors of the rest of the Arcadis. On the floor was something Albert had only seen a few times in his life–carpet.

"Woah," he quietly let out.

The Peacekeepers led him inside, closing the door behind them. It must've been the Command Sector. It was fit for the Leaders in Albert's eyes. They began to escort him past rooms full of beautiful furniture, entertainment devices, and other luxurious items. As he walked past one room, he saw a steak with some broccoli on a table.

Steak? Broccoli? The rumors were true then. The Leaders got to eat real food while the Workers had to eat synthesized, bland food. That annoyed him.

All of it was shocking. Albert had never been to the Command Sector and had never expected to. It was magnificent and luxurious beyond his expectations as well. It was clean and new in appearance.

"This way," a Peacekeeper said.

They led him into a large, round room. In the center was a white table surrounded by chairs. Built into the table were computers, facing each chair and displaying information on a 3D screen made of light. There was a massive window at one end of the room. As Albert walked in, he saw twenty-five chairs around the table, but only five people sitting at the table.

The Leaders. Unlike the Workers who wore jumpsuits with boring colors, they all wore clothing full of bright colors. They all had strange and bizarre hairstyles as well. Their skin glowed too, full of implants and devices attached to them through surgery. Each one stared at him as he entered.

"This is Worker 4270, as requested."

"Thank you. You may leave now."

The Peacekeepers nodded and left immediately, leaving Albert alone and nervous.

"He–" Albert began.

"No one asked you to speak," interrupted one of the Leaders.

Albert immediately became silent, nodding to show that he understood.

"Now, Albert," one said, leaning forward. "You recall who I am?"

It was a man by the name of Benjamin. Albert nodded.

"Good, then you remember our deal."

Albert did. It was only a few weeks ago when Benjamin, escorted by six Peacekeepers, had met with Albert in his room in the Residential Sector. It was there where they gave Albert a choice between opportunity and oppression.

"You're not special, Albert. We have many like you among the Worker population. We hear what they hear and know what they know. They too, have promised their loyalty and knowledge to us in return for protection." Benjamin told him.

"A few have already failed us. We know that you already understand what happened to them." said another Leader.

Albert nodded again.

"You've done well so far. You've proven your loyalty by reporting all the information you could on the 'Thrash Games incident' and aiding in the arrests of those who assaulted Peacekeepers. I'm sure your reward was well appreciated." Benjamin stated.

Albert grinned broadly and nodded enthusiastically

"Wonderful," Benjamin remarked.

"Now, we have a new task for you, Albert." said the first Leader who had spoken.

"We've received news of a rebel group among the Workers. They call themselves the Defiants. So far, they seem to be just a small group of troublemakers." said another Leader.

"But we're not fools. We know what could happen if these 'Defiants' gained any form of power. It could destroy the station. We want to maintain order. Your job will be to spy on the Workers. Gain any knowledge you can of the Defiants, ask questions but don't look suspicious, and report back to us. Simple. Can you do that?"

"Yes," Albert said.

"Good," Benjamin said.

"Do remember what you are doing, Albert," began another Leader. "There are around a thousand people on this station. They all depend on the station and us to survive. With civil unrest in the Worker population, the delicate balance that keeps us all alive is threatened."

"Yes, and with the help of you and many others, we'll stop that unrest," Benjamin said.

"It starts and ends with the Defiants," said the first Leader.

"You may go now, Albert. The Peacekeepers will escort you back to your room," Benjamin said.

Albert nodded and turned around, preparing to leave.

"Ah, ah! Wait."

He stopped.

"Remember, many have failed us. You know what happens to those who fail us, and I trust you will not join them. Speak of this to no one, and take this secret to your grave. I will assure you that you get your protection and that the Peacekeepers know who you are," Benjamin said.

"You are dismissed," said the first leader.

Albert began walking again, moving out of the room to meet an elite Peacekeeper. Meanwhile, he caught the beginning of another conversation between the leaders.

"Eight hundred Workers, three hundred Peacekeepers," Benjamin said, "I know most of you are not worried, but I worry for our stability."

"The incident at the Thrash Games has indeed made matters worse, but it made our responses justified. The Workers respond to order and discipline. As I said, send troublemakers to the Deck, and send dangerous offenders out to space."

"Come on," said the Peacekeeper.

Albert nodded and followed.

The Peacekeeper led him along the elaborate and luxurious corridors, eyeing him. Albert had a grin as he walked, quite pleased to have gotten on the good side of the Leaders. He did feel a slight twinge of guilt. The thought of betraying Thaddeus and Simon felt terrible.

Albert believed that if they were in his shoes, they'd take the offers of the Leaders too. He was also sure that if he put in the good word, he could keep Simon and Thaddeus safe. Still, he felt worried and guilty.

"What are you grinning about?" asked the Peacekeeper.

"A luxurious shower and a steak."

The Peacekeeper glared at him.

"Don't think you're invulnerable now that you're one of the Leader's hounds. We know who you are, but if you cross the line... I'll beat you myself. Fucking smug Workers."

Albert's grin faded.

Traps

10:38 AM, March 21, 2100

"How's your arm?" Sam asked.

"A lot better," Oliver said.

"Do the bandages need replacing?"

Oliver paused, pulling back the sleeve of his smart suit and gazing at the bloodied bandages around his forearm.

"Yeah, it's time."

Sam nodded and stood, walking across the small campsite and grabbing a bag from a reinforced crate. He walked over to Oliver with the bag, placing it beside him.

"It's not too bad. Isn't as bad as when I found you."

Oliver grimaced in uneasy anticipation.

"Can't believe I almost died out there," he said, looking out across the early morning wasteland.

It was a clearer day than most, with the sun rising slowly over the polluted sky. It bathed their campsite in sunlight. Even so, Oliver didn't feel warmed by the sun's embrace. The only thing that kept him warm was his smart suit.

Sam began to unwind the bandages. The gunshot wound was slowly healing and sealing. The edges were dark and scabby, while the interior was white and red. Oliver made a gagging gesture with his tongue and looked away, closing his eyes in disgust.

"I can't believe you found your way back," Sam said. "I never knew this place even existed. But, I never really ventured past that town we cleared out."

"I hope you liked the books I brought from there."

"I did. They're going to be very useful in the future,"

Oliver looked at the dark tunnel leading into the bunker. It was ominously silent. He felt unsettled by staring at it as if the concrete tunnel would erupt in mutants.

"Ow," Oliver winced as Sam cleaned the wound.

His gaze turned from the tunnel and to Sam, watching him as he re-bandaged the wound.

"I was lucky that the town is only an hour's walk out from here," Oliver said.

"Damn lucky," Sam said, finishing the bandages. "All righty, you're set."

"Thanks," Oliver said, "What's the plan for today?"

Sam sat down on a plastic bucket across from Oliver.

"Same as the last two days; build more traps and check the ones we've built," Sam replied.

"Sounds like a plan,"

Oliver grabbed his Railshot Rifle, checking the ammo contents and its energy levels.

"You sure we're clearing out the bunker with these traps? There were a lot of mutants when I was in there," Oliver said.

"Well, they're human mutants."

"And?"

"And they don't reproduce fast enough to overcome the amount that are dying every night from my traps."

"All right, let's get going then," Oliver said, standing up.

Sam stood and grabbed his pipe rifle. Before they left the campsite, he went to everything and secured it down in case of a Doomstorm. Oliver helped. The first thing they tied down was their tent, then their supply pile, and then a few floodlights. Once they secured everything to the ground, they began walking.

"You think the house is okay while we're gone?" Oliver asked as they began walking into the wasteland.

"I hope. Don't jinx it," Sam replied.

"Well, even if something does happen, we have this place now."

"How big is it under there?" Sam asked.

"Huge. I think we can fit a few hundred people in there. I didn't get to explore the entire residential area, but I know there's plenty of space for families in that area."

"Families?" Sam repeated.

"Families. There's enough for a small city. We're not selfish, are we? Can't condemn all the people out here to wandering the wasteland when we have space, food, and water."

"Water and space, but I don't know about food," Sam said.

"They gotta have some sort of agricultural area under there. I just probably missed it."

"You're right," Sam told Oliver. "I just don't trust people."

"I don't either. I just hope they respect some sort of deal if we make one. We exchange all the good stuff about the bunker for loyalty," Oliver said.

"Loyalty? Really?"

"What else do we have?"

"Bad ideas and bad dreams," he said.

Oliver shook his head.

They arrived at the first trap after a few minutes. Oliver immediately saw three pale corpses around the trap, facing a pole with a mutant head mounted on top. The cartridge trap. It was one of Oliver's favorite traps, consisting of bait on a pole surrounded by hidden bullets. Sam rigged the bullets in a way that if something put pressure on them, they shot off.

"Ay, we got three!" Sam cheered, walking over to the trap.

Oliver followed him, carefully trailing as they examined the mutants. It appeared that each one had stepped on a cartridge trap, got a bullet in the foot, and then fell onto more of the traps. Blood still seeped from each bullet hole in the corpses.

Sam carefully stepped across the trap and grabbed a corpse, Oliver doing the same. They lifted the body with one heave.

"Let's just toss each body over the traps before we move them," Sam said.

Oliver nodded. The pair swung the body back and forth three times before throwing it a few feet away. Once it landed with a thud, they moved onto the next body.

Sam slowly stepped over the traps that were still live, Oliver following him.

"Where are we moving them?" Oliver asked.

"Just out of the way where something can eat them," Sam said, leaning down to pick up a corpse.

Oliver grunted as they lifted another body. He was grateful for having gloves as he looked down at the skin of the first mutant. It was pale, yet somewhat grayish. Its body was covered in tumors and oozing boils, and its skin dropped flakes on the ground.

"Egh..." Oliver groaned in disgust.

The pair dumped the body behind a dune, carrying the other two and doing the same. Once they moved the bodies, they began to walk to the next trap. After a few minutes, they arrived.

"Scree!"

The sound came out of nowhere. Oliver jumped in surprise as he heard it, raising his gun.

"Woah! Woah! Relax. It's stuck," Sam said.

Oliver slowly lowered his gun. In front of him was another pale mutant, knee-deep in a spike trap. It was completely stuck, spikes impaled in its leg from ankle to thigh. The creature writhed and pulled, trying to escape with futile attempts.

"Just distract it," Sam told Oliver.

"How?"

"Like... Poke it or something; go in front of it and antagonize it. I'll go behind it and bash its brains out."

Oliver stared at the wriggling fiend before going in front of it and poking at it with his gun.

"Ha! Ha! C'mon!" he shouted at it, trying to provoke it.

The creature snarled and swiped at him, trying to claw at his gun and arm. As it did, Sam walked behind it quietly.

Sam brutally rammed the end of his pipe rifle into the mutant's head. The first hit dazed the mutant, the rest smashing its head into the ground until its skull cracked. Oliver stared at it as it went limp, leaning over and looking at the spike trap it fell into.

"Uh, Sam?" Oliver began.

"Yes?"

"How are we supposed to get it out of the hole?"

Sam looked down at the mutant.

"Uh.... Good question."

"Next trap?" Oliver suggested.

"Next trap."

The pair began walking across the dunes again. As they came upon the next trap, Oliver saw it was empty.

"Darn, nothing," Sam said.

"Ssshh! Do you hear that?" Oliver asked, raising a finger.

The two looked around. Gunshots echoed across the wasteland, sounding like whispers to the pair.

"How far away do you think that is?" Sam asked.

"Pretty far away."

"Should we investigate?"

"I don't know. It's right on the doorstep of our new place, though," Oliver said.

Sam looked down at his pipe rifle, then up in the general direction of the gunshots.

"Let's go check it out," Sam said.

Oliver nodded and followed Sam as they burst into a jog. As they moved out into the windy expanse of the wasteland, the gunshots grew louder and louder.

Sam dropped and slid behind a dune. Oliver did the same, creeping up beside him and looking down onto a road. A group of twelve people all were hiding behind the walls of a ruined building, keeping their heads down as six people behind a car shot at them.

"Woah," Oliver let out.

"There's a child with them," Sam whispered.

Out of the twelve people, only four shot back while their attackers all shot at them. They appeared to be nomads. Each one carried all that he or she had on their backs, wearing ill-fitting and worn gas masks. Their bodies were thin, and they had dirty, hole-filled clothes.

Their attackers were almost the same. There was barely a difference between the group, their attackers, and Oliver and Sam. They were all survivors.

"What do we do?" Oliver asked.

Sam laid beside him and stared as the two groups below them exchanged shots.

"Look," he pointed out, "Those are the guys that attacked us."

"Wait, how do you know?" Oliver asked.

"You can't tell? Their guns and masks."

"I didn't fight them off, Sam. I barely remember that whole thing." Oliver told him.

"Right, right. We gotta take them by surprise. If we run down behind them, I think I can take out two with my gun, and you can take out the rest with yours."

Oliver gazed down at the struggle before looking at Sam and shrugging.

"Fuck it,"

"All right, One... Two... Three!" Sam whispered.

As soon as he said three, the two sprinted down the hill. Sand and dirt flew into the air as they came crashing down, the pair aiming their guns at their surprised targets. Sam's aim was spot on as one attacker fell, Oliver pulling his trigger a moment after.

Sparks of energy came from the gun as scrap metal sprayed out into the group. In the blink of an eye, Oliver shredded everything in front of him. Three of the attackers dropped dead, wounds covering their bodies. A scream came from another one as the metal hit her, her legs and arms covered in gruesome wounds. The other one turned and shot at them.

Oliver and Sam dove for cover as bullets whizzed past them. As they hit the ground, the other pair began to flee. Oliver watched as they tried to escape, the wounded one shambling forward in pain.

With one clean shot from Sam, she fell to the ground with a distant thud. The other attacker looked behind and gasped, beginning to run as fast as possible at the death of his comrade.

Oliver stared as he disappeared over some dunes, slowly standing and looking at the corpses lying in pools of blood. It was horrific. Metal had completely shredded their bones and flesh, leaving strands and pieces of their bodies everywhere. He felt a twinge of guilt. It didn't feel so bad to kill these people.

Not at all. They had attacked Oliver and Sam and were attacking these nomads with a child. Were their lives that worthless? Oliver told himself it was justice.

Sam reloaded his pipe rifle.

"You can come out now! We're friendly," Sam shouted toward the ruin.

Oliver glanced up from the bodies. The group of twelve carefully walked out from the old ruin, expressions of disbelief beneath their gas masks.

"Holy hell, strangers. You saved us," one of the men said.

"No problem," Sam replied.

Oliver stared at them. They still had their guns ready but didn't point it at them. Still, he didn't trust them. Regardless of his guilt, Oliver was ready to blast the group of twelve with his gun. As he watched their movements carefully, Sam spoke.

"Why were they attacking you guys?" Sam asked.

A tall woman carrying an aged hunting rifle replied.

"We don't know. I assume that we probably entered their territory, and they thought they'd get some easy supplies off of us."

"You're nomads then?" Sam asked.

"We're just people trying to survive," the woman responded.

"So are we. I'm Sam, and my friend here is Oliver."

"Nice to meet you. I'm Mary, and this is my group."

Sam looked at Oliver and whispered.

"Should we ask them to help us clear out the bunker?"

Oliver looked at him and shrugged.

"We don't know who they are. Even so, they seem friendly enough,"

Sam turned back to the woman.

"If you guys are looking for shelter and food, we can provide. There's a bunker not too far away from here that we're clearing out from mutants. Once we get it clear, there'll be space, food, and water for everyone. We're willing to share if you guys can help us," Sam explained.

Mary paused.

"Well, I'm grateful for the offer." she began. "Give us a second to talk about it."

Shelter

The sirens loudly began to let out their blaring calls, filling the city with their deafening song. Immediately the city was sent into a panic, everyone rushing to gather their things. Shops closed, supplies strapped down, and people retreated indoors or into the subway system beneath them. Soldiers and guards ran everywhere, aiding civilians as they tried to take shelter. The winds picked up and blew loose things away.

"Come on, Rose, come on!" London said.

Rose ran beside him with her rabbit in hand, London holding her other hand and guiding her along the streets. He glanced behind them as they ran to the capitol building of New Uruk, his eyes widening. Behind them was a massive wall of sand reaching up to the sky. It was quickly approaching the city, enveloping building after building in its monstrous embrace. It was a Doomstorm.

The people of New Uruk were well prepared. As they ran indoors, they closed and blocked their doors. Once everything was tied down and secured, people hid under tables or in sturdy rooms. Those caught outside were escorted by soldiers who risked their lives to take them to the subway system below.

London ran with Rose as fast as he could, picking her up and sprinting as the Doomstorm drew closer. The limp in his leg slowed him down slightly. As they ran, he saw Archie running toward him from another street.

"Archie!" London called out. "Over here!"

Archie saw him and ran over immediately.

"Are you guys okay?!"

"Yes! Come on. We're going to the capitol building!" London said.

Rose clung to London tightly as Archie nodded and ran with the pair. Within a minute, they were at the stairs of the capitol building, windswept sand beginning to obscure their path. They arrived at the front of the building just in time.

"Wait! Wait for us!" London shouted.

The guards closing the building's front storm doors stopped, looking outside as the three bolted between the doors and came to a stop inside.

"Oh, thank God," London said in relief.

"That was close," Archie said, panting heavily.

The guards looked at them and then looked outside one more time before closing the doors. The hefty, metal doors closed with a thunk. They closed the outside world off, leaving the Doomstorm outside as it enveloped the city in howling wind and biting sand. Outside there were small bunkers and hidey holes, built for those unlucky enough to get caught outside. Meanwhile, the sirens continued blaring.

London put Rose down slowly. All three of them brushed sand off of themselves, London and Archie still panting from the sprint to safety.

"Not a great start to our meeting, but we made it," London said.

"Damn Doomstorms," Archie growled. "I've lost a few people to them before."

"That's just how it is. I have too," London said.

"What do we do now?" Rose asked, looking up at London.

"Wait out the Doomstorm, Rosey. We can do what we planned to do anyway," London told her.

Archie nervously smiled as they began to walk into the building.

"You excited to learn how to read, Archie?" London asked, walking beside him and holding Rose's hand.

"Can't wait. Reginald told me the capitol is full of books."

"I've heard all about it from him. Books, paintings, statues, everything."

"Yo, you ain't a tough teacher, yeah?" Archie asked.

London made a half-smile and shook his head.

"Not at all. Rosey here says I'm the best teacher ever."

"He is!" Rose said with a wide grin.

They stopped as they entered the main part of the citadel. The citadel itself was a massive factory building that was cleared out and refurbished. Instead of a factory floor, there were hundreds of bookshelves, research tables, and art pieces. In between it all were guards, scientists, and military personnel.

London stopped in amazement.

"Woah," he said.

He watched it all. In between the bookshelves and along walls were works of art. Statues ranging from ancient Greek works all the way to strange modern art from the twenty-first century were everywhere. There were paintings such as depictions from ancient Egypt to pieces from the middle of the twenty-first century, many of them being copies.

Among it all were researchers and scientists, dressed in gray, monk-like robes and painted gas masks. London had never seen these people before, gawking at their strange outfits. It was as if he had entered the Library of Alexandria. In one area were military personnel clustered around tables, hunched over maps and arguing with each other.

London looked upward, spotting a large, empty council room. The council room was the brain of all of New Uruk. It was where they governed New Uruk. London had learned that there were two governmental parties in New Uruk. Nine elected officials ran New Uruk, four in each of the two parties and one acting as a judge for decisions made for both. The law of New Uruk was their word, aptly called the Mandate of the Council.

As London and Rose ogled the gigantic capital building from inside, a guard walked up to them.

"Halt citizens, what is your business here?" the man asked, holding a pressure rifle in his hands.

"Oh, uh, we're just here to read and take shelter from the storm outside," London said.

The man looked at all three of them and eyed them for a moment.

"Very well. You will be under watch. Please do not cause trouble and obey the law at all times. I will also ask you to restrain from interacting with any of the military officials," the guard told them.

London and Archie nodded.

"We can do that," London said.

"All right, have a good day, folks," the guard said, returning to his post.

London led Rose and Archie to a table between some bookshelves, sitting down with Archie.

"Funny guy," London said.

"Halt citizens!" Archie said in a mocking voice, saluting at the same time.

They both chuckled.

"What are we starting with, London?" Archie asked after they had their laugh.

"Something simple. Rosey, can you get a children's book? Oh, and get something for you to read as well."

Rose nodded and skipped away, going to one of the gray-robed researchers in gas masks and asking for the book she wanted.

"A children's book?" Archie said in an insulted voice.

London snorted at his reaction.

"Relax, it's just a book. We'll start simple and work our way up to more difficult books."

Archie let out a grumble.

Rose returned with two books and laid them on the table in front of London and Archie. One was very thin, a book meant for kindergartners with fun illustrated characters. Another was a medium-sized book with a wolf depicted on its front.

"Thank you, Rosey," London said, taking the two books and examining them.

He slid the thin one to Archie first.

"Here, read through this for a minute, and then tell me how hard it is."

Archie looked at the book, glancing up at London before opening it. Meanwhile, London read the cover of the book with the wolf.

"*White Fang?*" London said, flipping it around before giving it to Rose.

"I thought the wolf looked cool," she said.

"I've never heard of that book. Tell me how it is when you're done with it, Rosey."

Rose nodded and sat beside him, beginning to read the book while Archie slid his book back to London.

"It's..." Archie began, embarrassed to speak. "It's kinda hard."

"Don't worry, Archie. It'll take you a while, don't be ashamed," London said.

He opened the book to the first page.

"Here, let's begin. What does the first line say?"

Archie squinted.

"The... be-ar... In the forest..."

"Good, it's bear."

Slowly they read through the book, London correcting Archie along the way as they went through page after page. It took a while, but Archie was a quick learner. They took a break once Archie finished that book, moving on to more challenging books as time passed.

It had been four hours, the storm outside still raging on. The wind howled along with the sound of the sirens, sand biting the barricaded windows of the capital. London occasionally looked upward in worry. No matter how the Doomstorm bit and chewed at the city, nothing collapsed or gave in.

Schemes

3:02 PM, July 11, 2185

Life on the Arcadis carried on. Simon continued his work as dictated by the Tasking Stations, keeping secret his new connections. The Defiants hadn't invited him to their cause yet. Sometimes, at lunch or dinner, Thomas would join Simon, Thaddeus, and Albert, discussing which rumors were likely true.

They spoke quietly, discussing calmly each rumor or piece of news of the tyranny they lived under.

As the days passed, the Peacekeepers became more violent as more instances of civil disobedience occurred. During one lunch call, Thaddeus joined them covered in bruises from a beating by a Peacekeeper. Even though he was a giant man, he told them that he didn't dare fight back, not yet.

Simon became more and more nervous, often avoiding most conversations outside of the mess hall table with his friends. He was suspicious of everyone and everything. He didn't dare read his book or speak in a place that could have surveillance, and he dared not speak to someone who could be a spy for the Leaders. Simon didn't know who could be a spy. He guessed someone desperate, someone seeking to get ahead of the other Workers.

Now it was June 11th, after the lunch call.

"Worker 4221, Hygienics Sector, lavatory maintenance," the Tasking Station ordered.

"Gah..." Simon let out.

Lavatory maintenance was a terrible job to do since it was in the sector where they all cleaned and relieved themselves. He knew it was better to have things fixed rather than having the sector flood with a feces-water mix. Simon had heard a story about that happening a long time ago and cringed at the thought.

A Peacekeeper walked up to him, firmly grabbed his arm, and scanned his Individual Chip.

"Worker 4221, that line," he indicated.

Simon nodded and joined the line.

"Hygienics Sector!"

The line began moving, Simon marching along with the rest of the Workers going to the Hygienics Sector. He looked around slightly at the others. For a moment, he felt grateful for his general jobs centered around technology maintenance. Simon knew the other men and women around him would likely be cleaning toilets and showers.

Eventually, they arrived at the sector. The Peacekeepers that had accompanied them said nothing as the Workers began to spread out to do their tasks. Simon walked past them, glancing into small, cubic showers as he moved. Soon, he was in the lavatory, a big room full of toilets for all the workers to share. He walked down each row, stopping at some of the toilets.

The ones that had issues had red marks on them, markers for Simon to know which needed repairs. He stopped, kneeling in front of the first toilet and checking how it flushed. It took him a few minutes to figure out that the button for flushing had broken. Simon fixed it in a few seconds before moving on to the next toilet, a few toilets down that also had the same red mark.

Simon continued down, fixing four toilets before coming to a fifth one that required some dismantling. First, he had to take off the top, and then he had to lie down to examine the inner mechanisms and Ignium-powered circuits of the toilet. As he worked, Simon zoned into his task.

At the same time, a Peacekeeper approached him, his boots clicking on the floor in an intimidating way as he approached. The man stopped and let out an order. Simon wasn't too sure what he said and was too afraid to ask what he had said. He assumed it was an order to work faster since the other Workers might've done, so Simon sped up.

Blunt baton strikes abruptly came down upon him, sending intense pain through him. One hit his leg, a few hit his chest and arms, another on the side of his neck, and then one on his side. They were sure to leave bruises. Simon shielded himself and screamed.

"Did you not hear me?!" the Peacekeeper growled.

"N-No!"

"I said that one of the other Workers found an issue with the shower!" he yelled, "Get up!"

Simon struggled as the Peacekeeper smacked him with the baton, only stopping to grab him roughly and drag him to the showers. In a second, the world was a blur before Simon hit the hard floor with a thud.

"There's your technician, now fix the shower!" the Peacekeeper ordered aggressively.

Pain coursed through Simon, but he willed himself to all fours. Abruptly, a hand grabbed him and pulled him to his feet.

"Are you good?" asked the man who pulled him to his feet, another Worker.

"Y-Yeah," Simon stuttered.

"Hey, c'mon, let's fix the shower."

"Yeah, what's wrong with it?" Simon said, groaning slightly as his body ached.

"Just some issues with the control panel, one of the buttons doesn't work."

The Peacekeeper stared them down as Simon entered the shower, taking off the panel and quickly fixing a worn connection to the button that didn't work. Once he finished, he checked the button. It worked perfectly.

"There," Simon said, "Working button."

"Thanks," said his fellow Worker.

Simon stepped out of the shower and glanced at the Peacekeeper that was staring at them.

"What are you looking at?! Back to work!!"

Simon hurried back to the lavatories and began fixing more toilets, soon wrapping up and waiting for the rest of the Workers. Once they finished, they each went to a Tasking Station and got escorted to different parts of the Arcadis.

The rest of the day was terrible. Simon's whole body ached from the beating he had received, and he was covered in more bruises than Thaddeus had when he had received a beating by a Peacekeeper. That night, at dinner, he told them about the beating the Peacekeeper had given him.

Simon approached the table, sitting down with a groan.

"Woah, jeez, what happened to you?" Albert whispered.

"Peacekeeper," Simon said.

Thaddeus stared at him, a twitch of anger in his eyes.

"What?" he asked.

"I got beaten by a Peacekeeper. I was fixing a toilet in the Hygienics Sector, and it turns out a shower needed fixing. He came over and told me, but I didn't hear him, so he just beat me with his baton."

Thaddeus's face turned red with anger, his fists becoming white as he clenched them.

"He beat you because you didn't hear him?" Thaddeus growled.

"Yes,"

"Ay, Thaddeus, buddy, calm down," Albert said. "Don't draw attention."

"Hey, Thaddeus, I'm fine. At least he didn't send me to the Deck or something," Simon said.

Thaddeus looked at them both, then sighed and tried to calm down.

"Fucking bullshit. The Defiants need to hurry their shit up so we can stop this shit," Thaddeus said.

"Shut up, for fuck's sake, don't say that name here," Simon whispered.

Thaddeus paused for a second and then shook his head and remained silent.

The next day came. Simon woke up to the sound of Genetrix awakening the station. He groaned, rolled out of bed, and followed the general morning routine. Morning hygiene, exercises, then straight to breakfast. He followed the crowd to his mess hall, walking slowly and groggily with everyone else.

He looked around as he walked. Something felt off. Simon glanced around for a moment and then was bumped into. He almost lost his footing.

"Woah! Sorry there! Hey, you dropped this."

Simon looked at the man. He hadn't seen him before and didn't know him. Quickly, he stuffed a plastic piece into his hand and walked off. Simon looked at him as he disappeared, then looked down at the plastic piece. He was surprised when he flipped it over and saw words carved into it.

"Welcome."

Infestation

"What do you remember about the layout, Oliver?" Sam asked.

Oliver sat on the plastic bucket and looked at the group of six around him.

"It's a maze," Oliver began.

He stood and started to drag his boot in the sand, creating a sort of map.

"A lot of it is just hallways. Everything is tall, and pillars hold up the ceiling," Oliver said.

Mary leaned forward on her hunting rifle.

"Pillars? It's a bunker. What do you mean pillars?"

"Like Greek columns. It's something more than a bunker. It's like an underground palace," Oliver said.

"That's.... strange," she said with audible disbelief.

"Very. Everything connects to the hallways, and there are sections. Every time there's a crossroad in the halls, there are signs giving directions. When I went in there, the medical wing was the first left from the entrance," Oliver told them.

He walked to the other part of his sand map.

"To the right, I think was a maintenance wing, but I'm not sure. Ahead was the atrium, which was at the center of everything. From there, I figured out that the whole place isn't just one level," Oliver explained.

"Jesus.... The place sounds huge. How many mutants?" asked Tom, one of the able-bodied men.

"A hundred?" Oliver guessed, "I don't know. There was a flood that chased me when I escaped. We've been clearing their numbers pretty good, but there's a lot. I don't know if we should try to push into there today."

"We have guns," Mary stated. "And if we need to, I'm sure we can hold them at bay while retreating."

"We might need fire," Sam pointed out.

"We don't have a lot of wood, but fire could help. The mutants in the bunker are nocturnal hunters and live in water. I'm sure they don't like fire," Oliver agreed.

"Where do you propose to get fire from?" Mary asked, raising her brow.

Sam raised his finger.

"I have a collection at the house. I can bring a few pieces and light them aflame," he told her.

Mary pursed her lips in thought and then nodded.

"I'll send some people with you, Sam. Bring back plenty of wood, and then we can start clearing out the mutants." Mary said.

"It's a plan then," Oliver said determinedly.

They stood and shook hands. Before leaving, Sam grabbed a few items, while Mary commanded two people to go with him. As Sam left with the people, Oliver and everyone else waved goodbye. Sam waved in response, soon disappearing over the dunes.

Oliver watched him, now left alone with the new group. He felt anxious to be around all these strangers. His trust was thin despite their friendliness. Who knows? They could cut his throat after they cleared the bunker. He turned, gazing at all of them. They were a family. All ten gathered around the fire with blankets and tarps to protect them from the wind and sand.

He looked down at the ground. Oliver had a family once in the old world with his parents. He hadn't thought about them for a long time. Oliver tried to keep those memories suppressed, along with the memories of the many groups he had been in. Each one had failed, but he always survived. Maybe this time was different?

After a moment, Oliver grabbed a plastic bucket, walked over to Mary, and sat beside her.

"Hey," he said.

"What's up?" she responded.

"Nothing much. Just came to talk while Sam is getting wood."

"Three hours? That's a long haul for wood."

"It is. I'm sure he's done tougher. We all have," Oliver said.

He paused as a wave of sand hit his visor.

"How long has this group been together?" Oliver asked.

"Three years, I think," Mary replied,

"It's 2100, in case you wanted to know," Oliver told her.

Mary paused in surprise, looking at him.

"Wow, it's been that long?" she asked.

Oliver nodded.

"How old are you?" he asked.

"Well, if it's 2100, I should be twenty-eight. How about you, Oliver?"

"I'm thirty-seven; I still can't believe it's been twenty-one years," Oliver responded. "Feels like yesterday. All the fear, destruction, and death. It's still fresh."

Mary frowned.

"It's a harsh world, but it's our world now," she said with a gloomy tone.

"Well, everyone in the past didn't believe we'd make it, but here we are," Oliver said.

Oliver looked up toward the dark bunker tunnel some distance away from the camp.

"Are you excited to clear the bunker out?" Oliver asked.

"I'm happy," Mary told him.

"Happy?" Oliver repeated.

"Yes, happy. I'm happy that my people will finally have a place to live in. If we clear out that bunker and if it has everything you said it had, then they'll be safe. No more Doomstorms, no more hunger, no more thirst, no more freezing. It's an easy place to defend too. That means less fighting, fear, and bloody battles. I've lost two due to fights with other survivors," she told him.

"I understand. I'm hoping for all that too. Maybe this is the place where everything starts. It'll be a new cradle of man, a new place for civilization to grow. Maybe this is where civilization is reborn?"

"Maybe. Just as long as my people are safe," Mary said.

Mary's intentions were clear enough: to protect her people and herself. Oliver still didn't trust her. He was hopeful, though; if the two groups merged and took control of the bunker, it would be a powerful advantage over other survivors in the wasteland.

He knew that it would be easy to defend from attackers. In Oliver's mind, that mattered less than its value. He could trade its value for loyalty. Oliver imagined that people would give their loyalty and services in return for protection, food, water, and space. It was reasonable. If he was in their shoes, he'd do that, too.

It felt good. After so many years of living at the mercy of the world, a little power felt good. Oliver cracked a smile under his mask.

Three hours droned on as the group sat and waited. They huddled around their fire, sitting, and enduring the wind. As they all waited, they spoke among themselves. A few spoke with Oliver, exchanging stories of funny times and hard times in the wasteland. He learned about their backstories and who they were before they joined the group.

After three hours passed, three figures appeared on the horizon. Oliver stood as they approached, squinting to make out Sam and the two people who went with him. In their arms was wood. Sam walked to the camp and dumped the wood into a pile, loudly grunting as he did.

"Welcome back," Oliver said.

Sam panted and looked at Oliver.

"Good to be back. That was a long haul," Sam said.

"Don't you have a cart or something?" Oliver asked.

"I think it's broken," Sam paused. "Don't apply logic to this."

Oliver chuckled and patted him on the shoulder, "Good to see you back. You ready to clean our new home?"

Sam looked over to the entrance of the bunker, letting out a long sigh and nodding.

"Yeah, yeah, I won't let a little bit of wood tire me out," he said.

"Mary!" Oliver called, "Are your people ready?"

"We are. Come on, everyone! You heard him! Load your guns and bring ammo!"

Mary stood, hunting rifle ready. Sam prepared his pipe rifle, loading in a bullet. Oliver grabbed his Railshot Rifle, checking its charge and metal capacity. It was all coming together. Three people grabbed pieces of wood and lit them on fire with Oliver's tesla lighter, while the rest had flashlights.

Oliver proceeded to lead them to the tunnel. The group marched carefully along as they descended into the darkness, flashlights and torches ready.

"Stay together," Oliver said. "The torches should keep them at bay, so if they surround us, we need you three to defend all sides of the group."

The group halted as they arrived at the great doors which separated the bunker from the outside world. A few of them gasped as they saw the naked statues holding up the ceiling, the intricate carvings on the door, and the face gazing down upon them above the door. Oliver glanced at them once and then moved to the door.

It was still closed. Memories of terror filled Oliver's mind as he approached it. He remembered the whispering growls of the mutants and their grotesque forms. Oliver hated the mutant animals of the new world, but he hated the human mutants more. Some were born in the new world, but many were victims of mutagenic bombs during the resource wars in the old world.

Oliver was scared of them but felt sorry for them as well. He knew that many of them were scared. They were people once, with families and dreams that they forgot when they lost their minds.

He let out a shuddering breath as he placed a hand on the door.

"Keep your guns ready," Oliver said. "We don't know what's behind this door."

Sam came to his side, the two moving back and charging into the door. A loud metallic groan echoed through the tunnel. It barely budged. The two charged into it again, and then again. After a few pushes, they made a gap that could fit one person. Oliver warily walked forward into the darkness, flashlight on and rifle ready.

The hall was empty. Oliver assumed the mutants were nesting during this time of day. Sam came in a moment after, pointing his pipe rifle into the darkness.

"Holy shit, you weren't kidding," he remarked.

One of the men with guns came in after.

"It's beautiful," he said.

"It's perfect," Mary stated.

Oliver looked behind him.

"Two torches in the front, one in the back. Watch the corners, and listen for anything," Oliver ordered.

The group gathered together. Oliver and two people with torches led in the front, while one person with a torch followed in the back. He walked slowly. They began to pass the stone columns holding up the ceiling, gazing at the art pieces in between.

"Woah," said one of the women.

"Are those paintings? And statues?" asked one of the men.

"Quiet," Oliver said.

They approached the first crossroad in the halls. Oliver went over to the metal sign that still lay on the floor since his last visit. He knelt and read the worn letters—medical wing to the left, maintenance to the right, and the atrium ahead.

Oliver stood and pointed ahead, taking the group to the atrium.

"We'll clear out the residential wing first if we can find it," Oliver said.

The bunker halls were silent, only disturbed by the footsteps and scared breathing of the survivors. Oliver had his guard up, listening for mutants. Eventually, the group arrived at the atrium. Oliver shone his flashlight up at the ceiling, gazing at the recreation of the Creation of Adam. He looked around, struggling to recall where the residential wing was.

"This way," he whispered.

The group followed behind, looking around with their flashlights and waving their torches. No mutants had appeared yet, though the survivors were all nervous.

Oliver went down a staircase and through a hall, carrying on through a few turns. Eventually, they arrived at the residential wing. Oliver stopped.

"Everyone be quiet," he whispered.

They stopped, holding their breath. Oliver listened. The gargled breathing and rasping growls from the mutants were heard from each room, Oliver glancing into one to see a pile of pale mutants sleeping.

"How do we start?" Sam whispered.

"Guns blazing?" Oliver suggested.

"We need to be careful so that we don't get swarmed," Mary whispered, "And we need to put out enough firepower to keep them back."

Oliver nodded.

"We can clear one room and use the doorway to bottleneck the mutants?" Sam suggested.

"That works," Oliver said.

The group moved into one room, approaching a pile of sleeping mutants. Oliver walked forward, pointing his Railshot Rifle directly at the center of the pile. He exhaled and pulled the trigger.

Gore and guts splattered everywhere as metal shredded the pile of mutants. In an instant, they were annihilated. They were all dead. For a moment, he felt triumphant and powerful. It was easy. Then the feeling disappeared instantly.

"Graah!"

"Scree!"

The entire wing erupted in cries of alarm.

"Torches to the front! Block them out! Guns ready!" Mary shouted.

The three people with torches went to the front of the group, guns ready. The hallways flooded with footsteps. Oliver shakily held his gun, ready for the horde. Abruptly, a flood of mutants collided into the door frame, every mutant trying to crawl over each other to get to the survivors.

"Fire!!" Oliver shouted.

Bullets and metal hailed upon the mutants. The swarm bottlenecked in. The few that got into the room hissed and shielded themselves from the flaming torches. Oliver smiled. They were afraid of fire. The group kept shooting. They alternated between reloading and shooting, keeping a continuous flow of projectiles.

Blood splattered everywhere, squeals of pain filling the air. With fire and bullets, they kept the mutants at bay, thinning the swarm. Soon, the horde began to retreat, leaving a few dozen corpses on the floor.

"Push out!" Mary shouted.

The three people with torches went forward, followed by everyone else. The mutants ran from them, falling as precise shots hit them. The group began to move along the halls of the residential wing, clearing each room and destroying nests. Oliver was filled with adrenaline as he reloaded and shot, shredding every mutant that dared approach them.

It was bloody and horrific, but he was too focused. He felt exhilarated. They were succeeding, and everything was going according to plan.

With every mutant dead in the residential wing, Oliver turned his sights to the underground reservoir. He remembered the terror that shot through him when he saw the eyes in the water. This time would be different.

"What's next?" Mary asked.

"There's a bunch at the reservoir," Oliver said, "Come on."

Oliver burst into a jog, the group following him.

"I think we woke up the entire bunker," Sam pointed out.

Oliver listened to the hallways. There were footsteps and figures everywhere in the dark. Now and then, they encountered a few mutants, simply blasting through them as they ran.

"We woke a lot up with our guns, and the rest with our scent," Oliver told him, "There was none when I first entered, and after a while, there were more and more. I think my scent woke them up."

"The more we kill, the better," Mary stated.

They ran through the turns and halls, soon arriving at the reservoir. Oliver looked around. The stalls were to the left, and the beach chairs were along the water. He walked over to the water, shining his flashlight into the murky depths. Dozens of eyes met the light, shining back as he pointed his rifle.

Metal sprayed into the water, hitting a few mutants as the eyes moved toward them.

"Shoot into the water!" Oliver shouted.

"Two torches in the front, one watching the hall!" Mary shouted.

They began firing into the water, blood pooling in the darkness as mutants died.

"Scraaaw!"

Mutants jumped out of the water, rushing at the group and stopping as they had torches waved at them. As the mutants shielded themselves, bullets brought them down.

"Watch out!"

"Over there!"

"Keep shooting!" Mary shouted.

The group killed everything that moved, lining the floor and water with corpses. Oliver killed the most, spraying body parts everywhere.

"Kill them all!!" he shouted, relishing the carnage.

Rose

4:14 PM, August 18, 2154

Rose walked beside London as they ventured past the merchant stalls. It was a busy day in their neighborhood. There were stalls and merchants everywhere, each one screaming out what their goods and prices were. There were carts, boxes, weapons, food, live animals in crates, and more among the merchants as people walked around to buy and sell.

Along with the guards and citizens were workers out in the street. Some were fixing Ignium-powered lights or machines, while others were sweeping up sand from the last Doomstorm. Some laborers were out of factories and workshops already, joining the crowds of consumers.

London led Rose from stall to stall, purchasing goods. As they walked, Rose looked around at all the goods in the market with a big smile. Tomorrow was London's birthday, and she wanted to get him something. Rose was unsure of what to get him. A new weapon seemed improper, while a card was dull and hard to obtain.

"Five filters?" London asked, holding a handful of crossbow bolts.

"Yes," said the merchant in front of him.

"They were three last week."

"I know, I know. It's the war, London. They're making us send a lot of supplies to the war front for the soldiers, so it's harder to make money back here in the city."

"Fucking war..." London mumbled, "All right, I understand that the war is making everything hard. Here."

Rose watched as London paid five gas mask filters for the crossbow bolts, gazing at his reluctant glare at the merchandise. He sighed as they left the stall, moving through the market again.

"London?"

"Yes, Rosey?"

"Is the war going to end soon?" she asked.

"I don't know, Rosey."

"Are we safe?"

"Yes, I think so. It's far outside the city; I know that."

"Are you sure?"

"Yes," London said, stopping and kneeling beside her, "Don't worry, Rose, even if the war comes here, I'll protect you. No matter what."

She leaned forward and hugged him. London smiled and held her for a while, soon releasing her and carrying on with their business.

"Ah, London, how are you today?"

London approached the merchant's stall and nodded.

"Pretty good," London said, "Watcha got for me today, Will?"

"Premium cuts! Got some Thresh Horn flanks today, fresh from the hunt." Will said.

"Show me,"

Rose watched as Will leaned under his stall and pulled out some fresh, heavy pieces of meat. Thresh Horns, iron lung animals that looked like deer mixed with elks were among Rose's favorite animals to eat. As London and Will discussed prices, she gazed past the stall and into the building behind Will.

Behind him was an old, brick house rebuilt into a butcher shop. Inside she could see a few workers handling meat, moving animal parts around, and cleaning them. Rose wasn't disturbed by the sight of blood and flesh being handled and gazed curiously inside.

"Thirty filters for these two flanks," Will said.

"Thirty?" London repeated.

Meat was expensive in New Uruk. It was hard to get, so it was a high-class commodity. Even so, that didn't stop London from haggling.

"They're fresh flanks."

"How about we do twenty?" London suggested.

While the two began to haggle, Rose tugged London's arm.

"What?"

"Can I explore the market?"

London looked around them and then nodded.

"Sure, just don't wander too far off," he said before returning to haggle with Will.

Rose gleefully grinned and looked around the marketplace, slowly beginning to venture through it. There were many strange and interesting sights. She skipped around from stall to stall as she searched for something suitable for London's birthday.

The first few stalls she found sold weapons. She gazed at each cruel and deadly device on sale, examining them before shaking her head. They were too expensive, and London already had weapons. Next, she looked at the stalls selling animals, staring at each strange mutant animal with fearful awe. Those were too expensive, and she didn't like any of the animals.

Finally, she found a strange stall placed near an alleyway. Rose approached it. Her eyebrows scrunched in curiosity. The man at this stall had a full-visor gas mask, a mean resting scowl, and a missing eye. He leaned on a wooden post holding the stall up, brooding over all of his items like a dragon upon gold.

This stall seemed interesting. It had many strange and ancient devices, items from the old world such as Smart Wrists, toys, implants, and more. She approached the stall slowly, somewhat afraid of the man with the missing eye.

"E-Excuse, mister?"

"Huh? What?" he let out, looking down at her, "What do you want?"

"How much is this?" she asked, pointing at a Smart Wrist.

"Five hundred filters, too much for someone like you. Go away, ya rascal, before ya steal something," he growled.

Rose stared at him and backed away. She'd have to find something else.

She sighed and began to explore the market again, passing all the stalls from before until she reached the other end of the market. Just when Rose was about to give up, she spotted a very interesting stall. Manning it was a girthy man who seemed somewhat wealthy, his clothing and gas mask in high condition.

His stall had candy. There were candied meats and plants, hard candies, and soft candies. Rose's eyes widened for a moment at all the sweets in front of her, and then immediately went up to the man.

"Excuse me," she said.

The man looked down at her, leaning over the table of his stall.

"Ah, hello there, younglin'. Lookin' for some candy, eh?"

"Yes, how much for that?" she asked, pointing to some soft reddish candies.

"That there? Twenty-five filters."

Rose frowned for a moment.

"Can you make that twenty?"

"No can do," he said, shaking his head, "I gotta make a living here. Hop along,"

"Please?"

"I said hop along. I ain't got no time to be arguing over prices."

Rose grumbled, then returned to London.

"Find anything interesting, Rosey?"

"No," she said in an annoyed voice, "Nothing."

London patted her back and began to walk home with her.

"What's wrong?"

"Nothing, just some mean merchants."

"Hmm, yeah, they all have attitudes here. If anyone's too mean, just take me to them, and I'll set them straight." London said with a smile.

"Thanks," she said, returning the smile.

They walked through the marketplace and eventually turned into an apartment complex, going into one of the buildings and going to their home. As soon as they arrived at their apartment, London unloaded the goods he had bought and begun to sort everything.

The apartment they lived in was like any other apartment. It wasn't too big, but it was suitable. There was stuff everywhere, piled and sorted against the walls, laid on furniture, and put on shelves. One of the rooms they used for storage was filled to the brim. There was power in the apartment, though water had to be brought home in containers from community wells and fountains.

As soon as London finished unloading the stuff, he slumped down on a couch.

"Ugh..." he groaned, laying his head back, "That was a long day."

"Hey, London?"

"Yes, Rosey?"

"Can I read one of your books?"

"Sure, take whatever you want. I'm gonna take a nap."

Rose smiled and went into the main bedroom where London had piled all of the books he hadn't donated to the capitol library. She grabbed one and sat on the bed, waiting for her plan to be set in motion.

It took thirty minutes before London fell into his nap. Rose waited for him to snore before doing anything, closing her book immediately once he did. She snuck across the apartment, tiptoeing to check if he was asleep before going to her room. Her room, like any other part of their home, was messy and full of stuff.

She sifted through the piles and piles of goods and trash before she pulled out a hidden box. Rose opened it, gazing at all the gas mask filters inside. It was her piggy bank. There were all sorts of filters inside of it, Rose counting twenty-eight filters. That was perfect.

Rose tiptoed across the apartment again, checking on London one more time before going out onto the deck of the apartment. Most homes in New Uruk had at least one door or window with a pulley system, which made it easy to receive goods or send goods to the street below. Rose was light and had figured out a few weeks ago that she could use the pulley system.

Carefully, she held onto her "piggy bank" box and grasped the rope attached to their apartment's pulley system. She leaned and pulled a switch, immediately grasping the rope again as some cogwheels came loose and slowly delivered her down to the street. Once she was on the ground, she burst into a sprint and ran to the marketplace of their neighborhood.

Rose joined the crowds of citizens and merchants trying to get their last deals in before the marketplace shut down for the evening. She ran to the candy merchant, presenting her box immediately to the merchant. He was surprised by her sudden appearance, then chuckled at the box as he took it into his hands.

"What's this?" he asked in a mocking voice.

"Filters. I want the red candies, please."

"And you think this box is gonna be enough for th-" he began, stopping as he opened the box.

"Yes, there are twenty-eight filters in there." she said with a smile, "You can have twenty-five if I get my candy."

The man stared at her for a moment, then nodded. Slowly, he took out twenty-five filters. Rose made sure that he took nothing more. Once finished, he gave her the box and an old milk jug filled with the candy she ordered.

"Thank you," she said with a smug smile.

The merchant only nodded as she skipped off.

Before anyone could see her or follow her, she slipped into the alleyways leading to the market and snuck between fences and hidey holes. There were a lot of small and sneaky spots like these inside New Uruk. She knew most of these secret passages and holes were used by other kids, many using them to escape angry merchants they had stolen from. Rose had learned about these passages from a kid who was a known thief.

Soon, she arrived at the apartment complex she lived in and quickly snuck to the rope. With another flip of a switch, the pulley lifted her to the deck she had left from, slowly sneaking inside of the apartment once she got up there. London was still fast asleep. Before anything, Rose hid her "piggy bank" and then went to London.

"London!" she whispered, shaking him.

"H-Huh? What?" he blurted out, snorting awake.

"I got you a birthday present," she said excitedly.

London sat up and let out a quiet groan before looking at her.

"That's wonderful, Rosey. What did you get me?"

Rose gave him the milk jug of candy, watching him raise his brow in surprise.

"I bought you candy!"

"You did?!" London asked, his eyes lighting up.

He took the milk jug and looked inside.

"Wow, thank you, Rosey. How did you afford this?" London asked, scrunching his brow in curiosity.

"I saved up for it. Do you like it?" she replied with a big, proud smile.

"I love it," he said, "Thank you."

London turned it and shook the candy out onto his hand.

"Have you ever had candy, Rosey?" London asked, moving his hand toward her.

"I don't think so. Have you?"

"Never. It's old-world stuff." he said, "Come here, sit."

Rose went and sat beside him. London broke a piece of the candy in half and gave it to her.

"Let's try it together," he said.

Rose nodded, removing her mask with him.

"Ready? The first piece of candy in three, two, one!"

At the same time, they munched down. The candy was soft and sweet, with a pleasing gummy texture. Both of them smiled in surprise at the taste. The taste of candy to them was indescribable, like eating physical happiness and luxury. They looked at each other, laughing at each other's expression of awe.

"Wow," London said.

He felt like a father and felt that he was living up to the promise Rose's father made him make. Her smile of joy over his reaction to his gift was a reminder. It reminded him that Rose was the only person or thing that mattered to him, her survival and well being the only thing he truly strived to care for.

"Thank you, Rosey. Best birthday gift ever."

Traitor

12:08 PM, August 23, 2185

Simon sat uncomfortably at the mess hall table. Normally, he'd be in mess hall four talking to Thaddeus and Albert by now. This time, he was in mess hall five. He had never been to another mess hall for anything beyond repairs and maintenance. A sense of dread and anxiety pulsated within him as he looked around the table at faces he had never seen before.

Beside him was Thomas, quietly chewing his food. Simon did the same. No one had begun the conversation yet, and no one seemed inclined to do so either. Around the mess hall, just like mess hall four, were Peacekeepers eyeing everyone down.

Weeks of work had led to this moment. Simon had been involved in a web of secret messages, plans, and sabotages to meet these men and women in front of him. They had orchestrated it perfectly. Just like how he had joined the group, he too had "bumped" into people. Simon was a secret soldier in an even more secret war.

He thought back to it all for a moment. People had passed messages to him, which he passed onto others. These short meetings were swift, quiet, and quickly finished before any Peacekeeper could catch on.

It was all thrilling. It was thrilling to be a mouse hiding beneath the cat's nose, and it was all a big game that meant life or death. Simon had played well, to his surprise.

They all looked around the table. The silence was somewhat uncomfortable.

"So, welcome to the first meeting of the 'Electronic Repair Group,'" Thomas whispered.

Each person at the table gazed at him, taken aback for a moment. There was more silence.

"We only have so much time. This meeting is for creating a plan to overthrow the Leaders," said one man.

"And who are you?" asked a woman.

"Another man who wants freedom, just like all of you."

"Hey, we're all brothers and sisters here," said a third man.

"Introductions aren't necessary. Just a plan. Have any of you come up with anything?" Thomas asked.

They looked at each other, searching each other for a plan.

"Chaos. Start a battle in one of the mess halls, and spread it to the others. It'll be a chain effect. There are more of us than there are of them, and most of the Peacekeepers follow us around now."

"Stupid, they have weapons, and we don't," said another woman.

"No, no, that'd work. Just not yet. Everything around us can be used as a weapon, but not everyone considers that. We need something that can deal with the Peacekeepers," the second man stated.

Simon gazed at each person as they spoke. After a while of arguing, he leaned forward and spoke.

"You're all missing the obvious. Have none of you studied the Arcadis? All you need to do is sabotage the air vents going into the area where the Peacekeepers sleep. You'll kill them all in their sleep. Once that's done and discovered, chaos will ensue. All you have to do is spread the word among the Workers before all hell breaks loose, and we'll be unified."

He paused to eat.

"With the main bulk of the security force gone, we'll overwhelm the rest, and the station is ours. Simple. All we have to do to start is to get a man to sabotage something in their area, then someone like me could get assigned and do the rest."

Each one of the Defiants blinked in surprise. Simon smiled at them.

"Perfect," Thomas said, "That's perfect. Don't you all agree?"

"I agree."

"Same here."

"We have our plan."

They ate for a while longer before the voice of Genetrix filled the station.

"All Workers report to the appropriate Tasking Stations for their assign-ments."

They looked among each other and stood, nodding to each other.

Simon did his assignments that day with renewed energy. He felt brave, invincible as if no Peacekeeper or Leader could hurt him. He knew all he had to do now was wait. Simon didn't know who was the one that was going to be assigned to do the task since it was random and skill-based. It could be him, or it could be someone else. Generally, Simon didn't feel like this, but this time he felt ready to accept the task.

Days passed. With them came more messages, more bumps, and more sabotages to direct other Defiants around the station. Sometimes, they failed, and sometimes they succeeded. He had kept Thaddeus and Albert up with the news, but he had kept some secrets. Regardless, both of them knew something was up.

A week and a half had passed since the meeting.

"What is the news, Simon?" Thaddeus asked.

"Nothing so far. Waiting for our 'plan' to happen," Simon said, eating his lunch happily.

"Did you guys choose a date or something that you ain't telling us?" Albert asked.

"No. It'll happen randomly. Could be today, could be tomorrow, could be any time." Simon said.

"Good luck, brother," Thaddeus said.

"Yeah, you'll need it," Albert said.

"Thanks, guys."

Once more, Genetrix put an end to lunch.

"All Workers report to the appropriate Tasking Stations for their assign-ments."

Simon looked at his friends as if it was the last time he would, proceeding to put away his plate and walking to a Tasking Station. Albert stood behind him, smiling and nodding as Simon glanced back before approaching the statue. He scanned his Individual Chip and waited for the machine to assign him a task.

"Worker 4221, Peacekeeper Residential Sector, air vent maintenance."

Simon's eyes widened for a second, his body recoiling by a few degrees.

"Wow, Peacekeeper stuff? Jeez, good luck, man," Albert said, patting his shoulder.

"Yeah.... Be careful out there, Albert."

"You too."

Simon waited for a Peacekeeper to direct him into a line, then waited for the line to take off to the Residential Sector. His heart was throbbing. Simon felt ready, even though fear and dread strangled him. He was alone in this task. Four Peacekeepers escorted him, each one of them looking at him with suspicion. He had to do the plan carefully.

They arrived at the Residential Sector a few minutes after, passing through it and going to where the Peacekeepers lived. Simon waited patiently as they passed each security door leading to the sector, counting three ID-locked doors before they arrived. As they entered, Simon looked at the conditions in which the Peacekeepers lived.

The Peacekeepers, to his shock, lived like the Workers. They had small rooms with few belongings. He could see all the Peacekeepers that were off duty, only a few being off duty during "daytime" hours. Simon was marched to the main hub area where they already had a vent panel open.

"Here's the air vent. Get to work," a Peacekeeper ordered.

Simon didn't even look at her, simply beginning to work. Anxiety coursed through him, and he tried with all of his will not to shake. As the Peacekeepers waited with bored expressions, Simon crawled into the vent and moved around. He didn't bother to ask them what the problem was since he could figure it out, and he didn't want to get beaten again.

As he worked, he eavesdropped.

"Are you guys excited for the next Thrash Games?" a Peacekeeper asked.

"The next one? Fuck, after the last one, I'm not so sure."

"Oh yeah, you were caught in the brawl. How did that go?"

"Fucking terrible. Look, don't tell anyone, but I missed a few years ago when the Workers were calm, and we could be lazy. Not this business. I like keeping the peace, but I don't like beating the fuck out of these Workers because they can't keep in line."

"Hey, it's their fault that they don't obey."

"Rumors, man, rumors, it gets them riled up."

"Buncha bullshit."

Simon found the issue, a cut piece of Ignium circuitry attached to the main controls sticking out like a sore thumb. Now was the time. Simon crawled to it and attached it again.

"Hey, are you done in there? I don't wanna wait here for your ass."

"Almost! There's a lot of wear in here." Simon responded.

"Hurry up, damnit!"

His hands were shaking. Simon glanced out the vent before weaving the circuits and wires around, replacing certain parts with mastery. In a minute, he had created a ticking time bomb. Simon had weaved the circuits just right so that they would pop in six days, during "night time" hours when all the Peacekeepers were sleeping. Once the circuits popped, air would stop being pumped into this part of the Residential Sector and suffocate all the Peacekeepers.

Simon crawled out and glanced back into the vent before putting the vent grate back on.

"You done?" asked a Peacekeeper.

"Y-Yes, just some minor issues," he said with a smile.

"There he is! Arrest that man!" shouted a familiar voice.

Simon looked over to where the voice had come from, his heart skipping a beat. Fifteen Peacekeepers approached him, led by a sight he couldn't believe: Albert.

"Arrest him for treason against the Leaders!" Albert shouted.

"A-Albert! What are you doin-" Simon began.

All four Peacekeepers leaped onto Simon and took him to the floor. Simon landed so hard he was dazed. Before he knew it, there were cuffs around his arms, and a taser held ready to his neck. Albert looked down at him, Simon staring at him as the Peacekeepers lifted him to his feet.

"What the fuck, man?!" Simon shouted.

"Take him to the Deck!" said a Peacekeeper.

"Hey, hey, hold on! Let me say goodbye at least." Albert said, "I'm never gonna see him again."

The Peacekeepers looked at him.

"Hey, I could get the Leaders to sentence you to the same fate," Albert threatened, the Peacekeepers nodding.

"You're with them?!" Simon growled, trying to throw himself at Albert in a fit of rage.

"Yeah, I know. Thomas was right. The Leaders do have spies everywhere."

"Since when were you with them?"

"I'm sorry, Simon,"

"Albert.... Albert, why? We grew up together."

"Survival. Pure and simple. The Leaders are trying to keep us all safe, and I wanted to be on the winning side. You're a brother to me, and I wanted you to join m-."

Simon spat at Albert.

"You disgust me. Fuck you!"

Home

Oliver stood and looked out across the wasteland. The sun was rising steadily over the sandy dunes, beams of light piercing through the pollution haze. It was calm. The wind blew steadily, twisting and turning between all the dunes. Moments like these made Oliver wish he had a cup of coffee.

He was alone. Behind him was the tunnel leading into the bunker. It was home now. Oliver felt that he had earned it with blood, sweat, and tears. Clearing the mutants out wasn't easy, and removing the blood and bodies was harder. Now the entire group lived in the bunker. Though they still had a lot of work to do to refurbish the place, agriculture was underway, and the group had water.

A proud feeling embraced Oliver. The group was prospering. Under the leadership of Mary, Sam, and himself, they had so far worked through every challenge. The group had even grown as they went out to comb the wasteland for supplies, occasionally bringing in desperate survivors. Instead of twelve people, they were twenty-six, all working together.

Since the beginning of the new year and century, a lot had changed. Oliver had gone from a lone survivor to a leader. At the beginning of the year, he scraped by to survive. Now, Oliver had consistent shelter, water, and food. His body had grown healthier. The group had even begun working on air purifiers inside the bunker, making his skin healthier and less irritated.

Oliver looked down. Carefully, he pulled back the sleeve of his right forearm. The gunshot had healed, leaving a scar in place of the bullet. He smiled thinly.

It was a painful memory, but it was worth it. The blood, sweat, and fear from that experience led him to the bunker.

He looked at the time on his Smartwrist. It was soon eight o'clock. With a final look at the sunrise, Oliver turned and disappeared into the tunnel. He arrived at the doors going into the bunker, finding them closed. With two knocks, one of the doors opened.

"Welcome back, Oliver."

"Thanks, Stephen," Oliver said, sliding inside.

Oliver walked into the first hall of the bunker. They had fortified it with barricades and walls meeting anyone who entered. Behind the walls were cots, supplies, and Ignium lamps. Generally, they had three people guarding the door.

"Did you hear anything last night?" Oliver asked.

"Nothing."

"Good," Oliver said, "Keep up the good work."

"Will do!"

Oliver went through the little camp, waving at the other two guards before walking farther into the bunker. It was only a few weeks ago that Sam had restored the power. Now, as Oliver walked past the statues and paintings between the pillars, he could see them clearly. He strolled along, taking his time.

He still had trouble navigating the mazes but was developing a pretty good mental map. After following a few twists and turns, he arrived at the agricultural wing. Oliver walked inside, looking around. It was a massive area, consisting of hundreds of shelves lined with crop containers. A few were tipped over and destroyed, while the rest were empty.

Sam and a few others were already inside, repairing and planting.

"Hey, Sam," Oliver said as he entered.

"What's up? How was your morning stare into the wasteland?" Sam asked, smiling under his mask.

"Well, it's still empty out there. I think the pollution haze has gotten thinner, though," Oliver told him.

"Thinner? Well, it's been over twenty years without any consistent sources of pollution. It should clear up one day," Sam said.

"One day. Maybe it will be green again, with blue skies." Oliver said.

"Maybe," Sam said. "We might not be there to see it, though,"

"I would want to."

"Well, maybe that doesn't matter; maybe it's our job to make sure that happens. With the books you gave me, I was thinking we could try to use electricity again. Of course, I have to repair everything using Ignium in here first, then slowly convert."

"It's why I gave them to you. How long do you think it will take?" Oliver asked.

Sam sat beside the shelf he was working on and looked up at Oliver.

"A few years. Maybe a decade. I have to learn how to do it, then I gotta teach some other people, and we gotta have the supplies for it," Sam said.

"Well, we're not going anywhere," Oliver said. "We have the time."

Sam looked at the shelves, waving his tool to gesture at them.

"We'll have these ready within the week. I just gotta get the reservoir pumps to pump water over here, and we should have this all going."

"That's great. What seeds do we have?"

"Carrot, potatoes, cucumber, all sorts of stuff,"

"No tomatoes, I hate those," Oliver said.

Sam chuckled.

"What if everyone else wants tomatoes?"

Oliver gazed at him for a moment and snorted.

"All right, fine, but keep them away from me."

Sam stood, lifting the shelf he was fixing, moving it into the row it was a part of. With a satisfying click, it connected to the shelves adjacent to it.

"Are we meeting with Mary today?" Sam asked.

"In a while," Oliver said, checking his Smartwrist. "We should probably get over to the atrium."

Sam nodded and walked along the rows of shelves, examining them before exiting out into the hall.

"So, how is this place compared to the shack?" Oliver asked.

"Better," Sam replied. "Moving everything from over there was a pain.

It's good to have the shack, though. In case anything ever happens, I can go there."

"Maybe we shouldn't have let them find out that it existed?" Oliver asked.

"Maybe; I have a few other places that I haven't even told you about."

Oliver raised a brow at him.

"Ah! Don't worry. If something happens, you're coming with me," Sam assured him.

"Got worried for a moment," Oliver grinned.

"I wouldn't leave you behind," Sam told him.

"Thanks, Sam, I wouldn't leave you either."

The pair went through a few halls.

"What do you think of Mary's leadership?" Oliver asked.

"It's pretty good. I think we balance her out. She's a bit tough and cares a lot about her own group," Sam said.

Oliver nodded in agreement.

"You think everyone else is okay with us leading?" Sam asked.

Oliver gazed at someone as they walked, waving as the pair went by.

"I think so. We've been doing pretty good," Oliver said.

"I don't look forward to leading a hundred people or so," Sam said. "But I think we can handle it."

"Definitely."

Eventually, they arrived at the atrium. After descending into the bookshelf maze, they navigated themselves into the middle. Mary was already on a chair, reading a book, and waiting for them. As they walked in, she shut the book.

"Hello, Oliver. Hello, Sam," she said.

"Hey," they said in unison.

Sam sat down on a sofa, Oliver choosing a chair opposite him.

"What are we talking about today?" Sam asked.

"I have a few ideas," Mary began, "We're going to have an increasing population as time goes by. We need to establish law, order, all that. With more people, we need to make sure food and water is given out equally."

"We should also have some system of defense other than three guards and a barricade at the front door," Oliver pointed out.

"That too," Mary agreed.

"Those are good ideas. I also think we should name this place. We can't just call it the 'bunker,'" Sam stated.

"Law first," Oliver said. "No murder, no stealing, no waste?"

"Simple. If we need to expand, then we will," Sam said.

"How will we deal with water and food?" Oliver asked.

"Rationing. Especially if times get tough. We have someone who gives out food equally. We won't starve anyone. It's worked for my people, especially during hard times," Mary said.

"Rationing works perfectly," Oliver said.

"Hold on, not everyone eats the same," Sam pointed out.

"That's true," Oliver said.

"Of course. We can give food out depending on certain circumstances." Mary said.

The meeting continued for an hour as they cycled between law, rationing, establishing a government, and making a system of defense. As the meeting neared an end, they hadn't all agreed on everything. Instead of arguing for too long, they decided to brood on their ideas and moved onto another topic.

"About the name for this place..." Sam said.

"We can call it something like... New something? New Denver, or New Austin, or something like that," Mary suggested.

"Egh, I don't like that. It gives honor to old-world cities and the old-world people who destroyed the planet," Oliver opined.

"We can name it something original? Maybe mash some words up? Wastehaven, anyone?" Sam said with a big grin.

Oliver shook his head.

"We are not naming this place Wastehaven,"

Sam threw his hands up in the air.

"Why not?! It's perfect! It's a haven in the wasteland!" Sam said.

"Something better, please," Mary said, rolling her eyes.

"Bah, you guys will probably come up with something terrible," Sam stated.

"Well, I've been doing some reading, and I think I have a good name," Oliver told them.

Mary leaned forward in her seat.

"What is it?" Mary asked.

"Patria. It means homeland in Latin," Oliver said.

Sam raised a finger.

"Ay, I actually kind of like that name," Sam said.

"It's.... Weird, but interesting. It might grow on me," Mary said, cocking her head slightly.

"Hey!" came a voice.

The three looked up in surprise as someone shouted Mary's name. It was one of the door guards.

"We got some trouble at the door. I think you guys should come and see this," the man said.

They all looked at each other in alarm.

"What the fuck?" Sam said.

"Come on, come on!" Oliver said, standing up and breaking into a jog.

The other two stood and followed him, navigating their way out of the maze. The three ran up the stairs and down the hall to the bunker doors. As they got there, they heard the doors shut.

"Holy shit! Are you okay?"

"Grab some bandages! Anything, go!"

One of their people ran past, glancing at the three as they approached. As they got to the door, they saw ten people. Five were strangers, another three were part of a looting group that went out into the wasteland, and the last two were guards. Oliver looked over the group. Blood covered one of the scavengers, and there were originally four people that went out.

"What happened?!" Mary asked in alarm.

"We got attacked and lost George, and Greg is heavily injured. I don't know if he will make it. We found these people as well, and they already lost someone," explained one of the looters.

"Who attacked you guys?" Oliver asked.

"We don't know. We think it's that other group outside the bunker that's been attacking us for a while."

"God damnit, those fuckers won't leave us alone," Sam growled.

"Who are these people?" Mary asked.

"Survivors, miss. We found your people getting attacked and came to the rescue. We tried our best. I'm sorry," responded one of the newcomers.

"Wait, we can't just let these people in," Mary told Sam and Oliver.

"They're welcome," Oliver announced.

Terrorism

11:23 AM, August 24, 2154

London walked through the market with Alisa, eyeing the goods at each stall. They both had their weapons with them, London with a crossbow on his back and Alisa with a shotgun on her back.

"War has gotten that bad, huh?" London asked.

"Patria has pushed closer to New Uruk. Look, I know it's dangerous, but we're not going to the front lines," Alisa told him.

"Supplying the war front is dangerous work, though. A lot of caravaners die doing that," London said.

"It's for a good cause, London. Plus, we're skilled, and we'll get paid a lot."

"It's dangerous, Alisa. I'm thinking about Rose when I say this."

They stopped by an alleyway, London leaning against a wall as he stared at Alisa.

"I understand that, London. Look, we're gonna go out of business if Patria begins cutting into trade routes. If we wanna get anywhere in this business, the filters from delivering supplies will help us."

London sighed and gazed at the ground, pressing his lips together as he thought about it.

"I'll consider it. It's just dangerous work."

"I think we should do it. I've spoken to Archie about it, and he agreed; Reginald is still on the fence."

"I don't blame him. How's Margaret lately?"

"The same. She's still sick, but she can handle dealing with trade at her stall."

"I think I might pay her a visit before getting ready with the next caravan. I'll talk to Rose tonight about supplying the war front."

"All right, just be smart about this, London," Alisa said.

"I will. See ya," London said, waving her goodbye.

"Later," she said, doing the same.

London walked into the street again, looking around the marketplace before heading right. The group's business was on the other side of the neighborhood, a trade building built into an old-world business with a garage beside it. They bought it from the city officials a few months ago and had completely renovated it. It had transformed from an abandoned building into a breathing business that caravaners visited daily, which had earned London and his group some reputation.

He took his time as he strolled down the street and viewed all the goods up for sale. Recently, he had noticed a shift in customer consumption with more clothes sold than usual. London knew that this was in preparation for the arrival of winter, which was harsh in the wasteland; the pollution haze that blocked out the sun made winter even more bitter.

Eventually, London arrived at the other side of the neighborhood, spotting Margaret. As usual, the old woman was sitting in her spider chair behind her merchant's stall, doing business with a caravaner. London waited for them to finish before approaching Margaret.

"Hello, Margaret."

She squinted, smiling as her old eyes recognized him.

"Ah, hello, London. How are you, dear?"

"I'm good. Just wanted to check in. How's the business doing city-side?"

"Hunkey dorey. We near about beat the amount of sales that we had last month already. Sho'nuff, we'll be buying some new wagons and Scab Boars and expanding the business. That's horse sense, I tell ya."

London softly grinned.

"I can't wait. We'll hire some people and really get the business rolling."

"That's the right idea, deary."

"What's your view on supplying the war front?" London abruptly asked.

"The war front? I reckon it ain't that bad of an idea. It'd put a smile on my face if we can help stop them vermin Patrians."

"It'll be dangerous though," London told her.

"My Reginald knows what to do about them Patrians. Don't you worry dear,"

"All right," London said, "I gotta be going. See ya, Margaret."

"Goodbye, dear."

London turned and walked away. That wasn't the answer he was entirely expecting, and he was unsure if Margaret understood fully what was going on. Regardless, the most important opinion would come from Rose. He began to walk home, strolling through the marketplace again, and viewing all the goods for sale.

There were goods everywhere; animals there, clothes here, food and weapons over there. It was nice to see that even during a war, New Uruk prospered in trade. It was what kept the city alive. He paused and stood aside as some wagons passed through the middle of the street, looking as large Scab Boars pulled them. Each animal was massive, letting out "orf" sounds as they pulled.

Once they were gone, he continued again and walked past a factory, glancing into the workshop full of workers. London paused as he noticed some commotion inside. He stared, mouth slightly agape as he saw six people pull out their guns and run into the street, another one pulling out a strange device. London gasped in horror and dove for cover.

A deafening explosion shook the ground, dust and debris flying from the factory as the six men with guns began clearing the street.

"For Patria!"

"Death to New Uruk!"

London was dazed from the shock of the explosion, rolling behind a stall and producing his crossbow.

Screaming and gunshots filled the air, the marketplace devolving into a pot of chaos as people ran from the six shooters.

A minute after the shooting began, sirens started singing their songs of terror.

Meanwhile, London hid in the stall he had dove behind, panting quietly and holding his crossbow. It already had a bolt ready to fire. He was shaking in fear, his fists white as he clenched the crossbow and his breath quivering. Another explosion in the distance echoed across the city, followed by more gunfire.

"Spread out! Kill the hiders!"

The Patrians began to spread out, quickly killing as many people as possible before the city guard could establish a defense. London slowly crawled to the next stall and peeked over, watching as a woman approached the stall he had been at before. As soon as she rounded the corner, London aimed his crossbow and fired.

In the blink of an eye, the crossbow bolt whizzed through the air and hit the woman in the throat. She let out a gurgling sound as she fell to the ground, landing with a thud. She twisted and clawed at the bolt. Before growing limp, she rolled over and stared at London before flattening out in her own blood.

London's heart skipped a beat when she hit the ground. Dread filled his heart as he gazed at her struggle, staring for a moment at what he had done. London had killed many people in his life, but it never got any easier to do.

Soon, he moved to the next piece of cover he could find. The other four shooters were far away, the fifth actively clearing stalls.

Every gunshot marked a dead merchant that London had known.

As much as he felt guilty, he wouldn't let people he knew die while he stood aside. London waited for his moment, occasionally peeking to watch the shooter. He reloaded the crossbow and prepared himself.

London burst up from the boxes he was hiding behind and ran toward the shooter, aiming the crossbow and firing. The string came down upon the bolt and fired once more in the blink of an eye, finding its mark on the shooter's side. He cried out in pain as it hit him, falling to the side in surprise.

In a matter of moments, London pounced upon the man and viciously shoved the bayonet of his crossbow into his throat, stabbing twice before the man was dead. London dropped to the ground beside him. His heart was thundering. The man twitched and gurgled from the stab wounds, thrashing slightly before bleeding to death in front of London.

More gunshots rang out as London gazed at the body in front of him.

"Oh my God, oh fuck..." London whispered.

London let out an angry growl and reloaded the crossbow, looking around the street. Another one of the shooters had noticed that her comrades were missing and had come back. London was ready, waiting in ambush. As soon as she was close enough, he popped up and shot at her.

The bolt cut through the air, whizzing toward its target and missing. It flew straight past the woman, barely grazing her before hitting something else behind her. She let out a surprised yelp and ducked, running to the other side of the street before beginning to shoot at London.

He gasped and hid behind the stall he had shot from, wincing and closing his eyes as bullets landed beside him. He loaded another crossbow bolt while cowering, waiting for another moment to shoot. The woman continued to shoot at him, pausing for a moment. It was his chance. London popped up again and fired, only for a bunch of bullets to shred the wood holding the stall up.

The world spun for a moment before he hit the ground, shielding himself as wooden splinters showered upon him. He heard footsteps as the woman approached. London didn't have time to load his crossbow. Instead, he knelt and hid behind the stall again, waiting to pounce up and stab the woman.

Time seemed to slow, the footsteps getting closer and closer. She was only a few steps away.

Abruptly, he heard a shotgun blast, a loud thud following it. London looked around and then peeked over. The woman lay dead on the ground, thrown off of her feet by the shotgun. Only a few feet away was Alisa, along with twenty other guards.

"London! Are you okay?!" she shouted.

London stood up slowly, staring at her with his mouth open in astonishment.

"I-I'm okay! I'm okay!"

"Come on then. We need to evacuate to the subway!"

Deck

Simon didn't fight as the four Peacekeepers dragged him out of the Residential Area and across the Arcadis. Lines of Peacekeepers and Workers walked past him, giving him glances of indifference, concern, or anger. Simon glanced at the Workers, his brothers, and comrades, that he suffered with in this rat cage.

They continued, going farther and farther down the Arcadis. Simon had never seen the Deck and knew very little of it. He searched his mind for all the rumors that he had been told of the terrible place and could only recall a few. With all his heart, he hoped that they wouldn't shoot him out into space.

They walked until they passed the Storage Sector, Simon glancing at a line of Workers leaving the place. Abruptly, he began fighting and kicking to slow down the Peacekeepers escorting him.

"Thaddeus!" he shouted.

Thaddeus, who was in the line, looked at him in shock.

"Thaddeus, hide who you are! Six days! Six days!!" Simon shouted before being bludgeoned and dragged away.

All the other Workers had heard his words. The Peacekeepers in Thaddeus' line looked at the line before shouting their orders to carry on, disregarding Simon's words.

Simon glanced back as they dragged him forward brutally, watching Thaddeus glance back and then carry on. He hoped the message would spread

173

to the Defiants. It had to. His body ached from the beating, and he didn't dare do anything to receive another beating.

They took him farther away from places he knew and deeper into the unknown. The escort moved through a few halls before arriving at a final hall. At the end were two Peacekeepers guarding a locked security door, the pair staring as the group approached.

"Another one?"

"Caught by a Leader Hound," a Peacekeeper said.

One of the Peacekeepers at the door put in a code, waiting for the heavy door to slowly slide open.

"Damn, those Leader Hounds have been catching a bunch of traitors. Smart move to get spies among the Workers."

"That's why they're the leaders."

Simon glanced back as he was led into a tunnel beyond the door, watching the heavy security door close and lock behind him.

The artificial gravity of the Arcadis weakened as they approached the Deck, Simon losing his footing once as he didn't expect the sudden shift of gravity. Soon, they were floating; the Peacekeepers held onto special bars along the tunnel as they moved, Simon kept helplessly in between them.

They got to a second security door that opened just as slowly as the last one, the Peacekeepers inside taking Simon into their custody. The four escorts left without a word, handing Simon to his fate. The Peacekeepers in this part of the Arcadis stuck to the floor with magnetic boots, taking him to a small room.

Simon got a good look at the Deck as they moved him. It was a huge cube consisting of at least three hundred cells with windowless doors. He swallowed as he gazed at the cells. Soon, he was taken to a small room and strapped down onto a chair.

"W-What are you going to do to me?" Simon whispered.

The Peacekeeper strapped him down to the chair, glanced at him, and then carried on with his work.

"Oh fuck..." Simon said to himself under his breath.

First, the man took out an electric razor, beginning to shave Simon's hair.

Simon sighed anxiously as he watched his brown hair fall to the ground, soon vacuumed and burned in a small vaporizer.

Second, the man pulled out a large needle. Simon felt his heart drop as the Peacekeeper approached, laying a hand on Simon's arm and slowly pushing it in. It went into his skin easily, stopping as soon as it touched his Individual Chip. Abruptly, energy surged through his body, Simon crying out in pain as he shook from the shock. That must've been the termination of his identity.

Third, once the man finished and Simon was stunned by the shock, he released Simon from the chair and stripped him, giving him nothing in the way of prisoner clothes. Naked, Simon was led out of the room and guided in zero gravity past all the cells.

Simon was still stunned from the shock and didn't even bother with the idea of fighting back. The Deck was eerily silent, and it felt as though he was the only one there. Was this place a tomb? Was he going to starve to death here as his execution for being a traitor? Simon could only imagine.

The Peacekeeper stopped at a cell and opened it, pushing Simon in and watching him drift to the other end of the cell. Abruptly, the man closed the door and left Simon in total darkness.

Simon looked around the cell. It must've been a tomb. It was a square room with nothing in it except the hard walls. No toilet, no bed, no chair, no table, nothing. It was just a blank room that he floated in. Simon began to hyperventilate, looking around in the pitch-black darkness and fumbling in the air. Occasionally, he'd hit a wall and bounce in another direction.

"No, no, no, no!" Simon whispered.

"Let me out, dammit! Don't leave me here!" he began to shout, unable to slam on any walls.

No matter how much he screamed or flailed, no one heard him. He was trapped.

Time felt slow here, as if seconds crawled like minutes, minutes like hours, and hours like days. Eventually, he calmed down and tried to accept the darkness that he floated in. His heartbeat sounded as loud as a train, and eventually, he wished he could silence his breathing.

Simon couldn't tell what bothered him first. The darkness? The lack of company? The cold? He shivered and hugged himself as a ball, continuing to bounce off the walls and trying to become comfortable.

Whenever he fell asleep, he tried to stick himself in a corner and only began to float when he lost consciousness. It was maddening. Simon felt exhausted after a while and hungry. For a moment, paranoia took over, and he panicked over the idea that he'd starve to death here. That couldn't be right. They had to feed him! He convinced himself that they needed him.

He calmed down again and then had another panic attack over not being able to sleep comfortably. His stomach began to hurt as the hours passed, growling and rumbling. Simon also felt the need to relieve himself but fought it. He wrestled with both feelings for hours until Simon couldn't hold it and had to relieve himself.

Disgusting. He shrieked once or twice when the waste touched him, thinking it was some demon in the darkness here to eat his soul. Often, he felt nauseous and dizzy, though he had nothing to vomit up. The worst came in minor hallucinations, shapes and hands reaching out in the darkness to touch him or try to pull him.

Simon was screaming in terror as he drifted toward a clawed hand, thrashing as he tried to swim away before the door opened and flooded the room with light. A Peacekeeper grabbed Simon and guided him out of the cell, carrying him along to the small room again and throwing Simon in. Simon screamed this time, terrified of what could happen. He was strapped down to the chair and slapped until he stopped screaming.

"Shut up!" the Peacekeeper growled.

Simon hyperventilated but stopped screaming.

The man stood in front of him and stared into his eyes.

"Who are the Defiants?" he asked firmly.

"I-I don't know. I don't know, please! I don't know anything."

The Peacekeeper took out the same needle from before, pushing it into his arm.

"Who. Are. The. Defiants?"

"Please! I don't kn-"

Power surged through the Individual Chip. Simon thrashed and cried out in pain before his torturer repeated the question.

"I don't know! They're a group of rebels working against the Leaders! I don't know any names, though!"

Again, the power coursed through him.

"Gaha!! Okay! Okay! I know one man, Thomas! I don't know his last name!"

The torture session continued for what seemed like an eternity until the man was satisfied and threw him back into his cell. Simon floated back into the darkness, hopelessness filling him as he returned to the hellish box.

Hallucinations tormented him once more, his starvation and desire for water making it worse. Mercy was only given a few times in small morsels tossed into the cell. Simon only had a few moments to know where they were before he was left to guess what was his waste and what was food and water.

The torture continued over two more sessions. Simon's condition grew worse. He tried with all his might to fight the insanity of isolation and torture, hugging himself and having attacks of insanity often. To cope, he tried to speak with himself, trying to stay sane.

"What's that, Simon?" he asked himself.

"Nothing. What's your favorite book?" he replied after a pause.

"The Omnipotent Eye and Individuality by Carl Kavanaugh."

"Oh, that's my favorite too!"

"It's a great book, one of a kind."

"Do you hear that, Simon?"

"I think so. What is that?"

"Are they coming?"

Simon looked around in the dark.

"N-No! Not again! Please! I'll tell you anything!" he began begging, hearing a noise outside his door.

All of a sudden, light flooded into the cell as the door opened. Simon screamed and begged, trying to get away.

"Simon!"

"W-Who is that?" Simon asked in a fearful voice.

"T-Thaddeus!" Simon shouted in joy and relief.

War

"How much ammo do we have?" Oliver asked.

"Nearly fully stocked," replied the man.

"Guns? Is everyone who can fight armed?"

"Almost everyone that can fight, just a few people who aren't armed."

"I want the people who can fight armed. Make sure everyone knows what to do, check the barricades, do everything to prepare. There will be no slip-ups today," Oliver told the man.

"Will do," the man said, nodding and running off down one hall.

Oliver felt a tingling sensation throughout his body. He was stressed and nervous. News had just come of an incoming attack on Patria itself. Oliver nervously gripped his trusty Railshot Rifle, which was fully charged and fully loaded. He felt worried, but he felt that the people of this newly established city would be ready.

He marched along the halls impatiently. Oliver knew their attackers well. The people of Patria now referred to them as the Outsiders, creating a sort of barbarian idea about them. Oliver had fought them before establishing Patria, a story told by the scar on his forearm.

Patria had been born from war. The fight between the new nation and the Outsiders was no longer a skirmish between survivors. Even though it was no longer a war for just food and water, the reason for fighting remained the same. It was a fight for survival. Oliver knew this well. Whoever controlled the bunker controlled the future.

The bunker was the key to civilization, a brand new home of humanity. Oliver believed Patria would build the civilizations and empires of the future. To him, these simple roots were a cradle. Inside the bunker were space, food, and water, while outside, there were Doomstorms, starvation, and the cold, polluted air.

"Oliver!"

Oliver turned around.

"There you are!" Sam said. "I've been looking for you."

"Hey, Sam, what's the news?"

"All the traps outside are armed. Barricades at the door are ready, and everyone is at their posts. I told them to hide and make the place look vacant. The ones at the front of the tunnel have periscopes, so they'll alert us when they see the Outsiders."

"That's good. I should have a man arming the rest of our fighting force."

"Those bastards won't leave us alone," Sam growled.

"Do you blame them? We control Heaven in the wasteland, and they don't."

"It's just needless fighting. If they had worked together with us from the beginning, maybe more people would still be alive," Sam said in a disheartened tone.

"If they hadn't attacked us, we might not have found this place," Oliver pointed out.

Sam sighed, "You're right."

"When are the Outsiders coming?" Oliver asked.

"An hour supposedly," Sam told him. "A couple of lookouts saw a huge group marching over here and warned us."

"An hour is plenty enough; we'll be ready for them," Oliver said with a grin. "They won't know what hit them."

"There's a few dozen we have to fight. Once they get through the traps around the tunnel, they'll try to push into the bunker. We have a defense there that we should be at. Your gun will do good in that space," Sam said.

"Where's Mary?"

"Already with everyone else, making sure we're fight-ready," Sam said.

"Let's go join her."

Sam nodded as they ran along the halls of the bunker. People rushed past them. Those who couldn't fight ran with supplies, running with medics and soldiers who carried boxes of ammo and medical supplies to the front entrance. As the two arrived at the doors, Oliver saw the defense was all put together.

Wooden and metal walls stood against the coming enemy, reinforced by sandbags and barbwire. The doors were opened, revealing the rest of the defense going all the way out of the tunnel. There were rifles, shotguns, crossbows, and all sorts of weapons among the defense. Everyone looked nervous and impatient. Oliver felt the same.

"Mary?!" Sam shouted.

"Over here!" she shouted back.

Mary walked toward them, holding her aged hunting rifle.

"What's going on? Are we ready?" Oliver asked.

"We're ready. They'll never get to the door," Mary said with a confident tone.

"I should've written something on those traps," Sam said with a chuckle. "Something like 'Love, Sam.'"

"And how is everyone?" Oliver asked, looking at all the soldiers as he ignored Sam's comment.

Mary looked at them and sighed.

"They're trained, armed, and nervous. It's the waiting that's getting to them,"

"It's getting to us all," Oliver said.

"Should we give them a few inspiring words?" Sam asked.

"I'm not one for speeches," Mary said.

"Speeches?" Oliver repeated, looking around.

"Oliver, you should do it," Sam suggested.

"Wh- No!"

"Come on, just a few words!" Sam pushed.

"Just do it, Oliver, it won't matter when we're fighting anyway," Mary told him.

Oliver groaned, "Fine, fine,"

He stood and walked to the middle of the small army, grumbling quietly. Oliver looked around, the soldiers staring at him as he prepared himself.

"P-..." he stuttered.

With a growl, he gathered some courage.

"Patrians!!" he shouted.

Everyone stopped as his voice echoed through the hall.

"Listen to me, friends, brothers, and sisters," he began.

"Today begins the war for our survival! This is no longer a petty war, my friends. This is no longer a fight for mere scraps! This is a fight for home, for people, and for family."

Oliver moved his arms as he spoke, gesturing nervously as he used the power of his voice.

"Look around you! Those around you, they are your people. Trust in one another! This battle, and the ones to follow, will lead Patria into glory.

"Remember, friends! The enemy is out there! The Outsiders want to take your family, your people, and your home. They want to take Patria from you!

"Will you let that happen?!"

"No!" some people shouted in response.

"No! These Outsiders have not fought for what you have! Patrian blood, sweat, and tears built this new nation! Patrian blood, sweat, and tears will build the new world! We are the forefront of civilization!

"The Outsiders are barbarians! They are destroyers! Will you join me, friends? Will you keep Patria safe?!"

"Yes!" more people shouted.

"Then fight! Fight for Patria! Fight for home! Fight for family! The Outsiders are coming, and we will push them back! We will send them running across the wasteland! Together, as one people, we will hold Patria against all who threaten it! For Patria!"

He raised his gun above his head as he shouted Patria's name.

"For Patria!" they all shouted.

Oliver smiled proudly and walked over to Sam.

"How'd I do?"

"They're excited, that's for sure," Mary said.

"Meh, could've been better. We'll work on your speech-giving skills later," Sam said, patting his back.

"Hah, All right," Oliver said. "I'm going to the front of the tunnel."

"Why?" Sam asked, raising a brow.

"I wanna see when they get here," Oliver told him.

"All right," Sam replied.

They shook hands and separated. Oliver walked along all the barricades, nodding to all the soldiers who looked at him. He felt a warm glow on him as they looked at him. He felt like they trusted him, believing in both him and themselves. They were still nervous but empowered by his words.

Oliver sat by the soldiers at the very front of the tunnel. Eight people were ready to defend with him, each of them greeting him as Oliver joined them. Three had periscopes, staring into the wasteland while the rest hid.

"Seen anything yet?" Oliver asked.

"Nothing, sir," one said, handing him a periscope. "Take a look."

Oliver took it from her and looked through it. All he could see was the wasteland, vast and empty with nothing in it. He grinned. Oliver couldn't see any of the traps that Sam and his team had planted, which meant the Outsiders wouldn't either. He handed the periscope back.

"Tell me if you see anything,"

"Yes, sir,"

Oliver sighed and laid there. He nervously began to move his leg and sweat, his nerves slightly getting to him. For a long while, there was nothing but the wind of the wasteland and nervous breathing. The minutes droned on as if time stood still. For a few minutes, Oliver thought the Outsiders weren't coming.

"Oliver, Oliver!" the woman whispered.

"What? What is it?" Oliver asked.

"I see people; look," she said, giving him the periscope again.

Oliver took it and gazed through it. He saw dozens of people, each one armed with a different weapon. They marched over the dunes, eyeing the tunnel as they approached. Oliver gasped, giving the periscope back.

"I'm going back into the tunnel. Retreat if you guys can't hold the entrance.

We'll choke them in here," Oliver said.

The woman nodded.

"Good luck, sir,"

"You too."

He slowly slid down into the rest of the tunnel, proceeding to run and hide behind some cover.

"They're here! Everyone get ready and be quiet!"

The tunnel became still and silent. People held their breaths, guns ready as they heard footsteps outside. Left, right, left, right.

Oliver gasped as the traps went off. Screams and explosions filled the air as Outsiders died to cartridge traps, spikes, and mines. The ones who fell into spike traps screamed the most. As the Outsiders closed in on the traps, the soldiers at the front of the tunnel opened fire.

As they started firing, arrows and bullets rained upon them. They hid as the bullets pelted their cover, keeping them down as Outsiders advanced on them. A few tried to shoot the oncoming invaders, only to fall dead to enemy fire. The others that remained slid down the tunnel and retreated, shielding their heads as an explosion destroyed the first installation of cover.

The traps continued killing people. Oliver had his Railshot Rifle ready, pointed toward the cloud of debris in front of him.

"Attack!"

Outsiders ran into the tunnel, shooting at the defenders as they tried to push in.

One shot from Oliver shredded them, another taking out more men. As he shot, so did his allies, killing all the soldiers that ran into the tunnel. For a moment, the rush stopped. Oliver prepared his gun again.

A second wave came. Soldiers with metal shields and old-world bulletproof shields ran with rows of soldiers behind them.

"Fire! FIRE!" Oliver shouted.

Metal shrapnel dropped a few invaders as they pierced the metal shields and dented the bulletproof shields. In return, a volley of arrows and a hail of bullets came from behind the shields. Oliver dropped behind his cover as he heard bullets whiz past, blood spraying on his clothes.

He looked to his left, watching as a Patrian slid down onto the ground beside him with a bullet hole through his mask.

"Fuckers!" Oliver growled.

He popped up and shot again. Oliver couldn't tell who dropped as he dove for cover again.

"Oliver! Retreat!"

He looked around, spotting Sam waving to him.

"Come on!" Oliver yelled.

The Patrians with him followed, running behind the next set of barricades. As they did, the Outsiders took the first set of barricades. Oliver slid behind the barricades and rolled, hiding as arrows went past him.

"Oliver! Are you okay?" Sam asked.

"Yes! They're pushing forward!" Oliver said.

"They walked into the next trap, don't worry. Just need a few more to advance!" Sam told him.

They crawled up against the barricades. Sam held a remote and a periscope, sitting and staring through it as the sounds of gunfire filled the tunnel.

"Are they advancing?!" Oliver asked, attempting to shout over it all.

"They are! Almost! A few more past the barricade, and I'll blow it. Almost... NOW!"

The remote clicked, followed by an ear-piercing explosion.

Caravan

"London, I want to go!" Rose cried.

London knelt and hugged her, picking her up.

"I'm sorry, Rosie, I can't bring you," London whispered.

"Why?! I want to go. I can fight!"

"You're too little, Rosie. We're going to the war front; it's too dangerous."

London held her as she cried, shushing her.

"London, it's time to go," Alisa said, standing behind him.

"No! You can't go! If it's dangerous for me, it's dangerous for you too!" Rosie protested.

London sighed and carried her over to Margaret on the other side of the street, setting Rose down in front of her and kneeling.

"Rose, I promise I'll come back safe and sound. I always have."

"Don't you worry, little thing," Margaret said. "He'll come back fit as a fiddle."

"You know it," London said. "I'll be okay, Rose."

Rose sniffled and nodded, hugging him one more time. London held the hug for a while before standing and walking to Alisa. She nodded to him as they walked to join the rest of the caravan, London hopping onto the spear-gun in the back of his wagon. Archie joined them, four soldiers following him.

A man climbed onto the front wagon of the caravan, holding a horn.

"Y'all got your backers tight?!"

"Ay!"

"Whips ready! Move out!" he shouted, blowing a horn.

As the Scab Boars heaved forward, London heard a scream.

"London!!" Rose screamed.

London turned and watched as Rose ran after him, reaching out for him.

"Please don't leave!!" she shouted.

As she ran, someone caught her and held her back. She turned and struggled, trying to free herself as the caravan left. London watched, Rose slowly stopping her struggle as she gave up and broke down into tears. As the caravan turned down another street, London looked down and put his hand on his gas mask.

"Fuck..." he whispered.

"Fuck, I hate goodbyes," Archie said, sitting against the side of the wagon's back.

"Who doesn't?" Alisa asked.

"Especially with her," London said, letting out a sigh.

The caravan traveled through the city slowly, passing all the factories and businesses full of busy workers. London gazed at them, leaning on the speargun in front of him.

"I can't believe we're going to the war front," Archie said with a dejected frown.

"First time to the war front?" a soldier beside him asked.

"Y-Yeah, first time."

"Ah, don't worry. At least you guys aren't fighting, just delivering supplies."

"It's still dangerous," London stated.

"That's why we're here," another soldier replied.

"I'm happy that we're doing our part to help," Alisa told them, "Tired of delivering water when people are dying out there."

"How far out is the front?" Archie asked.

"A few hours," the first soldier said.

"Gonna be a long ride," said the second. "Just relax."

Archie sighed.

"I'll try."

They left the gates of New Uruk. The caravan stopped as they opened the gates, waiting for more soldiers to join them before going out into the rest of the city. As they rode, Archie and Alisa conversed with the soldiers. London, meanwhile, was silent. He was watchful, cautious of the shadows. No mutants would dare attack such a large group, but the Patrians could be anywhere.

If they were able to perform direct terrorist attacks inside the city, it was reasonable. London heard recently that the war was going badly and that the Patrians were pushing closer and closer to the capitol. He could only imagine what horrors would happen if they got to the city.

"How's the war actually going? Sounds like you've been there," London asked the first soldier, cutting into the current conversation.

"Terrible. We lost the last big battle to them, and they keep sending devastating raiding parties into our territory."

"Yeah, they have a lot of soldiers too. Fuck, man, men, women, and children."

Another soldier let out a groan.

"Kids. It fucking screws with you," he said. "I know a few buddies who are messed up after fighting child soldiers."

"They have children fight?" London asked in disbelief.

"Yeah, people don't matter in Patria. Only their usefulness."

London looked out at the horizon. He couldn't imagine Rose as a soldier. He could imagine her terrified with a gun as bombs exploded and people died around her. It was terrible to imagine.

"Child soldiers, that's fucked up," Archie whispered, shaking his head.

The conversation quieted as they dwelled on the dark matter. London leaned against the spear gun and looked down, shaking his head as well.

The caravan carried on into the wasteland as they left the ruins of the old city behind. There were fifty wagons, each with at least six to eight people riding along. Everyone had weapons, armor, and ammo. Each scab boar had armor, each wagon fortified, and every spear-gun manned.

The winds of the wasteland blew softly today, thin currents of sand blowing across the landscape. Each wave slithered like a snake, moving through short blades of yellowed grass. London's gaze narrowed. Grass.

London thought about it. He was forty-six years old and had spent his entire life in the wasteland of the new world. The world, to him, had always been dry and desolate, paired with the eternal pollution haze. But, recently, he had noticed changes. The weather seemed gentler, the haze thinner, and nature had begun to appear.

For most of his life, Earth was relatively barren. To see the return of nature and plants was simply bizarre. London knew that what he saw before him were pioneer species, just as hardy as all the survivors in the wasteland. These plants were a mercy as well, helping to feed and sustain the animals of the wasteland.

The caravan carried on for hours. Occasionally, London joined the conversations between Archie, Alisa, and the soldiers. As they rode, he was always watching the horizon. Sometimes, they passed ancient dead trees. Other times, they passed ruined buildings, billboards, and power poles.

"You grew up in New Uruk?" Archie asked a soldier.

"Born and raised, west district."

"Oh shit, you're west? Same here; I used to work in the workshops before the factories came along," said another soldier.

"What is that?" Alisa whispered and squinted.

"What is what?" Archie said, looking around.

London straightened up on his spear gun, looking in the direction they were going. Ahead of them were multiple plumes of smoke, rising high into the sky. London's face turned into a surprised expression. The soldiers of each wagon looked over as well, immediately preparing their weapons.

The horn of the front wagon blasted.

"Whips, drive push!"

All the Whips urged their Scab Boars forward as they heard the command. With loud "orf" sounds, the beasts heaved and pulled. As they did, a second command went down the line.

"Soldiers, guns ready! Gunmen, get your road needles ready!"

London gripped the two handles on the spear gun and rotated the entire thing. His heart was already beginning to pound from excitement and nervousness. It seemed the Patrians had attacked their destination. Would they still be there? Was the caravan in danger? All these questions and more went through his mind.

As the caravan moved toward the smoke, they began to see occasional blast craters, foxholes, bodies, and small fires among the landscape. Ahead of them was a small town of around twenty buildings. There was destruction everywhere. Ruined vehicles, pieces of cover, sandbags, and barbed wire littered the town. People also walked among the corpses.

Each living person wore the symbol of New Uruk. Relief hit London as he noticed the symbols on their armor. Most of the men looked tired, battle-weary, and relieved as the caravan rolled into sight.

The wagons rolled into the embrace of the old world town. London looked at the ruins, staring at the bullet holes, arrows, and blast marks everywhere. On the faces of the men who stood guard was fear, yet relief.

Again, the horn of the caravan blew.

"All stop! Soldiers, out! Unload y'all's backers!"

London joined everyone as they got off the wagons, proceeding to help unload the supplies they had brought from New Uruk. He moved heavy boxes, listening to commands to see where he would go. He held medical supplies, so he was directed to an old bar that had become a field hospital. He went inside as he arrived at the building, immediately having the stench of blood and the sound of pain greet him.

Medics and doctors ran everywhere inside, rows upon rows of injured soldiers sitting before London. Many of them were heavily injured, yet the ones who weren't too hurt smiled.

"Help has arrived, y'all!"

London looked at them. He could tell from a distance many had shell shock. Their empty stares were fixed upon something yards away. They were numbed, seemingly unaware of his presence. London could stand right in front of any of them, and they would look through him. It was as if something inside of them had died, something maimed by the horrors of war that London could see in their glassy eyes.

He walked further inside, carrying the box in his hands to a spot full of supplies. With a grunt, London put the box down and turned around, preparing to leave before being stopped.

"London, is that you?!"

London looked toward the voice.

"Finlay?"

"London! Aren't you a sight for sore eyes?!" Finlay said, walking up to him.

London looked him over. Finlay was almost the same as when he left to join the war, though he now had soldier armor. On his armor was blood and medical crosses. Finlay walked up to London and shook his hand.

"I didn't expect you here," London said. "I wasn't even sure if you were alive."

"Takes more than fucking Patrians to make me stop kicking."

"Is it as bad as they say out here?"

"Worse. Follow me; I'm on break."

London followed Finlay as they walked outside. Finlay took him to a wall out of earshot near some sandbags. London watched him take out a flask of alcohol. As he caught London eyeing them, Finlay smiled.

"This was pretty expensive but well worth it. You want a sip?"

"No, thanks, I don't drink."

"Suit yourself. Anyway, situation out here is worse than what they say. I get boys under my care daily," Finlay began.

He lifted his mask and took a sip.

"Look, most of those boys are young, London. Eighteen, twenty. Half of them in there will either bleed out or succumb to infection."

"What?"

"Yeah, harsh truth about war. Fighting doesn't always get you. Morale is shit, especially with the Patrians constantly pushing us back into our territory."

"Any end in sight?" London asked.

"End of the war? Not for a long time. I hope the Patrians don't win, or we're all getting executed. The best thing for you is to get back to New Uruk, my friend."

Rebellion

10:23 AM, September 8, 2185

Thaddeus drew Simon out from the cell, gazing at his friend in the light.

"My God, what did they do to you?" Thaddeus whispered, eyes wide with shock.

Simon squinted and blinked at him, his eyes adjusting to the light.

"How long have I been in there?" Simon asked immediately.

"Six days. You did it, Simon. Your 'plan' worked," Thaddeus told him.

Simon hugged Thaddeus immediately, tears rolling down his cheeks from relief and joy. Thaddeus held him for a few moments before Simon let him go.

"Come on, Simon, we got clothes and food for you," Thaddeus said.

Simon was led along by Thaddeus as they parted from the cell. There were other Workers around the Deck, all of them working to free each person sent to the Deck. He glanced into each cell, seeing the starving and decrepit survivors of the terrible conditions.

His comrades that had freed him wielded anything for a weapon. Some had stolen weapons and armor from Peacekeepers, while others had pipes and bars torn from parts of the station.

The pair went into a small torture room, Thaddeus closing the door and allowing Simon to sit down on the chair.

"Here, take this," Thaddeus said, offering him a container of water and food.

Simon took it gratefully, eating immediately like a starving dog. In under a minute, it was all gone. He paused for a brief moment after, leaning his head back on the chair and then looking around the room. It took him a few seconds before he noticed the body of his torturer against one wall, needles, and other torture devices crammed into his bloody body.

Simon was surprised but took satisfaction that the evil man had gotten what he deserved. Simon watched as Thaddeus grabbed his body and began to strip it, getting his powerful hands bloody.

"What happened?" Simon asked.

"You sabotaged the air system in the Peacekeeper Residential Sector, right?"

Simon nodded.

"Well, you timed it just right. The circuits popped in the night and suffocated most of the Peacekeepers. Some got out, but that's when we realized what was happening. Rumors had been spreading to be prepared for something, and as soon as we found out what was happening, then we knew it was time."

Thaddeus stripped the man naked and left the armor pieces floating in the air. Thaddeus had taken some Peacekeeper armor from somewhere and pulled out some of Simon's clothing from a pocket. He unfolded it and gave it to Simon. Simon put it on and then accepted the armor stripped from the other Peacekeeper.

"We rushed the Peacekeepers in the Residential Sector first. They didn't survive the crowds. From there, we've been gathering weapons and uniting forces to deal with the rest of the station. It's complete chaos up there."

"Where's Albert?" Simon asked.

Thaddeus gave Simon the Peacekeeper's tesla baton, then looked at him with a frown.

"I haven't seen him."

"He's the one that betrayed me, Thaddeus. He didn't know what the plan was, but he caught onto what I was doing and got me arrested. He's a spy for the Leaders."

Simon's eyes glared in anger, clenching his jaw with narrowed lips. Thaddeus could tell this was the truth.

"Albert? But he's your best friend!"

"I didn't suspect it at all. Think about it, Thaddeus. Where did he go during the Thrash Games? It all happened right beneath our noses," Simon explained.

"And the others don't know anything."

"There are more spies among us."

"Can you fight, Simon?" Thaddeus asked.

Simon was weak from all that he had gone through, but he felt somewhat renewed. He thought about it for a moment, then closed his eyes and nodded.

"Come on then, it's time for us to buy our freedom," Thaddeus said, helping Simon to move out of the room.

They continued through the Deck until they reached the first heavy security door, moving past a few floating bodies of both Workers and Peacekeepers. As the pair moved up the tunnel, Simon slowly felt the artificial gravity of the Arcadis return. The second security door also had a few bodies, most of them being Peacekeepers that had been caught by surprise.

Eventually, the full strength of artificial gravity planted Simon's feet firm to the ground. He leaned on Thaddeus for a while, his legs shaking and wobbling. His breath was heavy, and every joint ached. Simon was grateful for the return of gravity and slowly regained stability the further they went. Soon, he was slowly walking by himself.

The station was in anarchy. In only a few hours, all order had been destroyed. There were corpses everywhere, consisting of Peacekeepers that had been beaten to death by swarms of vengeful Workers or Workers that had died due to lethal force from the Peacekeepers. Each Tasking Station laid in pieces, and wreckage littered the station's halls.

Simon gazed at each body in surprise at first, then horror, and then finally, cruel satisfaction. All the beatings, executions, and inhumane cruelty was being repaid tenfold. It was finally time to be free.

"We've taken the Storage Sector, Nutritional Sector, Hygienics Sector, and the Residential Sector so far. The Peacekeeper Residential Sector is a no go zone. We've faced some issues, but we've beaten most of them. We're trying to break our way into the Development Sector, but the Developers have barricaded themselves and have Peacekeepers waiting for us," Thaddeus explained.

"There's enough Ignium around the station to create something to destroy the barricades," Simon said.

"You're right. Our biggest problem is the Leaders. When everything hit the fan, they barricaded themselves inside of the Command Sector with most of the surviving Peacekeepers. So far, we haven't been able to get in."

"Why?'

"Heavy resistance from the remaining Peacekeepers trying to save their skins, and all the fortifications leading to the Command Sector."

Simon stared at Thaddeus for a second as they walked.

They joined up with other Defiants. All of the Workers had become Defiants and were running around securing their parts of the station. There was chaos, commands ringing through the air, and attempts to establish order. Most of the Workers were mad with the chaos, screaming, laughing, and destroying things in their new freedom.

Simon glanced at the men who were celebrating, closing his eyes in thought.

"Thaddeus,"

"What?"

"There's a way we can get in. The Peacekeeper Residential Sector leads to the Command Sector. All we have to do is restore air to that area. They won't be expecting it, and they won't be guarding it."

"We thought about that, but none of us can reach the vents without needing to go back for air. We don't even know which vent was busted. Until then, we're stuck trying to go into the other ways."

"I know which vent. I just need to get to it," Simon told Thaddeus.

They continued walking until a man ran past them, waving a metal bar and screaming.

"Everyone! Go to the Development Sector! We're breaching the barricades! Go! Go!"

Thaddeus looked at Simon.

"Do you wanna go help them?"

"I can try."

They immediately took off to the Development Sector, following a frenzied swarm of Workers that rushed to the fighting. As Simon jogged with Thaddeus, he heard explosions in the distance.

Each explosion was loud and echoed through the station, followed by a rumbling that shook the Arcadis.

The pair arrived at the scene just in time. There was still smoke in the air from the explosions, with sparks flying from Ignium connections built into the walls and doors around the blast site. Someone had caused some sort of explosion, and now the way was open.

A horde of Workers crashed into the Development Section, colliding with the Peacekeepers who met them with brutal force. Each side swung at each other, taser batons taking down Worker after Worker. In return, the Workers swung their weapons. They used stolen taser batons and makeshift weapons, denting the armor of the Peacekeepers and bloodying them.

"Kill them all!"

"For the Defiants!"

"Death to the tyrants!"

Thaddeus and Simon moved in together, joining the blur of violence. Left and right people fell, being beaten or trampled by the savage horde. Eventually, they worked through all the Peacekeepers and spread out through the Development Sector. They rushed past most of the Developers, some of them stopping to beat a few. The Developers were respected since they were the doctors and caretakers of all of the Workers since birth.

All of the Developers were terrified, cowering as the horde spread out and killed the fleeing Peacekeepers. In a matter of minutes, the Development Sector was taken and liberated. The Defiants were victorious. They all broke out into cheers and celebrations, shouting their victories out.

"You hear that, you sons of bitches?! The Arcadis is ours!"

Simon was in the middle of it, panting and wobbling slightly. He leaned on Thaddeus, taking a moment.

"Hey, you good?" Thaddeus asked, holding him up.

"Y-Yeah, just tired."

"Hey, it's him!"

"It's Simon!"

"It's the man who freed us!"

Simon looked around in confusion as the crowd surrounded them, cheering and chanting his name. He regained his balance and stood, gazing as Thaddeus smiled and joined the crowd, cheering.

"Simon! Simon! Simon!"

It seemed word had spread of his deed, and they were grateful. Simon was unsure of what to do, so he raised his fist straight into the air. The Workers around him mimicked him.

"Victory is ours! The Leaders shall fall!" he shouted.

Council

"Pull back!"

"They're flanking us!"

Oliver hid behind the concrete wall as the chaos went on around him. Between the gunfire, shouting, and screams of death, he couldn't tell what was going on. As bullets and arrows flew past, he gathered his courage. Oliver waited for a pause in the oncoming rain, popping up as soon as it appeared.

As soon as the scrap metal flew out into the ruins, he hid once again.

"We need to retreat back to Patria!" he shouted to his comrades.

"We need these supplies!"

"We've lost too many people already! We've lost!" Oliver shouted.

As he spoke, another soldier fell dead to arrows and bullets. Oliver gasped as the corpse hit the ground with a thud, blood oozing from the wounds.

It was a disaster. Oliver had left the bunker with thirty people and high hopes today. They were going to loot a town for supplies for Sam's new project. Instead, thirteen of them were dead among the rubble, while the rest were fighting for their lives against the superior numbers of the Outsiders.

Oliver was still surprised over how quickly the ambush crashed down on them. The Outsiders had them nearly surrounded, and it seemed that they were behind every corner and wall.

"We're retreating NOW!" Oliver barked out.

"Yes, sir! Come on, let's go!" shouted a commander.

The Patrians moved as a group. With tooth and nail, they fought out of the old world buildings, piercing a hole in the Outsider offensive. Oliver was one of the last to retreat. As his comrades ran into the wasteland behind him, he shot and brought down Outsider after Outsider.

Each shot kept the Outsiders at bay, buying the Patrians time. Oliver pointed, shot, hid, and repeated until he ran out of ammo. His gun only sparked and fizzled as he pulled the trigger.

"Crap!" Oliver cursed.

"Push forward!" came an order from the other side.

Abruptly, he swung the rifle, the entire thing crashing into the face of an Outsider as he rounded the corner. The man had no time to get up as Oliver smashed his gas mask with his boot, proceeding to turn and run. As he retreated, Patrian soldiers shot at the Outsiders, halting their advance as their leader got to them.

Once among them, Oliver led them over the dunes. The Outsiders had won this battle. As Oliver ran, he seethed in hatred and bitterness. This loss was part of a string of defeats against the Outsiders over the past month, all of which had caused tension in Patria. The people of the bunker were worried, and the three leaders were at odds with one another. Each one was paranoid. Recently trust had started to fade among them.

"Let's go! Let's go!" Oliver shouted, urging his soldiers on.

As they ran through the dunes, he looked behind them.

"Watch behind us! Outsiders could be on our tails!" he ordered, pointing behind the group

They moved on, each person heavily panting. Oliver was exhausted, and his muscles ached. Patria wasn't too far away. After a while of running, they ran into a patrol circling the border of their small nation.

"What's going on?" asked the captain of the patrol.

"We lost," Oliver said bitterly. "The Outsiders secured a new loot location."

"Is anyone hurt?"

Oliver paused, glaring at the man through his gas mask. The man gazed back at him, quickly becoming silent.

"I want your patrol to stay here in case they pursue us. If they do, retreat back to Patria and warn our defense," Oliver commanded.

"Yes, sir."

"Let's move!" Oliver shouted.

The soldiers carried on into their territory, relieved to be on home ground. They arrived at the tunnel leading into the bunker. Outside there were fortifications, along with a little lookout tower. The soldiers were hailed with joy as they returned; the joy quickly faded as the guards saw how many were missing.

Oliver passed the tower and walked into the tunnel. Rage exuded from him. The guards only nodded or quickly welcomed him back, attempting to avoid his anger while still showing respect. He ignored them, walking through the doors of the bunker and into the halls beyond. His soldiers followed him.

After they got inside, he stopped and turned around.

"You're all relieved for today," Oliver told them. "Someone notify Mary and Sam. I'm calling a meeting now!"

He was aggressive in his tone. They all jumped in surprise as he relieved them, two quickly running off to get the other two leaders. As they ran away, Oliver began punching and kicking his rage into a wall.

"Fuck! Fuck! Fuck! God damnit!" he shouted.

After a minute or two of beating the wall, he exhausted himself and calmed down. Oliver stood there for a moment. He recalled everything. The looting run had gone almost perfectly. They found almost everything they needed among the ruins and had begun collecting them. As they did, the Outsiders attacked.

He remembered the chaos of the first few minutes as Patrians died. They were completely surprised. Was it arrogance? Oliver wondered if their early victories in the war had made them blind. He brooded on what could have changed those events. After a few ideas, he settled on one thought. Blood.

The Patrians needed to end the war. If they did, they would be the undisputed rulers of the wasteland and have all of its goods to themselves. It would cost blood. Blood, Oliver thought, was something he was willing to give. He began to walk to the atrium, arriving after a few minutes and finding himself in the middle of the bookshelves.

Oliver sat with a tired grunt, waiting for the other two to arrive. As he did, he slowly reloaded the Railshot Rifle. It was a calming process to do it like this. It was satisfying to put new Ignium batteries in the weapon, and the sound of metal poured into the ammo container was even more satisfying.

Eventually, Sam and Mary arrived. They sat down opposite one another, tension filling the room. Each one glanced at the other, hints of contempt or distrust in their eyes.

"We lost," Oliver began.

They looked at him silently.

"We lost thirteen people. We lost thirteen good Patrian people, we lost a potential looting spot, and we lost another battle," Oliver continued.

Mary moved to speak. Oliver immediately cut her off.

"We're losing this war."

"We know that, Oliver," Sam said. "We're all trying to lead Patria to victory here. The new project is underway."

"We're all trying? I lost thirteen good people today!" Oliver shouted. "Is this project gonna lead us to victory, Sam?!"

"Yes! It will, Oliver!"

"Don't think for a second we're not trying, Oliver," Mary growled.

"I've been working night and day for Patria. I haven't slept in three days just to help everyone. It's thanks to all of us that Patria has held together. I've been guiding everyone. Sam's given us water, food, and is working on giving us air. You've been fighting since the first day to keep us safe, and we're grateful," Mary told him.

"Yeah, how are the crops? We've been going out to prevent starvation, and you two are worrying about air," Oliver said. "I've almost been shot every time I went out there!"

"What do you suggest then?! Total isolation in here?! Leave the rest of the wasteland to the Outsiders so they can build around us?!" Mary shouted at him, holding out her hands.

"I suggest blood!" Oliver barked, smacking his hand with a fist.

"Blood?" Sam repeated, recoiling slightly.

"Blood. Enough skirmishing over old world ruins and wasteland dunes. We need to amass everything we have and strike the heart of the Outsiders.

Take them by surprise like they did to us today, kill their leader, destroy their forces, and watch the rest run into the wasteland."

"And how are we going to do that if you can't defeat the Outsiders in most battles?" Mary asked, clenching her jaw.

"Can we calm down?!" Sam shouted over both of them.

They grew quiet, staring at him.

"Look, with the war machines I'm making, we can hit their heart easy. They'll be fast. We can take them by surprise, burn everything down, and kill their forces before they even know it," Sam told them.

"They're not even ready yet, and we haven't tested them!" Mary said.

"They'll work, trust me."

"When are they done, Sam?" Oliver asked.

"Soon. I just need more time and a few more supplies," Sam said.

A small wince came from Sam as he said, 'supplies.'

"Supplies?!" Oliver growled as his voice raised.

"Oliver, calm down! He's almost done. We have a few more hardships until we have a weapon to win this war. We just need to sacrifice a little more," Mary told him.

"All I've done is sacrificed, and people are still dying."

"People will die, Oliver! They're okay with that. They're fighting for you to achieve a dream of a better tomorrow for their home. They're fighting for what you said! They're fighting for home, family, and Patria. Nobody here thinks that this will come without pain."

"I'd die right now if Patria would live to see a better tomorrow. I'm sure Mary would sacrifice like that too. We are all in this together, right?" Sam said.

Mary nodded.

"We still need a plan for if the machines fail," Mary said.

"They won't fail. There hasn't been a battle with vehicles for years. It's a thing of the old world," Sam said.

"But what if they do fail?" Mary asked.

"They won't! The Outsiders will be destroyed before they even know what we hit them with."

"Don't be unreasonable, Sam. There must be a plan."

"There is no plan," Oliver told Mary, "This is do or die."

Enmity

1:14 PM, September 8, 2154

"Load up! Load up! Whips, at the ready!"

"Come on, London. Only two more," Finlay said.

London heaved and grunted as they lifted an injured soldier into the back of a medical wagon.

"Fuck, these guys are heavy!" London groaned.

"Preach," Finlay told him. "We're almost done."

The two went back inside the field hospital, picking up another soldier and taking her out to the same medical wagon.

"London! London!"

Alisa ran up to London, Archie at her side.

"You riding with us?"

"No, I'm riding with this wagon. The injured need a good gunman to watch over them." London told her.

"Patria is attacking soon. We don't know when, but if they hit us before we get to New Uruk, the injured soldiers will be the most vulnerable," Finlay added.

"I understand. Good luck," Alisa said, waving once and walking back to her wagon.

"See ya at New Uruk!" Archie told the two, turning to follow Alisa as they went to their wagon.

London grunted and climbed onto the wagon in front of him with Finlay, London proceeding to get on the wagon's spear gun. It was loaded, its pressure tanks were full, and there were plenty of spears in each ammo barrel near it. A minute after he got on, the entire caravan was ready.

"Y'all got your backers tight?!" screamed the front Whip.

"Ay!"

The horn of the front Whip echoed across the ruins of the old world town. Loud 'orf' sounds came from the Scab Boars at each wagon as they heaved forward under the command of each Whip.

Finlay sat against the side of the wagon near London, taking out his alcohol flask and sipping from it. He swallowed and sighed.

"To think, in a while, this place will be full of Patrians," Finlay said, leaning his head against the wagon side.

"Why aren't we staying to fight?" London asked.

"War front is getting pushed back. In other parts of the line, they've already been pushed back a mile or so past where we are. Matter of time before this place gets surrounded."

Finlay took another sip.

"We might be back here, who knows? They're taking the injured back to New Uruk so they can get the proper care they need. The rest of the soldiers are going back to be reorganized and sent out to fight at another position like this town."

"I just hope the war doesn't reach New Uruk," London said.

"Worried about Rose?" Finlay asked.

"Always," London told him.

Finlay sighed and took another sip.

"I'm tired. How far is the ride home again?" Finlay asked.

"A few hours."

Finlay thinly smiled.

"As long as I'm getting away from this damned war. Been too long since I saw the streets of New Uruk."

"We'll be happy to see you back."

"I wish I could stay forever."

"I don't blame you."

Finlay took another sip of alcohol. London leaned on the spear-gun, eyeing the horizon. Sometimes, he'd rotate the spear gun platform, checking all around them for a surprise attack.

"Hey, Finlay?"

"Yeah?"

"What happened to Tommy?"

"I don't know," Finlay began, putting his flask away. "I went through basic training with him, and we stuck together for a while. The guy actually has a lot of stories to tell if you can get him to talk."

"He can talk?"

"I know, I was surprised the first time too. Told me a story of how he learned to shoot."

"How'd that go?"

"Something along the lines of him stealing his father's gun, going out to shoot at some mutants, shooting it and not expecting the recoil, and returning with a bruise across his face."

London chuckled.

"Interesting first time," he remarked.

"Yeah. Anyway, we got separated going down to the war front a while back. Of course, I got sent to every field hospital outside the war front, which is lucky. Medics in actual war zones drop like flies or come back wrong. While I got sent off to save lives, Tommy got sent to do the actual fighting. Haven't seen him since; he could be dead in the sand or out fighting right now."

"I hope he's alive. I hope we win the war and can get the group reunited."

"Same here. I guess we just kinda got sucked up into this war, and it split us apart," Finlay said.

An hour and a few more sips of alcohol passed as the caravan carried along into the wasteland to New Uruk. It was somewhat windy, with tall currents of sand coursing through wasteland grass. London spoke with Finlay, Finlay sometimes pausing to tend to a soldier while London eyed their surroundings.

"How long has the war been going on?" London asked.

"Near a year now? I think? Somewhere back in February is when the first attacks from Patria began."

"Why?"

"New Uruk and Patria met a few months before the beginning of the war. Wasteland empires, I guess, meeting through expansion. Patria was growing Southward, and New Uruk was going Northward. New Uruk immediately tried to open up trade routes, while Patria gave us an ultimatum; assimilate or be consumed."

"Just that?"

"Yeah. Patria sustains itself with its war machine. As long as it keeps its war machine going, it keeps its empire going. It expands outward, consuming everything in its path. People either join it or get destroyed by it. New Uruk decided against joining since it would destroy the people and their way of life."

"Thank god, I wouldn't want Rose out fighting in some war. I heard they use child soldiers." London said.

"They do. Usefulness to the country; it's what keeps Patria going."

"Disgusting is what it is," London stated.

"Winning the war more like it," Finlay remarked.

"We'll push them back."

Finlay frowned and shook his head.

London looked at him for a moment before going silent. As the conversation died down, London stretched and leaned on the speargun in front of him. He felt sad. It felt horrible to see the shell shock on the faces of the soldiers, to see men crying for their mothers while holding their bloodied wounds, and to imagine the fear they must all be going through. Their sacrifices were for the good of New Uruk, but at what price?

He sighed and thought about it, eyeing the horizon all the while. He spun the speargun once, then twice, and then another time until something caught his eye. London squinted at it, trying to make out what it was. It seemed to be a small dust cloud. After a minute, there were other dust clouds.

"Ay! We got some larks fixin' for us!" London shouted.

As soon as he shouted, the warning went up and down the caravan.

"Y'all heard him! Gunmen, get your road needles ready! Whips, heat 'em!"

With that, the front Whip blew his horn. The caravan was in full speed as the Scab Boars "orfed," heaving and running as they pulled the wagons. At the same time, the soldiers who could fight readied their weapons while the spear gunners, the Gunmen, readied their spearguns.

London checked his spear gun, examining the spear loaded in it and checking the connections between the gun and the gas canisters. Once finished, he rotated the platform and aimed for the incoming dust clouds.

The sounds of Ignium engines began to come into earshot as the dust clouds grew closer, whooping and screaming following them.

"Patrians! Ambush!"

With that shout, a hail of arrows, spears, and bullets came from the hills and dunes on either side of the caravan. They had fled from the dust clouds straight into an ambush. In return, the soldiers on the wagons fired their weapons. London rotated the speargun, his eye catching glimpses of the symbol of Patria on each soldier. The twin-headed dog of tyranny.

"London!" Finlay shouted, "Shoot them!"

The speargun platform rotated around as Finlay shouted, London aiming at a Patrian soldier.

The pressure inside the spear gun built as he pulled the trigger, a massive metal spear flying forth from its resting spot. It spun and whizzed through the air, piercing straight through the scrap armor of a Patrian. The spear went through him, impaling him to the ground.

London had no time to dwell on the death of the man. His heart thundered, a rush of adrenaline coursing through him as he avoided arrows and spears. London grabbed a spear from one of the barrels beside the gun, shoving it into the spear gun and cocking the contraption. Once more, he rotated the gun and aimed for another attacker.

The second spear shot out from the gun, whizzing through the air with dangerous speed. It flew across the wasteland sand before cleanly missing its target.

"Fuck!" London growled.

Once more, he grabbed a spear and shoved it into the gun. He cocked it back again and prepared to fire.

By the time he had finished, the dust clouds in the distance had descended upon them. Patrians upon small, fast vehicles with Ignium engines began to circle and drive through the caravan. Each vehicle had a driver and a shooter. The shooters shot at the Whips and the Scab Boars, the drivers going between wagons to scare Scab Boars into separating from the rest of the caravan.

London turned the spear gun around, aiming at one vehicle as it approached.

The spear shot from the gun, flying out in the blink of an eye. It flew across the air and crashed straight through the front wheels of the vehicle, piercing into the engine underneath. As soon as the spear hit it, the entire thing flipped and sent the Patrians on it flying into the sand.

"Hey! Hey!!" Finlay shouted, trying to get the attention of their driver, "Get us the fuck out of here! The caravan is lost!"

At the same time, another Patrian vehicle sped past in front of them. Finlay ducked as the driver fell forward to the ground, wheels crushing the driver as the terrified Scab Boars bolted off with the wagon in tow.

"Damn it! London, keep firing!" Finlay shouted, hopping to the front of the wagon to try to take control of the Scab Boars.

London shot and watched as another spear impaled a Patrian soldier with a gun.

Finlay pulled at the reigns and yelled commands at the Scab Boars, failing to control them as the caravan descended into chaos. Patrians closed in all around; vehicles sped everywhere, Scab Boars broke free from the wagons while soldiers dropped like flies.

London prepared another spear, pushing it into the gun and cocking it. Once it was ready, he looked around for his next target while trying to make sense of the chaos around him. Left, right, behind him, and then his eyes widened.

"Finlay! Look out!"

A Patrian vehicle crashed into the side wagon. The world began to spin as London, the injured soldiers, and Finlay were sent flying into the air. It all felt like it was in slow motion until London hit the ground. The force from the impact stunned him, leaving London to lay on the ground in pain.

It took London a while to recover as he looked around. The world was a blur. The Patrians closed in on the caravan, bombs being tossed at trapped wagons while soldiers were executed at point-blank range or dragged away. The battle was lost. The realization hit London like a truck, knocking the spirit out of him as he struggled to get away.

"London! London, get up!" Finlay shouted.

At first, Finlay's words and his figure were a blur. London didn't quite understand what was happening as Finlay dragged him to his feet, only to fall again as a Patrian smacked Finlay with the end of his gun. London watched from below as the two struggled, the Patrian beating Finlay to the ground before turning the gun and firing.

London gasped in horror, watching blood spray from Finlay's corpse. A moment after, another Patrian was on top of him. He could barely struggle as he, too, was beaten with a gun, the beating almost knocking him out. The thought of death was so close, and London believed that surely this was the end.

His last thought was of Rose. He thought of her smile, how she giggled at something funny, or the delighted expression she had when she learned something new.

Just as London believed his death was a few moments away, he felt himself being dragged away by two pairs of hands.

Skyfall

The Deviants gave the Developers a choice: fight, or stand aside until the revolution was over. Most of them stood aside, while some chose to take up arms and fight. Now it was on to the next sector, the Command Sector.

They spread out throughout the Development Sector, searching for weapons and possible things to use as explosives to blast their way through the security leading to the Command Center. For a while, it was fruitless. As they searched, the voice of Genetrix rang out to order the Workers to lunch, though she was now ignored or screamed at.

After a while, they found old escape pods in the far end of the Development Sector. Simon approached one, walking in with a bunch of Workers with awe and suspicion. Simon guessed that these connected to the original purpose of the Arcadis: orbiting Earth until it was habitable again and restoring humanity's dominion on the planet.

There were lots of supplies inside: seeds, tools, weapons, and more. Simon looked at everything before stopping to stare at a few space suits. He stared longer at them, and then it clicked. These were what they could use to repair the air vents and take the Leaders by surprise. Simon immediately grabbed one, beginning to put it on while some of his confused comrades gawked at the strange sight.

Once he was in, Simon stretched and adjusted the spacesuit a bit. In seconds, reserved air filled it, and the suit became airtight and ready for space.

211

"Thaddeus! Thaddeus!" he called out, walking out of the escape pod.

"What, wh- holy shit, what are you wearing?" Thaddeus responded, tilting his head with confusion.

"It's a spacesuit. Come on. We don't have time to talk. I'm going to the Peacekeeper Residential Sector," Simon said.

Thaddeus understood after a moment of piecing it together, then looked at the Workers around them.

"Hey! Gather the other Defiants and meet me at the Peacekeeper Residential Sector. Gather as many as you can! We're ending this revolution!" Thaddeus shouted.

The Workers paused for a moment, then went to gather people.

Simon and Thaddeus were off, running as fast as Simon could go to the Residential Sector.

"Tools! Tools, I need tools," Simon said, stopping at a Tasking Station.

"They busted all the Tasking Stations, Simon," Thaddeus said.

Simon searched for buttons on the station and then snatched Thaddeus' taser baton. He began tearing and kicking the Tasking Station open, leaning down and zapping some circuits inside. It was useless. With a frustrated growl, Simon continued kicking and beating the Tasking Station; loud metal thunks heard before a loud metallic ting caused him to stop.

He leaned down and opened a lid, a pile of supplies and toolboxes falling out.

"Hah!" Simon let out.

He grabbed a toolbox he needed and began running with Thaddeus again, bolting down each turn arriving at the Residential Sector. They continued running until they came to one of the security doors leading into the Peacekeeper Residential Sector.

There were three bodies slumped on the floor around them, all of them Peacekeepers caught in the first rush of the revolution.

"Help me out here," Simon said.

The pair approached a body, heaving it up and carrying it through the door. Simon pushed the body's arm into the scanner of the door and watched as it beeped and opened the door. Air immediately began to be sucked into the sector. Simon walked through the door and turned around, gazing at Thaddeus. He nervously nodded to Thaddeus once, watching as the door closed in front of him.

"Good luck!" Thaddeus shouted.

Once more, Simon was alone. He was tired, exhausted to the point where his legs frequently wobbled and often lost balance. He was weak but determined. He was going to finish what the Leaders had started.

It was eerily silent here. Simon glanced into each room he passed, looking at all the corpses. His plan had killed so many, at least a hundred Peacekeepers laying dead in their beds or on the floor. He felt on edge. Simon looked around him as if the corpses would stand up and try to stop him.

He arrived at the vent that he had sabotaged. It was where Albert had betrayed him. Simon looked down the hall behind him, remembering the fifteen Peacekeepers that followed Albert. A spy. How had he never known? He felt like a fool.

Simon exhaled anxiously, and then turned to the vent and opened it. He crept into it and slid along inside of it. Inside the spacesuit, the vent felt stuffy and tight. He had to squeeze and inch his way through the vent, crawling to the circuits he had destroyed. Simon procured his toolbox and went to work.

This circuit connected here, this Ignium conductor put here, that melted wire removed and replaced. Simon felt pleased. His bad circuitry had worked perfectly. Still, a guilty feeling in the back of his mind nagged, Simon's memory flashing back to each suffocated corpse. With a final click and solder, the Ignium circuit guided energy correctly once more and air flooded into the Peacekeeper Residential Sector.

Simon crawled out of the air vent, his boots meeting the floor again with a quiet click. He slowly took off his helmet, breathing in the air that flooded into the area. Success. Simon walked across the sector, stopping at the security door and opening it. A loud cheer caused him to jump. On the other side of the door were dozens of Workers, Thaddeus at the front.

"He's fixed the air! Go! Go! Charge!" Thaddeus shouted. "For the Defiants!"

Simon joined the charge. They ran across the enter sector before arriving at a security door, using another body to open it.

"From behind! Go, go!" screamed one of the Peacekeepers inside.

The frenzied horde flooded the Command Sector. Simon cried out with Thaddeus, crashing into one of the Peacekeepers caught off guard. They pummeled the man, Thaddeus bringing his weapon down over and over until a puddle of blood formed beneath him. He panted and then helped Simon up.

"Come on, brother!" Thaddeus said.

Simon stood and joined Thaddeus again as they merged with the crazed horde. Ahead of them were formations of Peacekeepers, shields, and weapons ready as they marched forward. The Workers attacked relentlessly, flinging themselves at the shields and trying to rip them away from the Peacekeepers

Then the Peacekeepers began swinging, zapping and killing Workers and advancing.

"Move forward!" was heard from a Peacekeeper commander.

The tide shifted backward as the Workers realized they couldn't take this formation on. They threw their weapons at the Peacekeepers, people picking up chairs and other things to toss at them.

Simon looked around. The Command Center was beautiful and full of luxurious things. Each table, chair, and light was magnificent. He paused and looked at a table with a few plates on it. He was surprised to see a real steak on it, along with some delicious looking vegetables. The rumor was right; the Leaders did eat real food.

He felt enraged, joining Thaddeus and a few others to toss an entire glass table at the Peacekeepers. It knocked a few of them down, but before the Workers could take advantage of the attack, other Peacekeepers went around and held them at bay.

"Thaddeus, we're failing; what do we do?!" Simon asked.

His heart was beating insanely, sweat dripping from him as adrenaline coursed through him.

"Open fire!" barked a Peacekeeper commander.

"I don't know, we just gotta keep fi-' Thaddeus began.

The crowd screamed in terror as gunshots filled the sector, bullets piercing the crowd. Simon shielded himself, stumbling backward. Thaddeus did the same, abruptly falling to the ground as a bullet pierced his head. Simon gasped in horror, reaching out in vain.

"N-No! Thaddeus!" Simon cried out.

"Move forward!" the Peacekeepers shouted.

The formation continued forward, bullets whizzing past Simon. He couldn't stop to mourn his friend. Simon glanced at the oncoming Peacekeepers, then turned and ran with the escaping Workers. He ran as fast as he could, ignoring the cries of agony from his body.

"Break formation! Find and destroy!"

The Peacekeepers began to spread out, chasing the Workers as they fled. Simon ran with a few of his comrades. They couldn't stop and hide, a bunch of Peacekeepers hot on their trail. Simon glanced behind him. Workers beside him died one by one as bullets pierced them. He ducked and weaved, trying to avoid getting hit as the others fell.

They ran into the Development Sector, Simon bolting past lab equipment and using cover. The Peacekeepers charged in, blasting a bunch of Workers who leaped out to ambush them. Simon was petrified for a moment as he watched each body fall.

He got up and sprinted, being pushed by the oncoming Peacekeepers into one part of the Development Sector. In a panic, Simon sprinted into an escape pod and closed the door. He held it for a second before hearing thuds on the other side.

"You two! Get him out and kill him! The rest of you with me!"

Simon listened as they tried to open the door, then began trying to break it down. Simon looked around in a panic, running over to the front of the escape pod.

"No, no... Come on, come on..."

He scoured his mind, trying to remember everything he knew about the Arcadis. He pressed buttons, pushing until the escape pod lit up and hummed to life.

"Welcome," said an AI voice similar to Genetrix.

Simon listened to it as it began to speak, glancing back and paying little heed to the AI.

"Shut up!" he growled, pressing more buttons.

"Fucking get the door down! He's starting the pod!"

"Please insert coordinates," said the AI.

The two outside hammered harder at the door. Simon pressed another few buttons, listening to the AI call out a launch sequence. The hammering stopped, a loud thunk being heard from outside the door as another door covered the port.

"Takeoff initiated," the AI voice said.

Simon leaned his head back in relief. He had escaped the Peacekeepers. Then he let out a gasp. The pod had trapped him in as it prepared to go to Earth.

"Please strap in and prepare for launch,"

Simon's eyes widened as he inhaled sharply.

"W-Wait! Wait no! Stop!" Simon shouted, standing up and pressing more buttons.

Nothing worked. Simon ran down to the other end of the escape pod, trying to unlock the door. Futile.

"Takeoff in ten... Nine.... Eight..."

"Fuck! Fuck!" Simon said, looking around.

"Seven... Six..."

Simon screamed and ran to one of the front seats, strapping himself in.

"Five... Four... Three..."

He was hyperventilating, closing his eyes as he heard the AI countdown.

"Two... One... Takeoff."

Loud thrusters ignited behind the escape pod, pushing it forward before automatically directing it to Earth. Simon stared in awe as the polluted planet filled the front window, his breathing slowing until he stopped and just stared in complete astonishment. He had just lost one of his best friends, the other had betrayed him, and now he had lost his home.

There was no way he could stop the pod or no way he knew of. Simon sat there, trying to accept it. Everything was lost.

The pod smoothly traveled through the expanse of space, propelling him toward the alien planet. He had no idea what to expect.

Thirty minutes passed. Simon eventually gained the courage to leave his chair, walking around and trying to remember what he knew of Earth. Pollution filled the air, making it a toxic planet with little to no life. He needed food, water, and oxygen, all of which were here on the ship. Simon had his spacesuit but grabbed a gas mask and gun as well.

Eventually, after an hour, the ship's AI rang out again.

"Approaching Earth. Please buckle in and prepare for landing."

Simon immediately ran back to the chair and strapped himself in. Earth was now the only thing he could see through the windshield, the pollution haze coming closer and closer. The AI spoke as the pod got closer to the atmosphere, telling Simon how many kilometers away from the surface it was and how long it would take.

The pod rumbled and shook as it re-entered the atmosphere, a shockwave forming in front of the pod as friction built up. Soon, the intense temperatures rose, the inside of the pod becoming hot as Simon covered his face in terror. The AI continued to speak, thrusters outside helping to slow the pod before a huge parachute in the back opened up.

Simon opened his eyes, watching as the pod breached the pollution haze. It was thinner than he thought, the pod emerging below to the tremendous sight of Earth. There were oceans, mountains, and sandy deserts everywhere. He could see dust storms, clouds, and more as the pod continued to descend. Simon recognized the Americas as the surface drew closer. The pod directed itself toward North America, Simon realizing that those were the coordinates he accidentally put in.

The pod slowed down tremendously as the parachute and thrusters did their jobs. The AI spoke again.

"Prepare for landing."

Simon tensed up and prepared himself again as the Earth drew closer and closer.

"Landing in one minute."

"Oh God," Simon whispered.

"Ten, nine, eight, seven, six, five, four, three, two, one..."

The pod crashed into the Earth, Simon being thrown around in his chair as the pod slid through the Earth, abruptly rolling over as it hit something and tumbled for a few more yards.

Objects flew around inside. Simon shielded himself as the pod tumbled. He opened his eyes for a second, seeing a shape fly toward him. One moment he was looking at the shape, the next, everything was gone.

Advance

6:09 AM, September 8, 2100

Oliver ripped the tarp aside, revealing his motorcycle. Dust and sand came from it as it was disturbed, slowly settling on the ground. Oliver smiled. It was still in great condition since he last rode it.

"Is this it, sir?" asked the Patrian soldier beside him.

"This is it," Oliver said.

He walked around it, examining its beautiful shape for a moment before hopping on and starting it. The engine thundered to life as if it was a beast awakening from hibernation. Slowly, he moved forward with it and patted the back.

"Hop on, we gotta get back before the assault," Oliver stated.

The soldier nodded and got onto the back end, holding onto Oliver. He accelerated slowly at first, getting onto an old-world road before hitting it. In a matter of moments, Oliver was thundering across the wasteland, zipping past everything in the morning darkness.

"Holy shit!" screamed the soldier, holding tightly onto Oliver.

Oliver laughed ecstatically. It had been a while since he last rode the motorcycle, and it lifted his spirits. The recent few days had been a dark time for Patria. With the completion of the war machines, everyone was preparing for battle. Anxiety and worry filled the Patrians, and Oliver had never felt more stress.

"This is power!!" Oliver shouted as the terrified soldier clung to him.

The spot where Oliver hid his motorcycle disappeared in seconds. Each ancient billboard or power pole went past just the same, the motorcycle soon carrying Oliver to the old world town he had looted with Sam. The motorcycle shot through between the old world ruins, going through the town in under two minutes and leaving it behind.

They were again in the wasteland. The wind blew on Oliver as he drove, moving along the twists and turns of the road. Eventually, he went off the road. A cloud of dust followed behind him as he drove over the dunes, heading straight for Patria.

As he drove, Oliver whooped and cheered in excitement. He couldn't wait to see the expressions on his soldier's faces as he arrived at full speed.

"S-Sir?! Should we slow down?!"

"Relax! We're almost there!"

Oliver sped through the territory of Patria, driving past an empty outpost. After a few minutes of bolting across the wasteland, he arrived at the tunnel leading into Patria. Oliver came to a gradual stop, looking around as he arrived.

The Patrians were already assembling. Out of a population of over a hundred and twenty people, seventy could fight. Each one was armed and ready for warfare. Sam and Mary were already out with them, Sam grinning as he watched some Patrians get onto his war machines. He had made a total of fifteen.

Each one was small and fast, capable of safely carrying two people. Oliver thought they looked like old-world ATVs protected by scrap metal. As he rolled over, Mary got on one and gazed at him.

"Welcome back, Oliver," Sam said.

"Good to be back, especially on this baby."

The soldier riding with Oliver slowly stumbled off.

"Holy shit..." he whispered.

"Took him for a ride, huh?" Mary asked, chuckling

"I probably went over ninety," Oliver said as he laughed aloud.

"Not funny!" the soldier said, to which the three leaders burst out cackling. After a few moments of laughter, they all calmed down.

"It's a scary day. I don't know how these machines will do," Sam said.

"Don't say that; you'll make everyone nervous. They'll run fine." Mary told him.

"Does everyone know what we have to do?" Oliver asked.

"Yes. The people on foot will go first and wait for us. Once there, we'll drive into the camp with the machines and start causing havoc. As we do that, the soldiers on foot will push in and destroy everything. With surprise and our combined efforts, we should be able to scatter the Outsiders into the wasteland," Mary detailed.

"Flawless," Sam remarked.

"If it works, we finish the war," Oliver said.

"All right, I'll stay behind. We still need leadership in Patria, and in case anything happens," Sam said.

"Smart," Mary stated. "We'll be back in no time. Hopefully, we'll be back with all the supplies that the Outsiders have stolen from us."

"Is everything ready?" Oliver asked.

"Should be. Is it time?" Mary said.

Oliver nodded and walked in front of their entire fighting force.

"Patrians!! Today is the day of our victory! We will finally secure the wasteland for ourselves and destroy the Outsiders!" Oliver shouted.

"I know you've all experienced loss and are worried about today! But don't worry! You are Patrians! We are strong together! Don't let the sacrifices of the past be in vain! Trust in one another, and we will secure a better future for Patria!"

"For Patria!" Oliver shouted, raising a fist.

"For Patria! For Patria! For Patria!" they shouted.

Oliver smiled and lowered his fist, walking over to Sam.

"You still suck," Sam snickered.

Oliver grinned.

"You do better, then," he replied.

Mary looked at them and shook her head, walking over to their small army.

"You know what you all have to do! Soldiers on foot go first! Do not attack until the war machines arrive!" Mary shouted. "Move out!"

As she gave the command, the Patrian foot soldiers began walking. There was no order as they moved, not like soldiers in the old world who marched. They weren't truly soldiers. They were just survivors, fighting for home and family. Oliver watched them walk out into the wasteland, a worried frown on his face as they did.

"When do we go?" Oliver asked.

"In a while. The soldiers have to get there first; then we come in after. It'll all happen fast, and the machines are loud, so we need all the surprise we can get," Mary told him.

Oliver nodded and got onto his bike again, looking at the line of war machines before him. Each one had two armed Patrians and carried a good amount of firebombs. He gazed at all the weaponry. Oliver wondered how many Outsiders they would kill today, and he wondered how many Patrians would die.

As he stared at them, the soldier from before and Sam walked up to his motorcycle. The soldier got on with a reluctant sigh, while Sam went up to Oliver.

"Be careful out there, Oliver," he said.

"I always am. I'm just worried about everyone else. They are what make up Patria, and if they fail, then Patria could go with them. So much work for nothing, you know?"

"They're fighting for you and Patria. It's sort of a dream they share with you. Don't worry. I got enough firebombs to level a city on these war machines," Sam told him.

"And the soldiers know how they work?"

"Yep, just pull the trigger and toss 'em before they cook your hands."

"Simple enough," Oliver said.

"I really do hope you guys win. If the war ends, everything will be how it was before. No more unstable leadership, no more infighting, and no more fear."

Oliver glanced at Sam for a moment as he talked about leadership.

"No more death," Oliver added, "Everyone in the wasteland will come to Patria to be safe. No more risking their lives out here trying to survive off of other people."

"Yeah, one people, one leadership, as it should be," Sam said.

"Yeah," Oliver said quietly, disliking Sam's tone.

As Oliver moved to speak again, Mary stood on her war machine.

"All right, everyone! Let's take it slow and move out! When the Outsiders' home comes into view, full speed ahead! Light as many fires as possible! Every kill counts!" Mary commanded.

"For Patria!" the soldiers shouted in reply.

The air filled with the thunderous sounds of Ignium engines, all of which were drowned by the power of Oliver's motorcycle as its engine came to life.

"Good luck, Oliver!" Sam said, grinning and winking at him.

"Thanks, man..." Oliver said.

To Oliver, the wink was strange. Regardless, he moved the motorcycle to the front of all the machines. The soldiers began to follow him as they left Patria behind, Oliver glancing one last time back toward Sam. Sam stood there, waving them goodbye. Oliver shook his head, driving over the dunes as the tunnel to Patria disappeared.

"How far away is it, sir?!" asked the soldier hugging Oliver.

"On foot about forty minutes. It'll take us at this speed around twenty!"

The soldier paused. "How long would it take us if we went full speed?!"

"What? You wanna go full speed?"

He stuttered.

"N-No, sir! Just curious!"

"Probably five minutes or so? Have you been out to their territory?"

"No, sir! I usually join the patrols around our territory!"

"They live in tents around an old warehouse in the middle of the wasteland!" Oliver told him.

"An old warehouse?"

"Yeah! We're gonna burn their tents! They hide in the warehouse during Doomstorms, so if we burn everything down, they have nowhere to go!"

"Sounds good, sir!"

The war machines followed him, some of the Patrians whooping and cheering as they went along. Oliver glanced back occasionally. Many of these Patrians were young and had never ridden in cars or old-world vehicles.

These war machines were foreign to them and felt like race cars even though they were slow.

After a while of driving, they caught up to the infantry. They were all running by the time the machines got there, charging toward their destination. In the far distance, Oliver could see the warehouse surrounded by tents. That was perfect. He glanced back and signaled to Mary, who nodded and stood up.

She began to wave her hand in a circle, signaling for the drivers to go full speed ahead. Oliver shot forward on the motorcycle, the war machines following as they raced to the warehouse. He left them behind easily, Railshot Rifle ready and mounted on the front of his motorcycle.

"Are you ready?!" he shouted.

"Yes, sir!"

"Let's kill some Outsiders!!"

Separation

4:23 AM, April 13, 2156

It had been over a year since the battle. London still clearly remembered the screams and terror of warfare, the primal fear instilled in the last moments of someone struggling to live. He recalled all the deaths he had witnessed, especially Finlay's death. The moment of blood spraying out of his body was ingrained in London's mind, always there to remind him in the darkness of night.

London laid silently beneath the inadequate shelter of the tent shared by him and three others. He stared straight ahead, a thousand-yard stare upon his face. He, along with the three other men in the tent, was a prisoner of war. Each of them was from New Uruk, sharing the same fate as many other unlucky soldiers. London was the only person from the caravan that had survived for so long as a prisoner.

He glanced at all three of them. Like him, they wore thin hide clothes that provided little protection against the rough sand, toxic air, and the cold. All of them, including London, had irritated and burned skin. They also had gas masks, though they were terrible. Most of them were old gas masks, given to them by Patrians who had broken them or worn them down. Because of the condition of his gas mask, London's lungs constantly stung, and he coughed often.

With a long sigh, London ran his fingers down the frame of his body. He was incredibly thin, no longer the strong forty-year-old man who heaved and lifted heavy boxes for the caravans. Instead, London was a beaten and bruised

225

slave. His fingers danced around his ribs, sliding across his malnourished flesh.

A few coughs escaped from his mouth as he tried to sleep. For most of his life, London had had nightmares that kept him up. Many were from memories of being chased or attacked, moments of pure fear. Now, fresh memories of horror were what kept him awake. Flayed bodies, dead children, all of it tormented him. Every image was lucid, a dancing demon on his mind.

"Wake up!!" shouted a voice.

London startled awake, immediately sitting up in response to the voice. The other three war prisoners did the same, following London out of the tent and into the embrace of the morning sun. It was windy today. The sands kicked up high, coursing and dancing through wasteland grass.

The camp was already being taken down and packed, prisoners from two other tents emerging after London did. Altogether, there were twelve of them. The Patrians were quick to line them up, two overseers beating and whacking them as the prisoners obeyed orders. London looked around as they lined up.

There were twelve prisoners and around fifty armed Patrian soldiers. London had learned during the months spent in Patria that there was a main army currently used to fight New Uruk, and then hundreds of raid groups. Some of these raid groups consisted of soldiers in training, generally staying within the borders of Patria and keeping the nation safe from invaders.

Raid groups sent to rove the wasteland consisted of trained and veteran soldiers. These groups either attacked settlements or hit the back lines of Patria's enemies. The group that attacked London's caravan was one of these raid groups. The group London was in now was one of the raid groups that patrolled Patria.

"At attention!" shouted one of the overseers.

The prisoners stood at attention, waiting as the Patrians prepared to leave. The Patrians didn't tell the prisoners where they'd go today or what work they'd do. Instead, they told them to wait. Once the group was ready to leave, they began marching in a single line, following the Patrians.

London shuffled with his comrades. His head lowered meekly like the other prisoners. The winds blew sand and toxins against them, threatening to throw their weak bodies across the earth. They were stubborn, keeping their footing as strong as their wills.

Walking through Patrian territory felt eerie to London. It was vast and sparse, a huge conquered territory that was triple the size of New Uruk's territory. Spread throughout were villages and military outposts that consisted of half-buried buildings designed to withstand Doomstorms. At the center of it all was Patria's capital, a city surrounding an underground fortress.

London was curious about what the capital looked like compared to New Uruk, though the Patrians never took him there. Instead, he was dragged around Patria and forced to do labor. For London, the days droned by and became a blur. The only time he could recall a day being different from the last is when something grotesque stood out in his memory.

"Walk faster!" screamed an overseer.

The prisoners shuffled faster in response to the command, every one of them staring at the ground to avoid a beating. There was not a hint of hope or defiance in any of them, especially London. He only wanted to stay alive. London had one hope that kept him going; the hope that one day a Patrian would make a mistake and he'd get his chance to escape. That day was far off, but London was patient.

The group carried on until they found a road of stones, going in two directions. The leader of the group ordered them north and further into Patrian territory.

No one paid too much attention to a row of flayed war prisoners lined beside the road as they walked, each prisoner erected as a warning. London glanced at each corpse. Each body spread out like a starfish, their limbs attached by ropes to wooden poles and their backs flayed open. In the flesh and in their eyes crawled flies and maggots, feasting on the decay. London had seen bodies like this so many times that it barely fazed him as he kept walking.

London knew what was going to happen as they walked. He had heard from the Patrians that there was a new military outpost in the area. This meant one thing for London: road work. It wasn't the worst form of labor, but it was still terrible. For another twenty minutes, they shuffled. The group was slow, moving beneath the rising sun as they followed the sand-covered stones making up the road.

Eventually, they arrived at a fork on the right. The leader of the raid group took the left turn, leading them across more stones until the road disappeared into the sand. There were already three other groups here, bringing two hundred slaves and Patrian soldiers to build the road.

A shovel was shoved into London's hand immediately as they arrived. A moment after, a new overseer came and directed them to the construction site. The sound of picks, shovels, and grunting filled the air as London joined the workforce. He questioned nothing, functioning like a weak machine as he began to clear out dirt and make way for stones.

Every road led to Patria.

London's body agonized as he sweated and grunted, moving the shovel back and forth to move the dirt. Every time London slowed, someone hit him.

"Keep working!"

"Let's go! Move those stones!"

When London wasn't shoveling, he was carrying stones or using a pickax. He ignored his legs when they burned and tried his best to disregard how hungry he was. There were no breaks. It was all hopeless, endless torment which bruised and bloodied him. Still, London kept going. All he needed was one thought to keep walking, one thought to keep working, and one thought to keep fighting: the thought of Rose.

Meanwhile, in New Uruk, the city was buzzing as the morning market came to life. People started trading or went to their jobs, working in factories, doing construction, or many more jobs all around the city. In one apartment, the morning had just begun.

Rose jumped slightly as the mechanical clicking of the spider wheelchair entered the room.

"Good morning, Rose," Margaret said.

"Good morning to you, too, Miss Margaret," Rose responded.

"Oh, dear, you don't have to call me Miss."

"Sorry," Rose whispered.

"No need to be sorry," Margaret told her. "I see you made breakfast?"

"Yes!" Rose said with a smile. "I made something with the veggies from the greenhouse down the street and some meat from Jeff."

Margaret smiled and moved her spider chair to the dining table, examining the plate of food at her spot.

"Looks wonderful, dearie!" Margaret said. "Jeff gave us quite the deal on those cuts."

Rose looked at her empty plate, waiting as Margaret moved her mask and slowly began to eat.

"Did you see where Reginald went?"

"He went out early to join the water caravan," Rose told her.

"That man is hankering to get shot with those no 'count Patrians pushing closer every day. I reckon he'll be fine; Reginald's never been a yaller dog," Margaret said. "Sho' nuff, I'm sure he'd try to send them Patrians running back home if he could."

Rose giggled.

"Are we gonna go trade today?" Rose asked.

"Yes. We have that deal with Riley today. If that varmint has any horse sense, he'd best give good deals."

"Didn't he try to scam Reginald?" Rose asked, raising a brow.

"Yes, he did. Reginald gave him an old fashioned whooping for it," Margaret said with a grin.

"I'll make sure to give him a whooping if he tries to scam us!" Rose declared, giggling with Margaret.

Margaret soon finished her meal, putting her oxygen mask back on. Rose quickly took the dishes and put them away, joining Margaret as the spider wheelchair strode to the door. As they got to the door, Rose opened it for Margaret.

"Thank you, dear," Margaret said.

Margaret and Reginald's apartment was on the second floor of the apartment building, right beside one of the busiest markets in New Uruk. Lately, with the war encroaching on the city, merchants had been trying to sell their entire stock. For Rose, Margaret, and Reginald, it was a prosperous time.

Rose was hopeful that the war would turn in New Uruk's favor and knew the benefit of buying up everyone's stock before it did. Margaret had told her that when the war ends, they could sell everything back for a much higher price. The idea excited Rose. She remembered how she started a business, practicing trade deals with kids in her neighborhood while London was off doing caravan work.

London. Rose gazed at the ground sadly as they went down the stairs. She was eleven now, and it had been four days since her birthday. London wasn't there, and he wasn't there for her last birthday. It had been a year and a half since she learned about the fate of London's caravan.

She grew stronger with age, more intelligent, and mature. Regardless, she still cried at night thinking about him. In her heart and thoughts, London was still there, helping her grow up and comforting her when she cried. Even so, all she wanted was to hug him one more time.

"What's wrong, dear?" Margaret asked as they walked out into the busy street right outside their apartment building.

Rose shook her head a little.

"Thinking about London again?" Margaret asked.

Rose didn't answer. Margaret stopped her wheelchair, gently grabbing Rose and hugging her.

"Oh, I understand, dear. It's okay. I'm sure he'd be very proud of you if he were to see you now."

Rose stopped herself from crying, silently hugging Margaret for a while before nodding.

"I'm okay..." she whispered. "It's still hard."

"I know, dear. I know what it's like to experience loss. It never really leaves you, but it helps remind you how much you love him. It reminds you so that you never forget about him. Remember, dear, he'll always be with you, right there," Margaret said, pointing to her heart.

Rose nodded in understanding. Margaret smiled and started the wheelchair up again.

"Come on; I'm sure Riley's waiting with something rotten."

Rose walked side by side with Margaret as they went through the busy street. As they did, almost everyone stopped to greet Margaret. The population of New Uruk respected her, both for her status as an elder and for her status as a great trader. Some people even greeted Rose, many people calling her "Trader Mouse."

"Hello, Miss Margaret!" said one woman.

"Good day to y'all!" said a man.

"Stay strong out there, Trader Mouse!" said Jeff, their meat vendor.

The pair carried on through the busy streets, soon turning and arriving into an alleyway. This alleyway already had some people in it. A few tents and tarps setups held various small businesses. Rose glanced at the traders and merchants as they walked by, catching pieces of conversation between them and their merchants.

Eventually, they arrived at a large stall covered in lights. It was like a tent. Surrounding it were shelves, making up the walls with a small entrance that led inside. Inside of it were some small tables and a large, main table. The pair moved inside, Margaret taking it slowly as the wheelchair barely squeezed through the entrance.

"Ah! My two favorite people!"

Rose's expression immediately soured as she saw Riley. He had an arrogant air about him as he sat opposite them on a chair, his boots resting on the table in front of him.

"How are you guys?" he asked.

"We're doing well, thanks for asking," Margaret said, keeping her tone cordial.

Rose walked into the tent, looking around at the bookshelves and tables. Junk laid everywhere, particularly consisting of shiny things. Lights, glass, old-world screens, and tech, it was all there.

"Take a seat, take a seat!" Riley said, overly friendly.

Margaret quickly shot him a dirty look as Rose sat down on the only available chair across from Riley.

"Oop, sorry," he said, awkwardly smiling.

"I have no time to waste, so let's get to this lickety-split," Margaret said, marching her wheelchair right up beside Rose.

"Right! Right! What was it that you wanted again?"

Margaret was quiet.

"R-Right, the Ignium cores," Riley started.

"How many of them?" Margaret asked.

Riley leaned forward and put his elbows on the table, looking at the two.

"Four, of course. You didn't think I'd forget?"

Rose glared.

"You have four, right?" Rose asked.

"Right here," Riley said. "One, two, three, and four!"

As he spoke, he turned around and grabbed the Ignium cores from behind him. They were large, round batteries that weighed around ten pounds. Each one had a gray metal body with four glowing blue strips going down from the top. Riley let out a grunting sound as he moved each, placing them on the table with a thud.

"Tada! Four Ignium cores, fit to power any engine or household!" Riley stated.

Margaret and Rose looked over them. From the bottom to the middle, the light strips glowed brightly, growing duller toward the top.

"Riley, I'm fit to be tied," Margaret said with a displeased tone.

"W-What?"

Rose immediately planted her knife between his fingers, missing his flesh by only an inch.

"They're not fully charged!" Rose growled.

Riley immediately pulled back.

"Holy shit! Control your kid!"

"Don't you tell me what to do with her, Riley. I knew you were a fool after you tried to scam Reginald, and now you try to scam us? You think I was going to pay four hundred filters for half-charged Ignium cores?"

"No, no! I didn't know they were half-charged!" Riley said.

"Don't lie to me, Riley. You're a worse liar than you are a scammer! The only reason we trade with a varmint like you is because you can get items that other merchants don't sell. Now, if you ain't lookin' for a whooping from little Rose here, I'd suggest you better fix these cores."

"All right, All right! I ain't looking to get stabbed. I'll fix 'em!"

Rose pulled her knife out of the table, a smug grin under her mask.

Terra

Simon slowly opened his eyes, letting out a loud, pained groan as his consciousness returned. He sat there for a few moments. It took him a while to figure out where he was, his eyes scanning the interior of the escape pod. Slowly, he undid the safety straps tying him to his chair, and fell to the floor.

"Gah!" he blurted out.

He huffed and breathed heavily, gradually working his way to his feet and stumbling across the escape pod. Simon fell onto another seat, landing with a thud and releasing another groan.

"F-Fuck... Come on, Simon," he told himself.

Food. That was the first thing he needed. Simon slowly shifted over to one of the containers he had searched during his journey to Earth, opening one and digging in it desperately. Like a starving raccoon, he tore and pulled at a few food and water containers, savagely devouring everything and gasping in relief after.

"Oh... Thank God..." he whispered.

For a while, Simon sat and recovered. Occasionally, the escape pod would shift or make a noise. Outside, there was a continuous howling sound, a deep and quiet sound that Simon never heard. Eventually, Simon recuperated and stood. His spacesuit was hot and stuffy, sweat pouring from him as he grabbed a gas mask and put it on.

The sounds outside continued. Simon glanced at the windshield, seeing that the escape pod was half-buried in the ground. He couldn't see out. A weapon, he needed a weapon. Simon walked around the interior of the pod, slowly gathering supplies. Out of one container, he grabbed a bag. In another, he procured food and water that he stuffed into the bag. Finally, he opened a heavy, metallic container.

Inside was a set of weapons, either Ignium powered or regular, gunpowder weapons. It seemed that the creators of the Arcadis were ready for their descendants to return to a hostile Earth. He grabbed a gun, a heavy energy rifle with a few Ignium charges for ammo, examining it for a moment.

It was a white weapon that was sturdy, a glowing white circle above the trigger telling Simon that it was at full charge. He recognized the model of the gun. It was the kind that would super heat matter using Ignium inside of an insulated chamber, melting it and then sending it out at the speed of a bullet. Simon knew it was a very dangerous weapon that could both melt faces and cover.

Simon, with his new weapon, felt brave. He put a bag around his shoulders and approached the door. He was nervous. What was outside? What dangers did Earth hold? He couldn't imagine it. Before he left, he secured his gas mask tightly to his face. Simon was shaking as he reached for the control panel for the door, slowly pressing a button and listening to the door open.

His breathing intensified as the door slid open, and he took his first steps into the great unknown. Immediately, the light of the sun piercing through the pollution haze blinded him. As his eyes adjusted, Simon's jaw dropped in awe.

The wasteland met Simon in its full glory. Around him were rolling hills of sandy wasteland, along with the occasional ruin from the old world. To his surprise, there was yellow grass everywhere and small, weed-like blooms seen throughout the rolling landscape. Simon listened. The howling he heard in the pod was wind, currents of sand dancing among the waving stalks of yellow grass. He had never heard wind before.

He blinked and looked up. He had never seen clouds from below or stood on dry, sandy soil as he did now. Simon was astonished, so amazed that he could barely take it all in. That's what the sky looked like, that's what the sun looks like from down here, and that's what grass is like. Slowly, Simon began to walk away from the escape pod. He closed the door and gave it a farewell, hoping to come back.

For now, Simon needed help. He held his gun, ready for anything. He didn't know what to expect here in the wasteland. Were there still humans? Were there animals out to eat his flesh? Simon carried on over hills and plains, weakly moving each leg and taking in his surroundings.

Soon, the ground beneath Simon became harder, causing him to pause. With a few kicks of his boots, he unearthed a cracked, asphalt road. He knew some about roads, how they were used by cars to travel from city to city in the old world. After a moment of thought, he decided to follow it.

Sometimes an old, dead tree stood alone in the landscape. Other times, there would be a collapsed ruin of some forgotten building. Rarely, Simon saw shapes in the distance, wild animals that passed him with little more than a glance. So far, none had attacked him. They were living proof to Simon that Earth was habitable, but he didn't know how breathable the air was and didn't dare to test it.

Simon gazed at the occasional, small body of water hidden among the rolling hills. Each one was an oasis, greenish plant life surrounding each one that he saw. Simon wondered how toxic the water was. Soon, he approached one and stared at the murky, green water in front of him.

He had never seen a body of water up close, the only sight he could compare to being the sights of Earth's oceans from space. Simon timidly reached his foot to the water. He kicked some of it onto the dry sand and stepped back.

"Heh... That's cool," he whispered.

After gawking at the water, Simon carried on exploring the desert wasteland. He had little skill in navigating, but he was smart enough to try and leave a trail of breadcrumbs behind him to the escape pod. Sometimes, he grabbed a rock and piled it with other rocks or planted a stick or a rusted metal post straight up in the ground. It required a lot of effort from him, but he was not willing to get lost.

Simon walked for a while. He stopped as he spotted some weird shapes in the distance. After a moment, Simon approached them with his gun ready.

As the distant haze made way for him as he walked, he gradually made out what those shapes were. They were houses. Simon's feet began to move a little quicker as he approached them, his heart beating excitedly. Would there be people here? Would they welcome him?

Eventually, he got to the first house and stared with broken hope.

"No... No..." he whispered.

It was a ruined house, something from the old world that had piles of sand against it. The windows had blown in, and the front door was on the ground, buried in sand. Simon slowly approached the house and entered, gun ready. It was empty. There was sand everywhere, piled up on old tile and carpeted floors. The house creaked and groaned, an old ancient standing against the winds.

He stepped out of the house after searching it, admiring the strange architecture of the old world. Was this really how people used to live? Simon walked back out to the road and looked around. Occasional fence posts stood between the houses. He was unsure if this was one of the old world suburban neighborhoods or just a collection of houses.

"Hello?! Is anyone out there?!" he called out.

Nothing. There was only an eerie silence. The world seemed empty, quiet, and alone. It was as if Simon was the only human on Earth, left alone with only animals and patches of yellow grass. It felt hopeless. He fell to his knees, reaching down and picking up a handful of sand.

Simon had lost everything. His childhood friend had betrayed him. His other best friend had died; he had lost his home and everything he owned. Simon had nothing except for the supplies from the escape pod. Maybe this was better than the Arcadis. Nobody would beat him here, or order him around, or treat him like an animal.

It took him a while to accept it all. Simon contemplated the idea of creating a farm and living out the end of his days by himself in one of these houses. No, no, that wouldn't do. Not yet. Simon scraped up the last of his strength and hope and continued forward down the road. As he walked, more and more houses began to appear, soon mixing with old buildings like restaurants and power stations.

He glanced up at some ancient street lights as he walked, squinting at them and trying to understand what they were. As he walked, Simon realized that he was approaching a city. In the distance, there were the silhouettes of skyscrapers. Ruined houses were everywhere, the remains of a suburban neighborhood enveloping him.

Simon stopped in front of a rusted automobile frame, examining it and trying to figure it out. He had learned about old-world cars a long time ago, and the memory faintly appeared in his imagination as he recalled it. To him, it was a strange and alien thing, made even more alien by the hostile environment.

He continued walking, moving beneath the remains of a few leafless trees and looking at each one of them. Simon had seen images of trees before and felt a little saddened by each dead one that he passed.

Abruptly, something clicked under his right foot. His right leg was pulled out from under him, Simon falling back and hitting the ground before being dragged upward.

The fall was hard, and the world once again became black as his consciousness left instantly.

Blood

The motorcycle sped across the wasteland soil, thundering toward the camp. As it did, Oliver heard a fiery explosion behind him. He glanced back. His eyes widened as he saw the explosion, bits of flame raining everywhere. One of the machines had exploded, killing both of the riders.

"Sir?! What do we do, sir?!" asked the soldier, clinging to him.

"Nothing! We can't do anything!" Oliver said.

"S-Sir?!"

"Eyes on the prize!"

Oliver sped toward the camp. People ran in panic as the attack began. Some were panicking, some were moving for refuge, and most were getting ready to defend themselves. Oliver aimed the Railshot Rifle as he drove toward the tents and the defenders, ready to punch a hole to race through.

It felt as if everything slowed down as he drove. Oliver felt his heart beating, the motorcycle thundering, and the excited breaths of the soldier behind him. Oliver aimed for a few surprised men, exhaling and pulling the trigger as he came toward them.

Sparks flew from the rifle as the metal left it, each shard flying through the air. The men were shredded by the metal, blood spraying everywhere as they fell to the ground. Oliver bolted past them, driving into the camp. People were running everywhere in panic as he arrived. It was perfect. Oliver saw the chaos as a plan coming together; with the Patrians losing the war, the Outsiders did not expect any attacks on their main base.

Oliver shot the rifle over and over again. Metal flew everywhere as people dropped dead from the deadly scrap. Each shard pierced through tents, barricades, boxes, everything. As Oliver shot, he sped around the camp as fast as possible, attempting to cause havoc.

Another fiery explosion echoed in the distance. Oliver didn't look back. Instead, he continued to drive around the camp, blasting through tents and killing Outsiders. All the killing was bloody and brutal, though the only part Oliver relished was revenge. It felt good to pay back for all the dead Patrians, and it felt good to secure a future for his people.

As he drove around, the war machines finally arrived. Thirteen war machines raced between the tents, soldiers on each machine throwing firebombs as they did. Soon, the foot soldiers followed. Screams filled the air as the Patrian assault descended like a flood, rushing into the camp like a frenzied horde.

Any defense the enemy had crashed down in futility. As the lit fires raged and consumed tent after tent, thick smoke filled the air. Corpses and blood were everywhere. Oliver continued blasting people with his rifle until it ran out of ammo. As he tried to reload it, he saw a shape out of the corner of his eye.

Abruptly, he ducked. Oliver heard the wind cut above him, a gurgling sound following it and ending with a thud. He turned around only to see a corpse. The soldier that had ridden with him now had a hatchet in his neck. Blood oozed from his neck as he writhed for a moment silently before falling limp.

"N-No!!" Oliver shouted.

He hopped off the bike to try and help the soldier, grabbing his limp body and looking him over. It was too late. The ax had hit hard and fast, quickly ending his life with a clean cleave. Oliver swore in rage. As he held the body, a woman ran at him while waving another hatchet and screaming.

Oliver shot up immediately as she got close, hitting her right in the mask with his gun before she could swing.

She flew off her feet, Oliver leaping on top of her. He was merciless. Over and over again, he smashed her mask in with the gun, cracking the glass and breaking her bones. He didn't stop as he heard the bones break. Oliver continued hitting until she stopped moving, letting out a vengeful scream as he hit one last time.

Oliver panted and stood with a wobble. He gazed at her mangled face, staring at the blood-stained glass of her broken gas mask. He didn't feel guilty over killing her. She had tried to kill him and had killed another Patrian, so Oliver told himself it was justice.

Another fiery explosion occurred as he stood there.

"Sir!! Oliver, sir!" a soldier shouted.

Oliver gasped and straightened up, gun ready as a Patrian ran up to him.

"Sir, are you all right?"

"I'm fine," Oliver hissed. "What's going on?"

Oliver looked around as he spoke. Patrians were everywhere, shooting and killing. Some had gotten into melee combat, brutally butchering people just as Oliver did to the woman. In the rush of battle, they were just like him.

"We're winning, sir. They have no defense, and we got into the warehouse before they could block it off."

"Get their leader. I want him dead, and anyone who defends him," Oliver commanded.

"Yes, sir," the soldier began, pausing for a moment, "Sir?"

"What?"

"Mary's dead. Some of the machines fell apart and exploded," the soldier told him.

Oliver stared at the soldier, trying to process what he just heard.

"Go," Oliver said.

"Sir?"

"Go!!"

The soldier backed up and ran off to join the fray. Meanwhile, Oliver reloaded his Railshot Rifle and looked around. Mary was dead. He couldn't believe it. Sam's war machine killed her. Oliver paused as paranoia took him. Maybe that's what the wink meant. Maybe Sam had somehow rigged her war machine to explode so he could eliminate one of the leaders of Patria, and then he could kill Oliver to become the sole ruler.

Oliver asked himself if Sam would do that. He was unsure. He kept thinking about the wink and all the fights they had during meetings. Oliver remembered the distrust, the foul glances, and the stress of leadership. He decided he would find out himself.

He raised the newly loaded Railshot Rifle and jumped into the battle once more. Soldiers rallied to him as they rushed to kill every Outsider, joining his charge toward the warehouse. As he ran, Oliver took in the carnage. The heat from all the fires baked the air, paired with the smell of cooked meat as the flames engulfed corpses.

The screaming never seemed to stop. The attack was ruthless, and it seemed that only a few Patrians had died during the whole thing. Oliver burst into the warehouse as other soldiers followed him. Immediately, fire met him. Other Patrians had already broken in there, all of them already fire-bombing the tents inside and murdering people who had fled into the building.

Oliver joined them, beginning to shoot his gun. The deadly metal scrap flew again, going through tents, flesh, and out the walls of the warehouse. As he took down Outsider after Outsider, the Patrians began to grab people from a large tent. Each person was dragged, beaten, and taken outside.

"Patrians!" Oliver shouted. "Take their supplies and burn the rest! For Patria!"

The soldiers heard him and chanted.

"For Patria! For Patria!"

Oliver followed the Patrians, who captured some of the Outsiders, leaving the warehouse and escaping the smoke.

"Outsider scum!"

"What should we do with them?"

Oliver walked to the Patrians with the Outsiders. There were four Outsiders, all of them struggling against the overwhelming group of thirteen Patrians.

"Hold on!" Oliver commanded. "Line them up."

The Patrians looked at him before picking up each Outsider. They lined them up, keeping them on their knees and holding their heads up. Oliver approached them, gazing through each gas mask. All of them had hateful expressions, growling in pain as the Patrians held them still.

"Who are these Outsiders?" he asked his men.

"We took them from a big tent, sir. There were plans and maps in there; we think it was where they planned attacks on us. One of these four could be the leader."

"Which one of you is the leader?" Oliver asked.

They didn't respond.

"Who is your leader?!" Oliver shouted, smacking one with the end of his gun.

The man Oliver struck groaned.

"Who is it?!"

"Me," said one of them.

Oliver stared at the man who spoke. He had an old-world gas mask with a wide visor and wore tough leather clothes. Underneath his mask were gray hairs and scars. He seemed old and looked like he grew up in the old world. Oliver didn't consider this. Instead, he focused on extermination.

"Lay him on the ground," Oliver commanded.

"W-What are you doing?" the man asked.

Oliver walked up to him, Railshot Rifle ready.

"You won't get away with this, bastard tyrant!" the man shouted as he struggled.

Oliver pointed the Railshot Rifle down, quickly pulling the trigger.

He closed his eyes as gore splattered everywhere. The man's head, neck, and shoulders became nothing as Oliver shot the rifle. As he opened his eyes with a cold expression, he felt no guilt. The Patrian men holding the man down let go of his body, backing up in slight horror.

"Kill the other three," Oliver said.

He turned away from them, beginning to walk back to his motorcycle. As he did, he heard three gunshots echo behind him.

Oliver went through the camp. Most of the tents had collapsed from the flames, falling upon charred corpses and destroyed supplies. Oliver checked his Smartwrist. The assault had only lasted for an hour. In one attack, they had ended the war and brought a peaceful, Patrian reign over the wasteland. He had a thin smile over their success.

As he mounted his motorcycle, he looked at the corpse of the soldier who had volunteered to go with him. He sighed mournfully. Slowly, Oliver looked around at some of the war machines that had exploded during the attack. He gazed at the burned corpses around them, a vengeful rage coming over him.

Sam was behind this. Oliver had a feeling that he had rigged Mary's machine to explode and was hoping that Oliver would die to the Outsiders. That's what the wink meant, and that's why he stayed behind. Oliver wouldn't have it. The motorcycle thundered once more to life as Oliver started it and turned it around.

He left the destruction behind, glancing back only once to see a huge pillar of smoke. Soon, the motorcycle was speeding back across the wasteland. This time Oliver didn't have his army following. He went as fast as possible with the motorcycle, going through the wasteland in ten minutes.

The motorcycle came to a stop in front of the bunker entrance. Oliver hopped off, Railshot Rifle ready.

"Oliver?"

The few guards placed at the entrance were surprised to see him.

"Where's Sam?!" he asked viciously, spitting Sam's name out.

"We don't know, sir! He's inside, but that's all we know!"

Oliver proceeded to walk past them, moving past the metal doors and into the halls of Patria. He ignored everyone he walked past, searching every hall and room. Sam wasn't in the atrium or the agricultural wing.

"Sam!! Where are you?!"

Oliver shouted for Sam as he walked around.

"I'm right here, Oliver,"

Oliver paused as he entered the room that Sam had turned into a mechanic's shop. There, right in front of him, was Sam. He was holding a wrench and gazed at him with a plain expression.

"You rigged those machines, didn't you? So you would kill Mary? Thin out our assault a little, so I'd die too?"

"What?"

"Don't tell me those were accidents. You're better at your work than that."

Sam stared at him with wide eyes, slowly moving forward. Oliver eyed his every movement, slowly readying his gun. Abruptly, the wrench in Sam's hand was flying toward Oliver, hitting him in the mask. The visor cracked with a crunch as it hit Oliver. Sam ran toward him and swung a fist, only for Oliver to smack him away with his gun.

He fell onto the floor, crawling away from Oliver. As he did, Oliver tore off his own gas mask and threw it aside. On his face was a cold, wrathful expression.

"You bastard, I always knew it," Oliver growled.

Oliver pointed the Railshot Rifle, preparing to fire before another metal piece hit him.

"Fuck you!" Sam shouted as he tackled Oliver.

They both fell to the floor, the rifle falling to the side as they exchanged fists. Oliver ignored the pain of every strike, throwing elbows and fists at Sam. For a moment, he was winning. As he took the advantage, Sam kicked him off and crawled away. Oliver gasped as he watched Sam crawl for his gun, Oliver turning to grab something.

Oliver saw spears, all makeshift and laying together in a pile. Near them were large devices, gun-shaped with gas canisters attached to them. Oliver threw himself forward, grabbing a spear and standing. He flew around, running at Sam as he grabbed Oliver's rifle. They met at the same time.

"Raah!!" Oliver shouted.

Sam's eyes widened as he turned around and aimed the gun, watching as the spear went through his own throat. As the spear pierced Sam and went through to the floor, Sam pulled the trigger of the Railshot Rifle.

Metal flew out from the devastating weapon. Each piece annihilated Oliver's right forearm, taking everything up to his elbow. Pieces of metal also shredded his side. Blood sprayed everywhere. Oliver stumbled back for a moment, watching as Sam became limp before he fell back.

Fear

London grunted and shambled along the sands of the wasteland. He was frail and starving. His once-powerful muscles had withered away, and his hope was a small flicker. A few months ago, London still had strength. Now, he was a completely broken man. Soon, he knew he'd collapse, the wasteland eventually enveloping him.

The same fate waited for the other prisoners of war who shambled with him, each zombie-like and half-dead just like London. They too would eventually collapse. The Patrians ordered them along, beating and whipping at them while hissing cruel words. It'd bring them joy to watch London collapse.

He was truly unsure that if someone saved him that he'd live to recover. Everything hurt. The painful pangs of hunger were long gone, but his joints and pale flesh ached unbearably. When the Patrian overseers struck him, London felt nothing. It was somewhat blissful as if their attacks went straight through him.

"Faster!"

London coughed and heaved forward.

"Come on, you slow fuckers!"

London didn't know the date, but he assumed it had been a long time since he had seen Rose. He pondered on what she was like now after so long. Was she still alive? He wondered if she was growing into a strong young woman and wondered if she could grow up well without him.

That hurt the most. Not the hitting, the starvation, or the aching in his joints. It was the thought of Rose. He had no choice but to go on the caravan trail to the war front, and he knew the price. London wished that he could have gone back and hugged her harder. As he stumbled forward with the other prisoners, he recalled his last promise to her.

"Rose, I promise I'll come back safe and sound. I always have."

Not this time. London took some solace in knowing that he was here and that Rose was safe inside New Uruk. As the group continued on, one of the prisoners collapsed.

"Get up! Come on!" shouted an overseer.

In response, the prisoner weakly moaned.

"Stop!" he shouted.

The prisoner line stopped, all the prisoners lowering their heads as they heard the overseer stomping the man's head.

London winced slightly as he heard the prisoner's skull crack.

"Keep moving!"

London began to walk again, listening as the prisoners behind him had to walk over the body.

The minutes and hours droned on as the prisoners walked, following a road built by soldiers turned slaves. London had learned that the Patrians took soldiers from their enemies as slaves. Once they had conquered a population, those who weren't soldiers became forced citizens who had to pay taxes and gather resources for the empire they were now a part of. Children raised in these conquered populations would grow up to become soldiers or workers for Patria or killed if they couldn't do either.

It was a long, brutal process that London found disgusting. For New Uruk, they traded with new populations they met and eventually invited groups and factions into their nation. London, at that moment, felt grateful that he was on the right side of history.

The group walked past some flayed corpses lining the road. London barely glanced at them. Each one seemed rather fresh, which meant that these were newly executed prisoners or that the group was nearing the war front between Patria and New Uruk.

After a while, the remnants of war became apparent. There were blast craters everywhere, corpses, vehicles, and war machines littering the landscape. London looked up to see the remains of an old-world town. It was like the one that he had been to so long ago. He recognized this place; it was a trade outpost close to New Uruk, a place for traders from settlements outside of the city to stop at.

London's heart sank as he saw the remains of the outpost. Many of the buildings had collapsed, and there were Patrians executing people on the remaining rooftops. Traders. Some they hanged, others they flayed, and many they shot. The Patrians fed the unluckiest to ravenous dogs.

The prisoners and the soldiers with them walked past the town, soon joining with other prisoners. At first, only a few groups joined them and formed separate lines. Ten prisoners, twenty, forty. Eventually, there were a hundred prisoners, and then a few hundred until London could assume that there were at least five hundred prisoners.

All of them looked as starved and dispirited as he was. They marched in long lines, hounded and yelled at by Patrian overseers. As the lines moved, they trampled any prisoner that collapsed. London looked around. It was as if they were being herded, pushed together, and guided forward by the cruel commands of the Patrians.

The sounds of pained moaning, coughs, and shouting filled the air. London kept shambling, occasionally coughing as half-filtered air filled his lungs. It was a stinging pain. It got worse by the day, becoming almost as unbearable as his aching body. Every cough created a shockwave of pain through his body as well.

"Keep moving!"

Soon, the silhouette of buildings appeared on the horizon. As the prisoners and their overseers drew closer, London could see a city. It must've been the old-world city that New Uruk occupied. He looked in awe. The Patrians had succeeded in pushing the war front to the gates of New Uruk. Outside the city were hundreds of tents. Soldiers, slaves, vehicles, and work animals ran among them, all while a few dozen siege machines were pushed and pulled toward New Uruk.

London could hear explosions and gunfire, while large plumes of smoke rose from the streets leading to New Uruk. It seemed that they were holding their defense outside the walls surrounding the actual city, fighting in the streets and ruined buildings. The prisoners arrived in the war camps outside the actual old-world city just in time to see the fireworks.

The siege machines outside of the city fired, launching heavy artillery projectiles high in the air. The projectiles escaped the machines with deafening booms, arcing and coming down upon New Uruk. A horrified gasp left London as the machines fired. Rose. He hoped that she was in the subway systems, safe while the Patrians brought the city down.

"Stop!" an overseer shouted.

The lines of prisoners came to a stop. London watched as a group of armed Patrians approached. The one in the center was covered in armor and carried a long staff with a two-headed metal dog on top—the symbol of Patria.

"General!" the overseer said, saluting the man by putting his hand on his heart.

"There's no time to delay. How many are here?"

"Five hundred, general."

"Good. Take them to the front."

"The Hanged Eagle, general?"

The general nodded and waved him off, the overseer saluting and walking back to the herd of prisoners.

"Move! Move, you fuckers!"

Once more, the slaves walked. They scrambled forward, moving through the camp. There were dogs, male and female soldiers of various ages, and slaves setting up tents. Some glanced at them, spat at them, or yelled curses against the prisoners and New Uruk.

"Fuck New Uruk!"

"Come on! Come on! Grab two poles! Let's go!" shouted an overseer.

London looked ahead as the lines split up. Each prisoner paused and picked up two poles from a pile. Some were out of metal; others were out of wood. Such a simple load seemed strange. When it was London's turn, he struggled to lift the poles, growling with effort as his malnourished muscles screamed in agony.

He stumbled slightly as he straightened up, carefully joining the lines formed ahead of the herd. After five minutes, they were off again toward the city. As the prisoners approached the edge of the city where the New Uruk soldiers were fighting, a horn blasted.

"Pull back! Pull back!" screamed the soldiers.

With one horn blast, a horde of Patrian soldiers retreated from the city, leaving the New Uruk soldiers to recapture the streets of their home. With the soldiers came vehicles and armored war dogs, pulling back under covering fire. Once the Patrians had pulled back, the overseers began to move the prisoners into a long, straight line between the city and the war camp.

Once the line was complete, overseers began to move back and forth along the line. Each of them barked orders, forcing the prisoners to dig holes to put the poles in. They were specific, strangely checking each person and their limb spans before telling them where to dig. London didn't protest, digging his fingers into the sandy wasteland dirt where an overseer told him to dig.

London labored sluggishly, digging his fingers deep and getting sand crammed between his fingernails. After what seemed to be an hour, he had two holes. He then stood with an exhausted stumble and began putting the poles in each hole. London buried each, stuffing and packing sand to make sure they didn't fall. Even in the sand, the rest of each pole sticking out of the ground was taller than him.

By the time London buried the last pole, his energy had burnt out. As he struggled to pack the sand, he slowly fell forward and collapsed. It felt good, like falling into bliss as the sand embraced his face.

"Prisoner! Get up! These poles aren't sturdy enough!"

London didn't respond, unsure where the voice came from.

"Are you ignoring me?!"

London felt as a hard rod smacked him a few times, his body limply moving. It did nothing. London was already done.

"You there! Get these poles standing properly!"

London listened as he heard more digging, followed by a grunt. A second horn blast shocked a little life into him, London blinking as he felt his clothes getting ripped off, followed by his gas mask. London was naked but didn't feel vulnerable. He felt nothing as he was hoisted up and tied to the poles. The ropes spread London out, his wrists tied to the top of the poles while a box went beneath his feet. He hung forward due to the extra slack in the rope.

He tried to look around, spotting other prisoners being hoisted up the same way as him. London let out a weak wheeze, gazing ahead. He saw soldiers in the ruins, people of New Uruk who were too afraid to rush at the Patrian army and save the prisoners. It would've been futile anyway. London was sure to die soon, regardless.

Agonized cries came from London's left, London glancing over to watch Patrians cutting into the backs of the prisoners. Executioners. This was it. Each executioner had a helper who would hand them items, mainly fish hooks with long strings. London's head drooped as burning. Toxic air flooded his lungs freely.

Then he felt it. A pair of hands grabbed him as he felt pain at the top of his back. A knife. It slowly slid down his back, cutting from his shoulder, around his shoulder blade, down his spine, and stopping above his buttocks. The knife repeated the same on the other side. London groaned weakly and wheezed. His face grimaced, London unable to do anything as the knife slid. It cut downward, moving under his skin as if skinning a dead animal.

Once the knife finished, fingers worked under his skin and pulled it slightly; London let out a cry as his skin separated from his flesh. They didn't take it all off, letting go after a few seconds. Blood poured from the wounds, pouring down his legs and dripping onto the sandy dirt and wooden box below him.

The relief from the knife leaving didn't last long. Prickly pain shot through him as he felt small hooks enter the newly loosen skin. One, two, three, each hook went through his flesh with ease. After, a string attached each hook to the poles on either side. In the end, there were at least fifty hooks; London lost count after five.

London wheezed and bled, weakly leaning forward as he was unable to stand. As he leaned forward, the ropes holding his wrists, and the hooks in his back, stopped him from falling. Rose. He promised himself that she would be in his last thoughts. He held onto the hope that she was safe in New

Uruk or somehow able to escape with people who would keep her safe.

As London hung and cherished his memories with Rose, a speakerphone echoed from the Patrian war camp into the city.

"New Uruk! Cowards, sheep, all of the weak who hide in the city before me!" shouted a man into the speakerphone.

"Look at these dead men before you! They are broken! Worthless and tossed away like trash! They are your people! Each one was a strong soldier of New Uruk!"

"See how we have shattered their hope, their spirits, and their bodies! You shall all share their fates! Those who hide inside the city shall be forced to work for the glory of Patria, and your children will become glorious soldiers in our empire!"

He paused, grabbing something. At the same time, a set of footsteps crunched in the sand behind London.

"Behold now the power of Patria!" the general said, blowing a horn.

London gasped as the box beneath his feet was kicked out from underneath him. He dropped until the slack of the ropes and strings disappeared, each line snapping straight. As they did, the force tore the skin from his back and revealed his flesh to the toxic air.

He couldn't cry out in pain. It was impossible. London opened his mouth, yet nothing came out. Only the horrifying screams and gasps from the soldiers in New Uruk filled the air. Five hundred men were executed at the same time. Most died instantly, while some would suffer for hours until they bled out.

London hung, thinking of Rose. Her smile and laughter, that was the clearest thing in his head. London struggled to hold the picture in his head, slowly slipping away. Soon, all the pain in his body was gone, the world disappearing until everything was silent. Finally, there was peace.

Human

6:21 PM, September 8, 2185

Simon recovered once more from being unconscious, a dizzy feeling holding onto him. Now he had a headache as well. It took him a moment to realize that he was still hanging upside down, dangling from the rope trap that had caught his ankle. His gun laid below him, so close yet so far away.

He reached out for it, his fingers inches away from grabbing it. Simon swung a bit, struggling to reach the gun and moving back and forth. As he failed, his frustration built. His face was red, and his headache was unbearable.

"Gaah!" he growled, "Fuck!"

Eventually, Simon gave up and hung there helplessly. With no other option, he began to cry out for help.

"Help!! Anyone out there?!" he shouted.

After a minute, he tried again.

"Help!!"

Help didn't seem anywhere near. Simon hoped that this wasn't an ancient, unmanned trap. He hoped that he wouldn't starve to death here, not like this.

"Anyone! Please!"

Simon continued to hang, panicking, and trying to grab the rope around his ankles. His body was too weak, and he couldn't reach it.

Then he paused as he heard quiet scratching approaching. Simon gasped and tried to spin around to see who or what was approaching. The rope twisted slowly, bringing him around and then spinning him around again. Simon stared at the shape approaching him. It was a dog, furless and covered in rough tumors.

He had never seen a dog outside of pictures and felt his heart leap out of his chest. It stared at Simon as it approached. It began to bare its teeth, growling. Its teeth were broken, decayed, and wicked in appearance. Simon was now panicking, thrashing and flailing as he tried to free himself from the snare or tried to reach for his gun.

"No! Stay away!" he shouted. "Go away!"

The dog growled and barked at him, snapping and biting at him. It grabbed his spacesuit and tugged, Simon screaming and shouting in terror.

"Stop! NO! No, no!" screamed a voice.

As the voice called out, the dog stopped and released Simon. Simon continued to shield himself for a moment after, spotting a figure once he lowered his arms.

He watched as the figure approached, soon being able to make it out. It was an older woman with fading, strawberry-blonde hair and damaged tanned skin. She wore clothing made out of hide covered in thin metal plates, a sight completely alien to Simon. On her back was a large backpack with supplies hanging from it. There were also skulls and bones dangling from it, swinging back and forth as she walked. The strangest thing he saw on her backpack was a small oven on the left side with a chimney going out the top.

She had a gas mask and a hood on, and a sort of scowl beneath her mask. She seemed rugged, worn by the wasteland yet well-versed in its ways. In her hands was a heavy crossbow. A bayonet stuck out from the front of it, and a quiver of bolts hung from her hips. The woman approached Simon, looking him over.

"Sorry, Rex, that ain't food," she said.

She examined him, taking his weapon and inspecting it.

"Ain't that pretty as a peach," she whispered, taking off her backpack and strapping the gun to its side.

"You're a strange one. You're out here caught in one of my traps, wearing clothing I've never seen before. You out to steal on my hunting range?"

The woman pointed the crossbow at him.

"Gimme one good reason I shouldn't turn you into dog food, stranger."

Simon gasped and shielded himself.

"Wait! Wait! I'm not trying to steal anything! I just got here and stumbled onto this trap."

"Yeah? I reckon you're lying. What's your name?"

"Simon!"

"Simon? Haven't heard that sort of name around here before. You lying?!"

"No! No! It's Simon. I'm not from here. I'm not even from this planet."

The woman lowered her crossbow in disbelief and then burst out laughing.

"Is that right? That's just fascinating, spaceman. What planet are you from? Mars?"

"The Arcadis Station. I'm from a station that orbits Earth, and I just crashed and ended up walking until I stepped on this trap."

"You're saying that the meteor that just came down was you?"

"Yes,"

Her smile faded.

"Well, seems we could be of use to each other, stranger. How about this... I free you from this trap here, so you don't starve to death, and you could let me take a look at this... Spaceship of yours." she said.

"Sure! Sure, anything you want! It's a deal."

"All righty," she said.

She put her crossbow down and walked up to him. It took the woman only a moment to undo the trap, chuckling as Simon dropped to the ground with an "oof" and a thud. He let out a groan and sat up, stretching with a grateful expression.

"Oh my God, thank you," Simon said, standing up.

"No worries."

Simon stood there for a moment, wobbling and looking at the woman. She looked back at him.

"Name's Anna, nice to meet you, Simon. You look worse for wear."

"Worse for wear?" Simon repeated and furrowed his brow in confusion.

"Tired, sick, in bad shape," she responded.

"Oh, yes... I haven't gotten a lot of rest or food in the last six days. And I've been knocked out twice," he said.

"Well, I'm feeling generous today. Take me to your spaceship, and I'll nuss you right up at my home."

Simon wasn't entirely sure what "nuss" meant, but he nodded anyway. Simon began to lead the woman back in the general direction he came from. It didn't take long before his little trail of breadcrumbs appeared, piled rocks and erect sticks that he left in his exploration. Simon pointed it out for the woman and continued walking. The dog faithfully followed Anna as they walked, watching Simon carefully.

After a while, they arrived at the crash site. So far, no one had found the wreck. From afar, Simon could see how he landed, gazing at the trail left behind it. It seemed that it had landed, hit something, rolled, and buried itself in the ground.

"Here it is," Simon said, gesturing to the ruined vessel.

"What the hell," Anna whispered, surveying the wreck from afar.

"I wasn't lying..."

"I can see that,"

"There are some supplies in it. You can have them in return for your help," Simon offered.

The woman grinned beneath her gas mask and approached the escape pod. Simon followed, helping her open the back door. She began to take everything she could, stuffing all the supplies she could into her backpack. Simon helped, grabbing as much as he could in his weak state.

"This is a lot to carry," she said as she placed the backpack on her back.

"Yeah, it's for a group of people," Simon told her.

"Well, I'll have to be fixin' to return here to carry some more of this. Can you lock the door?"

"Yes, I can."

"Hop to it, and then we can be on our way outta here."

Simon nodded and followed her out, closing and locking the door shut behind them. Once he finished, they carried off in nearly the same direction they had come from. Now Simon was beginning to feel very weak. He willed and pushed his way forward, taking each step slowly.

"Stay with me stranger, my home isn't too far away," she told him.

"I'm fine," Simon said quietly. "I'm just tired."

Anna led Simon through the neighborhood again, carefully leading him past all her snares and traps. Simon was amazed to see her ingenuity, gawking at each strange and unique trap. They left the neighborhood and followed the buried road out into the wasteland.

Everything was new. Simon looked at dead trees, power lines, billboards, car frames, anything that they passed that looked interesting. Anna glanced back at him sometimes, noticing his awe.

"You okay there, stranger? It's just stuff from the old world."

"Yeah..." Simon responded, "I've just never seen this sort of stuff. Well, not outside pictures. It's weird."

"Well, I reckon you're ripe for storytelling."

"I could be."

"Well, you'll have plenty of time to tell me. I reckon you need a little more than nussin' before you're off into the wasteland."

"What do you mean?"

"Well, once you're all fixed up, you need to know how to survive. Letting you run off into the wasteland, well.... That's plain stupid, stranger. I'm sure something will eat you up like a pie."

"I... I'd be grateful if you could help me learn."

"Darn right, I'll make sure you're fit as a fiddle and give you some sense."

Simon chuckled and smiled.

"Thank you, Anna."

Eventually, they turned right off the road and passed two posts with animals' skulls on them. As they walked, they entered a property with a weak fence line surrounding it. There were also a couple of trees with rough bark, skeletal and leafless, along the fence. The pair walked past the fence line and onto the property itself.

At the center, on a hill, was an old house that had been repaired, fortified, and added onto by Anna. There was a watchtower at the top and a little radio dish, a silo beside the house, and a small barn a few yards away. Beside the barn were a few wooden grave markers, Simon counting four. All around the house were fields.

Simon squinted as he saw a figure walking along one of the fields. It took him a moment to realize that it was a rusty, old robot, the humanoid kind used in the old world. It seemed that Anna had repurposed it; the robot slowly plucked out weeds in the field.

He stopped as he heard dogs, watching as three other dogs ran to them and growled at him.

"Max, Rey, Jack! No! Be nice to the guest."

"Woah, you have a lot of dogs."

"Darn right; man's best friend is more faithful than anything else in this world, always has been true."

Simon looked at each one nervously, then continued following Anna to the house.

"Home sweet home. Welcome to my farm, partner."

Patria

Oliver smiled as he looked out upon Patria. He stood at the tunnel going down into the bunker, gazing out across the city around it. It was a huge city for being in the wasteland. There were hundreds of houses along the hundreds of streets, all built into the ground. The city was somewhat like a massive crater. Surrounding it was a wall that helped block out the weather and protected the city.

Occasionally, there were vertical turbines along the walls. They spun slowly and powered the city with electricity. Oliver gazed at one. Electricity was a gift to his people, and it was something produced from sacrifice and blood. It flowed through power lines all across the city, powering light bulbs, machines, and entire households. All of it was free.

Oliver was ninety-one this year and had grown bent and elderly in his old age. Instead of a regular gas mask, he had an oxygen mask attached to a tank that went with him at all times. He was still relatively healthy, but years of polluted air had damaged his lungs greatly. The only thing that bothered him was his arm. Everything below his right elbow was missing, which hindered him since he had always been right-handed. Oliver glanced at it, remembering how he lost it.

Sam. Oliver still didn't know who had betrayed who. Had it been Sam trying to seize power, or had it been Sam defending himself from Oliver? His memory was fuzzy, but he still felt guilty. Patria was a dream shared between both of them and had been built by both of them. Electricity was one of Sam's great projects, which Oliver had finished for him.

It was peaceful today, despite the buzzing of the city. The winds were calm, and the pollution haze seemed thinner today. Children played, and people worked. There were craftsmen, traders, and soldiers all at work in the streets. Everyone had a duty to provide for Patria, to give everything they had for the greater good. It's what the founders of Patria, including Oliver, had done to create Patria, so everyone had to follow their example.

Oliver thought of his soldiers. Patria had been born into war and was forged by it. Now, decades later, Oliver had turned Patria into a great war machine that used war to sustain itself. Most Patrians served as soldiers, though they did more than fight. Oliver's soldiers helped in not only the security of the nation but its infrastructure as well. They built roads, houses, and even entire towns as they expanded Patria's borders.

For a moment, he paused and gazed down at the ground. Oliver considered all the violence and all the suffering Patria had caused. Invasions, taming newly conquered populations, and executions. Patria was famous for flaying people during executions, which had given Oliver the infamous nickname of the "Flayed King."

He frowned. Oliver didn't feel bad about most deaths he caused. They were necessary. Each death had a purpose, like controlling the minds of the Patrian people or aiding in the assimilation of new peoples.

Oliver questioned himself. Was he a cruel dictator or a leader trying to do what was best for his nation? Oliver didn't know and never found an answer. Most of Patria respected and loved him, so he believed that he was doing something right.

"Oliver, sir?"

He turned around, looking down at a man kneeling before him. It was one of his generals, of which he had four. The man had a gas mask on and wore heavy armor. A twin-headed dog was painted on his chest. It was a symbol of Oliver's design. The dog was red on a purple background, surrounded by a gray circle.

The dog had many meanings. It depicted a mastiff, which was strong and powerful. Since it was a dog, it was loyal, just like how every Patrian citizen should be. Its twin-heads represented the new world and its harsh reality. Finally, one dog represented one leader, which was Oliver.

"Just call me Oliver, Chris," Oliver said softly.

"I want to respect you, sir. I apologize."

"It's fine. You may do it if you want to. What is it, my friend?" Oliver asked.

"I came to fill you in on today's report, sir," Chris told him.

Oliver nodded.

"You may stand. Come to my side, Chris," Oliver commanded.

Chris gazed at him in confusion for a moment before walking over to his side. He was a giant compared to Oliver. Oliver was short with old age, while Chris towered over him like a muscular tree. As he went to his side, Oliver turned and pointed out to the city.

"Isn't it beautiful?" Oliver asked.

Chris looked around.

"I'm sorry, I don't understand, sir?"

"That's okay. I'm referring to the city. Isn't it beautiful? Everyone working hard for the good of Patria, soldiers keeping us safe, children playing in peace. I grew up in the old world, Chris. This is how it was like back then. People were safe and happy, working through their lives just like the next person."

"Oh... It is beautiful, sir."

Oliver chuckled.

"I started this all. The first Patrians were a stubborn people, Chris. We fought and sacrificed so much, just for this dream. We starved and died, and now everyone has water and plenty of food. We sacrificed, and now I'm here to see the fruit of our labors."

Chris looked at him.

"Sir, I'm grateful for Patria."

"As you should be."

A brief moment of silence passed as they gazed at the streets.

"Sir?"

"Yes?"

"I still have to give you the report, sir."

"All right, let's go inside and talk," Oliver said, turning around.

Oliver was slow as he walked, carefully strolling down into the bunker.

"Tell me then, what's been happening lately?"

"We're winning in the northern wastes. Most of the northern tribes have been conquered, and we're currently trying to assimilate them."

"That's good news," Oliver said.

Oliver gazed up at the stone face staring down at him as the pair walked past the doors leading into the bunker. The interior halls were shiny and clean. Patrian soldiers were everywhere, either cleaning, patrolling, or waiting for orders from higher-ups.

"Hail the Flayed King!"

The soldiers greeted him with joy and respect. Oliver nodded and waved to them as they saluted to him, walking past them as they worked.

"How are things inside Patria?" Oliver asked.

"Stable, sir. Our roads are well maintained, taxes are paid, and all our citizens are loyal. We're working on establishing new cities, but that's a slow process, sir."

"I'm sure it is. Whatever it takes, Chris."

"Of course, sir,"

Oliver walked toward the atrium with Chris.

"How is the advance West and East?" Oliver asked.

"Going well, sir. There are fewer tribes in the East, which means more free land for us. The West and North are slow pushes due to all the resistance we meet, but we haven't been stopped so far."

"What about the South?"

"Well, that's what I was worried about telling you about, sir."

"Worried? Don't be worried. I need to know."

"We've met a new nation in the South. They call themselves New Uruk. It's a well-established nation in the southern lands. They trade and farm and have gathered a bit of control of the surrounding wasteland through trade."

"What about it?"

"It's organized, sir. It's located in the industrial area of an old-world city, and there's a chance they can produce a strong offensive against us should we attempt to invade them."

"We've won against organized nations before, Chris."

"I know, sir. New Uruk is bigger than those nations. When our emissaries met with theirs, they attempted to establish trade with us. Of course, we don't need their trade. We just need their people. The problem is that they declined our offer to join Patria."

"I assume you haven't sent the heads of their emissaries back to their leaders yet, have you?"

"No, sir. We have been careful not to start a war before Patria is ready. I already have the other generals prepared to discuss how we should approach this. That is if you wish to meet with them."

"Let's go meet them. I want to deal with this new nation."

"Very well, sir. They are already in the war room."

Oliver followed Chris to the war room. They went through the halls, passing the atrium and a few wings of the bunker. Eventually, they arrived in a circular room full of desks, tables, maps, papers, and everything to do with planning warfare. There were already three other people at a large table at the center, gazing at them as the pair entered.

The first one was Moe, who was a wide and powerful man with gray eyes. The second was Isabella, a woman with a stern, merciless look. The third was Joseph, the youngest and thinnest of them all. As Oliver entered, they rose and saluted.

"Hail to the Flayed King!"

Oliver smiled.

"You don't have to salute to me. We're friends here."

"It's tradition, sir," Moe said.

Oliver walked in and sat down in a chair, Chris joining them as they all sat around the large center table with a map on it.

"Before we begin today, sir, we have a gift for you," Chris said.

"Oh?" Oliver murmured.

"We finally found paint for you, sir. My men found them, while Isabella and her men found brushes and a canvas."

"We wanted to give you stuff to paint with, sir," Chris told Oliver.

"Thank you all. I've never been a great painter, but maybe it's something nice to do before I go."

They looked among each other. They had not chosen a leader to succeed Oliver, which was a subject of many debates.

"Now, Chris told me about this new nation, New Uruk. Tell me about it."

"Well, they're organized, sir. They have a very large population, though most of it consists of farmers," Joseph said.

"What's difficult with farmers?" Oliver asked.

Isabella leaned forward and circled her finger around the map in front of them, defining the area of New Uruk.

"Our scouts reported that the city is centered in an old-world city in an industrial area. That means they are already well fortified. That also means that with all the food they produce and their location, they're well-stocked. They have supplies and trade to go with them. If needed, they could produce supplies and equipment to fuel an army," Isabella told Oliver.

"We already have an army ready to go. We just need to secure our borders, recall our forces, and hit New Uruk. Their resistance of assimilation mocks our strength," Oliver said.

Chris responded with a warning.

"I advise caution, sir. These people aren't survivors in ununited tribes,"

Oliver looked between them as they all nodded in agreement with Chris.

"All right, all right, we shouldn't be hasty. As I said, recall our forces, arm as many men as possible. Everything should be prepared for a big war," Oliver told them.

"That will be done then, sir," Chris said.

"I'll have war machines made and machines to maintain supply lines, sir," Joseph said.

"How quickly can you produce them so that we're prepared?" Oliver asked.

"It'll take a month or two before we have a good amount for the beginning of the war. If all goes well, that will be enough," Joseph said.

"Good. I also want roads, forts, and everything else built as we move forward when the war begins. I don't want us losing an inch of ground."

"Nothing will be lost," Moe stated, "These are farmers after all. They can't possibly hold out against Patria itself."

"You're correct, Moe. These people, these... Farmers of New Uruk," Oliver said, "They will be an example of Patria's power. I'm sure defeating them will be a strong warning not to stand against us for everyone else in the South."

"No doubt about it," Joseph said.

"Sir?" Chris began.

"Yes?"

"Are you sure you want to invade New Uruk now? We still have the new cities to build, and we need to finish off the Northern and Western tribes."

"They will be finished off before the war begins. As for cities, I don't want to wait for them. I want to see one last good war before I die, one last beautiful demonstration of Patrian power in the new world. You wouldn't deny an old man that, would you?"

"I wouldn't deny you anything, sir,"

"Good. So, we are in agreement? War against New Uruk?"

They all nodded.

"Then I, Oliver the Flayed King, ruler of Patria, declare on New Uruk!" Oliver announced, standing up and raising his left fist.

The other four generals stood and saluted.

"For Patria! For Patria! For Patria!"

Revenge

6:08 AM, May 2, 2162

Rose laid beneath the protective cover of the tent, staring up at the top of it. She was in silent contemplation, a heavy crossbow beside her. She was wearing tough hide clothing covered in armor, and she wore a fine gas mask that had multiple red marks across it. Each mark was a number.

Rage. That was all that she could think of. It had been nearly six years since the death of London. She was seventeen now. The world had not treated her kindly through those years, and she had become hardened. Her only solace was the people who protected her. Margaret and Reginald had raised her, protected her, and kept her safe in place of London. For that, she loved them both. Margaret had become very sick, though Rose still remembered Margaret's sad smile as Rose went to fight in New Uruk's war.

She remembered everything as clearly as the day she experienced it. There were five hundred bodies, all flayed as a cruel insult to New Uruk. After the soldiers of New Uruk pushed the Patrians back into the wasteland, they allowed people to bury the bodies. Rose was among them. Reginald had tried to stop her, but it was no use.

Finding London's body, bloody with his skin torn apart, still haunted her. She could barely look at him. Her last memory of him alive was him going out to the war front, promising to come back, and her last memory of London was burying him in the wasteland sand.

Rose growled as her face grimaced in mental anguish.

"Why?" she whispered.

If he had not gone to the war front, he would never have died. She would never have had to cry herself to sleep, suffer nightmares, and grow up without him. That was the worst part, growing up without him.

"Why?!" she growled in a louder tone.

Rose's anger flooded her for a while before she sighed and calmed, her face relaxing as she shut her eyes.

"Time to wake up," said a voice.

Rose looked over at the tent flap as it opened.

"Gimme a minute, Tommy," Rose said.

He nodded and waited outside.

Rose slowly sat up. She hadn't slept all night and felt on edge thinking about the coming battle. Six years. New Uruk had been fighting for Patria for eight years and nearly lost the war the day of London's execution. They only pushed Patria back through the combined efforts of the city's defenders and reinforcements from towns and small cities within the nation of New Uruk. Today was the battle that would finish it all, the battle for the capital of Patria.

Rose walked out of the tent. It was still dark with the pollution haze looming above. Regardless, the hundreds of tents surrounding her were alive and buzzing. Soldiers were beginning to wake up, preparing their weapons and armor for the battle ahead. Tommy greeted her with a rifle, presenting it to her.

"Got this one from a Patrian officer; I thought you'd want it," Tommy said.

Rose grinned beneath her gas mask and took the rifle. Her crossbow was on her back, and there was a knife on her belt and on her boot.

"Perfect. You have ammo?"

"Plenty,"

She had broken her gun beyond repair in a fight with a Patrian, a fight that she had won. He was a tough fight, a memory painted on her mask as another mark.

"Are we already preparing to move out?" Rose asked, looking at the war camp surrounding them.

"Yes, the army is assembling. We'll probably all be ready to go before they sound the horn blast," Tommy said.

"Let's go join them then," Rose said.

The two began to walk among the tents. Soldiers were popping out of each tent left and right, joining the rush to assemble outside of the camp. The sounds of Scab Boar's "orfing" in the distance were heard, along with the engines of fast vehicles and heavy war machines. The pair continued along, scaling a small dune and joining the army.

There were hundreds of New Uruk soldiers in front of them, nearly five thousand men and women. They were farmers, craftspeople, factory workers, and medics— all turned into fighters who fought for the freedom of their people and the safety of their families. Among them were fast hit-and-run vehicles and heavy, tank-like machines.

Ahead was a sight that infuriated Rose. Patria. It was a massive city dug somewhat into the ground, surrounded by great walls. The walls protected against Doomstorms and violent winds. Hard clay, bricks, metal, and other tough materials composed their entire structure. Occasionally dotting the wall were vertical turbines that powered the city.

There had already been a battle to get here, and now New Uruk had been besieging the city from the outside. Rose gazed along the front lines, looking at each siege machine in front of the amassing army. They had been throwing boulders, bombs, firebombs, and everything they had for days now. Many of the turbines laid destroyed, the walls were crumbling, and the city gate was pummeled. Inside the city were pillars of smoke, rising high into the air.

Even as the army stood there, the siege machines threw projectiles into the city. Every time something exploded or collapsed a building, a cheer rose from the army. Rose's heart fluttered with excitement. As they stood there, the army prepared their formations and chanted.

"Death to the Flayed King! Fuck Patria! Death to the Flayed King! Fuck Patria!" they chanted.

Their voices echoed across the wasteland. There would be no speech. The soldiers didn't need it. The blood of their fallen comrades and their boiling fury from eight years of war and loss was enough. There would only be a single horn call. Rose looked at Tommy, Tommy glancing at her and giving her a reassuring nod.

He was her companion, her partner, and her protector in these battles. He had a shotgun, a rifle, and a brutal hatchet to dismember high-ranking Patrians. Tommy was especially well-known among both sides of the war to be a brutal torturer of Patrian slave-runners.

The army assembled after thirty minutes. They all moved into various formations, preparing to move on the city as the siege weapons pummeled buildings over the wall. As a barrage of shots flew over the wall, the sound of a loud engine echoed in the distance. Rose and Tommy turned to the sound, watching as a heavy, wedge-shaped vehicle shot past the army.

It drove straight for the gates of Patria, a loud horn of war blasting across the wasteland as it crashed through. It broke the gates off their hinges, each crashing down to the ground. Men and women shot from slits in the vehicle's armor as it drove into the city, causing chaos in its wake.

The army flooded forward. Patrians rushed to defend the gates and the holes in the wall, finding cover and shooting at the invaders. They used everything they had: guns, crossbows, bows, arrows, bullets, bombs, bolts, stones, everything, and anything.

Rose joined the surge of soldiers, Tommy by her side. They ran toward a spot where the wall had collapsed into a turbine. There were Patrians there to meet them, immediately firing at them. Both Tommy and Rose dove to the ground for cover while soldiers ran past them.

"Tommy, take the left!" Rose shouted, pointing to her left.

One down, two down, miss, another miss, three down. Rose reloaded the rifle, putting the clip in and cocking the bolt.

An explosion took out the Patrians defending the fallen section. Rose and Tommy began running again as part of the army ran over the debris. In a matter of seconds, the pair was over the wall. Rose looked over the city. There was destruction everywhere.

Rose could see clay and old-world scrap made up the houses and roads, partly dug into the ground so that three-story buildings had their tops exposed to the elements. They went up the wall and down into the street ahead.

The city was a maze dug into the ground, with bridges and walkways connecting between houses to make a somewhat three-layer street. The invading army received fire from above and below. Rose followed Tommy as he cleared their way to cover. It took only two blasts from his shotgun, a cruel, one-handed weapon that had its barrel sawn off, to clear their path.

"Where are we going?!" Rose asked, trying to shout over the sounds of anarchy around them.

"Straight to the center of the city! The rest of the city is underground. We'll find their elite forces and their leader there!" Tommy shouted in return.

One Patrian down. Once again, they were running. They followed other soldiers, fighting their way down streets, neighborhoods, and markets. Resistance met them everywhere as the Patrians defended their city, hiding behind walls and attacking from bridges.

The soldiers of New Uruk plowed through. Explosions went off everywhere, war machines pushing into the tight streets and screaming. There was nothing to match the terror of war. Rose and Tommy fought together, shooting Patrians one by one until their rifles ran out of ammo. Once they were out of ammo, Tommy began to use his shotgun, and Rose used her crossbow.

Rose rarely missed with the crossbow, bringing down Patrians left and right. One through the eye, one through the neck, and one right into a lung. Tommy, meanwhile, sprayed the streets with blood and gore as he annihilated body parts with his shotgun. More New Uruk soldiers met them, moving like a spear to the center of the city.

Patrian soldiers fell like flies before the marauding forces. Rose, caught up in the anarchy, was mindless. She shot and killed, feeling nothing as she killed men, women, and child soldiers. It was easy for her. She didn't see people, but shapes that were trying to kill her. It wasn't hard to kill shapes.

"Take the next street! Take the next street!" shouted a commander.

Rose dove for cover with Tommy as a barrage of arrows, spears, and bullets brought down soldiers around them. Chaos erupted around them, the Patrians holding their position as they slew almost every invader in the street. Reinforcements ran into a stalemate as they tried to push forward, being forced back by more barrages.

Tommy dragged Rose behind a wall, joining some soldiers as they glanced out to the Patrian defense. For a moment, they were all unsure of what to do. They looked among each other, a loud crash causing them to jump. A heavy, tank-like machine drove past them, breaking through the Patrian defense.

"Charge!"

Once again, they were running and killing Patrians. The New Uruk forces merged, soon arriving at the center of the city. Rose had expected some form of a fortress but was surprised when they arrived at a tunnel. Other soldiers had already gotten there before them, though they were rushing out of the tunnel.

"The upper city is taken! The bunker is next! At my signal, we move!" a commander shouted at the gathering soldiers.

As he spoke, a loud explosion sent a huge dust cloud out the tunnel, everyone shielding themselves.

"Go! Go! Go! Spare no one!" shouted the commander.

The army bottlenecked into the tunnel, the dust still clearing as they got to the end. Rose followed Tommy, looking around as the tight tunnel filled with the sounds of heavy breathing and equipment. They got to the end in a matter of moments. There they found the remains of a set of twin doors. They were heavy, tall doors made out of metal and engraved.

Beside them were the remains of two statues, the left one being the most intact. They seemed to be depictions of naked, muscular men holding up the walls. Above the door was a stone face, staring down at her. Rose thought it was a little strange but didn't give the faces much thought as they rushed into the underground portion of Patria.

Patrian soldiers met the New Uruk soldiers, both sides exchanging fire. The New Uruk push immediately slowed to a crawl. Dozens of soldiers fell before soldiers with hand-made shields were brought in, Rose and Tommy quickly hiding behind them. Inch by inch, the soldiers moved forward, soon breaking through their first obstacle.

Next came the choice to go left and right. The New Uruk forces split, following the lights in the ceiling. Rose looked around as they moved. Ornate pillars held up the tunnels they ran down, pieces of art, statues, and paintings, in between each. There were bookshelves as well. It seemed as if the Patrians hoarded knowledge and artifacts as well.

"Come on, Rose!" Tommy said, following a squadron of soldiers as they navigated the tunnels.

"Bring the shields!"

"Bogeys ahead!"

Once again, they reached another Patrian defense. The push came to a crawl again, the New Uruk soldiers hiding behind the heavy shields as the Patrians shot at them.

"Argh!" Tommy gasped, falling in front of Rose.

"Tommy!" she shrieked.

Tommy hit the ground, clutching his shoulder as he crawled back. A couple of soldiers grabbed him and moved him aside, another soldier taking his place.

"Medic!"

"Get a medic!"

"Tommy! Tommy, are you okay?!" Rose asked.

Tommy clenched his jaw in pain and held his shoulder, looking at her.

"Fuckers got me!" he said. "It's just a bullet wound."

"Medic!!" a soldier shouted.

Tommy looked at Rose as she tried to check if he was okay, watching her attempt to put pressure on his arm.

"Gah! Hey! I'm okay!" he said. "Calm down!"

"Bu-"

"Pull your shit together! New Uruk needs you. I'll be fine. Get back out there and fight."

Rose's face became pale, her mouth open as she shook from the surprise of Tommy's injury.

"I'll find you after the battle. You know what to do, just go! Go, damnit!"

As he shouted for her to fight, a medic arrived and tended to Tommy. Rose stood slowly, turning to look as the New Uruk soldiers broke through the

Patrian defense.

"Are you sure, Tommy?" Rose asked.

"Yes! This is your victory, Rose. Remember London, and take your revenge."

Rose glanced back at Tommy before running to join the soldiers again. She gathered herself. She shook off the shock, her eyes becoming focused as the rush of battle returned.

"Push forward!"

Rose ran with them, crossbow ready. She quickly ran through her bolts as they pushed into more and more Patrian defenses, clearing out section after section. It was as if this place was a giant bunker, something that was from the old world.

Soon, the squadron pushed into a lone tunnel. At the end of it was a heavy, metal door that was somewhat like the one at the beginning of the bunker. Getting it open only needed the last of their explosives. After an ear-piercing blast, the soldiers ran down the tunnel while the dust settled. Rose followed from behind, loading one of her final crossbow bolts.

They ran into a huge, circular room with a large table at the center, surrounded by chairs. There were smaller tables everywhere, covered in papers, pictures, and more. Rose assumed this to be a command room. The soldiers ran in, only to have their flesh melted.

Patrian soldiers wearing old-world military armor aimed plasma rifles at them. Rose gasped and fell to the floor as she saw them. Each time they fired, Ignium energy melted metal and shot it out. The result tore through flesh and bone, burning and killing many of the New Uruk soldiers.

Rose aimed and fired. A bolt hit its mark and brought one down, while bullets killed other Patrians. As Rose reloaded, everyone in the room killed one another.

Her final bolt met another victim. Everyone had fallen around her, leaving one Patrian left to kill her. She reached for another bolt, realizing that she was out. She charged forward with the crossbow, thrusting the bayonet into the man's chest. The two fell down to the ground. Rose grabbed the knife on the side of her boot and plunged it downward a few times.

"Hargh! Fu– Grah! Hork!" the man gurgled before becoming still.

Rose panted and stood up, looking down at the man's bloody corpse. She held the knife tight in her hand, blood dripping from the blade. She looked around. Everyone had died except for her. Soon, reinforcements would come, though she didn't want to wait.

There was a door opposite the one Rose had come in from. She approached it, opening it slowly and taking cover beside the door frame. She glanced and found only a single light in the room. The walls were covered in paintings, the artificial glow of the light illuminating them all.

At the very center of the room was a man, sitting a painting on a canvas.

"Don't shoot. I'm not armed," he said calmly, his voice sounding elderly.

"Who are you?" Rose asked with her bloody knife at the ready.

Beside the man was an oxygen tank attached to a device that seemed to be from a hospital. Rose could only assume that whatever it was, it was keeping the man alive.

"A man drawing a tree. Would you like to see?" he asked.

Rose looked confused. Was this who the Patrians were trying desperately to defend? She approached cautiously, keeping a few feet away from the man in case he'd attack her. As she approached, she noticed that the man had one arm and was wearing a mask similar to Margaret's. A tube attached the mask to an oxygen tank.

The man looked at her. He had brown eyes that carried the burden of a life full of pain and hardship. His skin, old and wrinkly, was covered in scars; he also had white hair as well.

"How old are you? What's your name?" he asked.

Rose was silent at first, unsure of what to think. The old man chuckled and then raised his arms. One arm was missing everything from the elbow down. The other that still had a handheld onto a brush.

"I'm almost a hundred years old, and I have a paintbrush for a weapon. I think you're safe."

She paused and then lowered her knife.

"My name is Rose. I'm seventeen."

"Seventeen... I've met many younger than you that have fought and died in this war. Brave children, all of them. I remember when children like you were in school and playing games, not fighting wars."

"Who are you?" Rose asked.

"Oliver. Nice to meet you. Do you like my tree?"

"Are you the leader of Patria?"

Oliver looked at her and sighed.

"Young people. We'll get there in a while. Do you like my tree? I think it could use some improvements," Oliver asked, gesturing to the canvas.

Rose gazed at the canvas. She was somewhat uncertain about what it was as she looked at the bark and the green leaves that loomed over greener grass. It was all beneath a blue sky.

"I'm sure you barely know what this is. Have you ever seen a living tree?" Oliver asked.

"No," Rose replied.

"Sad. I grew up in the old world, and we didn't have many trees either. I was born when some of the last forests died out. I did get to see green trees, though they were in greenhouses protected from the pollution. They were always so beautiful."

"Why did you draw this?" Rose asked, raising her eyebrows.

"It's a tribute to their memory. I'm sure there are still some trees and forests left on Earth, but they are very few. I also think it's a testament. It's a testament to nature and man, who survive regardless of the recklessness of humanity. I remember when we destroyed the planet, and then each other.

"Many believed that we would end all life on Earth back in the old world. I was one of those. But... Nature isn't so easy to kill. Life always finds a way, and it has for millions of years. The stupidity of man was just another mass extinction in a long history of mass extinctions. We also believed that we would cause the extinction of all humans. We were again wrong, for here we are. The wasteland is full of life after a hundred years, with humans rebuilding civilization."

He paused.

"I'm sure you don't care about any of that. It's probably just some forgotten thing from the old world to you."

Rose shook her head.

"It's not. I would've liked to see trees."

Oliver smiled beneath his mask.

"Well, you can have this painting. I won't be able to finish it."

Antiquity

Simon walked through the creaky, old house. There were objects everywhere, many of them being sturdy containers filled with food, ammo, and other supplies. He glanced at some of them as he put his backpack on, a medium-sized bag given to him by Anna. Scattered between the containers were rubbish, pieces of garbage, and old paper thrown about. There were also candles made from animal fat, all of them unlit and leaving the house rather dark.

The house itself was well fortified. Planks fortified the windows, all the walls had carpets and blankets nailed to them for insulation, and there were many more methods to keep the house stable. Simon had recovered since he crashed on Earth and had learned much about the wasteland. He had learned about the mutants, the pollution, and the weather. He was told by Anna that there was a kind of sandstorm called a Doomstorm, and they had existed for well over a hundred years.

Because of the Doomstorms, the main areas they resided in were in the basement below the house. There were beds downstairs, a kitchen, a furnace to heat it all up, and various methods of entertainment.

He approached the door, firmly grasping an energy pistol in his hand. Taken from the escape pod, Anna told him it would be much better than the heavy energy rifle from before.

Simon opened the door and stepped outside, his shoes crunching in the wasteland sand outside. Immediately, he heard the angry cries of Anna.

"Rex, get back here and stop being a lark!" she ordered.

She stood by a wagon, lifting a crate of goods into the back.

"All y'all get back here! Max, Rey, Jack, Rex! C'mon now!" she shouted, whistling.

The four dogs, out running in the fields around the harvesting robot, ran to her. She praised each and then ordered most of them to a side building off from the house. Rex, on the other hand, was ordered up onto the back of the wagon.

"What are we doing today, Anna?" Simon asked as he approached her.

Anna looked at him and approached the front of the cart, petting a creature that she had told Simon was called a Scab Boar. The large beast 'orfed' and leaned into the petting. It patiently stood there, ready to heave and tow the wagon attached behind it.

"We're gonna go out and do some trading." she said, "Hop in the passenger seat."

Simon nodded and went around the wagon, stepping up onto the passenger seat. The wagon creaked as he climbed it, letting out a final creak once he sat down. It did the same as Anna sat in the passenger seat. She had her crossbow placed at her side between them and pointed to a rifle hidden between the seats and the rest of the wagon.

"I know you ain't much of a shot, but if anything pops up to attack us, this'll take care of them."

"All right. Where are we going?" Simon asked.

"Trading," she said, whipping the reins. "Huyah! Get on now, Rufus!"

The Scab Boar snorted and moved forward, pulling the wagon.

"We're going to a city called New Uruk. Gonna trade this year's harvest for some supplies in preparation for winter."

"City?" Simon repeated, raising his eyebrows in surprise.

"City. What? Y'all on your fancy space station didn't think we'd be rebuilding down here?"

Simon turned his gaze downward and swallowed in embarrassment.

"N-No."

Anna chuckled as they rode along the main road going out of the property.

They left the house and the three other dogs behind, riding past the robot in the fields and out past the property line.

"I reckoned that. See, there's a lot you Raptured folk been missing these past hundred years since you left Earth," she said.

Simon noticed the squeaking of the wagon's wheels as they moved along onto the bumpy road to wherever they were going.

"We've survived here for all that time, all the generations since the end of the old world. It wasn't easy. You can bet on that. I nearabout die every year, but that doesn't stop me. There've been towns, cities, wars fought here, just like it's always been," Anna explained.

"So the Developers lied to us..." Simon whispered.

"What was that?"

"The Developers, the scientists on our station, lied to us about Earth being uninhabitable by humans. They estimated another century or so, even though there were rumors that we could go back now."

"They sound like a bunch of Goddamn idiots."

Simon gazed downward and nodded. Anna glanced over at him.

"Cheer up now, Simon."

"S-Sorry, I just kind of miss it."

"I don't blame you," she said. "You have every right to feel down."

He only nodded again.

The Scab Boar snorted and kept pulling the wagon forward, easily pulling it up a hill and further along the road. As they moved, Simon noticed civilization around him. Sometimes, ruined, empty houses loomed over the sandy wastes, and other times proof of what Anna was saying appeared: homes, properties, farms, and ranches.

There were people on these farms and ranches. Some of them had recently bought the properties. They were digging holes, preparing to create half-buried homes that could easily withstand the weather. Some people were out with their animals, casually holding their guns and whistling to guide their herds. Sometimes, these people would wave, especially those attending to their harvests. Simon, unsure of what to do, waved back.

"Seems you're not the only one out here," he said.

"Not at all. I'm one of the few people who moved out here and took a property before New Uruk began splitting up the land to sell to people who wanted to move out to the countryside. Darn city. Keeps us protected, but it also brings taxes."

Simon watched as another person on a wagon passed them, nodding to Anna, who nodded back. Simon looked back as the wagon passed, a kid with a gas mask staring at him from the back of it.

"How much farther?" Simon asked.

"About ten minutes now, hold your horses. We got all day."

Soon, the city appeared in the distance. Outposts marked the borders of the territory, filled with guards who patrolled around empty neighborhoods and shopping areas. A few paused to greet Anna. In the distance, Simon could see old, decrepit skyscrapers which have withstood the test of time. Even from a distance, Simon was amazed by them.

The wagon rolled forward deeper into the city. More and more guards and outposts appeared before they reached a big wall separating a large portion of the city from the rest.

"Slow down now, Rufus," Anna said, tugging at the reins.

They stopped in front of a large gate flanked by guard towers, guards with guns and crossbows staring down at them. A man with a shotgun approached.

"What's your business, partner?"

"Same as usual, doing some trading before winter comes."

"Who's this?"

"This guy? Found him out in my hunting grounds danglin' from a snare like a ragdoll. Nussed him right up, and now he helps on my farm."

"He don't look like he's from around here."

"He ain't, and I ain't in no mood for stories."

The man looked at Anna, then back at Simon.

"Well, if you vouch for him, I reckon I can let you in. Open her up!" the man shouted.

The gate squeaked and opened slowly, 'orfs' heard from the other side as large Scab Boars helped men open the hefty gates. With a firm crack, their wagon moved forward into the city. What met Simon's eyes almost made his jaw drop.

Among the ruins of the old city was a new city, New Uruk as Anna had told him. There were people everywhere, walking along the street, and doing their business. There were market stalls, soldiers, factories, and businesses inside old buildings, and more. It was a living, breathing city.

"Woah," Simon let out.

Anna cracked an amused smile at his reaction.

"Bet you've never seen anything like this."

"Never."

Simon leaned forward to look inside of the businesses, staring at the strange belt machines which helped workers mass produce products. He stared at each strange, mutant animal sold in the street and gawked at all the strange sights. There were weapons, armor, food, ammo, and anything else that could be needed being sold by merchants. Occasionally, at intersections of streets, there were big water containers full of free water for the people of the city.

What Simon found strange were the lights and the machines. They didn't seem to run on Ignium.

"This is New Uruk?" he asked.

"You got eyes, don't ya? This is the shining capital of the wasteland; the biggest and most powerful city 'round these parts," Anna said, gesturing in front of her with one hand.

They turned down another street.

"I've lived here for most of my life and have seen a lot of its history. I even fought in the war that made it the place it is today."

"It's amazing. You have factories, technology, markets, food..." Simon said.

"Yes, indeed. It's all right around here, and I reckon that New Uruk will rebuild the United States and lead it back to its former glory."

"What's with the lights and the machines? They look strange. I think I've seen that kind of technology before, but I'm not sure."

"That there is electricity, stuff from way back in the day in the old world."

"Electricity?"

Simon had heard about electricity a long time ago. His teachers taught him that it was an inferior form of power compared to Ignium.

"Darn right. Ignium's responsible for bringing down the old world. It's the reason all the trees, grass, and animals died. People here at New Uruk figured that they'd need an alternative, which was found in electricity. May be old technology, but it works just as well."

He had many questions as they passed a few more lights and machines, Simon squinting and trying to get a good look at them.

"Woah, Rufus, woah," Anna commanded the Scab Boar as they slowed down to a stop.

They halted outside of a business, Anna hopping off of the wagon.

"You stay right here, Simon. I'm gonna go handle some business."

Simon nodded and watched her circle around the wagon and walk into a building that likely used to be some sort of apartment. As he waited, Simon looked around him. He waved to some of the citizens of the city who passed, most of them eyeing him suspiciously. Simon felt out of place but was intrigued by everything he saw.

After twenty minutes, Anna came back with a few men who began lifting and carrying crates from the wagon into the store. Rex sat in the back, watching each man as he heaved the crates in. Anna joined him in the driver's seat again, waiting as the men returned and put different crates in the wagon.

"She's all good, Anna. Y'all have a good rest of your day," said the last worker as they finished hauling.

"Thank you, Caleb,"

"Anytime,"

"Move along now, Rufus!" Anna said, the wagon taking off again.

"What's in the crates?" Simon asked.

"Filters,"

"Filters?"

"For gas masks. We use them as currency 'round these parts."

Simon looked back at the crates and then frowned. He opened his mouth to question further and then shook his head.

The rest of the day continued like this. For hours they moved through crowded streets, stopping at businesses to pick up supplies. They bought dried meat for the winter and preserved vegetables, ammo, building supplies, seeds, clothing, and hide. Simon looked back at the wagon each time, watching the crates of filters being replaced by crates of supplies until it was so crowded that Rex had to lay on top of them.

Anna had a big smile beneath her gas mask as they left the city and passed back into the countryside.

"What did you think about New Uruk, partner?" Anna asked as they rode along.

"Amazing,"

"You're darn right. I appreciate your help on the farm since your recovery. Maybe one day you will want to own a property? Hell, I'll even help you get there."

"I'd be grateful," Simon said, smiling broadly at the idea.

The wagon continued along until the Scab Boar turned onto Anna's property.

"Hey, Anna?"

"Yes?"

"You said back in the city how you spent most of your life there. I told you my story, about the Arcadis and stuff... What's your story?"

Anna looked at him, not sure what to say for a moment before forcing a smile.

"Well, that's a long story."

"We have the rest of the day," Simon told her.

"You're right. Well, I don't know where to start. I guess when I was a child."

"That works,"

Anna ordered Rufus to stop as they arrived at the farmhouse and began to unpack their supplies, the dogs happily greeting them.

"Well, I don't remember much from when I was a younglin'. Before New Uruk, I was a nomad, wandering from place to place in the wasteland and trying to find a home."

"Nomad? All by yourself?"

"No, no, I'd have died. I was with a man, uh... It's been so long since I've thought of him."

A broad smile formed on her face.

"His name was London. He raised me and protected me. I even remember what he used to call me."

"What's that?"

"Rose."

Thank You!

Please accept my sincere gratitude for your support of my debut book. I hope you enjoy reading it as much as I enjoyed writing it!

If you like this book, you'll love what we have coming next. Join the VIP list to stay up to date on news and the latest releases! – https://etgunnarsso n.com/news/

To support me further, please leave a review and constructive feedback on the following websites or equivalent. Positive reviews will help other readers find *Forgive Us* and help me develop the Odemark series further.

- https://www.amazon.com/dp/B08R2X9C52
- https://www.barnesandnoble.com/w/forgive-us-et-gunnarsson/1138 505158
- https://www.goodreads.com/book/show/56375585-forgive-us

About the Author

E.T. Gunnarsson translates imagination into words for a living. His debut book *Forgive Us* was awarded Best Sci-Fi book in the 2021 San Francisco Book Festival and Best Post-Apocalyptic Book in the 2021 Fiction Awards.

Born and raised on a horse-rescue ranch in the Rocky Mountains (9,000 feet altitude!), E.T. now resides in central Colorado with his dwarfed Cane Corso and his lifelong interest in Norse myth and culture.

A storyteller from an early age, E.T. spent his formative years developing his writing skills on international role-play sites. He suffers from dysgraphia and cannot write by hand easily. E.T. is a home/online schooler currently pursuing a degree in marketing.

You can connect with me on:

- 🌐 http://www.etgunnarsson.com
- 🐦 https://twitter.com/etgunnarsson
- 📘 https://www.facebook.com/etgunnarsson
- 🔗 https://www.instagram.com/etgunnarsson

Subscribe to my newsletter:

- ✉ https://etgunnarsson.com/news

Also by E.T. Gunnarsson

Awards

Winner, Post-Apocalyptic – 2021 American Fiction Awards

Winner, Science Fiction – 2021 San Francisco Book Festival

Finalist, Science Fiction – 2021 Best Book Awards

Honorable Mention, Science Fiction – 2021 Hollywood Book Festival

Honorable Mention, Science Fiction – 2021 New York Book Festival

Runner Up, Science Fiction/Horror – 2022 New York Book Festival

Honorable Mention, Science Fiction – 2022 San Francisco Book Festival

Abandon Us

How hard must a man fight when the apocalypse arrives?

Civil war ravishes the country. The economy collapses. A plague spreads like fire, and pollution darkens the sky. This is the toxic world of Robert Ashton. A wasteland of broken dreams, death, tech, and mutants. But he is not alone.

He and his partner navigate life underground, where it is safer. Society has buckled, and working as a smuggler, Robert builds a criminal life to keep the two of them fed. But nothing lasts forever, and he is forced to return to the surface when the underground suffers a brutal military raid. What he discovers shocks a man who thinks he cannot be shocked anymore.

Robert emerges into the hellscape of the Third World War...

Inspired by current events, *Abandon Us* is the prequel to E.T. Gunnarsson's multi-award-winning book *Forgive Us*, a story readers call "**thrilling, brutal, and completely unique.**"

Remember Us

What is it like to return to Earth a hundred years after its downfall?

Two years ago, Simon, a revolutionary from the Arcadis space station, fled to Earth. The alien planet he finds is backward and primitive.

While Simon struggles to adapt, his newfound friend Anna guides him through life in the new world. One day, a mysterious explosion in the sky compels Anna and Simon to take the journey of a lifetime.

Across the new frontier, they run into the Father and his fanatical cult, murderers, and zealots who will stop at nothing in their search for "the Vessel." In a desperate race for time, Simon and Anna battle to stop a conqueror from finding the key to tyranny.

Made in the USA
Monee, IL
03 May 2023

32908158R00162